The Innocent And The Dead

The Innocent And The Dead

By R.S. Craig

Colophon: Body text and Chapter headings are set in Times New Roman

ISBN-13   978-0-9825151-4-3
ISBN-10   0-9825151-4-6
Publisher: Bennett Books, A Publishing Resource for Independent Authors, (317) 902-7254
Printed in U.S.A.
All paper is acid free and meets all ANSI standards for archival quality

1

Acknowledgements

Writing is not always a solitary endeavor. We all need support and encouragement, and I've received a lot of that from a few people to whom I owe a lot of thanks.

First of all, I have to thank my wife Joyce and our son Darren. I would not have finished this project without them.

I would like to thank all my writing friends, especially Kathy Watness for her excellent job at editing, Bob Sullivan for his guidance and encouragement. To bring it all into reality I have to thank Jerry Bennett of Bennett Books for his craftsmanship and expertise. Along the way I have received excellent instruction and guidance from members of The Avon Writers Group and the Indiana Writers Center. God bless you all.

Finally! This story would have never been told if not for the wisdom and charity of my main character – the real life John McCauley. I built this story around him.

Of course, I can't forget you, dear reader. I hope you enjoy this story as much as I enjoyed writing it. It was a lot of work. I wouldn't have done it if it had not been fun.

R. S. Craig

Indiana 1889

With no moon and no stars, the night was as cruel as the black sky above the frozen countryside. Inside the old farmhouse beyond the wood pillars of the front porch and the Queen Ann furniture of the front parlor, was a chill that couldn't be driven away with warm clothes or a hot fire. It was the chill between a child and her parents, between a woman and her husband, between a man and his conscience.

Samuel Hanson scooped hot coals out of the kitchen stove and laid them in brass bed warmers. Cold air leaking under the door from the back porch danced around his carpet slippers and bare ankles making him pull tight on the lower part of his long nightshirt and wool robe. One at a time he carried the bed warmers upstairs and stuffed them under the mattresses, lighting his way with a single candle flame that cast an orange glow and silhouetted his dark figure as he ascended the stairs. First Samuel shoved a bed warmer under the mattress in the room of his five-year old daughter, Alice. He did not speak to her; he did not look at her; and Alice noticed that his hands had a slight tremble to them for reasons she didn't know, and she felt she didn't dare ask. When he was finished placing bed warmers, Samuel settled into the bedroom he shared with his wife, Margaret.

Alice was having trouble with her bedtime prayer. "Now I lay me down to sleep. I pray the Lord my soul to keep. If I should … " The words that came next had not frightened her before, but on this cold January eve the words wouldn't come out.

"Go on, Alice," Margaret coaxed. "If I should die…"

"If I should die before I wake, I pray the Lord my soul to take." Alice looked up and asked, "Mother, if I die tonight, will I go to the devil?"

Margaret pursed her lips and squinted her eyes shut for a moment then said, "No Alice, you won't go to the devil. Now finish your prayer."

"God bless Papa. God bless Mother. And thank you again God for making Papa well again."

Alice got up and burrowed into the warm nest of bedclothes and mattress. She was still shivering, and not because of the cold.

Papa had been very sick, but Papa had gotten well again. "What made Papa sick?" Alice asked. "Did I make Papa sick?"

"No Alice. Papa had a tumor," Margaret straightened the quilt.

"What's a tumor?"

"That's a knot that causes great pain."

"How did he get better?"

"Good medicine. Now don't ask so many questions."

"I'm sorry." Alice always tried to be a good girl because children obeyed while adults ruled, especially the men. And the men often had secrets.

Alice knew Papa had a secret. What was it? A man, a stranger, had come to visit Papa after church that afternoon while Alice played with her dolls in her mother's sewing room. The door was ajar, and Alice heard the stranger say, "If you don't tell me the truth, I can't help you." Alice knew she shouldn't be listening to man talk, so she walked over to close the door. But her mother saw her at the opening and accused her of listening in on an adult conversation. No matter how hard she protested to the contrary, Alice still got a thorough spanking and went to bed that night with a cringe worthy sense of guilt.

"Goodnight, Mother," said Alice.

"Goodnight, child." Margaret stood and left. She did not kiss her daughter goodnight.

Alice covered her ears and cried when the train whistle wailed out beyond the plowed fields and deep forest. She couldn't bear that mournful sound on this sad night. All this trouble was her fault. She had no idea what she had done to make Mother and Papa so mad at her, but it had to be something very bad. She quietly offered up another prayer. "Please forgive me, Jesus. I won't do anything to hurt Mother and Papa ever again. Please forgive me. I love them so much."

By the time she heard the clock strike ten she'd stopped crying. Before it struck the half hour she was asleep.

* * *

First came the chill, and then came the thunder. Still under the shroud of night, the sounds of breaking glass, screaming, and gunfire shattered Alice's sleep. The cold air carried the sound so well she thought her home was being invaded until she looked over at her bedroom window and saw the flickering orange glow of a nearby fire. She hopped out of bed and ran to the window, shivering from the cold floor on her bare feet. The neighboring house was fully engulfed in flames, the view partially blocked by a row of oak trees between the houses. Men shouted at each other. There was more gunfire and again the sound of breaking glass. The neighbor's stable was on fire now, and the horses screamed.

She ran out of her room and saw her father dressed in his night robe, his back to her, staring out a window at the end of the hall. The flames of the nearby fire cast a red glow around his head and shoulders.

"Papa, what's going on at the neighbor's house? It's on fire!"

"Alice Hanson! Get back into bed," Samuel shouted. "Margaret, take care of her!"

"Oh no, no, no!" Margaret ran out of her bedroom, scooped the little girl into her arms, then carried her to her room. She put her daughter in bed and closed the curtains on the bedroom window. "This is nothing for a child to be seeing. Lie back down there and cover your head."

"But Mother what is going--."

"Nothing, child! Nothing is going on that you need to be concerned about. Now here, let's get you back under the covers."

"Mother, I'm scared."

"No, no! Now there's nothing for you to be afraid of."

"Why are they…?"

Margaret laid a finger on Alice's lips. "Shhhh! Be still! Everything's going to be just fine."

"But what's going on…?"

"Alice, be still! It's alright."

"But the people next door--"

"Those people can't harm you. They are being taken care of. They have been very bad, but they can't do you any harm."

"Why is Papa…?"

"Papa's fine. Everything's just fine, Alice. Now be still. Lie down there and be still."

Oh I'm being a bad girl again, Alice thought to herself. *Mother and Papa are mad at me again for being a bad girl. Help me, Jesus. Help me be a good girl again. I'm not going to cry. I'm not going to cry.* Margaret stroked Alice's hair and whispered in her ear. "It's alright. Shhhhh. Go to sleep."

I will go to sleep. I will go to sleep. Help me, Jesus. Help me quit crying.

* * *

The night was silent again after Alice quit crying and she quit shaking. Margaret stroked her hair and hummed softly while staring at the window with the fire glow flickering around the edges of the curtains. She would have fallen asleep beside her little girl had she not been so cold with fear and shame and dread and distracted by the candle flame hovering over her. Margaret looked up to see the candlelight casting grotesque light and shadows across her husband's face.

"Is she asleep?" asked Samuel.

"Yes."

"Good. Let's go back to bed."

"I'll be there in a minute."

"Now."

Margaret rose up on one elbow and stared toward the window. "God help us all."

"Don't judge me. It was my life. It was our lives, all of us."

"Yes, I know."

"I did what I had to do."

"I know."

* * *

Just before dawn Alice awoke and thought she heard a baby crying out in the woods beyond the plowed fields. The room was still dark; the night sky was still black. From somewhere in her twilight awakening, she could hear crying from deep inside the woods in the middle of a cold January night.

Alice awoke the next morning with sunlight streaming through her bedroom window. She eased out of bed and walked across the floor, peeked under the curtains, and saw the smoldering ruins next door. She shut her eyes, turned her head away, and wondered, *Who were those people?* Her parents had always referred to them as "the tenants". She hadn't even known their names. Why did somebody burn the house? Was there something wrong with them? Whose baby was crying in the middle of the night? Was it the neighbor's? Did the baby die? Did everybody next door die? Mother said they were being taken care of. Why did her father act so strange in the hallway last night? Why didn't he send for the fire brigade?

The fire had not burned away the chill, and the sunlight had not warmed her heart. The horror of that January night would haunt Alice Hanson for the next 90 years of her life.

Chapter 1

The Hanson Curse

It would haunt a generation yet unborn.

Margaret Hanson gave birth to a second child in the spring of 1891, but the world would never know the color of his eyes or the sound of his cry because the baby boy lay stillborn in the doctor's hands while his mother screamed with pain and horror. Shortly after that Alice heard the words "Hanson curse" whispered by the catty women with clucking tongues who hovered just outside the family circle.

The baby had no name, and Alice always thought that was so sad. She thought she heard the baby crying from out in the dark woods the night after he was born. But, of course, it was just her imagination, wasn't it? The baby was dead, poor baby.

Four other children were born after that. Vera came along in 1893, Katherine in 1895. Then came the two boys, Victor and Robert, around the turn of the century.

The boys grew up fast and died young in the First World War. Their sister Vera died of tuberculosis during the Great Depression. Katherine, beautiful Katherine with her mother's dazzling eyes and pretty face, died in a car crash in 1942, but not before she gave birth to the most favored child in the Hanson household.

John McCauley was born to a giddy little party girl and a troubled veteran of the First World War who came home and drowned his troubles with whiskey. John moved in with his grandparents and Aunt Alice at the tender age of three after his father Kenneth ran away, and his mother went to work and party in nearby Indianapolis.

Samuel Hanson had lost both of his sons. "But, by God, I got me a grandson," he declared.

John grew up tall and well muscled over the first sixty years of his life. His thick hair was still mostly brown shading into gray sideburns and framing a handsome face.

* * *

Before he and Margaret died at the end of World War Two, Samuel Hanson acquired over five hundred acres of prime bottomland in Forest County. Along with being a school teacher and John McCauley's primary care giver, Alice managed the farm quite well as she grew old. But by the 1970's, the Hanson slice of fortune had landed butter side down. Expenses rose, crops drowned in the spring rains, and withered in the summer droughts. Eventually it became clear it was time to cash in the land and make a living from real estate instead of farming.

John McCauley partnered with his old friend and classmate, Bob Parsons, to form Parsons and McCauley Realty. They parceled off all but twenty-seven acres around the old farm house; then sold half-acre plots to homebuilders including the south pasture where only weeds had grown and the sounds of gunfire, breaking glass, and screaming had all but faded from living memory- but not Alice Hanson's memory. The first excavator showed up on a spring day in 1978 to carve out a hole for the first house to sit there since 1889.

At the top of the stairs, in a room she had occupied since childhood, Alice sat in her favorite rocker and gazed out the window at the activity beyond the row of old oak trees. Outside a large Freightliner truck with a lowboy trailer had just off loaded a small Bear Cat with a front-end loader. The growl of the little engine was punctuated by a sudden backfire. The loud bang made Alice jump as her memory raced back to a cold January night when a stream of loud bangs had turned her little world upside down. All of that happened a long time ago, but she still wondered, "What next?"

From the bottom of the stairs Alice's niece, Louella Pritchett, called out, "Aunt Alice, I have your lunch ready. Guess what? John's here to join us."

Alice got out of her chair and yelled, "Good, I want to talk with him."

"Do you need help with your escalator chair?"

"I don't need help with that infernal machine." Alice's strong mind had been honed by years of teaching wily young school children who constantly tested her mettle while ninety-five years as a farmer's daughter had kept her body in shape.

Alice settled in her chair and spotted her nephew, John, standing next to Louella. As she rode down in the escalator Alice couldn't wait to ask, "John McCauley, did you close on that south pasture?"

"No I didn't," said John as he and Louella watched her closely from the bottom of the stairs. "Bob Parsons closed that deal."

"Why?" shouted Alice.

"Because he's my partner, and I was busy with another matter."

"I don't want him closing on another piece of this land, you hear me?"

"Alice, would you please be careful," said Louella. "You're getting yourself all in a tizzy, and you didn't buckle your seatbelt."

"Why shouldn't he close on some of this land?" asked John.

"Because he's a crook," said Alice.

"No, he's not."

"He's the son of a crook. Gerald Parsons took your Aunt Vera's farm like Sherman took Atlanta."

"I wouldn't know about that," said John. "The Second World War was on, and I was off in the army." The chair stopped at the bottom, and John said, "Here, let me help you over to the kitchen table."

"I don't need help," said Alice. "You can help me into my grave when the time comes, but not until then."

As they settled around the table for lunch John asked, "Aunt Alice why do you spend so much time during the day in that upstairs room? We made a bedroom for you out of Grandma's old sewing room."

"I know," said Alice. "And I hate that room. I don't belong there. My room is upstairs. Always has been, always will be."

"But the bathroom is downstairs," said Louella.

"So what?" said Alice.

"Well you're going to get hurt riding that escalator chair all day."

"Then get me a chamber pot for upstairs."

John broke up and almost choked on his vegetable soup. Louella frowned. "Aunt Alice please, not at the lunch table."

"We could convert my old room to a bathroom up there," John suggested.

"Are you crazy?" said Alice. "Do you realize how much that would cost?"

"No, but I could get an estimate."

"Forget it. You're not spending good money on a bathroom for this ninety-five year old body."

"Someday we're going to sell this house, and a second bathroom . . ."

"Can be added at the expense of the new owner."

John and Louella had learned long ago that any argument with their aunt always ended with Alice having the last word. So they let her have it and ate the rest of their lunch in silence.

* * *

After lunch John dried while Louella washed the dishes and Aunt Alice went back up to her room to watch all the activity in the south pasture.

John noted his cousin's worried look. "What's the matter, Louella?"

"Well, I hate to tell you this, but we had another incident last night."

"What kind of incident?"

"Aunt Alice called Sheriff Caldwell, claiming that somebody had abandoned a baby out in the woods on the other side of the cornfield. She swore she heard a child crying."

"What did the sheriff do?"

"He came out with a couple of men and made a show of looking around the woods. Then he had a long talk with Alice and told her they couldn't find anything. Surprisingly, she let it go at that. It wouldn't have bothered me, but the sheriff came to me at the motel and told me about it. He said it was the third time Alice had called him about the same thing." She paused in her scrubbing. "John, I'm getting worried about her staying here by herself all the time."

"She's been doing it for over thirty years," said John.

"You know as well as I do she's not the same woman who raised you and took care of her parents."

"Her mind is still sharp, and she knows her limitations. Louella, don't start talking nursing home. She would die within weeks if we put her in one of those places."

"Well let me ask you this. You grew up in this house. Have you ever heard a baby crying out in the woods at night?"

"No," he lied.

Chapter 2

The Undisturbed Earth

Fred Grider maneuvered the little bulldozer around in the south pasture to scoop out a foundation. He had been an equipment operator for twenty-five years, and he was good at it - when he was sober. He was sober now, but he still couldn't shake the feeling of somebody looking over his shoulder. Every time he shifted into reverse, he looked around to see who was behind him. There was nobody there, but his boss, Rick Mundy, and the building contractor, Dan Foster, standing off to the side, gave Fred some strange looks.

They think I'm drunk, Fred thought to himself. He kept digging and backing up, but the feeling that somebody had climbed up on the back of the little Bear Cat dozer stayed with him.

There was no way that any of the two men could have seen the human skull that Fred had unearthed while he was digging. It was now hidden in the mound of earth that lay beside the hole where the foundation would stand. In future weeks when the house was finished and the cinder block walls were backfilled with the same dirt, the skull would be buried again. Nobody would ever see anything extraordinary about the loose soil that had previously been undisturbed for almost a hundred years.

Murdered me. The whispered voice was inside Fred Grider's head. *Murdered me.* It was barely a whisper, but Fred heard it even above the noise of the Bear Cat engine. "*Murdered me.*"

Murdered? Who murdered? Fred thought to himself.

He stopped, got out of his seat and looked around the foundation hole he had dug. "What's the matter?" Rick Mundy asked.

"Nothing."

"What are you looking for?" asked Dan Foster.

"Nothing." Fred got back in the driver's seat and kept digging.

The voice kept whispering, *Murdered me. Murdered me.* As soon as he finished Fred jumped off the bulldozer, got in his own pickup truck, then drove away without saying a word to anybody.

"Where in the world is he going?" Dan Foster asked Fred's boss Rick.

Rick watched the little pickup truck disappear down the road and said with an embarrassed chuckle, "Well, I guess he's done."

"Does he take off like that all the time?"

"Ah, no."

"What's the matter with him?" Dan said, waving a hand at the road. "He kept looking behind him the whole time he was digging."

"I don't know."

"Is he drinkin' again?"

Rick glanced at the foundation hole. "He was stone cold sober when we came out here."

"That's not what I asked."

Rick bowed his head and offered no answer.

"He is, isn't he?"

Again, no answer.

"I don't want him back, Rick."

"But he was - "

"I mean it. I don't want him back out here."

Rick frowned. "We've still got footings to dig."

"Get somebody else."

Rick let out a sigh of resignation. "Yeah, yeah. Okay."

Fred drove around the country square mile and came back toward the construction site he had just left. He owed his old friend, Rick Mundy, an explanation. That presented a problem. He didn't have one. As he neared the truck that hauled the bulldozer, he stopped in the middle of the road and realized what a fool he had just made of himself. Then he caught sight of Dan Foster. *They know what I've done. They've found out what I've done. God, I'm in big trouble now.*

Wait a minute! What the hell have I done? I didn't do anything except my job. Maybe if I just told them what happened. What happened? How the hell should I know what happened? Nothing happened! Just go back and explain to them . . . Explain what? Then they'll know I'm guilty.

Guilty of what? Damn it man! Get a grip! Fred swerved around in the middle of the road just as Dan Foster and Rick Mundy caught sight of him. He sped back into town and fell off the wagon . . . again.

Chapter 3

Homer

The Old Dog Tavern sat at the end of a dead-end street in a dead-end town called Tanner's Grove. The sleazy little watering hole had a bar, some tables and chairs, a twelve-foot high ceiling painted with a film of soot from the old coal-fired furnace, and a liquor stash, some of it labeled, some of it not. Fly strips hung from a clothesline mounted over the bar. The old noisy window air conditioner sitting in a hole cut out of the front wall did little to cool the enormous room. The patrons sweltered in the summer. Once there had been a jukebox, but it had been smashed in a bar fight eight years ago. That was about the time the new owner, Max Carter, hired a bouncer who doubled as a bartender. His name was Homer. He never told Max or anybody else his last name, and that didn't matter since Max paid him cash out of the register, allowed him to stay in the upstairs apartment rent-free, and kept no record of him. He had no idea where Homer came from, but he was big with fists that could have doubled as sledge hammers, long hair tied with a black ban-danna, deeply lined face, olive skin, devilish brown eyes, heavy brows, a hair lip and bent nose. A single name was all Max needed. Who was going to question Max or Homer about tax forms or employment records and risk having his face and kneecaps rearranged?

Dust and cigarette smoke swirled in the sunlight streaming through the grimy windows. Even without a juke box the place was always noisy with the chatter of hookers, pimps, and hustlers with pockets full of cash and dope. Harvey Gutz, a dirty little goblin with a scruffy little mustache, was always the loudest one of all.

"Hey, Pappy, how about a head job?" yelled Harvey as Fred came through the door.

Fred glanced over at the bar and noticed a painted up blonde glaring at him. He waved his hand at her and Harvey, then sat down at one of the tables.

"Aw, you just came to get drunk, didn't you?" said Harvey. "Oh, well, your loss."

A mural stretched across the back and one sidewall depicted a steam locomotive passenger train with open pastures and forests behind it. It was the first thing Fred Grider noticed whenever he came in. He slouched in his chair as he admired the mural, nodding his head and shivering on the verge of delirium tremens.

Homer came up, slapped an empty glass on the table, and filled it with a clear libation out of a bottle with no label.

"What's this?" asked Fred.

Homer sat in the chair opposite. "Mr. Carter has a connection with a man in Tennessee. I thought I'd try it out on my best customer. Take a sip."

Fred tipped the glass up and took a gulp. He coughed and hacked until he blushed blood red.

"I said a sip, lard head." Homer grinned. "Drink it right, it goes down real smooth."

Fred caught his breath and took a sip the next time. He pointed at the back wall and asked, "Who painted that, Homer?"

"I did."

"Aw, you're lyin' to me now."

"That's my pride and joy, Fred; and don't you forget it. Ain't that right, Anna Lee?" Homer shouted at the old woman behind the bar. He got no reply.

"That looks almost like the train my Uncle Glen and I

rode to Cincinnati one time," Fred remarked. "He worked for the old New York Central, and we rode his pass all the time to Chicago, St. Louis, Pittsburgh." Fred took another gulp of the old Tennessee recipe and choked again.

Homer slapped him on the back and said, "Slow down. I need you to live long enough to put away the second bottle."

"When you gonna get food in this place?" asked Fred. "I'm hungry."

"What the hell did you come here for?" yelled the old lady as she carried a pitcher of beer to another table.

"Shut up, Anna Lee," said Homer. "Bring that stale sandwich you fixed me awhile ago."

She walked back to the bar and came back carrying a plate with a sandwich made of white bread and chicken breast, nothing else. Her thin hair was still all black and tied back in a bun exposing her forehead and the front half of her scalp. She had no teeth, was barely five feet tall, weighed less than a hundred pounds, and walked like her feet hurt.

Fred took the plate from Anna Lee and lifted the top slice of bread. "You got any mayo to put on this?"

"We ain't got no mayo," she said. "Be thankful for what you got. Any mayo around this place would probably spoil in a day and raise hell with your insides."

"Aw, shut up, you old bitch and get back there and wash them glasses."

Anna Lee said, "Damn it, Homer, quit talking so nasty to your mother."

Homer smacked the old lady on the butt as she turned and went back behind the bar.

Fred ate the sandwich and chased it with a sip of shine after every bite. All the while he kept staring at the painting of the passenger train on the back wall.

Suddenly, he heard a familiar noise inside his head:

Hisssss....Chug. Fred squinted his eyes and cocked his head to the right so his good left ear could hear. *Hisssss....Chug.*

"What are you lookin' at?" asked Homer with a chuckle.

"I ain't lookin'. I'm listenin'."

"What are you listening to?"

"Aw, hell, it's gone. You ruined it, Homer."

Homer wasn't the only one who ruined the spell. A burly hulk with a tattooed bald head sidled up to the blonde at the bar. "What's your name, honey?"

"Bambi," said the blonde with a sneer on her face.

"Aw, that ain't your name," said the hulk. "That ain't even original. How about flies in the snatch? That's a good name for you."

"What's your name?" asked the blonde.

"C.O. Jones."

"Ha . . . Ha." came the lame laugh. "Are you C.O. Jones, Senior or C.O. Jones, Junior? He he he."

"Don't fuck with me, lady," said the hulk as he grabbed her hair and yanked her head back. Her sneer turned to a look of terror instantly.

"Get your hands off her," said Harvey as he slapped the bald head from behind.

The hulk turned, backhanded him and knocked him off his stool. Homer jumped from his seat at the table and timed his approach so he was able to head butt the guy in the nose as he turned back to the blonde. When the hulk put his hands up to his face Homer kneed him in the groin. The big guy doubled over. With one hand on his collar and one hand on his belt, Homer escorted the bald dude out the front door.

"If you want some broken bones to go with that pain, come on back in. Otherwise get out and stay out." From behind, Homer gave him another kick in the gonads and sent him sprawling face down on the sidewalk.

When he turned his attention from the front door and back to the mural, the noise in Fred's brain came back and kept rhythm with the movement of his jaw. *Chew, hissss...chug, chew, hiss....chug.* Fred sipped some more moonshine, and the sound kept coming. *Hisssss....Chug.* After a few more sips, the locomotive came to life. Steam shot out in front of the wheels while black smoke poured out of the funnel on top of the boiler. Sparks flew out from under the drive wheels as the train lurched ahead. The steam whistle let out a loud squeal, and Fred slapped his hands over his ears. He followed the train as it rounded the corner of the back wall and came toward the front of the tavern, disappearing out the front door as it sailed through mid-air.

Fred stared out the front door and clapped his hands over his ears again to ward off the noise of the steam whistle that rattled all four walls of the grungy tavern. The loud hiss and chug of the locomotive and the loud clack of steel wheels rolling on steel rails faded in the distance.

"You starin' at me?" said the blonde at the bar.

Fred had been looking out the front window with a slack jaw and bug eyes as the phantom train disappeared in the distance. He neither saw nor heard anything or anybody else.

"That stare will cost you five bucks," said the blonde. "A quickie will cost you ten and do you more good."

Fred turned his back on the bitch and looked at the floor. Noise from the locomotive and its steam whistle got louder as the train doubled back and headed for the tavern. Suddenly bricks, wood and plaster flew in all directions as it smashed through the front wall, demolished the bar, then headed for the back wall carrying the mangled bodies of Anna Lee and the bar flies with it. Fred covered his head with his arms to shield himself from the flying debris. When he lowered his arms, the train was once again attached to the back wall; the bar and all its fly strips were back in place. Anna Lee was still bent over a galvanized tub washing glasses; and the front wall was back together. All the steam noises were silent. Harvey Gutz and his bevy of hookers and drug dealers were laughing at Fred.

"Don't just sit there and squirm," said the blonde hooker. "Get up and dance for us."

Fred got up and ran out the front door to his truck.

Chapter 4

"Not Again"

The wood frame for the ranch style house went up two weeks after Fred Grider parked his bulldozer and went off to get roaring drunk. The crew of carpenters worked until sunset on the last day of June to finish the job. Then one of the men, Tim Whitaker, piled up the left over wood scraps and set them afire.

"Hey, don't start a fire out there now," Dan Foster yelled at his stepson.

"Why not?" asked Tim.

"We're getting ready to leave. There won't be anybody here to watch it."

"So, it's all muddy around here. Nothing'll catch on fire."

"Just put it out, okay?"

Tim shoveled dirt on the fire and smothered it.

"College boy knows it all, don't he?" one of the other carpenters said to Dan Foster.

"Aw, Tim's alright. You just have to get his attention now and again. He won't be workin' for me too much more anyway. He starts a new job next Monday."

"Doin' what?" asked the carpenter.

"Radio announcer."

"Radio announcer? I didn't think he had sense enough to do something like that."

"He's got sense," Dan said with a keen edge to his voice. "He went to school for it. 'Bout time he got some breaks his way."

Everybody left and the countryside was peaceful. The daily racket of pounding hammers and stamping feet was gone. The space under the plywood floor was very dark and very quiet. It was also getting very hot. The red glow that came out of the ground blackened the floor beams and the plywood, and soon they were smoldering. Then it blackened the timbers of the walls and roof. By the wee hours of the morning, the new wood frame was completely engulfed in flames.

Alice Hanson watched the fire from her upstairs bedroom. She had already called the fire department while she watched the eerie glow of the flames in the window at the end of the hallway. She imagined seeing her father standing on the same spot watching another fire so very long ago. "Sweet Lord in heaven, not again."

* * *

They called it arson and held out little hope that anybody would ever be caught or that the insurance company would ever pay off. So Dan Foster and the carpenter split the loss and started all over again, just the two of them.

After the roofer, stonemason, plumber, and electrician took over, Dan drove by the house every day to make sure it was still standing. Every day he breathed a healthy sigh of relief.

And every day Fred Grider had a hard time shaking the feeling of somebody looking over his shoulder. He knew only one cure for it.

Fred sat staring at the mural on the two walls at The Old Dog tavern. The steam locomotive managed to stay in place, but the sound of steam kept hissing in his head. Homer filled Fred's glass and fed him chicken sandwiches to keep his stomach halfway healthy. Fred asked him, "What did you put in this glass?"

"Whiskey."

"Something besides whiskey in here. What did you put in that sandwich?"

"Chicken."

"You're lyin' to me again."

Homer leaned forward and looked Fred in his blood-shot eyes. "Where you been, ole buddy?"

"Home."

"You ain't been home. You stink too bad. Where you been?"

"Nowhere."

"Don't tell me nowhere. You been somewhere."

"I don't remember. I seen the sun come up twice. Have no idea where I was. All I know is I forgot somethin', and I can't remember what it was."

"Now you quit lyin' to me. You seen the sun come up more than twice. I can see something in those big brown eyes. It ain't pretty."

"No, it ain't. Sheriff been leanin' on me."

"What for?"

"I guess he thinks I had something to do with that new house burnin'."

"What new house?"

"The one over by the Hanson farm."

"That's what I figured." Homer leaned on his elbows and stared at Fred. "You take my advice, ole buddy. Stay away from that Hanson farm."

"Why?"

"Look behind you."

Fred looked behind him. "I don't see nothin'. What have you been drinkin'?"

"Coffee."

"What do you see?"

"I see a man bloodied and burned. And he's whisper-ing in your ear, 'Murdered me. Murdered me.'"

Fred looked up at Homer with a start and Homer laughed at the sight of goose bumps on Fred's arms. "I'm tellin' you. Keep away from there. Keep a whole mind in your head and stay away."

A vise like grip clamped down on Fred's left shoulder and made him jump. Harvey Gutz smelled of booze and sweat as he let out a high pitched laugh that sounded like a bicycle horn. "Hey, my man, what you need is a good head job to calm your nerves."

"Who the hell are you?" asked Fred.

"Aw, Fred, you've seen me in here before. I'm the guy with a babe who's going to cure what ails you. She's outside in the bed of my truck . . ."

"You keep her in the bed of your truck," said Homer. "I don't want to see her in here ever again suckin' some guy's pud at the bar."

"Well, I'll have her give him a hand job, Homer."

"Do whatever you want," said Homer. "Just do it outside."

"I ain't never seen you in here before," said Fred. "What's your name?"

"Sure you have," said Harvey. "All that booze has your mind messed up."

A tall skinny guy with a scarred face and a glass eye came up to Fred. "This here's Harvey Guts. That's his sister out in the truck. Ha ha ha."

"Shut up, Ron," said Harvey. "And it's Goots, not Guts. Quit makin' fun of my name."

"Lemme alone, the both of yas." Fred got up and staggered out the door.

Harvey shouted, "Come on man. Ten bucks for some head. You don't even have to shuck your britches if you don't want to."

"Aw hell, you're too smashed to get it up anyway," Ron called after him and laughed."

Chapter 5

His Goose Is Cooked

Trouble wasn't through with Dan Foster's new house. Just when he thought it was finished on the outside, the shingles started falling off. It took two different roofers three tries to get shingles to stick and not curl up. The stonemasons had to replace over half the stone veneer after it fell off, and two different painting contractors put three brands of paint on the outside trim.

By the time Ken Wallis came to hang dry wall, he had heard all the stories of trouble and bad luck. There was even speculation that the place was haunted. He laughed that off and told Dan Foster that his walls would be solid, and he'd have no trouble.

The day was overcast so Ken brought a pole lamp to light his work. He had already hung the drywall so all he had to do was tape and Spackle the seams and nail holes. For this part of the job, he worked alone. There was nothing in the house on this unusually warm but dreary November day but Ken, his lamp, and his tools, no radio, no idle chitchat, just work.

He started at 8:30. At 11:00 he heard the front door open and close. "Damn it, I don't need any supervisors," Ken muttered. "Dan, that you?" He walked from the master bedroom to the living room. Nobody was in sight. "Hey, Dan, where are you?" No answer.

He went out to the garage. Nobody was there either. "Dan?" he called meekly. No answer. Ken shrugged his shoulders and went back to work.

Another thirty minutes passed. *Why is it so quiet in here?* He started wishing he had brought a radio along. Some noise besides the scraping of his putty knife and somebody breathing would have been better than this. *Wait a minute, who's breathing?* Ken looked around and saw eerie patterns out the corner of his eye. Was that a bearded old man staring at him? No, it was just a smear of spackling compound over a nail hole. Was a giant dove about to sweep down on him? No, it was only tape and spackling over a seam in a corner of the ceiling.

Ken glanced at his watch, then frowned. Why had it stopped? It was his grandfather's old Bulova. Had he forgotten to wind it? He never forgot things like that. He looked outside. There was no sun, no sundial shadows to tell morning from afternoon. He shrugged, then finished the master bedroom and moved on to the bathroom.

The back patio door slid open and closed. "Hey, who's there?" Ken went to the living room. Again, nobody in sight. "Who's there?"

No answer.

"Come on, quit the crap. Who's there?" By now, he was walking around with a hammer gripped in his hand. He went from the living room to the kitchen, then to the garage, back through the kitchen and living room, down the hall and into the bathroom, across to the master bedroom again. He checked the two bedrooms across the hall. Nothing. There was nothing but naked drywall, smears of spackling, and pipes sticking out of the walls where the kitchen sink, bathtub, lavatories and stools would be.

But there was somebody behind him. *Who . . . ?*

"Damn it! Who's there?"

The front door opened and closed again. Ken rushed into the living room. Nothing. Nobody. He locked the front door, then the garage door. He laid a piece of wood in the patio door track to prop it closed and locked. "And stay out," he muttered before going back to work.

There was no other sound in the house but the scraping of sandpaper as Ken sanded and smoothed the dry spackling compound. Was someone whispering in the next room? He stopped to listen. Nothing. He walked from the living room to the hallway to the bedrooms. Nobody. He checked the bathrooms. There were pipes sticking out of walls, copper fingers pointed accusingly at him. *Get a grip, man. Come on, get a grip. Pipes . . . They're just pipes.*

Ken jumped when the thunder boomed outside and shook the walls of the house. A few seconds later, rain lashed at the windows and doors.

"Rain? I don't remember rain in the forecast. Damn it man, quit talking to yourself."

More time passed. How much time? He had no idea, but the sound of rain helped relieve the oppressive silence as he rushed to finish the job. He didn't even break for lunch.

Rain? Ken thought. *Are my truck windows up? Better check.* He ran outside and rolled up the driver's side window. When he came back, drenched to the skin, the front door slammed in his face. It was locked and the key was still in Ken's toolbox.

"Aw shit!" Ken wrestled with the knob and pounded on the door. "Hey, open this door." He pounded some more and looked through the little diamond shaped glass window. It had begun to fog, but etched in the fog was the outline of an ugly face. The long hair, broad nose and ragged mouth had been formed by fog turning into water droplets and running down the glass. The hideous face was massive, but the expression was sad. The broad mouth opened, and a low growl came out of the door. He had enough. Tools or no tools, job or no job, Ken darted into his truck, fired the engine, and sped off, gravel spewing out from under his tires.

The skin across the back of his neck prickled. He was being followed. He didn't know if something was in the club cab behind him or in the truck bed. But whatever had been in the house had followed him. He kept glancing in his rearview mirror and twisting around in his seat. There was nothing behind him that he could see, but it was there.

The rain lashed at the windshield and Ken could barely see to drive. Normally, he would have pulled off the road and waited for the storm to pass. He couldn't do that now. Something was after him. A sepulchral voice started singing and gurgling from the radio.

"Go and tell Aunt Rody
Go and tell Aunt Rody
Go and tell Aunt Rody
Her old gray goose is dead."

"That's it! My goose is cooked. My goose is really cooked." He began sobbing and laughing hysterically. The same lines played over and over as Ken fiddled with the dials, but he couldn't turn it off or tune it out.

Two miles down the road the pavement made a 90-degree turn to the right. Ken didn't see the curve and drove straight into the woods. There was heavy underbrush on either side of him, but the gravel of the old mining road he drove on was still there. None of that mattered. There was still something after him.

Up ahead lay an old strip mine turned fishing lake, surrounded by weeds as high as the hood of the truck. The weeds snapped as Ken's front bumper mowed them down. They were thick up to the water's edge, and Ken couldn't see for the tears pouring out of his eyes.

Without slowing down he drove straight into the lake. The truck hit the surface after being airborne for only a second, sending a wall of water and spray in front of it. The truck floated for just a moment, then started sinking.

"It's got me! Now it's got me! I really am dead! Oh, God, please help me! The truck's sinking! Open the door, fool! Get the hell outa here! No, don't open the door. The truck'll sink. The truck's sinking anyway. Roll the window down, idiot! Get out! Get out!"

Ken was underwater by the time he got his legs out from under the steering wheel and in position to squeeze through the side window. He stuck his head out of the cab, grabbed the roof, then heaved himself out and away from the sinking truck. His jeans, flannel shirt, and work boots were not made for swimming. Once they were soaking wet, they felt as heavy as a lead suit. He kicked and stroked as hard as he could to get back to the surface. But the cold water cramped his legs, and he sank deeper and deeper into the moss and weeds, deeper and deeper into the muddy bottom. How desperately he wanted to breathe! How badly he wanted to open his mouth and inhale a breath of air to chase away the fire of panic ripping through his head. *I want it so bad! Oh, I want it so bad! Oh God, please let me live. I want to breathe. I want to live! No! No! I don't want to die!*

Finally the cramp in his legs was no longer a pain, and the panic in his mind lost its grip. It all melted into a ringing that grew louder and louder. It grew so loud it sounded like a massive chorus singing to him, and it sang only to him. Finally he was at peace.

* * *

That night a worried wife called in the wee hours.

The ringing phone shattered Kathy Foster's sound sleep and she really didn't have the motivation to answer it. Finally she reached out and fumbled for the lamp switch, turned it on, squinted at the bright light, and picked up the receiver. "Hello?" she mumbled.

"Kathy Foster?"

"Yes?"

"This is Lori Wallis."

Kathy looked at the alarm clock on the nightstand. "Lori, my God, it's two-thirty in the morning."

"I know. I'm sorry to call you so late, but have you seen my husband by any chance?"

"No. Why?"

"I haven't seen him since he left for work this morning."

"Have you called the tavern?"

"No! I mean, yes. I called the tavern, the hospital, the sheriff." She began to cry.

"Lori, is something wrong with Ken?"

"I don't know. I don't know." Lori sobbed.

Dan rolled over in bed. "Is that Lori Wallace?"

"Yes. Ken has come up missing."

"Missing? Let me have the phone." Dan took the receiver and stretched the cord across Kathy's neck. She hauled the trim line phone off the nightstand and laid it between her and Dan. "Lori, this is Dan Foster. Did Ken go out to the new house at the Hanson farm this morning?"

"He said he was going to finish something. I don't know where."

"Well, did he call you anytime after he left?"

"No."

"What time did he leave?"

"Around eight o'clock."

"And you haven't seen him since?"

"No."

"Did you call the sheriff?"

"Yes."

"Did you go looking for him yourself?"

"Oh, for God's sake." Kathy reached over and took the receiver away from Dan. "Lori, was Ken alright when he left for work this morning?"

"Yes! Yes! I'm sure. Kathy, he's never done anything like this before. I swear to God!"

"Are you home by yourself?"

"No, Mother's here."

"Okay. Well, honey, I don't know what to tell you. If we hear anything we'll call right away, okay?"

"Okay." She hung up the phone.

Kathy Foster flopped back in bed and put the phone back on the nightstand as Dan got up and started getting dressed.

"Where are you going?"

Dan said, "I'm going over to the Hanson farm to see what in the world is going on now."

"Now? It's past two-thirty in the morning."

"I don't care."

"Dan, please. I don't want you going over there at this time of night."

"Why not?"

"It's not safe."

"Safe from what?" Dan took note of the look of horror on his wife's face. "Aw now, don't give me that crap about spooks and a haunted house."

"All I know is this damn job has been a nightmare. I wish you'd just walk away from that disaster. It's gonna run us into the poor house."

"You know I can't do that. If I leave a mess for somebody else to clean up, I'll never be able to build a house in this county again."

"Alright, but . . . please don't leave now. Please don't. It can wait till morning."

He stared at the floor a moment, shirt in hand. "Okay, I'll check on it first thing."

Chapter 6

What Next?

The house was just as quiet when the sun came up, as it had been when the sun went down the night before. When Dan Foster came through the front door, he found a wood tote box filled with tools in the middle of the living room floor. All around him, the walls were covered with plasterboard, their seams hidden with tape and spackling compound. The drywall was finished. Whew! Ken Wallis had done a good job as usual. But where was Ken?

Dan walked over and gently tapped the wood toolbox with his toe. He bent down and grabbed the large steel ring with the new house key. Why would Ken leave and lock the door without his tools?

Dan noticed a nail sticking up from the plywood floor. He took a hammer out of the toolbox and knocked it back down. Then he noticed that the house was deathly quiet. Casually, he thumped the hammer against the floor a couple of times to make some more noise. The house was too quiet. It was the first time Dan thought about a place being too quiet.

Dan jumped at the knock on the door and caught his breath. He went to answer it, and there stood John McCauley. "Hello Dan."

"Come in." Dan Foster breathed a sigh of relief and stood back as John entered.

"Something the matter?" asked John.

"No. Why?"

"You act like you've been spooked."

"No . . . No, it's nothing. What can I do for you?"

"Well, I was on my way over to the courthouse. I saw your truck in the driveway and thought I'd stop by."

"What for?"

John glanced at Dan's face as he pulled a notepad out of his pocket. He still looked spooked. "I think I have a buyer for the house."

"What house?"

"Ah . . . this house."

Dan chuckled. "Well, this house is hardly finished yet."

"The lady still wants to talk to you." He handed Dan a piece of notepaper. "Here's her name and number."

Dan looked at the note. "Emily Petersen. I know her. I did some remodeling for her after her husband died."

"Well . . . that's good." John walked around the unfinished living room and examined what had been done so far. "Ken Wallis did a good job with the drywall, didn't he?"

"Ken Wallis has come up missing."

"Missing?"

"His wife called in the middle of the night. She hasn't seen or heard from him since he came out here yesterday morning. He left his tools behind. No sign of Ken."

"No sign of any disturbance," said John.

"Yeah well, I think we've had enough of those."

"So I've heard."

Dan sighed, and his shoulders sagged. "You've probably heard I'm not in very good financial shape either."

"Dan, if you need somebody to cosign a loan, if I can help you in any way . . ."

"No!" Dan softened his voice. "I mean no, that won't be necessary."

John patted Dan on the shoulder. "You're a good man, Dan Foster. If you need help don't push it away." John headed for the front door. "Call Emily Petersen, okay?"

"I will."

As John turned to leave Dan called out, "John, could I ask you a question?"

"Sure."

"Look . . . ah . . . I've had a lot of trouble out here."

"I know. We just mentioned that."

"Well . . . I was just . . . Aw, forget it. I shouldn't even be thinking about that."

"About what?"

"About . . . Well, there's been talk about . . . Oh, about the place being not quite right."

"You mean haunted?"

"I didn't say that."

"Oh now, that's not a bad word. I've heard some rumors about that too. Mostly I've heard about a possible arson, bad shingles, bad paint. Of course there's always the ghost hunters, the mystics."

"Are you one of them?" Dan hastened to add, "Now I don't mean anything bad about that. It's just that . . . well, at your house you sometimes have people over to . . . ah . . . do some odd things."

"Like hypnotize each other, explore the hereafter, explore past lives?"

"Yeah. Your folks were farmers, church people. How did you get on to stuff like that?"

"I had to work a couple of jobs when I was young to keep Aunt Alice out of the poor house and save the family farm. One of the jobs was unloading trucks at a warehouse. I met an old man there who believed all sorts of things, things I'd never considered while growing up. Old Carson Sells taught me hypnosis, self-hypnosis, mind over matter. We even got into prenatal regression and studies about reincarnation. He taught me more about human beings than all my college professors. John paused. "Old Carson helped Sharon and me through a tough time when our daughter Lisa died."

"I heard about that. God, that must've been tough."

"It was. So . . . what does this have to do with a haunted house?"

Dan stood and pulled at his lower lip, then said, "I guess it doesn't. Aw, forget I even mentioned any of this. I'm sorry, John. I didn't mean to get anything started. Please, don't tell anybody I said anything about it."

"I wont." He pointed at the notepaper in Dan's hand. Call Emily Petersen."

"I will."

Chapter 7

Make a Deal

Dan Foster hesitated a day before calling Emily. He had negotiated real estate deals before, none of them this flimsy. When he finally called, she answered on the second ring; but Dan took a few moments to answer her back. "Is this…ah…Emily Petersen?"

"Yes. Is this Dan Foster?"

She sounded glad to hear his voice. "Yes, it is. How have you been?"

"I'm fine. Listen, I've heard all about the trouble you've been having. I have an idea that may save both of us some grief."

"I'm all ears."

"How much would you ask for the house if you sold it right now?"

"I couldn't sell that house now. The plumbing isn't finished. We're putting in the bathtub and lavatories this afternoon."

"Could a good handyman finish it if he moved in and bought the stuff and fixed it up himself?"

"Well . . . that depends on who he is."

"He's my son-in-law, Bill Barnes. He and Diane and their daughter are moving out here from the city. Bill lost his job last February; before that he lost his father to cancer; his daughter, Mary, was beat up on her way home from school. It's been a rough year and they need a change of scenery."

"You say Bill lost his job?"

"He's started a job with Carter Oil."

"Carter Oil? How'd he wind up with that bunch of thugs?"

"Well, it's a job. And Bill was smart enough to save some money before he got laid off."

"Yeah, but Emily, the place isn't livable. We're putting in new wiring and drilling a new well. The new well won't be in until spring."

"Well after the wiring and the well go in, how much do you want for the house as is. Bill and I can buy the rest of whatever needs to be added, and he can finish the work."

"Well, I'd have to have around 35 thousand. How does that sound?"

"That sounds very fair. Let's get together and close on it."

"Emily, if it weren't for Kathy, I'd kiss you!"

"Well, maybe in another life time."

* * *

On the second of May 1979, Dan drove by the new house and stopped to stare at the "sold" sign on top of the real estate banner in the front yard. He breathed his first sigh of relief in almost a year. "The next time I want to lose money I'll go to Las Vegas," he muttered. "I'm sure it'll be cheaper."

Chapter 8

House of Square Nails

Everything that was finished in the new house worked just fine now. In fact, everything worked so well that all of the windows and doors opened and closed by themselves. Nobody saw this happen. Otherwise there might not have been a moving van and pick up truck parked alongside the house on this fine spring day with the sun shining, the birds singing and a rambunctious ten-year old girl running around the house and looking in all the windows.

Her skinny arms and legs made her look like a tomboy. Her long chestnut hair and pretty face made her look like a queen. "Queen" Mary Barnes surveyed her domain and shouted, "Where's my room? Where's my room?"

"It's on the truck," said her father, Bill, pointing to the big moving van.

"This is so cool," said Mary. "There's nothing around us but country." Mary danced around the stone house with her arms outstretched. For as long as she could remember she had begged her parents to move to the country. Now here she was running around the yard of her new home surrounded by the biggest, most beautiful trees she had ever seen in her life. There was no big city traffic noise, and the closest house was a big, old, white, two-story structure behind a row of oak trees to the north. To the east, rows of corn separated the back yards from the dense forest. Open pastures stretched south, and across the road and off to the west a high bluff of jagged rocks was topped off with more dense forest.

"Hey, Mary, get out of the mud," Diane Barnes yelled.

"We've got lots of work to do."

Mary walked back toward the house, slapping her hands against her sides. "Oh, why can't we just enjoy the country for now? No more dirty streets, no more dirty alleys, no more dirty buildings, no more dirty air."

"No more lollygaggin'," said Diane. "Now get those shoes off before you go in the house. I don't want mud all over my new carpet."

"Where's Grandma and Charlie?" asked Mary.

"They'll be along in a few minutes," said Bill.

Bill Barnes didn't share his wife and daughter's enthusiasm. He wasn't looking at the pretty scenery. He pushed back the brim of his black cowboy hat, gazed at the new house, and wondered how he was going to pay for it. Diane walked up and tugged at Bill's arm. She laid her chin on his shoulder and kissed the side of his tanned handsome face. "It's going to be alright," she said. "Everything's going to be just fine."

"You bet. We'll make it alright."

But would they? Could they? So many changes had left Bill feeling helpless.

Doctors had failed to save Bill's father from the ravages of cancer last winter. The old man had weighed eighty pounds when he died. Bill could do nothing but sit outside his hospital room with his hands between his knees.

The safe haven of a secure job was yanked away a few weeks later. Bill had worked at Weber Fabrication for twelve years, making giant thermos bottles for liquid nitrogen storage. It was a non-union shop, and Bill had been cross-trained as a welder and machine repairman. Then the company felt the pinch of rising prices and shrinking profits, and sold their cryogenics department to a foreign-based company in Talladega, Alabama.

Upper management had promised to find jobs for all

furloughed workers; but, of course, it was a promise they couldn't keep. They lectured everybody about how to survive the trauma, but Bill was too shocked and stunned by the loss of his job to hear much of it. All he really remembered was that the work he had loved so much, and mastered so well, had suddenly gone south to a town with an Indian sounding name somewhere in the heart of Dixie.

On the day Bill walked out of the plant for the last time, he suddenly realized he had put his faith and trust in people who cared very little about his future and security, except as it affected their own purpose and bidding. His boss, Vern Decker, stopped him in the company parking lot and gave him one last piece of advice. "Bill, you're a damn good welder, best I've ever known. Quit worrying about what these people did to us and go your own way. You ought to start your own business. You'd be good at it."

Bill filed the fatherly advice in the back of his mind and took his pink slip home to Diane. They were both philosophical about it all.

"It can't get much worse than this," said Bill. "This is just about rock bottom. Everything has to go up from now on."

But the situation got worse. The neighborhood on the east side of Indianapolis was becoming more and more occupied by transient renters and landlords who abandoned their houses, then left the rest of the neighbors to cope with the rising crime. Mary had walked to a nearby grade school by herself for the first four years. In fourth grade an older girl beat her up on her way home. She might have been hurt a lot worse if an attentive neighbor had not come out of his house and ran the girl off.

Good ole Emily Petersen came to their rescue with the house at a bargain basement price and word about a job close by. The job was better than anything Bill had found by himself, but it only paid about half what he had been making. The house was well built, but it was going to take a lot of money to finish it and make it livable. Bill told Emily he would pay her back every dime she loaned him. She told him not to worry about it.

"Bill! Bill, help me!" Diane had a long wooden box half way out of the pickup truck bed when Bill snapped out of his reverie and rushed to grab the other end.

"What are you trying to do, kill yourself? I've got tools in that thing. It weighs a ton."

"Well, I was just trying to get stuff unloaded. You were just standing there doing nothing."

"Whoa! Slow down troops." Bill and Diane turned to see Bill's best friend, Charlie Boatright, coming up the driveway. Behind him Diane's mother, Emily Petersen, was struggling with an armload of clothes.

"Mother, let me help you with those," said Diane.

"No, no, just get yourself a load of clothes," said Emily. "Let Charlie and Bill handle that box. Hi, Mary. Hi, Bill. Well, we're all here. Isn't this gorgeous?"

"Yeah, gorgeous," Bill said flippantly. He looked around for Mary and spotted her sitting on the front door stoop scraping mud off her shoes. "Hey youngin', get over here and help your mother and grandmother."

"I've got something in my shoe," said Mary.

"What's in your shoe?" Bill ran over to Mary's side. "Aw for cryin' out loud. It didn't poke you in the foot, did it?"

"I didn't feel it."

"Take your shoe and sock off right now. Let me see it."

The rest of the crowd gathered around them. "What have we got here, our first casualty?" said Charlie Boatright.

Bill Barnes dug into the sole of Mary's shoe with his pocketknife. "Naw, it's just a nail."

"A nail?" shouted Diane. "Mary, let me see your foot."

"Mother, it's alright," whined Mary.

"Let me see it."

"It's a piece of an old square nail," said Charlie. It's probably left over from an old house or barn that used to be here."

"Mother, you're hurting my foot!"

"Hold still," said Diane. "Let me make sure. . ."

"Diane, she's alright," said Bill.

"Well where in the hell did that nail come from?"

"Diane, it was just a nail," said Bill. "Now let it be."

* * *

After three hours of unloading, they finally found the dishes. One of the movers carted in a box marked "Extraly Fine China". Everybody else chuckled at the imbecility behind his back.

"Put the dishes in the bathroom," said Bill.

"Why the bathroom?" asked Charlie.

"Because that's where we'll have to wash them until I get the kitchen sink in."

"Terrific," said Diane. "We should've moved in with mother. At least for a while."

"Diane, it's bad enough she loaned us all that money." Bill looked around to make sure his mother-in-law wasn't within earshot.

* * *

It was past five p.m. when Charlie and Bill got the gas dryer and washing machine hooked up. From the living room they heard Diane and Emily shouting at each other. "I'd better go referee those two," said Bill.

"Damn! Damn! Damn!" Diane darted around the garage looking in boxes, under piles of blankets and in every dark corner.

"What's the matter now?" asked Emily.

"I can't find my rose bushes," said Diane.

"Your what?"

"My rose bushes."

"They're in the trunk of your car. I moved them from the bed of the truck where they would get smashed," said Bill.

"Why didn't you tell me?"

"You were preoccupied at the time."

* * *

Bill Barnes and Emily Petersen strolled out the front door and watched Diane dig in the dirt by the light of the porch lamp. It was well past dark, and none of them had had any supper. "I'm gonna get us some fried chicken in town," said Emily.

"Never mind!" Diane sobbed and leaned against the stone wall.

"Never mind, I'm not hungry."

"Diane, what are you crying about?" asked Emily.

"Look at this damn dirt! It's all hard clay. You'd think we'd have decent ground out here in the country."

"Honey, it's the way they backfilled the foundation," said Bill. "All the hard stuff wound up on top. I'll get you some potting soil."

"Oh forget it! The garden stores are all closed by now."

Emily slipped over and put her arms around her daughter, then glanced at the tender little rose sprigs and their naked roots dangling in coffee cans of water. "Hey honey, I'm sorry I spouted off at you. Now look, it's not going to hurt those bushes to soak overnight. We'll get some potting soil in the morning, okay? Now go get cleaned up, and I'll go get us some supper."

Diane nodded, then Emily left for town to get some fried chicken.

"Nothing's going right with this house. Nothing," Diane said, watching her mother pull away in her old Buick.

"Aw, come on! Give it a chance, will ya?" said Bill. "Ya said so this morning. It'll be alright." He squeezed her shoulder. "We'll make it alright."

"I'm sorry. I just had a bad feeling about all this, that's all. It'll go away in the morning."

"Bad feeling about what?" Bill asked as they turned and entered the house.

"Folks, I'm gonna call it a day," said Charlie Boatright from the open garage door at the far end of the living room. "Sure there's nothing else I can do for you?"

"Why don't you stay and have supper with us," said Bill.

"Naw, I'd better be going." Charlie eased the door closed without saying another word.

Bill frowned. "That was abrupt."

"Oh, I probably scared him off," said Diane. "Baby, I'm sorry I acted such a fool today."

"Don't worry about it."

Mary gave both her parents a worried look as they passed through the living room. She had been ready to ask her dad when he was going to hook up the outside antenna so they could get a decent TV picture. Then she thought better of it. Instead she willed herself not to think that maybe all this moving was a bad idea. It was a good idea.

They slept in their own beds that night. In the morning Diane served breakfast out of cardboard boxes in what was still a strange kitchen.

"I had the most stupid dream last night," Mary said, fiddling with her cereal spoon.

"What was it?" asked Diane.

"Well, we were all in this horse drawn carriage, and we were going down this long dark tunnel. When we came out of the tunnel, the horse and carriage were on an old wooden bridge that went over a river. The river was way far below us. But the bridge only went halfway across. And that stupid horse kept trotting along. Finally, we all went off the end and started falling."

"Then what happened?" asked Diane.

"Nothing, I woke up."

Bill and Diane looked at each other in stunned silence.

"You're right. It was a stupid dream," said Bill.

"That's funny, I had the same dream," said Diane.

"You did?" exclaimed Mary. "Dad, did you have the same dream?"

"I don't remember."

"What do you mean you don't remember?" asked Diane.

"I mean I don't remember dreaming last night. Can I eat my breakfast now?"

Chapter 9

Salt and Pepper

When Mary Barnes was four she had two imaginary playmates. One was called Salt and the other Pepper. They lived in the real salt and peppershakers Diane had painted in a therapeutic ceramics class while she was still recovering from the depression of her second miscarriage. The first had come before Mary was born.

Salt was molded in the form of a fat lady with long blonde curls, a sunbonnet, and a hoop skirt. Mary shortened her name from Salt to Sal. Sal was a good old gal.

Mary played favorites with Pepper. She was molded in the form of Aunt Jemima when Aunt Jemima looked like Hattie McDaniel instead of Kim Fields. Mary was quite taken with her colorful contrast, the yellow headscarf, the black face, ruby lips, ivory smile, yellow dress, and white apron. She was so in love with the peppershaker that Mary named her Mrs. Pepper Jane Barnes, much to her mother's hilarious glee and her father's angry chagrin.

Mary lectured Sal and Pepper about their weight. "It's not good for you to be so fat." She always wanted her mother to tie a scarf around her head like Pepper's, with the knot tucked in just above her forehead.

Eventually Diane put Sal and Pepper away and forgot about them until she moved into her new house in the country. After two weeks, the Barnes family was still unpacking. At the bottom of a box marked "ceramics", wrapped in old towels for protection, Mary found Sal and Mrs. Pepper Jane

Barnes. "Mother, I found Sal and Pepper. They weren't lost after all."

"And they aren't broken," said Diane. She held each shaker in front of her and smiled. "Well, you two belong in the kitchen of our new house."

Chapter 10

Things They Can't See

Now that she was free of gravity, the Indian witch was free of the flesh, the ills of the flesh, the confinement of the flesh. She was just a spark of spirit and feelings and intelligence. She knew so much more now that she was unseen and unheard. But free as she was, she could not escape the terror of that cold winter night so long ago, and yet so vivid in pain and memory. The countryside around her was so peaceful. But her memories were so terrifying, filled with the noise of murder, fire, and butchery.

She could escape briefly by diving deep into the earth or nestling among the wood fibers and fabric strands of the house. One morning, while the sky was still orange, she found a new place to hide. The family was still in bed, and long shadows spread across the floor. A broad sunbeam came through the kitchen window and glistened on the ceramic figurines in the middle of the table. The witch found the fat saltshaker to be crude and disgusting. She thought the long blonde curls, white skin, and hoop skirt overbearing and pretentious; but the witch was overwhelmed by the color and grace of the ceramic figure that the "others" called Pepper Jane.

Such a fine figure of a woman, thought the witch. Such a stout woman she was with her ample bosom and bright smile. The witch liked Pepper as much as Mary had when she was little. She used a touch of magic to give life to the enamel and ceramic eyes, and a voice to the red ceramic mouth. They carried on secret conversations much like Pepper and Mary had. The witch told her about the horrible night so long ago when she and her entire family had been murdered on this very site. She told Pepper about the curse she had put on the Hanson family. Pepper's forehead wrinkled, and her eyes grew wet with tears at the telling of the witch's tales of magic and horror. She asked Pepper to tell her all about the Barnes family.

Because the witch was free of the restraints of the five physical senses, she could read latent impressions left by human touch. The loving touches of paint and brush and hand from Diane Barnes spoke to the witch and told her of Diane's trouble with child bearing. The loving caresses of little Mary told the witch of Mary's longing to live close to the forest and meadows of the witch's native soil. The witch even gleaned impressions from the indifferent touches of Bill Barnes. They told her of a troubled childhood haunted by memories of blood and sudden death. But the witch felt such coldness and indifference that she was only able to see blood splashing across a metal surface, hear the blast of a loud horn, and smell the strange odor of perfume.

The witch could make Pepper move from place to place now. She didn't need feet or legs like the woman who painted her or the little girl who played with her. She simply floated through thin air on the wind of the witch. But the witch told her that she had many places to explore and many creatures to inhabit. The cats and the crows and the hounds and the mice enjoyed her magic too. Besides the "others" will be getting up soon. Can't let them see such things yet.

The spirit of the murdered man possessed the body of Sal. He was the most troubled one because he didn't understand what had happened here. Were all these other people here to wreak more havoc like the men who murdered him in the middle of the night?

As the family began to stir, and the house came alive

with the sounds of footsteps and voices, the man slipped out of Sal's body and found a housefly to inhabit so he could stick to the wall and listen in on the conversations of the other people. Or maybe he would just float around by himself, unseen, unheard, and unfelt.

By night the air was quiet, but by day it was filled with the noise of hammers, and the screech of monstrous looking saws. What strange creatures they were. The "others" brought water into the space between the four walls through strange looking spigots and even flushed the waste of their natural functions with it. They harbored discarnate human voices in odd-looking boxes, and they displayed grotesque images on a glass screen in the front parlor. The house itself had a strange noise. It seemed to originate from a box-like steel contraption that sat in the attached carriage house. Here sat two strange vehicles that seemed to be propelled by some magical force. The door even moved up and down by itself. How strange.

* * *

Diane stopped the car just as the windshield hit a small rubber ball Bill had hung from the garage ceiling to tell her when she was far enough inside the overhead door. She came in the house with both arms wrapped around two huge grocery sacks. Nobody offered to help her. Was somebody following her? While the service door from the garage was still open, Diane turned to see … nobody.

"Hey, who's Coke can is this?" she asked as she sat the groceries down on the kitchen table.

"Not mine," Mary yelled from her spot on the floor in front of the television.

"Not mine," Bill called from under the kitchen sink, then went back to tightening the compression nuts on the faucet set.

Just as Bill came out from under the sink, he saw Diane smash the can flat with the heel of her hand. He might have been shocked at what she'd done, but Bill was preoccupied with hitting his head on the kitchen cabinet, yelling, "Shit!" and breaking wind.

Mary saw what her mother did out the corner of her eye. She walked over and picked the can off the table. Something was wrong here. Her mother was strong, but she wasn't this strong. She couldn't have done this, could she? Mary frowned and her heart began to race.

Something else didn't fit. Diane didn't bother putting the groceries away. She walked back out to the garage and began hauling bags of potting soil and more rose bushes out of the trunk of the car. *She's becoming obsessed with rose bushes*, thought Mary. *Why? What's making her do this? Did it have something to do with the house? There was something bizarre about this house.* The salt and peppershakers Mary had played with when she was little kept disappearing out of the kitchen and reappearing in the garage, the bathroom, and the back patio.

Mary knew no other security outside her parents' loving embrace, and now one hand of that embrace had suddenly turned grotesque and deformed. It was as though somebody had painted boxing gloves on the hands of the Virgin Mary, or vampire fangs on the Mona Lisa. A tidal wave of dread swept over her, and she tried to shake it by going back to the television and losing herself in the cartoon fantasy on the screen. Bullwinkle and Rocky were about to be ambushed again by Boris and Natasha. Suddenly it wasn't funny anymore, so Mary turned to another channel. Four people were carrying on a very dull conversation about the state's economy, but that was okay. Dull was good. Dull was comfortable. Mary sat and stared at the four stiff and stilted figures on the screen. After a few minutes she managed to stop shivering.

Chapter 11

The Face

Just before the sun went down, Diane put her garden tools away and came in the house. She was hot, tired, dirty, and sweaty. "Sorry I took so long." she told Mary and Bill. "I'll fix you guys some supper as soon as I get a quick shower. Okay?"

Bill and Mary grunted their approval from their perches in front of the television.

* * *

The door on the medicine cabinet swung open by itself. The sad face in the mist of the bathroom mirror stared at the vague outline of a female form behind the milky curtain. A shiny pipe coming out of the wall was spraying her with water while she rubbed soap all over her body. Diane finished her shower, rinsed herself off, and bent over to shut off the water. She straightened up and looked down at her lower abdomen. It was starting to bulge slightly. She knew she wasn't gaining weight. Maybe it had something to do with gravity. Maybe it had something to do with four miscarriages. Not age. Dear God, not age! She caught sight of another gray pubic hair, plucked it out with her fingers, and wrinkled her nose in disgust. Diane ran her hands over the backs of her thighs and buttocks then laid them across her abdomen. As soon as Bill hung the full-length bedroom mirror and she had some privacy, she thought she should examine herself more closely and see what Bill saw when he threw back the covers and pulled up her nightgown. God, what did he see? Was it still good for him? Or was he just relieving himself in the nearest receptacle?

Diane threw back the curtain and grabbed a towel off the rack. She dried herself off while she stood in the tub then got out and noticed the face etched in the mist of the mirror. The water droplets under the brow congealed and the eyes began to twinkle. Diane quickly wrapped the towel around her and clutched her arms in front of her chest. Just then Bill barged into the bathroom, lifted the lid on the toilet, and started urinating in the bowl.

"For God's sake, can't you use the half-bath off the bedroom?"

"Sorry, I don't have a stool in there yet."

"I thought you put one in there yesterday."

"It leaks."

"Terrific."

Chapter 12

What's Wrong With This Picture?

On June 15th everything was finished. The last light fixtures in the living room and Mary's bedroom were in, and there was finally a toilet stool that didn't leak in the half bath. Bill had been hard at work at his job and in his house since six o'clock that morning. After a nine o'clock supper, he flopped down on the floor to watch a little television.

"Bill, go take a shower before you fall asleep," said Diane.

It was too late.

Diane let him lie and went to bed a little before ten. Then it happened. Sometime after 3:00 A.M. the hall light went on by itself and . . . AAAAAAAAIIIIIIIEEEEEEEEE!!

Diane, Mary, and Bill met in the hallway. "Who screamed?" they all yelled at once.

"I didn't scream. Did you scream, Mary?"

"I didn't scream, did you scream?"

"I didn't scream."

"Well don't look at me," grumped Bill. "It was probably the television.

They all went into the living room and looked at the TV screen. It was filled with snow and softly hissed.

"See, I left the TV on," said Bill.

"Since when does a TV station sign off the air with somebody screaming?" asked Diane.

"Go to bed," said Bill as he flicked off the television set.

"Well, who screamed?"

"Nobody, Mary," said Bill. "Just go back to bed."

Mary couldn't sleep by herself that night. After a few minutes alone in her own bed, she jumped out and trotted across the hall and snuggled down with her mother. Nobody bothered to shut off the hall light. Sometime before dawn it shut itself off.

Chapter 13

Sunburn and Garden

It was now late June. Diane stood at the back patio door and looked out at the big green treeless yard and decided it was too big to be without a garden. She told Mary and Bill at the breakfast table, "Pam and I and our parents always had a big vegetable garden when we were kids. That house in the city had no space for a garden, but this one sure does."

That was on Friday. On his way home from work, Bill stopped and rented the biggest rear-tine rototiller he could find. Early the following morning, all three of them went out to measure off a garden that occupied most of the yard. Diane had planned out where to plant corn, beans, tomatoes, okra, cucumbers, spaghetti squash, and zucchini. Strawberries and rhubarb would occupy one end of the plot and raspberries would occupy the other. Bill and Diane were properly dressed in jeans, old shoes, T-shirts, and straw hats. Mary wore her usual warm weather play clothes, shorts, tank top, sandals, and no hat. She would be punished for that later in the day when the sun beat down from high in the blue cloudless sky.

Bill manhandled the rototiller while Mary and Diane smoothed out the dirt with rakes. Mary became fascinated with how well the tines tore up the sod and dirt and asked her mother, "Can I take a turn tilling the ground?"

Diane thought about Mary's request for a moment and said, "Maybe the two of us can handle that. I'll ask your dad when he comes down this way the next time. Come on. Keep raking."

Meanwhile, Mary became fascinated with the farmer and tractor in the neighboring cornfield. "Why is that man going so fast through the corn?"

Diane said, "Well Honey, that's a rotary hoe he's dragging behind him. He has to go that fast to make the tines on the hoe dig and throw the weeds out from between the rows." She smiled. "Come on, keep raking."

As Bill approached the spot where Mary was smoothing the dirt, she ran up to him and shouted, "Can I take a turn?"

Bill smiled. "Sure. I'll just walk behind you and keep an eye on you."

Diane would have protested doing all the raking herself, but the corn farmer had stopped his tractor and was walking toward her carrying a large thermos jug. He smiled and waved. Diane waved back. When he got close he said, "If I knew you folks were going to put in a garden, I would have brought out my three bottom plow."

"That's okay," said Diane. "I think we've just about got it licked."

"Awful lot of hard clay in there."

"I know. Bill says it's the way they backfilled the foundation."

"Yeah, I know. Tell you what I could do if you want. I could bring a load of horse manure over with the tractor and wagon tomorrow."

"Oh, I don't know."

"Don't worry. It'll be dry and won't stink. I shoveled out some horse barns just to get the manure for my own gardens. I kind o' overdid it, and now I've got a pile outside my barn that I need to get rid of."

"Sure, that would be great. We'd be doing each other a favor."

"Say, there's one more favor if I could ask. Could I

fill my jug out of your garden hose?"

"Oh, you don't have to do that," said Diane. "We've got ice in the house. Let us fill you up with ice and water."

"I'd sure appreciate that," said the farmer. He had a disarming smile, probably enhanced by dentures, a well-lined forehead, slim build, and well tanned face and arms.

When Bill and Mary approached, Diane took the jug and yelled, "Hey, let's take a break. Mary, take this in the house and fill it with ice and water." Diane noticed the sunburn glowing on Mary's arms and legs. "And get some aloe out of the bathroom and bring it out here. Then you need to get some long pants and a shirt on."

"And a hat," said Bill.

"I'm sorry about my manners," said the farmer. "My name's Marvin Schmidt."

"Bill Barnes. This is my wife Diane, our daughter Mary."

Marvin looked at Mary and said, "Do you folks have any cider vinegar? I always found that to be the best thing for sunburn. Being a farmer, I'm sort of a sunburn expert."

"We'll try that," said Diane. "Come on, Mary."

Bill killed the engine on the tiller and said, "Marvin, let's take a break. The patio is still in shade." They settled down in a pair of lawn chairs and fanned themselves with their straw hats.

"Nice family you got there," said Marvin. "Is Mary your only child?"

"Yeah, well, my wife has had a problem with miscarriages."

"Oh."

"You've probably got grandkids, don't you Marvin?"

"I got a couple of kids, no grandkids."

"Really?"

"Well, Daniel never got married. Janice married one

of the Hanson great grandsons. They've been to fertility clinics and everything else. Just can't have no babies."

"They ever find out why?"

"No. Now you may laugh at this, but I think it has something to do with the 'Hanson curse.'"

"The 'Hanson curse'?"

"Yeah, most folks around here don't know much about that."

"Tell me about it."

"Well, it's kind of a long sad story. You're sitting on old Hanson farmland in case you didn't know it. That's the old Hanson farm house next door."

"Actually, I didn't."

"Sam and Margaret Hanson had five kids. Your neighbor, Alice, was the oldest. She outlived every one of her younger brothers and sisters."

"Really? What happened to them?"

"One of the girls, Vera, grew up and married a farmer named Joshua Moorehouse. She died of tuberculosis during the depression. Now, they had two kids. One of 'em was Louella Pritchett. She owns the National Motel out there on Road 137. They were good people, too. Plain people, but Joshua and Vera both had hearts of gold. A lot of folks around here would have starved to death during the Depression if it hadn't been for them They let whoever wanted to come to the farm and plant little gardens for themselves. Joshua did his own butcherin', and he shared a lot of beef and pork with his neighbors if they didn't have nothin' else to eat. Cryin' shame about Vera. Good woman like that dyin' young. After that Joshua sold his farm to Bob Parson's father. It's the land just east of here where Bob built that big fancy mansion.

"There was another daughter named Katherine." Marvin chuckled. "Boy, she was a looker in her day. She married a man named Kenneth McCauley. Their son, John, is

Bob Parsons partner. They're selling all this old Hanson property. Poor Katherine was killed in a car crash back in the forties. She and her second husband both died in the crash."

"What happened to her first husband?"

"Kenneth started drinking pretty heavy after he came home from the First World War. He and Katherine were divorced soon after that."

"What about the other two kids?"

"Both of the boys were killed in World War One."

"Really? They were lucky enough to have two boys and both of them died in the war."

"Yep."

"What were they like?"

"Robert Hanson was a real hellion. He went out one Halloween and turned over twenty-seven shit houses."

"Twenty-seven? In one night? By himself?" Bill laughed.

"Well, I don't know about by himself. He got caught though, and he was in more trouble with his pappy than he was with the law.

"Now Victor Hanson. He was the apple of his mama's eye. A real good piano player. He might have amounted to something. 'Course he wound up like his brother. They both *had* to get married. Neither one of them were much more than teenagers."

"You're kidding. Shotgun marriages back then? I'll bet that didn't go over too good."

"A lot of things didn't go over well with them old Hansons." Marvin frowned and his mouth turned down as he looked over at the old farmhouse. "I never had a whole lot of use for those two. Samuel was always buying people's respect with money to build a new church and a new grade school. He and Margaret were always front and center to tell everybody how to live too. I got along with their kids and grandkids. Not many people I know had a whole lot of use for Sam and Margaret.

"Anyway, the two boys went off to war. Both of them got killed within six months of each other."

"What happened to their families?"

"They were both farm families. They lived at home for a while. Then the young widows eventually remarried, but they stayed close by. That was the thing back then. Families always stuck together. Not like that now. Cryin' shame. Not like that now."

"Were both of the Hanson parents alive when all this happened?"

"Sure were. Their mother Margaret died shortly after Katherine was killed. People said she died of a broken heart, and I suppose she did. The old lady came down sick with a cold one winter then got pneumonia. Well, she recovered from all that, and I'll be damned if a heart attack didn't kill her. The old man died in 1947. He just died of old age, of course. Meaner than a snake, just mean to everybody around him.

"Most folks back in the day said Sam was gettin' his due for all the shenanigans he pulled. Whatever they were. I was just a kid at the time, didn't know nothin' about it."

"All the Hanson kids had kids of their own?"

"Yep. Except Alice. She stayed a spinster all her life."

"How do you know all of this, Marvin?"

"Small town. You know how gossip travels."

"Yeah, I know small towns." Bill chuckled. "Sounds like your gossip goes back a long time."

"Well, I been a gossip hound since I was a kid. I heard most of it in church."

"In church?"

"I'd sit in front of a couple of old hens, waggin' their tongues, waitin' for church to start. I'd hear all kinds of stories."

Bill laughed. "But nobody ever told you about what kind of shenanigans old Sam Hanson did?"

Marvin glanced away for a moment and said, "Not a word."

Bill suspected Marvin was holding something back, something about the old days, something about the "Hanson curse".

"Well, I talk too much myself anymore," said Marvin. "But, Bill, I got to tell you this. The best of that whole Hanson clan is good ole John McCauley. Now he ain't like most folks around here. John's well educated, but he earned his keep. He worked and paid his own way through college and helped his Aunt Alice with the farm. I never knew anybody who worked harder than him, and I never knew anybody who was so determined to do right by friends and family.

"Darn shame about John and his wife Sharon too. They had a daughter years ago, but she died when she was only four."

"Oh no," said Bill. "What did she die of?"

"Something that made a high fever. Before they could bring her out of it . . . she just . . . passed. God, it was awful, pretty little thing, such a beautiful little tyke. That hurt folks all around here.

"After that John and Sharon kind o' turned to spiritualism, or whatever they call that weird stuff, when they talk to the dead and go into trance. Kind o' spooked me, but it didn't seem to hurt nobody."

Marvin got out of his chair just as Mary and Diane came out the door. "Here you are," said Diane as she handed over the big thermos jug. "All full of ice and water."

"Thank you very much, ladies." He looked at Mary's

glistening arms and legs and said with a chuckle, "You smell mighty purty."

"I stink like vinegar," said Mary.

"Well, that will take the sting out of the sunburn for sure. Thanks for the ice and water," said Marvin. "I'll get back to work, and I'll bring you a load of manure tomorrow."

As Marvin headed across the back yard to his field, Bill said, "A load of manure?"

"He's got a pile of old dry manure at his place," said Diane. "He said we could have it to soften up our garden."

"Great," said Mary. "Between me and the manure, this place will really stink."

* * *

Six weeks after everything began to sprout, Mary was on her hands and knees pulling at the thistles and dandelions and wincing at the fine needle sticks from the thistle leaves irritating her hands. Mary had skipped her mother's advice and left her garden gloves in the garage. At one point she heard water hitting the ground, and assumed her mother had come out with the garden hose to water the corn and tomatoes at the opposite end of the garden. When she looked up from the weeds she had been pulling, she saw what she thought was a dog trying to hide between the cornrows. Mary got up and went over to investigate.

"Oh my God!" Somebody was peeing in the dirt. Water for the garden wasn't coming out of a hose. It was coming out from between a pair of long dark-skinned legs. The woman attached to them had her rawhide dress pulled above her waist while she squatted over the dirt. "What are you doing?" Mary shouted.

The woman straightened up, let her dress drop around her legs, and turned toward Mary. She had long black hair tied in braids that hung down her chest. She looked at Mary with dark brown eyes and spoke in a guttural foreign tongue.

The dark-skinned woman ran down the row of corn, turned and ran along the side of the garden. "Hey, what do you think you're doing?" When Mary chased after her and looked down between the rows of beans, there was a black crow sitting on the ground. Suddenly the crow squawked and flew over Mary's head.

Where did the woman go? Where did the crow come from? Something at the patio door caught Mary's eye. She glanced over and saw Pepper Jane on the living room floor looking out at her. Somehow her grin didn't seem as friendly as it did before.

Chapter 14

New School, Nasty Water

The summer went too fast. Diane drove Mary to her new school to register in mid-August, but Mary wasn't sure she liked it at all. The old Millie Hartman Elementary School had been expanded several times. It sprawled over two full city blocks.

"Riding the school bus will be a new adventure for you, won't it?" Mary's grandmother, Emily, had said.

Yeah, big adventure. Yeah, big school. Yeah, new kids, new teachers. Let's go back to the city.

The big yellow beast with the flashing red eyes pulled up in front of the house in the middle of a torrential rainstorm as Mary went out to get on. She walked down the aisle and looked for a seat where she could be alone. There was one near the back. Great!

As the bus pulled away Mary noticed that a boy, four seats in front of her and severely marked with a gross case of acne, kept looking at her, then looking out the window. As the bus rolled on, the boy kept stealing glances back at Mary. *What's his problem?* She thought.

The bus stopped to pick up another girl, and the boy kept looking back at Mary, making her wonder what he had in mind. Was he going to mess with her right here on the bus? This wasn't a big city sidewalk. She thought she would be safe on the bus.

"Can you sit someplace else?" Mary looked away from her overt admirer and up at a fat girl standing over her while rainwater ran off her yellow slicker and onto Mary's book bag. She repeated, "Can you sit someplace else? Janet and I always sit here."

"Yeah, sure." Mary scooted across the aisle and sat next to a boy who smelled a little like gasoline. She clutched her book bag close to her chest and sat as close to the edge of her seat as she could while the boy kept staring out the window.

When they got to school, Mary tried to keep a crowd between her and the boy with the acne. He sought her out and tried to catch up with her. The rain had stopped, but she had to jump over puddles to keep her feet dry on her way to the front door.

"Hey come back," yelled the boy. "I'm not going to hurt you. I just want to ask you a question. Please stop. Please!"

Mary barged past a line of kids going through the front door. When she got inside the acne kid was right behind her. "Please stop. I just want to ask you something." He was making a scene with his squeaky voice.

Mary stopped and turned on him. "Who are you and what do you want?"

"My name is Donny Wallis. You live in that new house out at the old Hanson farm, don't you?"

"What about it?"

"Please don't be mad. I lost my dad out there last fall."

"Your dad? What does my house have to do with your dad?"

"He put up the drywall in your house. The day he finished it he disappeared. Nobody's seen him since."

"Oh. Well, I'm sorry about your dad. What did you want to ask me?"

"Well, it seems kind o' stupid now. I was gonna ask you if you'd seen my dad. He looks just like me except he don't have no pimples."

"Doesn't have any pimples." Mary corrected his grammar just to keep the upper hand and Donny off balance.

"Oh, yeah. Well, of course you probably haven't seen him. So I guess I just wanted to ask you if you'd seen anything unusual out there."

"Like what?"

"I don't know. Gee, you're not making this very easy."

"I'm sorry. I really haven't seen anything unusual."

"Are you sure? Some people say that place is haunted."

"Why do they say that?"

"Lots of bad stuff happened out there."

"What kind of bad stuff?" Mary's dark eyes flashed.

"The place burned when they were building it."

"I didn't hear about that."

"There's probably lots of things about that place you haven't heard about."

"Like what?"

"Like my dad disappearing." The boy turned and stomped down the hallway.

On the first day of school Mrs. Chambers' fifth grade class was treated to a substitute teacher, an ancient dowager named Miss Haverstick. She wrote her name on the blackboard and underlined the word Miss. Then she noticed a group of kids near the window holding their noses and fanning the air.

"What is going on over there?" the old lady thundered.

"Make him put his shoes and socks back on." One of the girls giggled and wrinkled her nose.

"Young man, why are you taking off your shoes and socks?"

"They're wet."

"How did they get wet?"

"It's been raining."

"I know it's been raining. Everybody else seems to have dry feet."

"No they don't."

"Mister, you'll find that contradicting me will only get you into more trouble."

"His feet are still wet," whined one of the girls.

"I see that."

"They stink!"

"Now that's enough! Young man why didn't you wear your rubbers to school if you . . ."

The whole class erupted in gales of laughter.

Oh no, thought Mary. *Why did she say rubbers? Doesn't she know any better than to say rubbers in front of a bunch of stupid boys?*

* * *

The worst part of the day was going back home. On the way to the bus Donny Wallis rushed by Mary, then turned and glared at her. On the bus Mary got a window seat sitting next to another girl she didn't know, who didn't bother to introduce herself. Nobody seemed very friendly at this school. Donny Wallis was pushy, but that wasn't friendly. So his dad disappeared while he was putting up drywall in the house. What did that mean? That he was rattling around in the walls someplace? Donny wanted to know if she'd seen anything unusual. Well, let's see . . . A woman peeing in the garden, Mary's mother crushing a pop can with one hand, Pepper Jane disappearing and reappearing in odd places. Other than that . . . oh, the dream. There was that stupid dream and that horse and carriage that went sailing off the end of a bridge.

Mary got off the school bus and stood in front of the house not wanting to go in. *This was not home.* The idea overwhelmed her. *It was a new house in the country where I always wanted to live, but this was not home.* The stone was gray and cold. The black roof was like a dark malevolent brow. The windows had the glint of evil eyes. But Mary went inside, and suddenly she felt very thirsty. When she got a glass of water, the smell of it got to her instantly. She dropped the glass in the middle of the sink and ran for the bathroom.

Mary was kneeling on the bathroom floor with her hands on the toilet bowl while she puked and prayed, puked and prayed. "Please God, don't let me lose my stomach in the john. Please God, don't let my head fall off in the john."

Diane ran into the bathroom and soaked a washrag in cold water then laid it across Mary's face. "My God, honey, when did you get sick?"

"Just now."

"Were you sick at school?"

"No, just now."

"Are you gonna throw up some more?"

"No, I'm through. I'm . . .I'm okay."

"Come on baby, let's go lay you down in your room."

As quickly as it had come on, the dizziness and nausea disappeared. But Mary's morose mood stayed awhile. She sat up on her bed and stared out her window.

"Mary, I still don't understand what made you sick," said Diane.

"There was something in the water."

"Something in the water? What did it taste like?"

"I don't know."

Diane ran to the kitchen and filled a glass from the faucet. Mary listened to the rush of water and thought it sounded like an animal hissing. She looked around the walls of the room and wondered if Donny Wallis' dad was buried in one of them.

Diane came back into the bedroom. "Water tastes fine. Are you sure it wasn't something you ate at school?"

Mary shook her head. "It wasn't anything at school."

"Somebody didn't offer you something they weren't supposed to, did they?"

"No! They didn't!"

"You lower your voice, young lady."

"Let's move away from here Mother," Mary said. "I hate this place. Let's leave today."

Diane's first thought was that awful day at Mary's old school. Distance seemed to help time do the healing, until now. "Mary, did something happen at school today?"

"No."

"Are you sure, honey?"

"Mother, please! Nothing happened!"

"Mary, I'm not accusing you of anything. I just want to make sure nothing happened to you."

"Nothing happened at school, Mother. It's this place. I hate it. I don't want to live here anymore."

"How can you say that? You've looked forward to moving to the country for so long."

"I don't care," Mary said through her tears. "I can't stand this place. I want to go back home!" With that she lay down on her bed and cried into her pillow, while Diane wondered what to do next. The nightmare was supposed to be over, but where was the dream of new sunshine? A cool breeze caught Diane's bare shoulder. She got up to close the bedroom window.

It was already closed.

She thought she heard a strange noise coming from under the house. There were so many strange noises out here.

All the plumbing in the house originated from a blue steel tank in the crawl space. The pressure switch and gauge attached to its bottom hummed with noise from the submersible water pump. When the gauge registered fifty pounds the pump shut down. All the pipes were quiet now except for a final popping and gurgling sound that shook the black well line. The plastic tube snaked across the floor of the crawl space, through the foundation wall, under the yard and out to the main well pipe sticking out of the ground. The well itself tapped into an underground stream that wound its way across the entire length of Forest County. The ghost of the murdered woman jumped in and out of the water screaming with glee. She was finally getting through to them.

Chapter 15

A Night Visitor

The city girl liked the country, but not when the sun went down. Diane could not get used to the tomb-like silence of the night punctuated only by the wind and rustling leaves. Bill had explained to her that the footsteps she heard in the hallway were the floor beams contracting with the cool evening air. Then he told her about the animal sounds.

Diane thought she had heard a baby crying out in the woods in the wee hours of the morning. "Oh, it's probably some stupid cat," Bill mumbled only half awake, "Cats sound like crying babies when they're having kittens."

"That's not it," Diane said. "I swear I know I heard a baby crying out there in those woods last night."

"Yeah, well, it could be sheep too. When they get sick they sound like crying babies."

"Sheep! When did you ever see sheep around here? Bill. . .Bill."

He was already sound asleep.

Later that night Diane awoke out of a sound sleep and saw light from the bathroom seeping into the hallway. The LED alarm clock next to the bed read 3:00 a.m. She waited for the bathroom door to close. She waited for the sound of the toilet flushing. She waited for the sound of Mary's footsteps. No flush. What's going on here?

Diane slipped out of bed and peeked into Mary's room. She found her daughter asleep so she went to turn off the bathroom light. Just as she got into the hallway, the light went out and left Diane staring into the darkness. She couldn't see anything, but she felt the sudden rush of what she knew was somebody running by her. But who?

"Biiieeell!" she screamed. "Bill! Bill! Bill!"

By the time Bill reached the hallway, he had tripped on the bed covers and banged his head on the bedroom door-knob. "What?" He yelled as he turned on the hallway light.

"There's somebody in this house!" Diane yelled. She was flattened against one wall, her eyes wide and her chest heaving with each breath. Bill reacted instantly. He ducked back into the bedroom and came back with both hands wrapped around a revolver and the barrel pointed straight up.

"Where in the world did you get *that thing*?!" Diane exclaimed.

"It's protection, okay?"

Bill crept down the hallway with his back to the wall, glancing both ways as he moved. Diane clutched at the wall as she watched Bill duck into every room and turn on every light in the house. Finally, he came back to Diane with the gun hanging limply at his side. "There's nobody here."

"There's somebody in this house!" Diane yelled.

"Yeah, I heard you the first time. And I'm tellin' you there's nobody here."

"Bill, I swear to God, somebody ran by me when I came to turn off the bathroom light."

"Diane, go back to bed."

"Are all the doors locked?"

"Yes, all the doors are locked."

"How do you know?"

"I checked them!"

"How about the windows?"

"Diane, get back in bed!"

"Bill, check the windows."

He grabbed his wife by the wrist and took her into every room to show her that every window and door was locked.

"What the hell do you mean yellin' your fool head off for anyway? If somebody had been in the house, they'd probably kill you just to shut you up."

When they came out of the living room and into the hallway, they froze at the grim figure in front of them. Standing under the incandescent glare of the hall light, Mary Barnes stared at her parents with eyes that looked like onyx stones set deep in her porcelain face. Her arms hung limp at her sides and her hair dangled straight in long, dark greasy locks.

Diane whispered, "Mary?"

No answer. Mary turned, went back into her room, and got back into bed. Bill and Diane turned to look at each other then went into Mary's room and turned on the desk lamp near the head of the bed. The little girl turned over and groaned but didn't wake up. Her long brown hair covered one side of her head like a sheet of silk.

"My God, Bill, what's wrong with her?"

"Nothing. She was walking in her sleep."

"But her face!"

"It's the way the light hit her. We were both hallucinating, Diane. We're just tired, okay? Let's go back to bed. Things'll be better in the morning."

Chapter 16

The Gun Moll

In the morning Bill discovered something terribly important was missing. "Diane, where's my pistol?"

"What do you mean? I sure haven't seen it."

"It's not here."

"What do you mean it's not here? Not where? Damn it, Bill. Why in the world did you bring that thing in the house in the first place?"

"I've had it for the past two years. I got it for protection, okay?"

"No, it's not okay. We've got to find that thing now!"

Diane looked in every dresser drawer, every table drawer, then under every couch, bed, and easy chair. Bill went to the garage and started pulling boxes, paint cans, and tools off every shelf. He dropped a pint can of red enamel paint that splattered the concrete floor with a deep crimson. The sight of the red paint made an air horn and a dull thud echo from deep inside his memory. It spooked him so bad he let out a yell, and Diane came running out to the garage to see what was the matter. She found Bill standing in the middle of the floor staring wide-eyed at the mess and shaking with fright.

Diane went up to him, touched him on the shoulder. Bill recoiled at her touch and shouted. "It's not here, okay? The damn gun isn't here!"

She backed away from him with a start and said, "Okay . . .okay, Bill. It's not here. What's the matter?"

"That's the matter, see?" He pointed at the red paint mess.

"We'll clean it up later. It'll be okay. You're gonna be late for work. Would you like me to drive you to work?"

He took a deep breath. "No. I can drive. I gotta drive anyway." He noticed her worried look. "Forget it, Diane. Forget it ever happened." He stomped out the side door of the garage, got in his pickup truck, and drove off.

* * *

Diane sat at the breakfast table sipping a cup of coffee while Mary ate her cereal. "Did you know that Daddy had a gun, Mary?"

"No."

"Did you see him with it last night?"

"No."

"Do you remember what happened last night?"

"No."

Diane carefully set her cup down. "Mary, are you alright?"

"Yes."

"Mary, look at me."

Mary ignored her mother and kept eating her cereal. When she was finished she got up from the table, slipped into the living room, then picked up her lunch box and book bag.

"Mary, where are you going?" asked Diane. *God help me there's something wrong with her.*

Mary left through the front door and cut across the front yard. Diane yelled, "Mary, come back . . ." Then she saw the school bus pull up just as Mary got to the edge of the yard.

The bus doors swung open and the lady driver glanced up at Diane running across the yard as Mary disappeared into the bus.

"Did you want something, Mrs. Barnes?" yelled the driver.

"Ah . . . no."

"Is everything okay?"

"Yes, everything's fine."

The driver looked to the back of the bus. "Did she forget something?"

"No. She's okay." *I hope.*

* * *

In the basement of the Millie Hartman Elementary School, a wooden table and a wooden chair sat beside the enormous boilers. Mary Barnes came down the stairs, eased over to the table, then put one foot on the chair. She lifted the hem of her dress and unstrapped her father's pistol from her upper thigh. She laid the piece on the table, put the belt around her waist, then went back upstairs to join her class-mates at recess.

Farley Mandon waited for her outside the basement door.

"Young lady, what were you doing down there?" asked the janitor.

Mary gave him a look that iced his insides and almost stopped his heart. Her eyes glowed like silver moonbeams, her lips turned thick and panic button red, and her grin showed pointed yellow teeth. She turned and walked out the side door to the playground.

Farley was still rubbing his eyes and shivering as Mary disappeared into the crowd of kids. *Did her eyes really glow? And what was that awful stench coming out of her mouth?*

The boiler room was Farley Mandon's domain. No-body else was allowed. Not kids. Not teachers. *Damn, what if that little bitch found my hooch.*

Farley trotted down the stairs and over to his wall

locker. He stood on his step stool and hauled up the twine that dangled a pint bottle of Early Times behind the locker. Two swigs and back into the dark corner went the booze. Farley popped two breath mints to cover the smell.

"I was seein' things," he muttered to himself. "I was seein' things. That little girl's eyes didn't really glow." Not like he'd seen in the eyes of a possum or dog when the headlights bounced off them in the middle of the night just before the wheels flattened them.

Farley looked at his watch, 11:00. "Screw it, time for an early lunch."

He hauled the lunch box out of the locker, walked up to the table, and stared down at something that he had seen only once before in his life. Lying there in the middle of the table, still in its holster, was a chrome-plated 357 Magnum revolver. Farley pulled the gun out of its holster, looked at the front of the cylinder, and saw that it was fully loaded with hollow point bullets. He couldn't believe his good fortune. He had wanted one since he saw a 357 in the hands of an old buddy at the Forest County Conservation Club. This one was a beauty and it was loaded with some stopping power.

The old man picked up the pistol and pointed it at the far corner of the boiler room. He closed one eye and looked down the barrel and imagined pointing the gun at somebody. Then he imagined cocking the hammer and gently squeezing the trigger. "Bam! There goes yer hair, teeth and eyeballs ya son of a bitch."

For the next half-hour he sat there eating his lunch with the gun on the table in front of him. Then he put the piece in his lunch box, took it out to his car, and locked it in the trunk. *Don't suppose that little girl put that gun down there on my table. Well, it's mine now. Can't nobody prove different.*

Chapter 17

The House That Scratch Built

Before Mary's big yellow bus pulled into the school parking lot, Bill Barnes was approaching an old house in the middle of Tanner's Grove. A simple sign in the front yard said that the house was not a home; it was "Carter Oil Company". Bill pulled into the neighboring alley and parked in back. He looked at the grim buildings, shook his head, and muttered, "Man, what a way to work. What a way to live."

He glanced at his watch: 7:40. "No sense in going in just yet." He opened his thermos of coffee and poured some hot eye opener into the cup lid.

When he was a young boy, Bill carried hod for a bricklayer, baled hay for his farm neighbors, and shoveled manure out of his uncle's horse barn. But driving a truck for Carter Oil Company was the worst job he ever had.

Herbert Carter had started the business from scratch after he came home from the Second World War. He groomed his two sons to take it over while he grew old and lived out the rest of his days with one hand wrapped around a whiskey bottle. After more than thirty years in business, the place still looked like scratch. The office, lunchroom, and drivers' staging area were in an old two-story frame house on Main Street. It needed paint, a new roof, new siding, or better yet, it needed a wrecking ball. The trucks were kept in a rusty, dilapidated pole barn surrounded by a gravel lot.

Sam Carter was the taller and skinnier of the two brothers and carried a hot temper. Max carried an even hotter temper and all the authority. God help anybody who forgot that. He was built like a tree stump; short, thick, hard, and mean. Max was the absolute ruler of all the property, including the Old Dog Tavern, and all the people in his company. It was obvious which he valued most. If a driver called in and said he had had an accident, Max's first question was, "What did you do to the truck?"

Bill worked for Carter Oil for two months before he discovered the existence of a third brother. Joey Carter ran the fleet maintenance garage for the company at his house just south of Tanner's Grove. The diminutive form of his name was used only because Joey was the youngest, not the smallest brother. He was over six feet tall and built like a Bermuda onion on thick stilts.

Being the youngest, he was the last brother Herbert had taken into the business. Joey had an even meaner and more unpredictable temper than Sam or Max. But he had a longer fuse so Herbert put him in a route truck. Everything went fine for six months, until a lone woman driver backed her car out of her driveway into Joey's truck parked alongside the road where he was dragging a fuel oil hose across a snow covered yard. The accident caused no damage at all to the truck, but it crinkled the back bumper and trunk lid of the hapless woman's car. Joey flew into a fit of rage, grabbed a pipe wrench, smashed the woman's rear window, and finished off her rear end. She locked herself in the car until a neighbor finally called the sheriff. By the time a deputy got there she was hysterical, and said that she sure as hell wanted to press charges. But she never showed up in court, and the charges were dropped.

Joey got in trouble again when he stood at a basement window watching a customer's fourteen-year-old daughter take a shower. There was no stall, no curtain, just a showerhead and faucet set on the wall. Joey said it wasn't his fault. He had to be there anyway to stick his hose in the fill pipe that ran to the basement oil tank. After that Max set him up with a house and a garage. He told him to "keep his greasy ass under his greasy trucks" and stay away from the rest of the business.

It was 7:45 a.m. when two denizens of the Old Dog Tavern, Ron Collins and Harvey Gutz, pulled into the opposite side of the parking lot in Harvey's battered pickup truck. Harvey had his cab radio turned up full blast, and the two of them were howling to the chorus of "Werewolves of London". Harvey and Ron took turns ducking down in the seat out of sight. Bill glanced their way and knew they were sharing a joint.

Bill couldn't stand the sight of Harvey Gutz, "the little rat-face runt." His unique talent for making his skull sound like a plunger clearing a clogged drain drove Bill to distraction. Harvey could swallow and sniff at the same time, causing a sucking sensation deep inside his head.

He said it made his ears feel good.

Bill wanted to feel sorry for Ron, the moron, but Ron's face kept getting in the way. He had a glass eye that sat in a patch of burn-scarred flesh extending from high on his forehead down to just above his upper lip, a reward for burning trash as a young boy. It was the one chore he relished, and he always enjoyed watching the flames consume everything in the trash burner while he stood too close to the fire.

One day a piece of flaming plastic flew out of the pile and landed across one side of his face cooking one eyeball and leaving ugly rivulets of flesh that constantly got infected and took over a year to heal. There wasn't even enough muscle tissue left to attach to the glass eye. The hideous white marble with the fake iris sat bulging out one side of his head.

Like Harvey, Ron had a talent for making bodily noises, but his came from the opposite end of his anatomy. He bragged constantly that he could fart on command. He would make a big production of it by screwing up what was left of his face, lifting one leg and--ppfffffttt!

"You're gonna shit yer pants one o' these days, Ron," Harvey warned him. "You drink a lotta beer. One o' these days it's gonna loosen them bowels, and you're gonna shit yer pants."

"Naw naw. I can always tell when one's gonna get too wet."

Bill got out of his truck a couple of minutes before 8:00. Maybe he could get into the office before Harvey and Ron finished blowing weed. He was wrong. His two favorite hemorrhoids were coming across the parking lot and closing fast.

"Hey Bill," yelled Ron. "Did ya hear the one about the nun and the bus driver?"

Bill tried to ignore him. *No Ron, I really don't want to hear the one about the nun and the bus driver.*

"There was a nun and this hippie. He he he he he."

"I thought it was about a nun and a bus driver," said Harvey.

"Well this nun and this hippie rode the same bus every day. Damn it, let me tell the joke, Harvey. Well, this hippie kept asking the bus driver how he could hit on the nun."

This was going to be too stupid and dirty even for Bill. He was about fifty feet from the back door of the office. Ron was still jabbering about a lecherous hippie, a cross dressing bus driver, and something about anal sex. He was too broken up in gales of laughter to finish the joke. Bill passed through the back door and hurried down the hallway to the front staging office where he picked up his route tickets for the day. Mercifully, Ron and Harvey ducked into the hallway lunchroom.

As he passed the last office on the left, he snickered at the sight of Sam Carter mashing wet plaster into a hole in the wall opposite the door. The day before, Sam and Max had gotten into an argument. Sam lost his temper and took a swing at his big brother. Max ducked and Sam's fist put a hole in the dry wall. As Max came back to a standing position, he planted his knee in Sam's groin. While Sam was still bent over holding his family jewels, Max made him walk across the street to the hardware store and buy whatever he needed to fix the hole.

"And if you charge it to the company, I'll **cut** your nuts out," Max bellowed.

Bill looked around for a desk, a table, anything to spread his paper work out and organize it. There was only one place with a table big enough for this mess. Regretfully, he went down to the lunchroom.

As he came in, he heard Ron ask Harvey Gutz, "How's your brother? He still sick?"

"Hell, yes, he's still sick," said Harvey. "He's got colon cancer."

"What's that?"

"Cancer of the gut."

"He still got that tube wrapped around his face?"

"Yeah."

"How's come?"

"So he can get oxygen."

"Well if he's got cancer of the gut, why don't they stick that tube up his butt?" For Ron it was an honest question. He didn't crack a smile.

Bill broke up and laughed hysterically. He knew Harvey didn't like him, and he really didn't care.

But Harvey had to ask, "What the hell's so funny?"

"Nothing," said Bill. "Except the thought of one of your relatives with a tube up his butt."

"Aw, fuck you, Barnes."

"And the horse you rode in on, Guts."

"Gootz, you asshole. Quit makin' fun of my name."

Ron said, "Oh oh, speakin' of assholes." He lifted one leg, squinted his good eye shut and cracked a bean in his britches. "I'll be Goddamned." He lowered his leg while a look of horror spread across his face.

"What's the matter, Ron?" asked Bill with a knowing grin.

"I just shit my pants."

Harvey howled with laughter and pounded one wall. "I told you you would, dipshit."

Ron walked out of the lunchroom like a bowlegged cowboy, down the hall, then out the back door.

Max Carter poked his head in the room and yelled, "Where's Ron Collins?"

"Went to shit and the hogs ate him," Bill shot back between tears of laughter.

Max didn't answer but went racing down the hall and slipped on a calling card Ron had left on his way out the door. His enormous hind quarters came down hard and ground his freshly dry-cleaned trousers into the goo. "Jesus Christ! Who the hell shit all over the Goddamn floor?"

Bill came into the hallway and admired the sight of Max Carter picking his fat hams off the floor with the excrement of one of his employees decorating one side of his pants. "Ron had a little accident while he was showing off."

"Aw hell! I'm gonna tell that son of a bitch to come to work with a diaper from now on." Max raced back down the hall, ducked into his office and commanded his younger brother Sam, "Cover the phones. I gotta go home and change."

"I see you do." Sam came out in the hall and watched his brother run out the front door, trying to keep the fresh wet mess away from his skin with his fingertips. Then he turned, doubled over with laughter as he and Bill Barnes exchanged red-faced expressions of glee. It would be the first and last time the two men would share a good joke on somebody else.

From another office came the shrill voice of Carolyn Marsh, the office manager. She was on the phone, shouting at an office supplier, accusing him of committing fellatio and having sex with somebody's mother. Bill tried to sneak by her office and down the hall when Carolyn yelled, "Bill Barnes, get your ass in here."

You called, horse face. Bill walked in just as Carolyn was backing her swivel chair up to the credenza behind her desk. He got a good look at her legs and miniskirt. She turned back around, pulled herself up to her desk, leaned over, and gave him a peek at some cleavage.

While Bill was ogling, Carolyn asked, "You got a truck report for me?"

"Truck report?"

"Yeah, dummy. You know, how much oil you put in your truck. How much fuel you put in it. I know that damn thing don't run on air."

"Oh, yeah. I'll get it."

"Hey! Come back here! I ain't through with you yet. I don't know what I have to do to get you route drivers to fill out your tickets right. We need the price per gallon, not just the total amount. We need the exact number of gallons down to tenths, and we need your signature as well as the customer's. Is that clear? You suppose you can handle that?"

"I'd handle it a lot better, lady, if you'd come down out of the clouds and yank that broomstick outta yer ass!"

Bill got out of Carolyn's office before her shocked expression turned to tears and jumped into the cab of the big LN 7000 delivery truck. "Oops! Forgot my cash purse."

He ran back into the staging area and grabbed the leather tote and ran past Sam Carter's office just as he heard him say, "Now settle down. Settle down."

"I can't settle down!" Bill heard Carolyn cry, "I'm up-set. I've never been treated like this before."

"Awwwww shit," Bill muttered to himself. He knew he was in big trouble, so he decided to stay out on the road the rest of the day and not call in. It would give him time to decide his next move in life, which he hoped didn't include the Carter family, their witchy bitchy office manager, their bubble gum and bailing wired trucks, and their firetrap office building. He was so preoccupied with where his life was go-ing Bill almost lost track of where the truck was going, and that there was a traffic light ahead, and a line of stopped traf-fic in front of him. By the time he stomped on the brake pe-dal, he came close to running into a motorcycle rider wearing an orange T-shirt that read "Can you see me now Asshole?"

Chapter 18

Lady in a Cage

Mary Barnes got out of bed that morning, dressed herself, strapped her father's gun to her leg, ate breakfast, went to school, deposited the gun in the school basement, and gave the janitor an evil glare before she went out onto the playground.

Then . . . she woke up.

She didn't remember one moment of any activity until she stood at the chain link fence separating the playground from the street. With her fingers laced through the wire, Mary held on to the fence with all her might and struggled to keep her grip and her balance. The moment of wakefulness had come like a lightning bolt. The sudden shock of seeing asphalt, green grass, cars, blue sky, houses and steel fence scared Mary so badly she gasped and yelped and cried. Then she started climbing the eight-foot fence. When she got to the top, her hands gripped the sharp pigtail twists in the fence wire and started bleeding.

A voice came from behind her. "Mary? Mary Barnes, what are you doing?" One of the teachers climbed up beside her and grabbed her wrists. "Mary, for heavens sake, your fingers are bleeding." The teacher tried to pry Mary's fingers off the chain link fence, but her grip was tight and she was afraid of doing more harm. "Mary, let go."

Mary turned to the teacher and screamed, "Help me. Please help me. I want to go home." One of the men teachers, attracted by the commotion, ran up to her, grabbed her by the hips and hauled her back to the ground.

In the nurse's office Mary's world started caving in on her. The smell of alcohol, iodine and cotton bandages; the feel of warm water washing over her bloody hands; the closeness of the tall, husky, big-bosomed school nurse drying and bandaging her hands; the commotion of so many voices around her made her shiver and wish she was anyplace but where she was.

Mary wasn't supposed to be here. She was supposed to be home just getting out of bed. How did she wind up here all of a sudden? Just as quickly, she found herself out of the nurse's office, then down the hall and walking into the principal's office where her mother ran and threw her arms around her. Suddenly it seemed like the scene at her old grade school in Indianapolis. An older girl had accosted her, but this time the culprit was unseen and unknowable.

Chapter 19

Slow Motion Rider

Bill Barnes didn't notice that the green Ford Escort passing him on the four-lane highway belonged to Diane who was carrying his daughter to a doctor's office. He was still fuming and carping over his lot in life when a voice from the past started playing over and over again. *Bill, you ought to start your own business. Bill, you ought to start your own business.* He couldn't get the thought out of his head. When he and his old boss parted company, Bill had relayed the fatherly advice to Diane. She had not taken it well.

"Are you crazy? We'll all starve. You're not starting a business." And that had been that.

Until now.

The prospect of running a business was scary, but it was becoming more and more attractive.

As he approached the stoplight at a major intersection with two lanes of cars stopped in front of him, Bill stepped lightly on the brake. The pedal went all the way to the floor. Bill's heart went all the way to his throat. He pulled up on the emergency brake lever. The brake cable snapped.

The terror of the moment forced Bill's brain to process everything he saw and everything he did in minute detail. As a result, everything seemed to move in slow motion. He shifted to a lower gear and steered sharply to the right to avoid the cars. Now on the narrow shoulder of the road, he was bound to tip the big truck over. Somehow he managed to get through the intersection without turning over or getting hit by oncoming traffic.

Two cars squealed rubber as the drivers slammed on the brakes, swerved to avoid hitting the big oil truck, and wound up hitting each other. Nobody was hurt, but two very expensive front ends had broken glass and metal scattered all over the intersection.

Bill careened down the highway, out of control, and headed for more cars, more babies in restrainer seats, more women with groceries in the trunk. In a panic, Bill steered the truck back to the left and bounced over into the grassy median in the middle of the four lanes. He was sure the dish shaped area of grass would rock and tilt the big truck and make it turn over. Instead, the lower gears and the soft grass brought the steel beast to a halt.

Several minutes later Bill's heart was still trying to pound its way out of his chest, and his white knuckles were still wrapped around the steering wheel when the sheriff's deputy climbed up on the driver's side fuel tank and peered in the window at Bill.

"Hey, bud, are you alright?"

Bill couldn't find his voice, but he nodded his head and kept staring straight ahead.

"Let's see if we can't get you out of this truck and into someplace a little more relaxing," the deputy said. "My car is parked right there in front of you. Now somebody else is going to handle the accident scene. You and I have to handle the paper work."

Bill couldn't answer anybody yet. He kept staring out the windshield and nodding his head.

"You sure you're okay?" asked the deputy.

Bill nodded his head again.

"Well, let's get you outta there. It's alright. Come on. We can handle this."

* * *

Herbert Carter needed a shot and a beer every morn-

ing just to make it through the day. As he watched the wrecker bring in the big oil truck, he knew he was going to need
another round just to make it through the afternoon.

Bill was already out of the cab of the wrecker and half
way across the gravel yard by the time Sam Carter came out
the office.

"Hey, what the hell's going on here?" Sam yelled at
Bill.

"Get your ass in the office! I need to talk to you and
your shit head brother."

Sam grabbed Bill by the shoulder. "You stand right
there, prick." Bill whirled around and slammed his fist into
Sam Carter's face. The tall skinny man went sprawling in the
dirt then bolted up and went after him.

Herbert rushed over and grabbed his son by the shirt
collar. "You leave that man alone. Bill's the best man I ever
hired for this job."

Sam batted away his father's grip. "You didn't hire
him, you old fart! **We** did. You haven't done a damn thing
around here in over five years. Now get outta my face!"

Bill, his face ashen and half his shirttail hanging out,
stomped into Max Carter's office. Max had been talking to a
well-groomed young man sitting just inside the door when
Bill turned to the visitor and shouted, "I hope to God for your
sake you ain't lookin' for a job here, sonny boy. Because these people will get you killed!"

"Hey! What the hell's the matter with you?" asked
Max.

"Here's your truck keys and my time card."

The large desk and small office were the only things
that kept Max from grabbing Bill in a hammerlock. "Will you
shut up? You got a phone call . . ."

"Your hunk of junk is outside on the business end of a
wrecker."

"Will you shut up? I'm trying to tell you . . ."

"You take your one-horse business and your junk trucks and cram 'em sideways!"

Max stood and leaned as far over the desk as his fat gut would allow. "Shut up! Shut up! Shut up and listen to me. You got a phone call this afternoon."

Sam Carter walked up behind Bill, slapped a hand on his shoulder, then shoved a piece of notepaper in his face. "Your wife called around noon. You're to go to this address. It's the Blackwell Medical Clinic."

"Oh."

"If you'd call in once in a while you would have got this a lot sooner." Sam was still dabbing blood off his nose with a white handkerchief.

Bill asked, "What did she say was wrong?"

"She didn't say!" Sam shouted. "That's for you to find out."

"Okay. Look, I'm sorry . . ."

"Get outta here," Sam shouted. "We'll mail your last check to you. Go on. Get outta here."

As Bill left the parking lot and hit the street, there was a reflection of Carter Oil Company in his rear view mirror. He didn't see it. All he could see was the road ahead and the wonder and worry over what had happened to his wife and child and what would become of all of them.

Chapter 20

No Need For The Nuthouse

Mary sat on the examining table and stared up at the doctor as he felt around her neck. "Why are you doing that?"

"I'm looking for lumps or an enlargement in your thyroid, Mary. Sometimes these episodes can be the result of an overactive or enlarged thyroid."

"I just want to get out of here and go home." Mary's voice cracked and she started to cry.

"It's okay now," said Doctor Blackwell. He put an arm around Mary's shoulders and took her doubled up fists in his hand. The cotton gauze wrapped around them was bloody but dry. "I think we can have the nurse put some fresh bandages on you while I talk to your mother. Diane, would you hold onto her while I round up a nurse."

Diane came over and slipped an arm around her daughter. "It's okay baby, the doctor's going to make you well again."

"What's he going to do, put me in a nut house?" cried Mary.

Diane said, "No, no. Of course not."

A petite young nurse came in and took over, greeting Mary with a smile before unwrapping the cause from her bloody hands. Clarence Blackwell and Diane went over to the doctor's office.

She paced while Doctor Blackwell sat behind his desk and motioned to a chair in front. "Have a seat."

"I can't. I've been a nervous wreck all night."

"Tell me about it. What happened?"

"We had an episode."

"An episode?"

"I thought I heard somebody in the house. When Bill and I searched the place, we found Mary standing in the hallway. She looked so strange."

"Strange? How?"

"She looked like a zombie. Her eyes had this evil look to them. Then she just went back in her room and went back to bed. Bill said she was just walking in her sleep."

"Has she done this before?"

"No, never."

"Is there any history of sleep walking in Bill's family?"

"None that I know of."

"Any history of hyperthyroidism in Bill's family?"

"No."

The doctor fidgeted in his chair, took a deep breath and went on. "Diane, let me ask you, has there been a lot of stress in the family lately? You told me about the incident at Mary's school in Indianapolis. I haven't seen any of you since then."

"Doctor Blackwell, we lost our insurance when Bill lost his job."

"I realize that, but I was about to ask, did Mary get over that episode?"

"Yes."

"How about the move to the country? Until that episode last night, how have you been getting along there?"

"Fine."

"Are you sure?"

"Well, Mary came home from school the other day very unhappy. She got a drink of water and got violently sick right away."

"Where did the water come from?"

"Out of the faucet in the kitchen."

"Really? You live on a private well or city water?"

Diane sighed and rolled her eyes. "I don't know. How am I supposed to know that?"

"Do you get a bill from a city water company?"

"No."

"You live out in the country, don't you?"

"That's right."

"Have you had your water tested?"

"No."

"I would have that done. It won't cost you anything."

Diane stopped pacing and looked at him. "That's fine, but what about this thing this morning? I don't understand why they had to haul Mary off the fence."

"It could be stress induced. It could be hyperthyroidism. I've seen this happen to children and adults both. They get up in the morning, go to school or work, spend the whole day in the office or classroom, and then they wake up; and they have no idea how they got there. Sometimes it goes away. Sometimes I've had to call in a specialist."

"A shrink, a head doctor."

Doctor Blackwell leaned forward in his chair. "Diane, don't stigmatize this. Actually I was going to call in a neurologist. But not right now. Right now I want to ask you, has Mary had a tetanus shot lately?"

Diane looked puzzled. "I don't think she has. Why?"

"Well, she has some pretty bad cuts from that school fence."

"Oh, for God's sake. I was so worried about her head I forgot about that."

When the doctor and Diane came back into the examining room and told Mary she needed a tetanus shot, she jumped off the table and headed for the front door. "I don't want a tetanus shot."

"Come back here, young lady," Diane commanded. She looked back at Doctor Blackwell and said, "We have a problem with needles."

"I don't want a tetanus shot," pleaded Mary.

"Mary, you could get very sick without one," Diane said. "Now sit down here and quit being such a cry baby."

"Why can't I just take a tetanus pill? I hate needles. You know I do."

Diane had to wrestle her daughter back into the hall-way waiting room where at least a half dozen other people were waiting to see the doctor, and they were all staring at Mary and Diane. "Mary, stop it! You're making a scene."

A man came up to Diane and put his hand on her shoulder. "Little lady, I wonder if I could help?"

"What?"

"I'm here to get an allergy shot myself. Perhaps I could take you and the little girl with me, and I could help her get over her fear of needles."

"I'm sorry. You'll have to excuse us. She's very upset right now."

"You're both upset. Maybe I can help."

"Well, I don't know . . ."

"Please. It can't do any harm. Let me show you." There was something about the warm smile, the thick mane of brown hair, the tall, trim body and the deep resonant voice that melted Diane's heart and made her give in.

"Oooookay."

"My name is John McCauley. And you are?"

"Diane Barnes. This is Mary."

"Diane, Mary, come over and sit down. Let's have a little talk.

"Now Mary, your mother tells me that you have a problem with needles."

"I don't have a problem with needles. That doctor has

a problem with needles. If he thinks he's going to stick me in the butt with one of those . . ."

"Mary!" Diane tried to stifle her daughter while looking around the hallway at all the people trying to stifle a laugh.

John McCauley said, "You know, Mary, you're right. That doctor does have a problem with needles. That's why he lets his nurse, Carla Jones, give shots. She gives shots that don't hurt.

"Hold out your finger . . . Go on, hold out your finger." John lightly pinched Mary on the finger. "That's what a shot feels like from Carla Jones. You see, some people, including doctors, don't know how to handle a needle. They stick it in too fast or too slow. They stick it in at the wrong angle or they push the serum in too fast or too slow. Carla knows exactly how to do it.

"John McCauley." The blonde, statuesque nurse came into the hallway and called for her next patient.

John got up to follow her then turned and motioned Mary and Diane to follow him. When they all sat down in the treatment room, Carla Jones turned and looked at the duo with surprise. Before she could say a word John said, "Carla, this is Mary Barnes, and Mary has a problem with needles. Somebody has given her a shot before and hurt her. Do your shots hurt, Carla?"

"Huh. . .why. . .no," Carla stammered.

"I didn't think so." John started rolling up his sleeve. "Now, I'm here to get my allergy shot. But I want Mary to watch so that she knows that you know how to handle a needle."

Carla finally chuckled then took the serum out of the glass cabinet and ripped a fresh syringe out of its cellophane bag.

"Now Mary, I want you to give me your finger again

and pay very close attention to what Carla is doing. She's wiping my arm with rubbing alcohol to keep out any infection. Now she's placing the needle at just the right angle." Carla inserted the needle, squeezed the plunger and pulled the needle back out in less than two seconds. John pinched Mary's finger. "Did you feel that? That's what I just felt. That's because she's good. Carla here is very good."

John McCauley rolled his sleeve down and got up to leave. He motioned Diane to follow him. Mary walked up to Carla and pushed up the short sleeve of her dress exposing her shoulder.

Back out in the hall Diane turned to John McCauley and asked, "Mr. McCauley you're not a witch, are you?"

He smiled. "It's just the power of suggestion. I've studied such matters for some time now."

"Nobody's been able to handle her like that, ever."

"She just needed the right suggestion."

"Thank you, Mr. McCauley."

"You're welcome. If you'll excuse me for being forward again, you're Emily Petersen's daughter, aren't you?"

"Why yes."

"You look exactly like your mother, and just as pretty if I may say so."

"You may." Diane's smile gave her cheeks a slight flush. "How do you know my mother?"

"Well, I sold her and your late father their last house just north of Coalton. She and your sister Pam still come to some of our meetings once in a while. I haven't seen your mother for a while. How is she?"

"You're the one," Diane exclaimed. "You do some sort of hypnosis or parlor magic at your house."

"We do something called prenatal regression. We explore the idea of reincarnation . . . who we were in our past lives. We do a little parlor magic too. Your sister hypnotized your mother one night and convinced her that the glass of water she was drinking was really straight bourbon. She had her feeling quite tipsy before she brought her out of her trance."

"Oh my God! I didn't hear about that," exclaimed Diane.

"Your sister was an interesting case. While she was in trance she related the life of a deaf woman in England in the nineteenth century."

"And now she works at the deaf school in Indianapolis. Fascinating."

Mary came up and stood beside Diane. John said to her, "That wasn't so bad, was it?"

Mary shook her head and took her mother's arm.

Diane said, "Well I'm very glad to have met you, Mr. McCauley."

"Say hello to your mother for me," said John. "And tell her we should all get together at our house sometime."

On her way to the front door, Diane met Doctor Blackwell again. "I'd like to see you again," said the doctor. "Just you."

"I'm fine," said Diane.

"Why don't you let me see about that?"

"I'm fine. It's Mary we should all be worried about."

"Call me, Diane. Please. For Mary's sake, for Bill's sake, for your mother's sake."

Diane looked at the doctor for a second and said, "I will. I promise."

Diane found Bill pacing up and down in the lobby. His hair was askew. His shirttail was still half out, and one shoe was untied. As soon as he saw Diane he rushed up to her. "What happened? Where's Mary?"

"Bill, keep your voice down. Mary stopped off at the bathroom."

"Well, what happened?"

"The school nurse called this afternoon. Mary had an accident of some kind."

"Accident? Is she hurt?"

"She's got cuts on her hands."

"Cuts? How the hell did that happen?"

"Shhhhh!"

"Don't shush me. How did Mary get cut?"

"She was climbing a fence."

"Why was she climbing a fence?"

"That's a problem, Bill. Mary doesn't know."

"What is this? Everybody wants a piece of my daughter."

Diane lowered her voice. "Bill, don't start with her. I just got her calmed down enough to get a tetanus shot."

Bill blew out a breath, then nodded. "We'll talk about it later. Come on, let's go home."

Chapter 21

No Water

As Bill drove home, his anger and frustration were tempered with the realization that he was going back to a wonderful wife and daughter who lived in a nice house where dear old dad had no job - again. But he thought he had it all figured out. He would tell Diane that he was going to get his welding gear back from his friend Charlie Boatright. He would put a business ad in the local newspaper. It would read: "Barnes Welding Company. No job too small; no job too big." Or something like that. He knew Diane would have a tizzy fit, but she would just have to get over it.

* * *

When they walked through the front door, Diane got busy fussing over Mary. "Let me see your hands, honey. Okay, they're dry now. We'll put fresh bandages on in the morning."

"We haven't had supper yet. How am I supposed to eat?"

Diane sighed and walked Mary to the bathroom. "Let's have a look."

Bill collapsed in a living room recliner and tried to find the right words to say to his wife. Finally, he just let her have it. "Diane, I quit my job."

"Bill?"

"Did you hear me?"

"Did you hear me? Get down here to the bathroom." When he arrived, Diane and Mary were attempting to wash their hands. "We have no water." Diane fiddled with the lavatory and bathtub faucets. No water.

"That's ridiculous." Bill went to the other bathroom off the master bedroom and the kitchen sink. No water. "Man, what kind of a brand new house has no water?"

"Maybe there's something wrong with the pump," said Mary.

"What pump?" Bill asked.

"The well pump. One of my teachers at school had to have her pump fixed the other day."

"What the hell does a ten-year old kid know about pumps anyway?" Bill muttered to himself. He went out in the garage and tried to look like he knew how to fix the problem. He found a furnace, a water heater, and a circuit breaker panel.

"Now, where does the water come from?" he muttered. "Let's see, out here in the sticks it comes out of the ground, right? Now how does it get in the house?" Finally a blue sticker on the water heater gave him a clue. It read: *F&H Heating and Plumbing. For emergency repairs call 555-4436.*

"Well, this is an emergency." So Bill called the number from the phone in the living room and let it ring and ring and ring and ring. Finally somebody picked up the other end and burped into the receiver.

"'Lo?"

"Is. . .this F&H Plumbing?"

"Yeah."

"My name is Bill Barnes. I gotta problem. We don't have any water."

"Check your circuit breaker?"

"The what?"

"Circuit breaker!"

"What has that got to do with the water?"

"Your well pump runs off your circuit breaker panel, pal!"

Bill slammed the receiver down on the desk in the living room and stormed out into the garage. He came back in less that a minute and picked up the phone. "The circuit breaker marked pump is on, pal!"

"You still don't have any water?"

"No!"

"Okay, okay. Gimme your address. I'll come out and look at it."

"Look at it? How about fixin' it?"

"Yeah, I'll do that too, but not until you give me your address."

"Forty-seven seventy-one county road 600W."

"I'll be there in a few minutes."

Bill hung up the phone and yelled down the hallway. "Somebody's comin' out to fix the pump. Diane, get down here. I got something to tell you."

Diane hovered in a corner of the living room, casting a nervous look at her husband slumped in a recliner. This wasn't going to be pleasant. "What is it, Bill?"

"I quit my job."

"You what?!"

"I quit my job. Now listen to me! I'm going to call Charlie Boatright and get my welding gear back."

She leaned forward. "You quit your job? My God, Bill!"

"That job was crap!"

She stabbed at the air with her hand. "It was a job!"

"It didn't pay worth a damn!"

"It paid something!"

He surged out of his chair. "Diane, listen to me!"

"Why should I listen to some asshole who just quit his job?"

"Diane, I'm starting my own business."

"You're what?"

"Diane, listen to me!" Bill clapped his hands in front of Diane's face to make her shut up. "I'm starting my own welding business. You'll see. We'll have money coming in like we used to. Things are going to start looking great again." Bill's expression was intense, but not reassuring.

"Great," Diane said. "We have a wounded daughter, doctor bills coming in, and no job. We've got a mortgage and no job. And you! You've got some wild-ass scheme to start your own business? Bullshit!" She burst into tears and ran down the hall into her bedroom and flopped across the bed.

She was still sobbing when she felt somebody's presence in one corner of the room. She rolled over to yell at Bill then gasped at the sight of the most powerful looking man she had ever seen. He had long black hair tied in braids, a big hooked nose, dark piercing eyes, and dark blue trousers held up with leather suspenders over a dark blue shirt. There were blisters and blackened flesh on his face and hands. Diane froze. She wanted to scream, but her tight throat wouldn't let her.

Her body shook and her head filled with a terrible buzzing sound. She felt herself sinking deeper and deeper into a dark hole in the ground, the big ugly man staring down at her all the while. Suddenly she sailed back toward the ceiling, then through the ceiling and above the roof. She came back through the roof into the living room. She looked at herself in the living room mirror and found no reflection. She ran to the bathroom mirror and found no reflection.

The floor dropped out from under her and she fell through a black hole in the ground again. At the bottom of the hole, Diane splashed into a pool of water so hot she thought she was going to boil. When she came back to the surface of the pool, kicking and coughing and sputtering, she saw a woman in a rawhide dress standing on a rock at the edge of the water. Her body glowed in the darkness of the subterranean cavern. She had a beautiful face with dark eyes and full mouth. She wore a chain and medallion around her waist. The medallion was made of silver bars in the form of an X bisected by a vertical line. Her long black hair was tied in twin ponytails that hung across her chest. She raised her arms straight over her head with her palms facing each other and formed an enormous electric spark between her hands that blossomed into a blue ball of fire. She threw it at Diane; and when it hit her, Diane went flying out of the water, up through the ground, and off through empty space.

Now she was falling again, and when she hit bottom this time she was standing in a dark room lit only by two candles. A man with long black hair tied back with a bandanna wielded a paintbrush. He used the full swing of his arm to make the blue paint splatter across one wall of the room. Suddenly, he seemed aware of Diane's presence and whirled. His head snapped back and forth; and, by his expression, Diane realized he knew she was in the room; but he couldn't see her. Then his gaze fixed on her, and he reached out his hand to touch her.

With her mind and spirit separated from her body, Diane was able to see and remember every detail of the man's face. His bushy eyebrows were massive; eyes were dark, skin was brown and wrinkled; and he had a hair lip creasing his mouth. But his gaze was terrifying, and Diane shot straight up out of the room and sailed back through the void of empty space with no sense of which way was up or which way was down. She curled up in a fetal position and squeezed her eyes tightly shut. A feeling of vertigo forced her to stretch out in a spread eagle position. There was no sensation of falling, but when she opened her eyes she was flat on her back in her own bedroom with Bill and Mary hovering over her with wide-eyed terror etched in their faces.

"Mother, what happened?" whined Mary.

"I don't know. I don't know."

"Diane, are you alright?"

"I'm okay. Just don't do anything right now, okay? Let me be; let the dizzies go away."

"Diane, you feel sick?"

"No, just get me a cold washrag, okay? I feel hot."

"No water, remember? How about a couple of ice cubes?"

Mary ran to the kitchen to fetch the ice, and Bill asked, "Diane, what happened?"

"Good question. I'll tell you what I saw if you tell me what you saw."

"What do you mean?"

"I wasn't here. I was somewhere else." Mary came running into the room and pressed two ice cubes on either side of Diane's head. "Oh, that's nice. Thank you, honey. Now what did you two see?"

"Diane, you were just staring up at the ceiling. I didn't think you were breathing there for a minute. Then . . ."

"Anybody in here need water?" Somebody yelled through the screen door. Bill went in the living room and let the man in. He was shorter than Bill and twice as big around. His enormous girth was clothed in a black T- shirt and blue jeans. The back of his shirt was decorated with an elaborately painted skull and the words Grateful Dead emblazoned around it. His long curly hair and bushy beard made him look like a fat dust mop. "Well, I can't get you any water from here. Where's your pressure tank?"

"What?" Bill asked.

"Your pressure tank. The tank that holds your water."

"How the hell should I know?"

"Which way to the garage?" he sighed.

"Follow me."

The man looked around the garage, then let out another deep sigh and said, "Aw, it's probably in the crawl space." He walked over to the circuit breaker panel and opened the door. "Look, I'm only going under this house once. I want somebody to stand by this pump switch here, see? When I pound on the floor and yell at you, I want you to shut this switch off, okay?"

"Okay," said Bill.

"By the way. You got stinky water out here I'll bet."

"It smells once in a while."

"It does more than smell. It probably stains your clothes and scales up your plumbing. We can put in a good water softener for you for about four hundred dollars."

"I don't know if we can swing that kind of cash right now," said Bill.

The plumber rolled his eyes and said. "Of course not. You'd probably have to float a loan, right?"

"Just get us water for now. Okay?" Bill snapped.

The man waddled around to the back of the house and looked for the crawl space hatch. When he found it, he popped the sheet metal door open and squeezed his mountain of blubber into the hole. He held his tools and parts in one hand and his flashlight in the other. It was starting to get dark and the man knew that by the time he finished under the house it would be pitch black outside. He hated crawling around under houses at night.

The house didn't appear to be that old, but the cobwebs between the floor joists made it look ancient and decrepit. "I'll bet he don't have his dryer vent hooked up right," the man muttered to himself. He batted cobwebs out of the way and searched the crawl space for a blue steel tank. He lay on his side and scooted along with his light and tools held up in one hand. His shirt rode up, leaving his bare belly exposed to the rough gravel. He felt rocks working their way inside his waistband. "Damn crawl spaces. Gonna gore me to death yet."

He waved his flashlight around again and finally found the pressure tank sitting on concrete blocks near the main support beam. He crawled over to it and pointed his flashlight at the pressure gauge. It read zero. He unscrewed the cap nut on top of the pressure switch and lifted the plastic cover. A probe of the wiring contacts with his circuit tester showed 220 volts. With a small end wrench, he began turning the adjustment nut. A blue spark jumped between the switch contacts and ballooned into a small sphere. There was a hum and the tell tale rush of water into the tank.

"Simple enough," he said. But what did he just see in the blue spark? "A face. Did I see a face in the spark? That's crazy. And why was the switch arcing like that?" The pressure gauge read fifty pounds. The pressure switch arced again and shut off. There it was again. The spark between the contacts of the switch swelled into a ball with a face inside it.

"God, I'm tired," he muttered. "Now I'm seeing things."

The blue sparks were making the crawl space smell with ozone. No, it wasn't ozone. It was something else, something sweeter.

He knew he should replace the pressure switch. *These yahoos will probably call me again in the middle of the night if I don't.* He pounded on the floor with his pliers. There was the thud of footsteps overhead. After allowing ample time for somebody to turn off the circuit breaker, he checked the voltage on the pressure switch. Nothing. Good. The idiot got that right.

The plumber opened the valve on the bottom of the tank and drained all the water. It sparkled in the eerie silver light of the flashlight. But it sparkled blue. What made it blue? Suddenly there were footsteps splashing through the puddle in front of him.

"Holy shit! Who's there?" he shouted. He waved his flashlight around the crawlspace to see who was running and splashing through the water. Nobody.

"How could anybody run through that mud puddle down here? God help me, there's nobody down here but me. Oh God, please don't let there be anybody down here but me."

He pulled in a breath. "Alright now, get hold of yourself." His round body rocked back and forth as each breath came with a giant heave while his heart raced.

Was that his own breathing he heard in these close quarters? Sure it was. He held his breath just to make sure. Silence. He hurried along, unhitching the wires from the pump pressure switch, unscrewing the switch assembly, and mounting the new switch, reconnecting the wires.

He pounded on the floor. "Okay, turn it on." The sound of his own voice shouting helped reassure him . . . a little.

The pressure switch hummed and sparked again. The spark swelled and turned into a face that quickly vanished. Water spewed out the boiler drain, and the man had a small flood before he got the valve handle turned off. The water was sparkling blue again. The pressure switch kept humming until the gauge read fifty pounds. Another click, a spark, and the switch shut off the flow of water into the tank.

But the blue spark didn't go away. It swelled until it formed a face with bug eyes and a mouth opened in a loud scream. The fiery sphere passed over his head and singed all the hair on his face. The man screamed and scampered across the rocky floor of the crawl space, scraping his knees and elbows and banging his head on the floor joists. As he squirmed out of the hatch window, the overhead door hook made a long bloody scratch down his back. He ran around to the front of the house, jumped in his truck, and roared off down the road.

Bill came around the back of the house to see what all the commotion was about. He walked around front, down the driveway and looked down the road at the taillights disappearing into the night. "Man, how'd he move all that blubber so fast?"

Mary came up behind him. "Dad, we got water back in the house."

* * *

Homer sat staring at the sunburst pattern of blue paint on the wall of the apartment. The walls in every room were painted black; the wood floors were bare; and there were naked light bulbs in the ceiling. The place had always been a crash pad. The middle-aged son of a bank president and the son's teenaged girlfriend had used the place to peddle dope until the local sheriff and the Drug Enforcement Administration caught up with them. There was no furniture save for an old mattress in the living room and another in the only bedroom.

"What are you doin' splattering paint on the wall?" asked Anna Lee.

"Need something in this dump," said Homer.

"What's you gonna paint now?"

No answer.

"I said, what - "

"I hear ya. Shut up. I'm trying to think."

"Don't hurt yourself."

Homer grinned. "We had a visitor just now. Pretty little lady."

"Who was she?"

"Couldn't tell. She wasn't all here. Just a little ghost of a lady. She was so scared. I tried to touch her and calm her down. She just sailed off into thin air."

"Did she die?"

"No. She just lost her skin and came sailing through here."

"I don't like it when you do that, Homer." The skinny old lady's voice had a whine to it.

"Do what?"

"Have all them creepy visions. You see things and it scares me."

"I'm having another one now."

"What is it? No! Don't tell me."

"I ain't tellin' you nothin'. But I'll give you a little hint." Homer came close to Anna Lee's side. He squinted his eyes tightly shut and opened his mouth wide. A tiny infantile voice began to wail, very softly at first, then becoming very loud. "aaaaaAAAAAAAAAAAAA!" It wasn't a man's voice imitating a crying baby; it was a voice that should have come from the vocal chords of a newborn infant. "AAAAAAAAAAAAAA!"

"Stop it! Stop it, Homer," yelled Anna Lee. "You doin' all them spirits and it's givin' me the awful creeps."

Homer suddenly closed his mouth and opened his eyes. "It was a baby, Anna Lee."

"I know it was."

"Well, they had no right to murder her. They had no right. You got that? No right. No right at all!"

Chapter 22

Grabbing A Wild Cat's Tail

"You sure you know what you're doin', ole buddy?" Charlie Boatright watched Bill lash the acetylene and oxygen tanks to the front of the bed of his pickup truck. He handed him his safety goggles and welder's hood.

"Put those in the front seat," Bill told him.

"You're real sure you know what you're doing?"

"Yeah, yeah." Bill jumped out of the bed and went back to the garage. "Come on, help me get the chop saw in there."

"No, no. Get the arc welder."

"Yeah, okay."

"Hey Bill, slow down man. Let's talk about this awhile."

"I ain't got time to talk. I got work to do."

"You ain't got work to do yet. You ain't even in business yet."

"I'm in business right now."

"Bill, you ain't no businessman. We both know it.

"Aw come on, Charlie. I thought we were friends."

"We are. That's why I'm asking you. Do you know what you're doing here?"

"You know damn good and well I do. Now get down there and help me boost this thing up in the bed."

Charlie bent down and grabbed the bottom of the arc welder control box and boosted it up to Bill. Then the two of them loaded the big power miter saw and some hand tools. Finally Bill slammed the tailgate shut.

"Bill?"

"What?"

"Come on in the house a minute."

"You're gonna give me a big lecture, aren't you?"

"Hey pal, this is ole Charlie talkin' to ya, okay? We've known each other since we were old enough to walk and talk."

"So?"

"So, I know something's eating you pretty bad right now, pal. What is it?"

Bill leaned against the truck bed and let out a deep sigh. "Charlie, I quit my job. Caught hell from Diane for that. Now I'm startin' my own business."

"Yeah, I know that."

Bill looked down inside the truck at nothing in particular for a moment, then he said softly, "Charlie, I'm scared."

"I know that too."

"I'm scared, Charlie, but I'm gonna do it anyway."

"You're no businessman, Bill Barnes."

"No, I'm a welder."

"Well, now, there's a few things you gotta consider, Bill. You got any health insurance? You gotta consider Diane and Mary."

"Diane's taken a job in the city. She's carrying our health insurance."

"Diane's lookin' kind o' peaked lately."

Bill gave Charlie a surprised glare. Charlie raised his hands to show he was backing off.

"We got insurance, Charlie."

"There's other kinds of insurance you have to carry with a business. Some of them you've probably never heard of."

"Yeah, I'm calling an agent tomorrow."

"You'd better."

"Okay. Okay."

"Bill, you gotta think about paying your own taxes now. Not just once a year, every quarter. You have to pay your own social security. Have you really thought about any of this?"

Bill gave him a sarcastic grin. "Well, what do you think?"

"I think not." Charlie interrupted as Bill started to say something else, "Bill, there's something else bothering you. What is it?"

"How do you know that?"

Charlie leaned across the truck bed and raised his eyebrows. "Ole buddy, you and I have known each other longer than we've known our wives. We've known each other so long we've been known to finish each other's sentences...just like married couples. You can read me like an open book and I can read you the same way. Right now your book tells me there's something besides jobs and money eating at you."

"You're reading something that ain't there, Charlie."

"Am I?"

"Yeah, you are."

He waved at nothing in particular. "Well, anytime you want to talk about . . . "

"No time! I got no time to talk about it. There's nothing to talk about, okay?"

"Okay, Bill. Okay."

Bill saw the hurt look on his friend's face and backed off. He wanted to apologize. Instead he looked away and said, "I gotta go. I'll see ya." Then he got in his truck and left.

* * *

"My God, do I really want to do this?" Bill muttered as he drove down the narrow county road. Till this moment, every crisis in his life had had an end that he could see from the beginning. His army boot camp had ended after eight weeks. His father's bout with cancer had ended in death. But now he had quit his job and was starting a business. He felt like he had grabbed a wild cat by the tail and was being dragged into a dark tunnel. Where would it end? What about Mary and Diane? They were being dragged with him. A small twinge of guilt ran through Bill as he thought about what Diane was doing right now.

Chapter 23

A Nightmare of Men

Diane parked her car in an open lot downtown and walked over to Delaware Street. She headed south three blocks to the offices of Morley Temporary Services. She could have saved time by walking down Massachusetts Avenue, but that would have taken her by a rescue mission, a hole-in-the-wall tavern, and an apartment house with derelicts passed out in the doorway. Along the way she would have been ogled and harassed by drunks sitting on the curb and urinating in the street.

How did all this happen? Diane wondered to herself. A few short months ago she and Bill and Mary had bought a nice house in the country. Bill had found another job and Mary was going to a nice school. Now everything had fallen apart: Mary's behavior at school, Mary's behavior at home. There were the strange noises in the house at night and the strange smell of the water and the crazy trip with the crazy vision she had a week ago. What was that all about? Then there was her brief meeting with John McCauley. Did he know something about the new house, the old farmhouse next door?

The traffic light turned green and Diane crossed the street. How did she wind up here? The steel gray sky above her, the black asphalt under her feet suddenly seemed unreal. She had worked for George and Maxine Morley as a temp before. Ten days ago she called them again after Bill quit his job. The bastard!

Maxine told her they had a permanent job opening in

their office, full benefits and all. Happy days are here again! The first day she showed up for work Diane got a very nasty surprise.

Maxine had promised her a position to match office workers with temporary jobs. George broke that promise. "Diane, I need your help in the back. My dispatcher quit yesterday. I need you to fill in until I hire somebody else." He had sweat dripping off his bald head and his big nose.

Diane had no idea what he was talking about until they walked back to the narrow hallway office partitioned by glass next to a dingy waiting room. The room was jammed with tables topped with cracked, cigarette burned Formica and tacky little plastic and tubular metal chairs. There were drunks with day old beards, clean cut guys, and guys so filthy she could smell them as soon as she walked into the dispatching area. They were sitting against the wall, at the tables, and leaning on the counter at the glass partition. George told her they were temporary day laborers for the industrial division and they were waiting for the day's job assignments. He showed her the employee index cards, the customer index cards, and the cash box for handing out cash draws against paychecks.

George was in a panic. He babbled on about this guy needing to fill out an application; this guy couldn't have a cash draw until he worked. The whole world seemed to be caving in on them. That first day Diane had to call the police to arrest a man who threatened to kill everybody in the office because he didn't get the pay he thought he had coming. She had to call an ambulance for a man having an epileptic seizure. She called the police again to break up a fight in the waiting room.

She kept hoping the nightmare would end soon when she overheard Maxine say to George, "I want Diane out of that back room. I want her out of there tomorrow. It's not right for a woman to put up with that bunch of bums. There are plenty of men who could handle that job."

But the men never came and now, on her sixth day at work, Diane was tugging on the front door of the office and cursing the day she heard about Morley Temporary Services.

She walked into the dispatching area and quickly scanned the board for the day's jobs to be sent out. She tried to ignore the little man at the counter window, but he kept yelling at her and pounding his fist on the counter.

"What do you want?" Diane asked.

The little man had a tongue that seemed to fill his whole mouth and he had a hard time talking through his toothless gums. Instead he kept pushing a piece of yellow paper at Diane, and pounding on it with his index finger. Finally she looked at the barely legible scrawl that indicated his name and below it: $2.00.

"I'm not going to give you a two dollar draw," said Diane. "You pulled that stunt on me before when you hadn't even filled out an application."

"Worked yesterday," the man mumbled.

"You didn't work yesterday. You walked off the job."

"Worked yesterday!"

"Damn it, Fred, you showed up for two minutes yesterday and walked off. If you want to work today, that's fine. But I'm not giving you a two dollar draw until you bring back a time sheet showing me that you worked." Diane backed up and busied herself with paper work.

* * *

While Diane was fretting about her lot in life, Max Carter was fretting about his. He was about to lose his primary source of wealth. He unlocked the back door of the Old Dog Tavern and climbed the creaky wooden stairs to the second floor apartment. The whole building reeked of urine, stale beer and cigarette smoke. At the top of the stairs he knocked on the door and got no answer. Impatiently, he let himself in with a key. He went straight to the bare mattress where Homer was asleep and snoring.

Max bent down and shook Homer by the shoulder. "Hey Bud, get up. We got an emergency."

Homer came awake with his fists clenched and his feet raised, ready for a fight. "What the hell?"

"Get dressed. I need you to go to the big city and get me some bodies."

"Again?"

"Again. The Old Dog is closed today, just today. Some asshole at the county health department pulled a surprise inspection on me yesterday and gave me one day to clean the place up or they'd shut me down."

Max paced the floor and struggled to catch his breath. "Now . . . I need you to go to the usual place and get me four bodies, preferably sober, who don't mind mopping floors and scrubbing walls. Tell them the usual, free beer on the house when they're done." He stopped pacing and looked Homer in the eye. "I need you to go right away."

"What am I drivin'?" Homer pulled on a stiff pair of jeans he had worn for the last five days, then sat on the floor to pull on a pair of day old socks and shoes with the soles held in place with duct tape. When he stood up, he still projected an image of intimidating force.

"There's a white van parked in front, keys are in it. Be damn careful. My brother Joey was supposed to fix the brakes on it yesterday. You might still have to pump 'em a little."

When Max left Homer's apartment, he either failed to notice, or chose not to notice, the mural that Homer had started on the wall adjacent to the door. It featured a sunburst of blue paint with a face drawn in the middle of it. The outline of the dark eyes, heavy eyebrows, and full lips were done in minute detail showing every eyelash, every detail in the irises, and every skin wrinkle. As Max exited the door, the eyes seemed to follow him. Homer took note of them, chuckled, and thought, *Tell all you know Great Grandma . . . What do you know, G.G?*

Homer knew he wasn't finished with the little mural. G.G. had other things to tell him . . . soon. She had come to Homer in a dream the night before and revealed her face that Homer had painted by candlelight before the sun came up. He would have congratulated himself on such a fine piece of art, but he had a strong feeling that something or someone had guided his hand in executing such fine life-like detail. He had to wonder, *what was behind those eyes? What terrible deeds did that spirit remember?*

* * *

Homer's mission was to drive to Indianapolis and park in front of Morley Temporary Services. There was always a crowd of street people milling around the entrance to the industrial division trying to decide if they wanted to work or just walk the avenue and beg a couple of bucks for a pint of booze. As soon as Homer parked the white van at the curb, everybody in the sidewalk crowd recognized him because he had been here before. Homer refused to tell them his name, but they all delighted in calling him Big Chief, Big Kahuna, or Top Dog. They called out to him and pounded on the side of the van.

"Hey Big Chief," one of the men cried out. "Where we gonna work today?" He knew he didn't have to wait for the Morley's to come up with a minimum wage job then make him wait a week to get paid. Homer's boss paid them a dollar an hour more and paid them in full at the end of the day plus a lively libation to satisfy their craving. Money was the only paper that changed hands.

One of the ladies in the front office looked out the window when she heard the commotion and recognized what was going on. She went to the day labor dispatching area and warned Diane. "Somebody's trying to steal our people again. We need somebody to go out there and get rid of that guy."

Diane looked at the tall husky woman with the thick neck, corpulent face, thick lips, and mousy hair pulled back in a ponytail at the nape of her neck. "Why can't you do that?"

The woman turned and went back into the main office. "Not my job."

"Where's Mr. Morley?"

"He's in a meeting at the Hilton." The woman disappeared around a corner without looking back at Diane.

Diane had nobody waiting on her at the window so she went outside to see what was going on. In the middle of the crowd, a ragged man in ragged denim clothes was trying to walk a straight line down a crack in the sidewalk. He lost his balance and fell on his butt as everybody laughed. A big man with long black hair tied in a blue bandanna watched him with his back to Diane.

"What's going on?" Diane asked nobody in particular.

The big man turned and looked Diane in the face. His gaze made her gasp as the sound of the men's voices, the gloomy sky, and smell of sweat and stale beer disappeared to be replaced by darkness, the dim light of candles, and the bizarre visage in front of her.

Diane recognized the man's bent nose, dark devilish eyes, hair lip and dark wrinkled skin. *It's him! It's the strange creature from a waking nightmare. Why is he here? Why am I here staring at his ugly face? Why am I back in that waking nightmare?"*

"Oh! Looky here," said the big man. "We meet again, pretty lady. Just look at you, all dressed up and looking like you're all business. And you got your skin on this time."

Homer roared and cackled, and the crowd of men joined in. Diane didn't hear anything but Homer's laughter. She didn't see anything but the piercing gaze of his big dark eyes.

Suddenly everything went black then she felt a painful snap in her lower abdomen. Diane was out of her body again sailing high above the downtown Indianapolis skyscrapers. She sailed up through the clouds and felt the heat of an unrelenting sun. She fell back through the clouds and came down with a rain shower that soaked the bare earth and sent her sinking through the mud and into darkness and unconsciousness.

When she came to, Diane was lying in the middle of the main office floor surrounded by a half dozen worried faces. Her first sensation was heat, mind-blowing body-roasting fire. Apparently her flush sweaty condition showed because one of the women fanned her with a desk blotter.

"Diane, are you alright?" Maxine Morley hovered over her face with an upside down look of horror. "Do we need to call a doctor for you?"

"No. Oh God, I'm so thirsty."

"Get her some water," said Maxine. "Somebody bring us a cup of cold water out of the cooler."

Maxine lifted Diane by the shoulders and let her lean back against her ample bosom while she wiped her forehead with a handkerchief. When somebody handed her a cup of water, she sipped it then began to cry. "Could I just go home now?"

"Diane, I don't think you're in any condition to drive yourself home," said Maxine. "Are you sure you don't need a doctor?"

"I'll call the paramedics," said the big woman with the fat cheeks. She started to walk away.

"No!" Diane shouted. "I just want to go home. I want to get out of here and never come back."

Maxine hugged her around the shoulders and whispered to her, "Now listen. There's no need for you to quit. I'm closing the industrial division until George gets back. He can handle it until he hires a man to run that operation. I want you to stay here and rest up, then go home and take a few days off. Come back Monday morning and we'll put you to work up here with me in the office division."

"Oh, Maxine, that is so good to hear." Diane took another drink of water and a deep breath. "How did I get in here?"

"Some ugly dude out on the sidewalk carried you in," said one of the worried women.

"Honey, how did you wind up on the sidewalk?" asked Maxine.

Diane wasn't ready to answer her. She thought about the trip high above the city, then she thought about the trip several nights ago when she sank into the ground, sailed high in the night sky, and landed in a strange room beside a strange man who reached out to her and sent her flying through space. She was sure he was the same man, but why was he here? Why did he show up on a sidewalk so close to her and so far from where she had seen him before? But where was he before? Where was *she* before? Was he following her?

Why me? What did he want with me? Was he a ghost? Was he evil?

Diane was aware of somebody talking to her. *Was she close by? Oh, It's Maxine.*

"Diane are you sure you don't want us to call a doctor?"

"No. I just want to go home."

"That's fine. Don't quit on us. You've worked for us before. You're a good gal to have around."

"Could I just rest a minute?"

"Take as long as you want."

* * *

Diane arrived back home at 1:15 that afternoon. It would be another two hours before Mary got home from school. Bill was in Greencastle picking up something for a customer and wouldn't be home until after supper. She was in the house alone now and she noticed how deathly quiet it was. It never seemed this quiet before when she was alone with Bill at work and Mary in school. Then it dawned on her. Diane had been outside working in the garden during the day and had no idea what it was like to sit inside the house and listen to . . . nothing. She went to the patio door and looked out at the weed-infested patch and sighed in disgust. Just a few days of working in the big city and not tending the garden had left it for Mother Nature to take over. She changed into jeans, denim shirt, and old shoes and walked out to pull weeds. Just before she left, the phone rang.

Diane picked up the wall extension in the kitchen. "Hello?"

"Diane, this is Maxine."

"Oh, hi."

"Diane, are you sure you're alright?"

"I'm fine."

"Say, I wanted to ask you . . . and I never got to with all the hullabaloo . . . that man that carried you into the office, do you know him?"

"Ah . . . no . . . I don't even know who carried me in."

"Oh, of course you don't. You were knocked out. What was I thinking? But anyway, he acted like he knew you."

"What did he look like?"

"Oh my, he was big and scary and looked like . . . something out of a nightmare."

"What made you think he knew me?"

"He carried you in, laid you on the floor, and said, 'Take care of my angel here.'"

"He said that?"

"Yes. Listen, this guy's been here once before. He pulls up to the curb and starts talking guys into coming with him, that he's got better jobs that pay better. And we don't have any idea where he goes or where he comes from."

"Maxine, I can assure you I don't know him. I'm certainly not in cahoots with him."

"Oh, I didn't mean to imply that. I certainly don't want you to think I'm accusing you of anything. We're just trying to find out who this character is and how to stop him . . . if we can stop him."

"Maxine, believe me, I wish I could help you. I just don't see how."

"Now Diane, I don't want you to worry about it. Get some rest and come back to us. We need you."

"Oh Maxine, thank you so much for the confidence . . . and the job. I'll be back."

They hung up and Diane felt guilty instantly. She didn't know who the big guy was, but she had seen him before. She just wasn't ready to tell Maxine the unbelievable details.

Chapter 24

Scary People, Scary House

The man and the two girls stepped down from the first passenger car behind the big locomotive and stood for a moment in a cloud of billowing steam. They turned and walked across the railroad station platform while the man glanced at the older girl's middle. She wasn't showing yet. Thank the Lord! He covered up his nervous feelings by tipping his hat to all the ladies that passed by. He carried on an inane banter with his oldest daughter then finally spotted the man standing beside the horse and carriage up ahead. He paid him for his trouble and hustled the two girls into the carriage.

Just before the horse trotted off, he leaned forward and asked the horse if they had met before. The horse looked around and grinned at him. Then the man leaned back in his seat and the horse turned and trotted out to the main road. As they rode down the gravel byway, it felt like somebody or something was pounding on his head. Then they started going down a long dark tunnel filled with stars. At the end of the tunnel, a wooden bridge stretched across a deep gorge with a raging river at the bottom of it. But the bridge only went halfway across the gorge, and when the horse came to the end they all went sailing off into midair. The youngest girl screamed and her sister started yelling, "Mary, Mary."

When Bill Barnes opened his eyes he was staring at a dark ceiling, but he looked over to see light streaming down the hallway. Was this part of the dream? No! The voice was real. It belonged to Diane. Where was she?

"Stop it! Make it stop!" Mary screamed.

Bill jumped out of bed and dashed to Mary's bedroom just in time to see Diane pulling on Mary's nightgown as they wrestled on the floor.

"What the hell are you doing to her?" Bill yelled.

Diane was in no mood for this. She helped Mary to her feet. "Get out of the way. We're going to the bathroom."

"Answer me! What did you do to her?"

"Bill, for God's sake she was having a bad dream."

"Bad dreams don't beat up on kids."

Diane doubled up her right fist, drew back, and shot a line drive punch into Bill's gut. He reeled back across the hall and thumped against the wall more in shock than pain. Diane and Mary brushed past him on their way to the bathroom. Diane turned on the light and shut the door.

Bill paced the hallway and yelled, "Would somebody tell me what in the name of God is going on here?"

A few minutes later Diane opened the bathroom door and took Mary into the master bedroom. "You sleep in here with me tonight."

Mary lay on her back in the middle of the big double bed. Diane left her with covers pulled up around her neck while she stared at the ceiling.

"Now would you tell me what you did to her?" Bill demanded after they stomped down the hall and into the living room.

"You bastard! You know damn good and well I didn't do anything to her."

"Then what were you two doing on the floor?"

"I was covering her up. She had welts all over her poor little bottom."

"How did those welts get there?"

"I don't know."

Bill waved his hands. "You don't know. You don't know."

In the master bedroom, Mary thought to herself, *They've argued before, but not like this. This is really bad.*

"Damn you! Damn you! What makes you think I would hit her like that?"

"You've hit her before."

"No, I've spanked her before. I never hit her like that. Damn it, Bill, that's exactly like I found her."

Stop it you two. Stop it! Can't you see what's going on here? Mary thought to herself.

Bill stepped in close, his face dark. "How did you find her?"

"I heard her scream, okay? I got up and I heard something or somebody smacking her. By the time I got to her room, she was on the floor just like you saw her."

"How did she get there?"

"I told you, I don't know."

Suddenly Mary jumped out of bed, opened the door, and ran into the living room and screamed, "There's something in this house. Can't you see that? Can't you see that?" She ran to the front door, heaved it open, and ran out into the night in nothing but her nightgown and bare feet.

"Mary, come back here," Diane shouted.

Mary was halfway across the yard when Diane came out the door after her. She looked back and saw the living room light shining through one window, her bedroom light through another. In between the two hideous eyes was the front door, a grotesque mouth spitting out evil looking creatures that Mary vaguely recognized as her parents. She had to run. But where would she go? The black top road stretched out before her into nothingness. She stopped just as Bill caught up with her and scooped her up in his arms. Mary waved her arms, kicked her legs, and screamed. It scared and sickened Bill so much that he buried his face in her shoulder and sobbed. "Don't baby! Don't do this to us. It's alright."

Mary screamed all the way back to the house. Finally, she fainted and went limp in Bill's arms.

She was vaguely aware of being put in the back seat of the car, doors slamming, an engine starting, moving to who knows where. Her parents whispered to each other. About what? *Who cares?* The buzz in her head made her shiver all over. She remembered somebody saying something about shock. She wasn't going into shock. Mary hyperventilated and fainted again.

When she woke up, strange smells and the feel of strange sheets in a strange bed surrounded her. Diane lay down on the bed beside her and held her close. "Go back to sleep, sweetheart. Daddy checked us into a motel for the night. Everything will be fine in the morning."

* * *

"You must not think bad thoughts."

What did she say? Mary wondered to herself. She was awake, barely hovering in the twilight between awake and asleep. She was drifting in and out, seeing the lighted face of a beautiful woman hovering over her.

"Now I don't want you to be afraid," said the lovely lady. "I have a gift for you. It's a doll, a very special doll. You and Pepper Jane will love it so much. But first you have to go on a long journey."

"I don't want to go," Mary said.

"Oh come now. You've traveled with me before. I know who you are. I know your father and sister."

"I don't have a sister."

"Of course you do. She's right there beside you."

Mary looked all around her. She was in black limbo. She reached out to grab something and caught two fistfuls of bed sheet. Mashing her face into the pillow made the dizzy feeling go away, and Mary drifted back to sleep.

This time she was back in the horse-drawn carriage, going through the tunnel of stars, going across the bridge. Oh, oh, the bridge was cut in two. The horse was still galloping. He pulled them all off into oblivion.

Mary heard the lady say, "When you hit bottom, I have something to tell you." But Mary could no longer see her face.

Chapter 25

The No Tell Motel

"More fornicators tonight?" Louella Prichett asked as she came into the office of the National Motel.

"Not tonight, Aunt Louella." Karen Mendel sighed as she took the wet umbrella and helped Louella off with her coat. "Really, they're not all here for illicit sex."

"There's a car at the end of the parking lot with a Marion County license plate. Who are they?"

"Well, I don't think they're fornicators," Karen said after hanging up her aunt's coat.

"Who are they then?"

"Aunt Louella! That's a man and his wife and daughter. They got here about an hour ago."

"How do you know? Did they all three come in to register?"

"No, just the man came in. But he was parked right under the neon sign, and I could see his wife and daughter in the back seat. They looked rather strange."

"How do you mean?"

"Well, they looked kind o' rumpled, like people who had just run out of a burning house."

"Let me see the register."

Karen handed over the old-fashioned register book. "They gave a local address."

"Barnes! That's the family that moved in right next door to Aunt Alice. What in the world are they doing here?"

"Ah, the gentleman didn't say. He was pretty shaken up."

"Well, didn't you ask?"

Karen just shook her head.

"Well, there might have been something on the police scanner. Why isn't the scanner on?"

"Because there hasn't been any emergency traffic for a long time tonight."

Louella reached for the phone. "I'd better call John and see if he knows anything about this."

Karen gently pulled it out of reach. "Not now. Look at the time."

Louella looked at the wall clock behind the desk and blinked. "Oh my, it's almost 1:00. Karen, I'm sorry I stayed so late."

"Don't think a thing about it. If I wasn't staying up late here, I'd be staying up late at home." Karen settled into an old style wooden office chair. Louella settled in another opposite her.

"Well, you know how it is. I can never get away from those people at a decent hour."

"So how did it go tonight? Did you have a good time?"

"Oh, yes. They were all very gracious. Of course they talked about things that were way over my head."

"Such as?"

"Well, the usual. You know--hypnosis, dreams, rein-carnation. Things like that."

Karen leaned forward a bit. "Did John hypnotize you?"

"Oh God, no!"

"Did you learn anything?"

"Well, did you know that people who are related in this life quite often are related in past lives?"

"Really?"

"Karen, it was so fascinating. There was a mother and

son there tonight who took John's course in hypnosis. That young man put his own mother in a trance and asked her if she knew who he was, and she said, 'Yes, you're my son. You have been before.' Then she described a life as an English duchess in the nineteenth century. She had sent her son off to boarding school when he was very young. Then he went off to sea as a young teenager. Later on John tried to hypnotize this young lad and take him back to his life at sea. I'm not sure John was very successful, but afterward the boy said he felt like he was in the crow's nest of a ship, and there was a gale blowing all around him." She looked at her niece. "I'm boring you, aren't I?"

Karen shook her head. "Of course not. Go on. This is very interesting."

"Well, then they got really deep. I think I understand the law of karma, but then somebody started talking about space and parallel worlds and something called time con. . .oh. . time con. . ."

"Continuum."

"Yes!" Louella's face lit up in pleasant surprise. "Karen, why don't you come over sometime? I could always get somebody else to watch the motel."

"I've never been invited."

"Well, I'll have to talk to John about that."

"Please don't do that."

"Why not?"

"I don't think Sharon likes me."

"Oh, of course she does. Sharon just takes some getting used to."

"It's not that. I just never got along with southern women. They always acted like they wanted to talk down to me."

"Now that's not true about Sharon. Besides, you're just showing your inferiority complex."

Karen rolled her eyes. "I don't have an inferiority complex."

"Sharon was asking about you tonight."

"Uh huh. Why am I thirty-two and still single, right?"

"Well, that's a good question, don't you think?"

"It's a fair question. The answer is I like my life just like it is." Karen rose to leave. "Good night, Aunt Louella."

Chapter 26

Robins and Tomatoes

Bill Barnes woke up the next morning in a strange empty bed. He bolted up and looked across the room---twin beds, strange room. *Where am I? Motel, oh yeah.* Diane and Mary were still asleep in each other's arms. Bill sighed and flopped back down in bed.

We gotta get outta here, Bill thought. *What the hell's happened to the house by now? Gotta get back and check on the house.* He eased out of bed, then dressed and gathered Diane and Mary's clothes. He'd throw them in the car and take his family home in their nightclothes.

* * *

"Did you have a nice stay, Mr. Barnes?"

"We had a very pleasant night." Bill forced a smile and dropped the room key on the desk.

As soon as he left, Louella picked up the phone and started dialing. When her cousin John McCauley answered, she barked, "John, what in the world is going on at the new house next to Aunt Alice?"

John sighed. "What are you talking about?"

"That new family that moved in next door to Aunt Alice is what I'm talking about. All three of them, the man, his wife, and their little girl just spent the night in our motel. They came in here in the middle of the night all bedraggled, then left just now."

"That's strange. Did they leave a mess or create a disturbance?"

"They were perfectly quiet. But I haven't checked the

room yet. You'd better believe I'm going to do that right now. Couldn't you at least make some inquiries among your real estate associates and see what's been going on out there? They do live next door to Aunt Alice you know."

"Louella, I know who they are and where they live. Now go check the room."

Louella hung up and fetched the key to room 16.

The place was spotless. Not a thing out of place. The beds had even been made. Louella suspected they may have tried to hide something so she pulled down the covers part way and sniffed the sheets. They were clean and smelled clean. Did they sleep in the beds or on the floor? Louella looked in the bathroom and found all the towels from the previous cleaning were still in place. She was about to go back and check the bill to make sure she had the right room, but she had just taken the room key. Of course it was the right room.

Something spooked her. Was it a feeling? A sound? No, it was the smell. The room smelled like the deep woods, and the smell raced to the back of her memory and illuminated an almost forgotten childhood encounter. Her throat tightened.

Something caught her eye. Louella recognized a doll made out of a cornhusk sitting on one of the end tables. Some of the leaves had been bent upward to look like arms. The hair was made of corn silk pulled out of the husk and brushed into the back of the head which was formed by cinching part of the husk to look like a neck. The face was painted on with some sort of red ink or paint.

Did it belong to the little girl that stayed here last night? *Surely not*, Louella thought to herself. Still, it might be a keepsake of some kind. Better return it personally.

* * *

As they drove down County Line Road, Diane looked

in the back seat at the blanket wrapped bundle of her daughter. Mary came awake and looked at her. "You didn't have a very good night, did you baby?"

Mary closed her eyes and shook her head. "Why did Daddy take us to a motel?"

"We just had to get out of the house for a night."

"Are we going back to that house?"

"Of course."

"No. No." Mary began to cry.

"Mary, remember how we used to travel in the car a lot, and we always said the best part was coming back home? Well, we spent a night at a motel. Now we're going back home." Diane reached back and patted Mary's tear-streaked face. "It'll be okay, baby. You'll see. Everything will be better."

* * *

"Now this isn't so bad, is it?" Bill had walked Mary and Diane all through the house then outside to the back patio.

"I suppose not." The gloomy look on Mary's face wasn't convincing. "There was something in this house last night."

"Do you see anything bad in the house now?" asked Diane.

"No."

"Neither do I," said Diane.

Mary turned to face both of her parents. "So which one of you spanked me last night?"

"I've gotta clean those gutters again I see," said Bill.

"Fine," said Mary. "Change the subject." She stomped across the yard toward the garden.

"Looks like we got visitors," said Bill.

"Where?" Diane watched Bill point at a pile of leaves and twigs on top of the electric company utility box beside the back door.

"See the nest?" We've got another family living with us." A mother robin swooped past Bill and landed on the nest. Four tiny beaks came out of the pile of debris, and the mother bobbed up and down to feed each baby.

From the edge of the garden came Mary's high-pitched scream.

Diane and Bill raced over to Mary who was bent over with her hands over her mouth. She turned to face her parents and giggled.

"What's the matter?" shouted Bill.

"He just scared me for a second," said Mary.

"What?" shouted Diane.

"It was a little baby garter snake. He's gone now."

"Where'd he go?" asked Bill.

"He crawled over there into the tomato plants," said Mary.

"Well don't scare him out of the garden," Bill ordered. "He'll eat bugs and keep them away from the plants."

"I know that," Mary giggled again.

"Oh look," said Diane. "We still have ripe tomatoes coming on." She lifted the hem of her nightgown and started picking tomatoes, dropping them into the makeshift sack of her gown.

* * *

Louella walked up to the Barnes's front door and knocked very gently at first. The storm door was locked, but the inside door was open and one living room light was on. She knocked again, a little louder this time. Then she stood back and waited a while, admiring the colorful rosebushes. The storm door opened and a massive fist crashed into her face. The force of the blow knocked her back several feet and she sprawled out on the front lawn looking up at nothing but blue sky. By the time she shook her head and looked back, a huge man with coarse dark features, blistered skin, long hair tied in braids, and dark blue clothes was standing on the front porch pointing his finger at her. Then he gave a sweeping motion with his hand, indicating that he wanted her to leave and right now.

It's him! My God, it's him!

Without taking his eyes off her, the man stepped backwards into the house. He reached around behind him, opened the storm door, backed through the doorway, and slammed the inside door. Louella couldn't move fast enough. She got to her feet, jumped in her car and roared off down the road. Five minutes later she was parked in front of John McCauley's house.

Chapter 27

The Man in the Woods

"The place is haunted," said Louella. Her hand shook as she raised a glass of orange juice to her mouth and took a sip. She coughed and took a deep breath. "There's a ghost in that house. My God, he's right next door to Aunt Alice. And that poor man and his family . . ."

"Louella, let's put the juice down for now," said Sharon.

"Oh Sharon, I've been a bad girl."

"Whatever do you mean?"

Louella coughed. "I think I'll try that orange juice again." Louella hoisted the glass, took a gulp and choked.

"For heaven's sake, sugar. Take it easy." Sharon held Louella's arms above her head as she coughed and gagged.

"It was him." Louella coughed. "I've seen him before."

"Him who?" asked John.

"The man. Big man. I've seen him before out in the woods behind Aunt Alice's house. I was just a little girl at the time, and I knew we weren't supposed to play out there, but a bunch of my cousins dragged me along anyway. That's where I saw him."

"What made you think he was a ghost?" asked John.

"I got separated from the rest of the kids. I fell down on the path. When I looked up, there he was standing right over me. I got up and started to run away; but there he was again, right in the middle of the path. I started screaming and he disappeared. He just vanished into thin air.

"The rest of the kids found me and took me back to the house. I didn't dare tell anyone what I'd seen. They'd think I was crazy." She sobbed. "Oh Sharon, I'm still being punished."

"You're not being punished, Louella. You saw a ghost. Lots of people see ghosts."

John came around the couch and picked up the orange juice glass from the coffee table. "Maybe we should spike this with something a little stronger." He walked over to the opposite side of the room and fetched a gin bottle from a sideboard.

"Oh, don't do that," said Louella. "I'm afraid my nerves can't take any alcohol right now."

"Then I'll drink it." John poured a splash of gin in the glass and chugged it down.

"John, what on earth are you doing?" asked Sharon.

"Oh nothing. I was just thinking about a dream I had about a ghost of another kind out there in the woods a long time ago."

"What was that about?" asked Sharon.

"Well, it's like this," said John. "Louella, contrary to what I told you before, I have heard a baby crying out in the woods behind Alice's house late at night. I guess I just forgot because it was so long ago."

He gazed at Louella for a moment, then came over and knelt in front of her. He took her chin in his hand and looked at her very carefully. "Louella, if that man hit you that hard, why didn't he leave any blood?"

"What?"

Sharon leaned over and looked at Louella. "It's true, honey. You don't have a mark on you."

Louella got up, ran into the bathroom, and looked in the mirror. She at least expected to find a fat lip, but she didn't. She turned around to find Sharon and John standing in the doorway side by side. "Well," she said, "I guess that means I'm going completely nuts."

"I don't think so," said John. "Come back in the living room. You could probably use that drink now."

As Sharon and Louella followed him into the living room, John went to the sideboard and refilled Louella's glass with gin and a splash of orange juice. He handed it to Louella who took a small sip this time. "You've both heard rumors about the Hanson curse?"

"It had something to do with the south pasture," said Louella. "And the woods bordering the south pasture. For some reason, Aunt Alice didn't want anybody out there."

"What was wrong with the south pasture?" asked Sharon.

"I don't know," said John. "Obviously there's something bedeviling the ground out there."

"I don't see any sense in just speculating about it," said Sharon. "Why don't we just ask Aunt Alice what went on out there?"

"I asked her at grandpa Hanson's funeral," said John. "She told me it had to do with something that people her parents' age didn't talk about."

"Let's ask her again," said Sharon.

"Just like that?" asked John.

Sharon waved her hand. "For heaven's sake, John Mac. You're a big boy now. There's no reason for you to be afraid of her. We only want to know what's wrong with a little piece of ground."

Louella took another sip of juice and gin and coughed.

* * *

As the three of them approached the front door of the old Hanson farmhouse Sharon said, "I suggest you two let me handle this."

"And why is that?" asked John.

"Aunt Alice likes me. Besides you two have alcohol on your breath."

Sharon was right of course. Aunt Alice did like her. Twenty years ago John worried when he brought his 22-year old bride home that the rest of the family might take a dim view of his May-December romance. To his relief and surprise, Alice and Sharon warmed up to each other instantly.

They found Alice in the downstairs sewing room opposite the front door. She was bent over her mother's old trundle operated sewing machine with her head down on her arm.

"Alice!" Louella grabbed the little 95-year old body by the shoulders.

"What?" Alice came straight up in her chair with a startled look. "Good Lord, Louella, are you trying to scare me to death?"

"Are you alright dear?" asked Sharon.

"Well of course I'm alright."

"Could I suggest a bed the next time you want to take a nap?" said John.

Alice braced herself on the sewing machine and stood up. "John McCauley, may I suggest you get down in the cellar and change the furnace filters like I asked you to a week ago."

"Alice, you could have fallen over and hurt yourself," said Louella.

"I was merely catching forty winks. I don't need a bed for that. A bed would have instigated an hour-long nap or more. I don't have time like that to waste."

Sharon shooed John and Louella to the opposite side of the room. "Aunt Alice, we have a question to ask you. Would you be so kind as to sit over here on the window seat with me? Oh the sun feels so warm when it comes through the glass like that, don't you think?"

Aunt Alice gave Sharon a sly grin. "Somehow I don't think this has anything to do with the sun."

"Of course you're absolutely right as usual. I'll get to the point. Alice, there have been some disturbances at the new house next door."

"It's haunted."

"I beg your pardon?"

"The place is haunted. It was haunted before it was built."

"Well," said Sharon with a broad smile. "It looks like we came to the right source."

"My dear, I educated half the adults in this township. Did you think I didn't keep up with what they're doing now?"

John asked, "Aunt Alice, what happened over there to cause all this? It had something to do with the Hanson curse, didn't it? It was something that happened a long time ago."

John noticed his aunt's eyes were starting to dance. She glanced at the door where Louella stood and her brow became more deeply wrinkled. Her eyebrows peaked in a contrite expression.

In her head, the words of Alice's mother replayed from her childhood. *These matters don't concern you. You were listening in. Weren't you?*

Alice stood and faced the window, gazing at the south pasture.

Please forgive me, Jesus. I love Mother and Papa so much. I didn't mean to hurt them.

Then she turned to face John. "Will you please change the furnace filters like I asked?" Her gaze shifted to Louella. "Since you're here now, would you mind fixing us all a bit of lunch."

Sharon said, "Oh I really wasn't . . ."

Alice interrupted Sharon with a hand on her shoulder. "That will be all for today, my dear. I buried the past with my father over thirty years ago. Let's go in the front room while Louella cooks and discuss something more up to date."

On the back porch John lifted the trap door to the cellar, went down three steps, and twisted the ancient light switch mounted on one of the floor joists.

He went over to the furnace, pulled off the side panel exposing the filter, and switched it with a new filter from a paper bag on a nearby shelf.

There was enough light for filter changing, but there were still dark corners in the old cellar John hadn't explored since he was a young boy. He took a penlight out of his shirt pocket and pointed it around the brick floor and between the old wooden shelves. The shelves had stored glass jars full of green beans, beets, and corn along with shallow wood boxes used to dry onions and potatoes. They were all empty now.

He saw nothing unusual anywhere in the old cellar until he looked under one of the shelves holding the old drying trays. Embedded in a knothole was a donut shaped stone. He pried it out of the wood with his pocketknife and recognized it for what it was immediately. But what was it doing in his aunt's house? What was it doing in the cellar of a home occupied by an Indiana farm girl, schoolteacher and surrogate parent with no patience for supernatural nonsense? Did Aunt Alice even know it was here?

He came back upstairs, went inside, and motioned for Sharon to come into the living room.

"What is it?" asked Sharon.

"Keep your voice down. I found a hag stone in the cellar."

"A what?"

"A hag stone."

"What in the world is a hag stone?"

"It was used to ward off witches."

"Witches?"

John glanced around. "Shhhhhh!"

"John, witches around this place? Around this family? What would any of them know about witches?"

"That's another mystery."

Chapter 28

A Worried Mom

Emily Petersen knocked three times then decided to let herself in. Her daughter Pam scolded her. "Mother, this is Bill and Diane's house. We weren't exactly invited."

"It's my daughter's house," said Emily as she fiddled with her key. "There's something wrong here. She doesn't call, she doesn't answer the phone. I never find her at home."

There was a retching sound coming from down the hall. They rushed to the bathroom to find Diane bent over the stool. There was drool hanging out of her mouth and hair hanging down in her face.

Emily grabbed a washrag off the towel rack, ran it under cold water, and slapped it against Diane's forehead. "Oh sweetheart, I didn't know you were sick. Are you going to throw up again?"

Diane nodded her head and braced herself for the next heave. Instead of vomiting she sneezed. "Dear God, no."

Her mother hugged her shoulders. "It's okay, honey. Mother's here. Go ahead and throw up some more if you have to."

"Could you wipe my mouth for me?"

"Of course, honey." Emily used the wet washrag to wipe Diane's mouth. "Are you okay now?"

"I gotta lie down."

"Okay. Okay."

"I gotta lie down."

While Emily and Diane staggered to the bedroom, Pam yanked some toilet paper off the roll and wiped some stray yellow ooze off the side of the stool. When she straightened up to wash her hands at the lavatory, the reflection of the dark figure in the mirror made her catch her breath. When she turned around, he was gone.

"Pam, get in here," Emily said. "Bring us some extra pillows out of the hall closet."

Pam stood in the doorway of the bedroom, her face chalk white.

"Pam, what's the matter?"

"Mother, there's . . . I . . .What did you want?"

"Bring us some more pillows. Pam, what's wrong?"

"Nothing. I'll be right back."

"Mother, don't bother. I'm okay." Diane propped herself up on one elbow and pushed her sweaty hair back out of her face.

"Diane, take it easy. You've been sick."

"No, no. I'll be okay. Mary was sick like this the other day. As soon as she threw up it went away."

"What made you sick?"

"I don't know, Mother. I asked Mary the same question. I don't know if it's something we ate or drank."

Emily jumped and ran into the kitchen.

"Hey Sis, what's the matter?" Diane asked as Pam came back into the room hanging on tightly to two pillows and easing onto the bed. "Pam, what's wrong; you act like you've just seen a . . ." Diane cut herself off, and the two sisters sat staring at each other daring the other one to say something.

The sound of running water finally broke the silence and Pam turned to shout down the hallway. "Mother, what are you doing?" No answer. "Mother?" The water kept running. Suddenly there was a thud, and Pam and Diane rushed into the kitchen to find their mother lying on the floor.

Pam grabbed her by the shoulders and propped her

up. Emily coughed, her eyes wide, then finally caught her breath. "My God, what happened?"

"Mother, what did you do?" shouted Pam.

"Pam, settle down. I'm alright. Just help me into the living room, will you?"

The girls lifted their mother by her shoulders while Emily said, "Easy now I'm still a little dizzy."

"Mother, you fainted," said Pam. "What made you faint?"

"Not now, Pam. Let me catch my breath."

"What were you doing?" asked Diane when they all settled on the couch.

"Well, I came in here to check on your refrigerator and pantry to see if anything was spoiling. Then I checked the water at the kitchen sink. I filled a glass and started to drink it, then the smell just knocked me out." She looked around with a dazed expression on her face.

"Mother, are you sick?" said Diane. "Mary and I got sick as soon as we took a drink."

"I didn't even take a sip before the smell got to me."

"What did it smell like?" asked Pam.

"Well, oddly enough, it smelled like some god-awful cheap perfume. The fumes were overpowering."

"Are you sick?" asked Pam.

"I told you no. How long has this been going on, Diane?"

"I don't know, a few weeks maybe."

"Has Bill been sick?" asked Emily.

"No."

"Is it just the water that makes you sick?"

"I think so."

"Well Diane, there's something in your well."

"What well?"

Her mother sighed. "You live in the country now.

You've got a private well. There's probably something polluting it."

"Great! What do we do about that?"

"Call the board of health. Have them test the water. Find out what's in it. Then call a good well digger."

"Oh God. What next?" Diane leaned on the arm of the couch and shook her head.

Emily slipped her arm around her daughter's shoulders. "What else has been going on in this house? I haven't been able to reach you for over three weeks now."

"Where shall I start? I went back to work at Morley's working in the office. Bill quit his job at Carter's and started his own welding business."

"Good for him," said Emily.

Diane frowned. "Yeah, good for him. For me, that means two full time jobs, one at Morley's and one keeping the books for Barnes Welding Company."

"No wonder you look so ragged out," said Pam. "Can't he hire somebody to do that?"

"He can't afford anybody right now; not until he gets some better cash flow." Pam didn't like her brother-in-law, but Diane didn't care or have the inclination to do anything about it.

"It's Saturday," said Emily. "Where are Bill and Mary?"

"He's out picking up supplies. Mary is at school helping out with the fall festival. Meanwhile I have work to do paying bills and ordering more supplies."

Pam leaned across her mother and laid a hand on Diane's shoulder. "You've got extra company, don't you?"

"Extra company?" said Emily.

"While I was in the bathroom, I looked in the mirror and saw an Indian-looking guy standing behind me. When I turned around he was gone."

"Oh God, he's still here." Diane buried her face in her hands. "I know there are things rattling around in this house. I hear them, I see them. Bill denies they're even here."

"What about Mary?" asked Pam.

"We had an incident with Mary the other night. She was rolling around on the floor screaming that somebody was spanking her. She actually had red welts on her bottom. We wound up spending the night in a motel." She took a deep breath. "When we came back home, everything was fine."

"Let me talk to John McCauley about this," said Emily.

Diane lowered her hands. "John McCauley? I met him at Doctor Blackwell's office."

"What were you doing there?" asked Emily.

"Well…ah…Mary…she kind of had a sleep-walking episode while she was at school. Doctor Blackwell thought it might be her thyroid."

Emily looked puzzled. "Her thyroid? Diane, why am I just hearing about this?"

"I'm sorry Mother. We've had a lot happening lately. It just didn't come up."

"My family is in trouble and it just didn't come up?"

"Mother please."

"When did this happen?"

"Three…maybe four weeks…no not four. I don't know. It was just before I started to work at Morley's."

"Then there's that stinky water," said Pam.

"What did John McCauley tell you?" said Emily.

"He said he knew you and Pam."

"Did he say anything about this house?" asked Pam.

"No. Why would he?" said Diane.

Emily motioned with her hand. "Well he sold your father and I our last house, and he sold me this house. This ground used to belong to John's grandparents."

"Then he had to know," said Pam.

Diane frowned. "Know what?"

"That the place, the land is haunted."

"Oh you guys, would you stop. This was supposed to be a good home for us after we moved away from the big mean city." Diane laid her head on the back of the couch. "I don't know what to do anymore."

"Well the first thing you need to do is call the health department," said Emily. "Meanwhile, I'll talk to John."

"What's he supposed to do about it?" asked Diane.

"Maybe he knows something that could help us out. Right now, I want you to make an appointment to see Doctor Blackwell yourself. You don't look well."

Diane rubbed her forehead. "I'm just tired, Mother."

"I think you're more than just tired, and I'm not sure any ghost story has anything to do with it."

"What about the ghost I saw?" said Pam.

"Pam don't make this any worse than it is," said Emily. "You girls were always seeing things in the dark when you were little. They all turned out to be nothing."

"Not this time," said Diane. "Not this time."

Chapter 29

Doc and Judy

Bill and Diane Barnes, John and Sharon McCauley had enough real life goblins on their hands. They didn't need any pretend spooks to celebrate Halloween. But on a hill high above Tanner's Grove, John's partner, Bob Parsons, and his wife were preparing for a very elaborate masquerade party. And for some strange reason their teenage daughter Judy was staying home on a Friday night.

"I just don't understand why a pretty 17 year old girl is staying at home with no school tomorrow," Bob said. "It's Halloween; and I know there's plenty of parties at her friends' houses. There's a ball game tonight for cryin' out loud."

"Bob, why don't you just leave well enough alone?" Norma Parsons adjusted the bodice on her floor length dress to make sure she was showing just the right amount of cleavage. "She says she has some homework to catch up on."

"You're not buying that, are you?" He glanced in the direction of his daughter's room. "She's up to something."

"That's because she has a mind of her own, just like her father."

"And her mother."

"Yeah whatever."

Bob Parsons strapped the saber and scabbard to his Confederate Army uniform and walked out of the bedroom and down the hall. "Judy, we're getting ready to leave."

Judy cracked her door open. "Wow, what a pair. Knock 'em dead, Rhett and Scarlet."

"Rhett Butler wasn't in the Confederate Army," said

Norma. "He was a coward."

"He was not," said Bob.

"Oh loosen up, you two. Have a good time."

Bob bounded down the stairs holding on to his sword and scabbard. "Come on Norma, we're going to be late."

"Will you wait? These hoop skirts weren't made for track stars."

"Judy, make sure all the doors and windows are locked when we leave. It's Halloween and there's going to be lots of pranksters out and about."

"Daddy, it'll be alright."

"Just don't take any chances, young lady."

"Okay, okay. Now just go on to your party."

Bob hesitated at the front door. "Norma, we're going to have a problem. How in the world are we going to get that hoop skirt in the front seat?"

"No problem. I'll just take it off."

"What?"

"My petticoats will cover everything else. I'll just put the skirt on at the party." Norma reached behind her and flipped the skirt away from the rest of her dress and stood there in her petticoats and bloomers.

"You're not going like that."

Norma ignored Bob and walked out the door.

"Norma, you look ridiculous."

Judy laughed as her parents went out the door. Bob turned on the porch, looked through the door glass, and told Judy to lock the door behind him. When he was satisfied the door was locked, he left.

Judy stayed to watch her parents pull out of the big circular drive that wound its way past the colonnaded front porch and immaculately tended flower gardens. When they were out of sight, she unlocked the door and ran to make a phone call.

"Bobby?"

"Yeah."

"It's Judy."

"I know."

"My parents just left."

"Thank you, Lord," he whispered into the phone.

"The front door's unlocked. I'll be upstairs in a nice . . . warm . . . bubble bath."

"I'll be right over." Bobby's voice almost cracked, he was so excited.

* * *

A thick white mist surrounded the house and rose as high as the second floor. The dark figure crept around the side of the big mansion and then scurried across the porch. He tried the front door knob. It was unlocked. *Hot Damn! This is going to be easy.*

* * *

Judy sat in the tub and caressed her naked body. She lifted her right leg and wiped off the suds, lifted her left leg and wiped off the suds. She heard the front door open and close and her heart leaped. *There he is, she thought. He knows where I am. Come and get it, Bobby.*

Long agonizing minutes passed. *Where the hell is he?* Judy wondered. *It can't be taking him this long to find the bathroom.* She giggled at the thought. She listened but heard nothing. She sighed and leaned back in the tub. Then she heard the floor creak.

If Bobby's trying to scare me, I'll strangle him. She slipped out of the bathtub, dried herself, then pulled on the dorm shirt that hung on the door hook. *I'm not scared.* But her hand shook as she turned the bathroom doorknob. With the door cracked open Judy peered down the hallway one way, then opened the door to look the other way. There was nobody in the hall. Was there anybody in the two upstairs bedrooms? She padded to the end of the hall farthest from the top of the stairs. Nothing was in her room. When she came back out in the hall, she screamed.

A monster stood under the incandescent glare of the overhead light. Long white hair obscured part of its face, but bulging, red eyes gleamed under the heavy brow. A long gray tunic covered the rest of the body. It raised its ugly head and flashed pointed white teeth and fangs. An ugly roar came out of the dark mouth.

The beast held a butchered human arm in its left hand and took a bite out of the raw meat that stuck out of the severed elbow joint. Blood dribbled down the rotten chin. From the long, delicate fingers of the severed arm, Judy guessed the beast had cut off the arm of a woman. *Am I next?*

She screamed, high and piercing. Her whole body buzzed with fright. She had never been so scared in her life. She backed down the hallway and grabbed the only weapon available, an end table with a rare vase sitting on it.

"Nooooo, oh, oh, oh!" Judy screamed and threw the vase and end table together with both hands. The monster batted the table out of its way, and the vase flew over the banister with a sickening crash to the living room floor below. Curiously, it looked over the railing at what it had just done.

Judy ducked into the end bedroom, then locked the door. *Oh God, what do I do now?* The bedroom window was two stories up and there was nothing below but hard earth.

The beast kicked the door open then waited. Judy crouched behind the bed. *What is it waiting for?*

The monster leaped and landed on the bed. Judy grabbed the bottom rail of the bed and flipped it up, tumbling the monster onto the floor and turning the bed over on top of him. She didn't realize that she was that strong.

With an open escape route, Judy darted out the bedroom door, then down the hall and down the stairs. At the bottom of the stairs another monster with a charred head, no mouth, and two enormous yellow eyes waited for her. Its body was completely covered with black hair.

Judy raced back up the stairs with the second monster in hot pursuit. When she got to the middle of the balcony she vaulted over the railing, landed flatfooted on the couch below, and bounded out the back door by the kitchen.

Where in the hell did all this fog come from? She thought as she darted across the back yard. It only took a few running steps to get out of the haze, but when she turned around to look back at the house she saw the heavy mist completely surrounded her home.

Doc, Judy thought to herself. *Doc will save me*. She ran across the yard, past the swimming pool, and out to the horse barn.

Judy flipped on the light by the tack room door and smiled at the gorgeous steed that whinnied in surprise. Judy ran to Doc, a big dapple-gray animal she had tried to save from the gelding knife. Her father had always wanted to have him cut for safer riding, but Judy had managed to whine and cry and get her way until the day Doc threw her off and almost broke her back. That same day Norma had the vet relieve Doc of his testicles. Much to her pleasant surprise, Doc showed Judy that he was still a very lively mount, which is what she needed now.

She let Doc out of his stall and mounted him in the wood floor hall. She rode to the trotting area to keep her bare feet out of the manure. She flipped the big door latch open, pushed the big slider back with a mighty shove, and rode off to the safety of the woods.

* * *

"Oh Jesus, we're in deep shit." Charlie Vanderhal and Doug Foley pulled their full head monster masks off and looked around the living room. Charlie shook his head in despair. "We're in deep shit. Deep, deep shit."

"What's the matter?" asked Doug.

"Look at that!" Charlie pointed at the shattered vase on the floor.

"So what's it worth? Couple hundred bucks?"

"A couple of hundred? More like a couple of grand."

"Aw bullshit!"

"Hey, the Parsons don't buy cheap stuff."

"So? She threw the vase at you. Let her pay for it."

"Damn it, Doug. It doesn't work that way."

"Well how does it work, boy wonder?"

"Let me think. Let me think."

"Forget thinking. Let's scram."

"Now wait a minute. This was my caper. It's my responsibility. And she was my girlfriend."

"She was never your girlfriend. Now come on, let's go." Doug pulled on Charlie's collar to drag him out the front door.

They were halfway across the front yard when Charlie stopped and yelled, "Oh my God, I forgot the fog machine."

"Aw shit, what did you do with it?"

"It's right by the front door."

* * *

Judy's long blonde hair flew out behind her while she and Doc bounded across an open field. But for want of a sword, she looked like she might be off to slay a dragon.

The forest ahead of them was so thick it looked like a solid black wall. Judy pulled back on the halter to slow Doc to a trot. When they got to the edge of the woods, she pulled back on the right side to bring Doc around parallel with the line of trees. When they came to a path that cut straight through the woods, Judy pulled to the left to make Doc go down the path. Instead he whinnied and backed up.

"Come on, Doc." She rocked back and forth on his shoulders then smacked him on the rump. Doc wasn't going anywhere. "Goddamn it, Doc, get the fuck going, will you?" Swearing at him didn't do any good either. Something Judy could not see or hear made the horse start and break into a full gallop down the dark path. Luckily Judy had a firm grip on the halter, but she almost fell off as her legs flew up in front of her. "Holy shit!" she grunted.

Doc plowed through the dark woods, then slowed to a trot when he broke out of the tree line on the other side. They were now in an enormous gravel valley that used to be the old railroad right of way. She had been across it many times on a county road, but this was the first time she had ever seen it isolated in the forest. From above, the bright full moonlight gleamed on the wide gravel track bed that stretched from northwest to southeast. Doc trotted aimlessly up and down the gravel path that was about half as wide as a football field.

Finally, Judy put it all together. *Moonlight, dark woods, Halloween, goblins that eat human flesh. Halloween pranksters.*

"BULLSHIT!"

Now she was mad. The front door had been unlocked for Bobby. And two bozos had just waltzed in with their goblin suits on to scare the hell out of her; and she had fallen for it. She tried to turn Doc around to head for the house. Doc would not turn.

* * *

Doug turned around to look at the fogging machine in the back seat. "Man, I hope you didn't burn that thing up. It sure smells hot."

"Don't even say that," said Charlie. I gotta have that thing back in school tomorrow, and it had better be in good shape."

"School? You borrowed that thing from school? Who let you have it?"

"My drama coach, Mr. Halston."

"Jack Halston let you borrow that thing?"

"Well, I kind o' borrowed it on my own."

"You mean you stole it? Charlie Vanderhal actually stole something? Man, what a stud."

"Shut up! I said I borrowed it, and I meant it. It's going back to the prop room behind the stage tomorrow."

"There's no school tomorrow. How're ya gonna get in?"

"The janitors will be there."

"They won't let you in."

Charlie smacked the wheel. "Aw shit!"

"Hey, we'll sneak it in Monday morning . . . somehow."

"Probably get caught."

Doug gave Charlie a crooked grin. "Was it worth it?"

Charlie smiled. "Yeah, it was worth it. Man you should o' seen the look on that little bitch's face when I turned on the hall light and bit into the fake arm."

"Yeah, I meant to ask you. How did you come up with a prop like that?"

"I got the arm from a busted mannequin at the department store where I work. I just hollowed out the end and stuffed it with strips of beef."

"Genius, pure genius."

"Scared the shit out o' Judy Parsons didn't it?"

"No."

"Whatya mean no?"

Doug smiled. "I saw her butt."

"What?" Charlie took his eyes off the road just long enough to give Doug an evil glare then drifted across the centerline.

"Hey, watch out!"

Charlie whipped the car back to the right just in time to avoid hitting an oncoming car. "When did you see her butt?"

Doug spent a few moments catching his breath.

"When did you see her butt?" Charlie repeated.

"When she jumped off the balcony. I was at the bottom of the stairs and she came down feet first with her back to me. Her dorm shirt flew up and showed her butt." Doug winked at Charlie. "Hope you don't mind."

Charlie said not one word, kept both hands on the steering wheel and stared straight ahead.

"Aw man, why do you want to chase after poon tang like that? Go find yourself a nice girl like Wanda Divens."

"Wanda Divens? Spread legs Wanda?"

"Hey pal, I know what you're after. Don't gimme none o' your crap, okay?"

* * *

Bobby Reston knew he was in big trouble with Judy Parsons. He just hoped she was still in a sexy mood. It had taken him almost an hour to get rid of Wanda Divens. He hadn't invited her over, but she came anyway. She was such an easy lay, but so hard to get rid of. And tonight he was saving himself for the most spectacular piece in the county.

Bobby knew he was driving too fast on the curvy road, but damn, Judy Parsons was waiting for him. Naked. In a bathtub. On the next curve to the left, he did what he knew was stupid and dangerous. He dove down inside the curve to maximize traction even though he was on the wrong side of the road.

Charlie Vanderhal and Doug Foley saw two headlights coming straight at them. They heard the sickening crash and felt the windshield and the dash against their heads and chest. They and Bobby Reston wouldn't feel anything else for a very long time.

* * *

Judy couldn't see in the dark woods, but Doc could. He jumped over deadfall and leaped small dips in the ground that Judy couldn't see. Coming into the forest a low hanging branch ripped out a hunk of her long blonde hair and almost knocked her off. She hoped and prayed that Doc knew where he was going. Fear had scratched the rest of her senses raw. She could feel every leaf brush by her naked arms and legs and hear every twig snap under Doc's hooves. Their minds and spirits were as one. Overhead a new danger soared above the trees.

The big crow screamed with rage as she circled the forest. The spirit of the murdered Indian witch had inhabited her body all day. There was going to be mischief in her dark realm of woodland ghosts. There was her loud scream and the cry of her murdered baby. Now it was time to work her magic. The big crow was a good vessel, and she would use it well.

She had them in sight now. She focused on the six-legged duo coming down the path. The witch folded her wings back to streamline the descent.

Doc felt the presence of harm descending from above. He knew something was after them so he quickened his pace, throwing the black bird's aim off. Instead of hitting her in the chest, the hard beak of the large crow hit Judy's forehead just below the hairline. She felt like she was falling backwards, then floating through the air. Then nothing.

The crow flew off into the night, still possessed by the spirit of the murdered Indian woman. The crow cried out as it swept up above the treetops, as it flew by the face of the bright moon, and as it flew over the fields of mangled corn-stalks and the green grass surrounding the new stone house.

The house was dark and quiet. The family was asleep and dreaming.

Chapter 30

Doc and Bill

In their dream Bill and Diane watched the horse pull their carriage through the tunnel, onto the bridge, and out over the gorge where the bridge only went halfway. The horse, the carriage, and all three passengers went off the end and started free falling through empty space. How strange, there was still the sound of hoof beats. Then there was the loud neighing of a real horse.

Bill was confused. What was real? What was part of the dream? Suddenly there was the loud bang of the barbecue kettle being kicked over on the patio. Bill came awake and sat up in bed.

"What was that?" he heard Diane ask while she rose up on one elbow.

"Stay here," said Bill. He was wide-awake when he jumped out of bed, then ran to the back door in a crouching position. Bill turned on the outside floodlights and the sight of the dapple-gray gelding with a long white mane made his heart leap.

As Bill watched the frightened horse kicking and galloping around his yard, the words of his Uncle Neville came to him from out of the past.

"A horse is too dumb to know how big he is, son. Don't let him bluff you. Show him who's boss."

Bill unlocked the back door and stepped out into the balmy October night.

"Bill, get away from him," Diane yelled from the patio door.

"Stay in the house, Diane. I can handle this."

"Handle what? Getting your fool head kicked in?"

"Shut up, Diane. He's been spooked. He don't need a lot of yellin' right now."

Bill didn't try to chase or corner ole Doc, but he didn't try to dodge him either. He gave him plenty of space, but when the animal tried to chase him off Bill stood his ground and didn't make a sound. Bill had always loved horses, respected their power and size and, with coaching from his uncle, he got over his fear of them.

Diane screamed, "Look out. He's going to kill you."

"Diane, I told you to stay in the house and keep still. You're making it worse."

When the horse ran at him then turned to kick with his hind legs, Bill dodged him with a quick sidestep. He danced around the flying hooves as skillfully as a boxer or bullfighter. There was no need to get in a hurry when collaring the horse. Time and confidence would calm him down. All of that would have worked out fine if it hadn't been for the screaming next door.

To the north of the back yard, Alice Hanson stood by the old oak trees. She looked like a ghost with her white nightgown blowing in the breeze and her white hair hanging down to her shoulders. "My God! You've killed them all!" the old lady screamed. "Why are you doing this? You've killed them all."

Bill yelled, "Diane, I can take care of this horse, but you're going to have to take care of that old woman. Get her back in her house, now!"

It was too late. Alice's screaming had frightened and enraged the horse as he ran around the yard kicking at phantoms in the dark. When he came by the small, frail figure of Alice Hanson, he let his hooves fly and caught the old lady with a direct hit to the side of her head.

Diane clasped her hands to her mouth in horror as she watched the wisp of a woman crumble to the ground. "My God Bill, he's killed her."

Bill knew he had to collar the horse now. He was heading right for Diane. Bill talked himself through it. *Be quick. Don't let him spook you too. Grab his halter now!*

Bill caught the end of the halter, ran about thirty feet alongside the horse until they got to the nearest tree. He veered to the left and put the tree between himself and the horse. When they passed the trunk, Bill ran around the tree wrapping the rope around it and pulling it up tight in a half hitch knot. Doc came up short on his halter and couldn't go anywhere. His eyes bulged wide with terror. Bill knew he couldn't do anything for him now. He would have to back off and let the horse calm down on his own. He ran over to Diane who was kneeling over the still form of Alice Hanson.

"She's alive and breathing," said Diane. "I can't tell how bad she's hurt. Let's get her in the house."

"No, let the paramedics handle her." He yanked off his T-shirt and covered the bloody gash along Alice's head. "Here, hold this to stop the bleeding. I'll call an ambulance and get some blankets."

* * *

Louella Pritchett heard the call come in on her police scanner as she sat in the office of the National Motel. She grabbed the phone and called her cousin. "John, get over to Aunt Alice's house now! There's been a call about a woman down at her address. I don't know what's happened. Please get over there now."

John McCauley said nothing. He hung up the phone and raced out of the house, barely remembering his keys and wallet. By the time he turned onto County Road 600W, he spotted several red lights flashing.

As he approached the old farmhouse he saw a very

large ambulance, two sheriff's squad cars, and a fire rescue truck parked along the road. At the back corner of the nearby stone ranch style house a familiar looking dapple-gray horse was tied to a tree. Bill Barnes, bare-chested in his bare feet and pajama bottoms, was stroking the horse's neck. Two ambulance medics were wheeling a gurney along the side yard with Diane Barnes running alongside.

John pulled up beside an ambulance then bolted from his car, leaving the door open. "What happened?" he asked, coming up to Diane.

"Oh, Mr. McCauley. The horse kicked her. We don't even know where it came from."

John glanced at the horse, then looked down at the gurney. "How bad is she?"

"She seems to be breathing okay, but it's a head injury. How did you find out about it?"

John looked at the horse again, then back at Diane. "My cousin called me. She heard it on her police radio."

"Mr. McCauley, I'm sorry you had to find out this way."

"That's alright. Do you know where she's going?"

"Where are you taking her?" Diane yelled at one of the medics.

"Cates Memorial." The man slammed the back door of the ambulance and came toward them. "Are you a relative, sir?"

"I'm her nephew," said John. "I guess I qualify as next of kin as much as anybody else."

"Would you come with us?" said the medic. "They may need your consent at the hospital."

John spared one last look at the horse as he headed for his car. He yelled at one of the deputies, "Sheriff, call Bob Parsons over on Orchard Road. I think that horse may belong to him."

* * *

Mary had been watching from her parents' bedroom window. The night was warm, but she shivered with excitement and thought what a strange place this was. With the appearance of the horse galloping around the house in the middle of the night, the place didn't seem so dreadful anymore.

She was having a hard time understanding her parents. They would fight like alley cats over petty things. Now they worked together to save an old lady's life.

Her father could be such a boor and then show so much savvy and skill in corralling a wild horse. He talked like he hated animals and constantly denied Mary's pleadings for a family dog. So why had he shown so much love and affection for such a big dangerous creature?

The night was quiet again when the squad cars and the ambulance left. Mary slipped out to join her parents on the front stoop.

"Come here, baby." Diane motioned Mary to sit beside her, then put an arm around her and kissed her forehead. "Did you see what happened out here tonight?"

"Yes."

"Isn't your daddy something?"

"He sure is."

"What in the world was that old lady screaming about?" wondered Bill.

"I don't know," said Diane. "It all kind of reminded me of our old neighborhood in the city. Remember the couple across the street that used to scream at each other every night?"

"Scream?" exclaimed Bill. "I thought they were going to kill each other. That's why I called the police on them!"

"Yeah well, we got a little loud ourselves sometimes." Diane chuckled.

"Loud?" exclaimed Mary. "You two weren't just loud. You were . . ."

"Hey, go get your slippers on," said Bill. "It's getting cold out here."

"No it's not."

Bill snapped his fingers and Mary ran into the house.

Now that they were alone, Diane decided to ask a rather delicate question about a very delicate matter. "Bill, you know I told you John McCauley helped Mary get over her fear of needles at Doctor Blackwell's office the other day."

"Yeah?"

"Well, Mother tells me he's a hypnotist."

"Oh yeah? Why?"

"Well, he helps people. He-"

"You know what this house needs?" Bill interrupted. "This house needs a front porch. I miss a front porch. Almost every house I've ever lived in had a front porch. That'll be my next project around here. Right after I enlarge the garage, we're gonna have a porch. Got to enlarge the garage. Got to be able to get trucks in the garage, big trucks."

Diane sighed and turned to look at the old farmhouse beyond the line of oak trees.

Chapter 31

Papa Was Bad

The news from the intensive care ward at Cates Memorial Hospital wasn't good. Alice Hanson was in a coma with tubes coming out of her mouth, nose and arm, while a urinary catheter came out from under her top bed sheet. Her head was wrapped in a gauze turban that covered one eye. The left side of her face was black and purple.

John McCauley stood at the foot of the hospital bed and wondered what a strange place for his aunt to be. For all ninety-five of her years, Alice Hanson had never been confined to a hospital, not even as an outpatient. She had spent her entire adult life caring for others and making sure her parents' farm didn't go into receivership. Alice had buried all her siblings and both of her parents. She and John had stood at the foot of her father's hospital bed waiting for the old man to die. Now Alice seemed to be near death, as John stood at the foot of her bed feeling very alone. The doctor had just left the room after telling him Aunt Alice had suffered a severe subdural hematoma.

For as long as he could remember, John McCauley had alternately loved and hated his aunt. Alice dried his tears and hugged away his fears. She was the one who kept him anchored and away from trouble while he was growing up, but sometimes the anchor got to be a bit much to bear.

He stared at his aunt's lips as they moved in and out and made him wonder what she was trying to say. John thought he heard a few faint sounds so he came around, sat on the edge of the bed, and leaned in close with one ear hovering over Alice's mouth.

"Papa was bad," came the faint words.

John leaned in closer and listened again.

"Papa was bad." How strange. How could she be in a coma with a breathing tube going down her windpipe and manage to talk at all? The voice didn't sound like Alice's, but like that of a man, hoarse and strained, but definitely the voice of a man.

* * *

Homer sat on the floor in his upstairs apartment staring at the blue sunburst he had painted on one wall with the black and white drawing of a woman's face superimposed over it. The eyes of the face followed Homer as he swayed back and forth.

The woman in the painting had told him that the child known in this world as Alice Hanson was without shame or guilt. She told him the child must go on to the after life knowing where the guilt lies and who owns the guilt for so much murder and mayhem. The woman said the child must not only know this, she must accept it and move on to the next level of her existence.

Homer's mind and spirit had come back into his body after they left the body of Alice Hanson fifteen miles away. He had his eyes shut and was still chanting very softly now, "Papa was bad. Papa was bad."

* * *

Robert and Norma Parsons had gone to a masquerade party looking like a dapper Confederate officer and his stunning, coquettish lady. Now that they were home, they looked more like refugees from Sherman's invasion of Atlanta. Bob was stripped to his T-shirt and gray trousers. He was on the phone with Sheriff Caldwell while his wife lay on a nearby couch stripped to her bloomers with a cold towel over her tear stained eyes.

"I know it's only a few hours till sunrise," said Bob. "But do you realize what could happen to her by then? How about that idiot you sent out here to investigate the breaking and entering? Can't you find something for him to do on this?"

"Excuse me, Mr. Parsons!" yelled Preston Caldwell. "I've got every available man ready to start looking for your daughter! Meanwhile, I've got three boys in the hospital from a head-on collision; I don't know how many calls about vandalism; and I've got all of 30 deputies to cover a county that stretches half way from here to Terre Haute. Now that's the best I can do, Sir!"

Both men slammed the phones down at once. Charlene Henderson, the woman dispatcher at the front desk, gave Caldwell a mock look of chastisement and shook her finger at him. "Yeah, yeah, I know," he said.

Charlene said, "We got a report from Cates Memorial Hospital on those three boys involved in the head-on collision. Apparently Bobby Reston took the brunt of the force. He was driving a little Triumph TR-7 . . . not much protection. He has numerous internal injuries and a very serious brain injury." She sighed and rolled her eyes. "They really don't expect him to make it through the night.

"The other two boys are in critical but stable condition. They're both heavily sedated. Looks like they're in for a long rehab."

Sheriff Caldwell shook his head. "Kids. They never get the message until it's too late."

* * *

Bob Parsons looked over at his wife lying on the couch.

"I won't live without her, Bob," Norma Parsons cried. "I swear, if anything's happened to her, I won't live in this world without her."

"Norma, don't talk like that."

"I mean it. She's my baby. I can't live without her."

"Norma, please!"

"No, not Norma, please! Bob, I swear to God! If she's dead, so am I!"

"Norma, stop it."

"So am I! So am I!"

Bob Parsons shook his wife then held her face next to his. "Baby, come on. I'm going to look for her now. We'll go together."

Bob Parsons put 300 miles on his Lincoln that morning. He didn't find his daughter.

Chapter 32

Lost, All is Lost

John McCauley stopped at an all night drug store and bought a thank you card for Bill and Diane Barnes. He used his fountain pen to add a personal note: *Our family is eternally grateful for your kindness and courage.*
John McCauley.

He bought a stamp from the machine and mailed it at a box outside the store.

The balmy October night had turned into a frigid November morning. As he drove south, John turned his car heater on and wished he had brought a warmer coat. When he approached the old Hanson farmhouse, he noticed light spilling out of the front windows at the Barnes home. Maybe he should thank them in person. He parked at the foot of the drive and walked up to knock on the front door.

Diane opened the door and smiled. "Mr. McCauley, come in." John stepped in and noticed that the whole family was in the front living room, and they were all still in their nightclothes.

"I see you folks didn't get any sleep tonight either."

"Heavens no," said Diane. "I was about to start breakfast. Want some?"

"No thank you. I have to get next door and secure the old place. I just wanted to stop and thank all of you for helping my aunt the way you did."

"It was the least we could do," said Bill.

"How is your aunt?" asked Diane.

"I'm afraid it's not good. There's so little they can do for her given her age and frail condition."

"I'm sorry," said Bill. "I wish we could have done more."

"You should've seen my dad collar that horse," said Mary.

"I wish I had, Mary. How did you manage to do that, Bill?"

"My uncle taught me about horses a long time ago."

"Did you talk to him? Calm him down?"

"Oh yeah."

"Interesting, interesting. Well, I want to thank you folks again. I can't imagine what Aunt Alice was doing out there."

"She was yelling about something," said Diane. "Something about killing people. She acted real strange."

"I'm sorry you folks had to endure this." John wanted to apologize for the haunting too. *Was this a good time to bring that up? Probably not.*

"Did they ever find out who the horse belonged to?" asked Bill.

"I don't know," said John. "He certainly looked familiar. I told the deputies to call my partner, Bob Parsons. It may belong to him." He turned back to the door. "Well, I've got to get next door and check on the old homestead. Thank you again for your trouble."

* * *

There's something in here. The thought dogged John McCauley as he entered the front of the old farmhouse. He closed the door and the clatter echoed up and down the hallway.

There had been a hag stone in the basement. What else was hidden? What other secrets did the house conceal? Did Alice know about them or just some of them?

John walked to the back door of the kitchen and threw the deadbolt shut. He re-entered the hall and glanced at the old grandfather clock at the bottom of the stairs. He was about to leave when he remembered something about the little table beside the clock. Alice had told him years ago that Grandpa Hanson's father had made the table. It was a simple piece with square legs, one drawer, and just enough top space to hold a phone and directory.

John had always wondered what was in the drawer, but it was always stuck. As a little boy he had caught Aunt Alice's wrath when he tried to pull it open. But now Alice wasn't here, and John had questions. He pulled on the drawer. It was still stuck.

He put the phone and directory on the floor and turned the table upside down. Then he went to the back porch and fetched a hammer and large screwdriver from a toolbox. John tapped on the back edge of the drawer, but it still wouldn't budge so he hammered a little harder. The front panel started to split. He was destroying a family heirloom, but did it really matter? John chopped around the back of the front panel until it was all knocked off the drawer. He righted the table and looked inside. What looked like an old ledger book was fastened to the underneath side of the table top with heavy tape. John cut the book out of the table with his pocketknife.

The book turned out to be Grandma Hanson's diary. The first few pages had been torn out. The top left corner of one page contained a single word: coitus.

What was a formal reference to sex doing in Grandma Hanson's diary?

The first full page was dated June 16, 1907.

I love my children dearly, but sometimes they can be such a trial. Vera almost killed her brother this afternoon. She nearly fractured his skull with a carpet thrasher. The doctor has been here most of the day bandaging Robert's head and watching his eyes for any signs of a concussion. So far there are none. I pray with all my heart that he is well in the morning.

Our dear Alice proved to be the most stalwart of the entire brood. She bandaged Robert's head and stemmed the loss of blood. She took charge of the dire situation and commanded Vera to call the doctor. I am very proud of her.

Samuel doesn't seem to be overly worried. He says Robert is the most hardheaded child he has ever known.

In the right hand margin, in another's handwriting, was a note: *Very aptly put, dear Margaret. And so true.*

Samuel Hanson had edited his wife's diary? John knew his grandfather could be mean to those closest to him. He hadn't realized his audacity extended to editing his wife's most private thoughts.

There were more pages torn out. At the top of the next full page was the end of a sentence: *who will judge us all.* Below was the beginning of the next entry dated February 10, 1918.

The church and the community have been very kind during our hour of greatest sorrow. The people around us are such a blessing, but sometimes the blessing can hurt. Mrs. Rothmoore came to me after the memorial service this morning, "How lucky you must feel to have been able to lay such a large gift on the altar of freedom," she'd said.

The altar of freedom? thought John. *Who gave a damn about the altar of freedom even in those days?* Of course she was referring to Robert and Victor's memorial service. Both of them had died in the First World War. How strange to think of them as Robert and Victor, not Uncle Robert or Uncle Victor.

John was only a year old when his family received the horrible news. In his memory the two boys had been nothing more than pictures with no character, no personality, no voice. There had been nothing to inspire love or hate or respect or pity. Not knowing was the saddest memory of all.

There were more missing pages. Once again the top of the next full page began in the middle of a sentence. . .*but I can't help but wonder, how delicate and intricate is the pattern of the human fabric. How radically it can be altered by the weaving or unraveling of one thread of human kindness or hate or love or indifference.*

A splotch of ink covered the rest of the page. It had soaked through the next five pages. Five pages with nothing, no handwriting, just a splotch of spilled ink. But they weren't torn out. As John turned each page he noticed that the five ink stained sheets were stuck as if riveted together. Something very thin and very sharp had left a puncture hole through each page. Why? What was going on and when?

The next entry was dated October 6, 1945.

Lost, all is lost. But the earth does not care. The good mother was born of fiery upheaval herself, and over the ages she adapted to the violence of human kind by covering the graves of the wicked and the good with the same soft soil that grows new crops of tall grasses and golden rod to dapple the green pasture.

There was a small ink dot below the paragraph that may have indicated Margaret was going to continue writing. But she didn't, and there was nothing on the last two pages.

There was one more entry. It was written on the inside of the back cover. There was no date, just a single sentence. *The consequence of something we cannot undo is punishment enough.*

Do? Undo? What did they do? John wondered. *What did the old people do?* He sighed and muttered to himself, "Too many ghosts, too many questions."

John snapped the book cover shut then realized that something didn't fit. He opened the back cover again and looked at the handwriting. It wasn't Grandma Hanson's hand. He thumbed back through the pages. It wasn't Grandpa Hanson's either. Who had written it? It wasn't Alice's handwriting. John had seen her writing before. Who did it? What did they do? What could they not undo?

The phone rang and John jumped, then caught his breath as he picked up the receiver. "Hello?"

"John Mac, where in the world have you been?"

Sigh. "What is it, Sharon?"

"Norma Parsons called over two hours ago. She and Bob came home from a party. Their house was ransacked and their daughter Judy is missing."

"Missing? Judy's missing?'

"Yes. Bob is out running all over the countryside looking for her."

"Why in the world is he doing that? Didn't they call the sheriff?'

"Of course they did. But you know how nobody moves fast enough to suit ole Bob."

"Sharon, go over and take care of Norma. Calm her down. I'll do my best to find Bob."

"John, there's something else."

"What is it?"

"The hospital called. Aunt Alice passed away about an hour ago."

John knew Alice wasn't going to make it, but when he heard the words "passed away," the shock of her never being close to him again hit him in the chest and knocked him senseless and speechless.

"Did you hear me, John?"

"I heard. I'll talk to you later."

As he turned to leave out the front John, heard a

pounding at the back door. He walked back down the hall and turned the upper dead bolt and the lockset in the door handle. When he opened the door he found a half naked girl, covered with mud and scratches, cowering on the back porch. "Oh my God, Judy. What happened to you?" He bent down, took off his jacket, and wrapped it around her shoulders.

"Where's Doc?" Judy cried. "I lost Doc." She looked up at John with blood all over her face and head. The big black bird had pierced a big scalp artery that bled profusely.

John was temporarily taken aback by the bloody mess on Judy's head. He took out his handkerchief and pressed it against her scalp. "Doc's in a safe place now. Here, let's get you back home."

"I can't walk any further," whined Judy. "I can't walk any further."

"It's alright, Judy. I'm going to call an ambulance.

"I'm so cold," she cried. "I'm so cold. Oh God, I can't stop shaking."

"It's okay Judy. I'll get you some warm blankets." As soon as he got Judy inside the back door, he rushed upstairs and fetched two blankets out of a hallway closet where they had been kept for as long as he could remember.

In spite of the extra warm layers, Judy still couldn't stop shivering. She shook all over as she rode in the ambulance, and she shook all over as the paramedics treated her wounds. At the hospital, the nurses put her in a hot whirlpool bath. She felt warm; but she couldn't stop shaking; and she couldn't stand or walk because her legs were cramped and uncoordinated.

The nurses dried Judy off as she lay on a gurney still shivering. One of them put an IV needle in her arm, and the warm liquid started to make her feel warm inside. She still shivered, now more from fright than anything else, so one of the ER doctors ordered a sedative. When the sedative took effect, Judy's eyelids got heavy and began to close. That's when the moonlight and visions invaded her head.

In the black of night Judy saw a pretty little doe and her fawn tramping through thick underbrush. A screaming woman carrying a crying baby crossed their path. Behind the woman and child there was the flash and bang from a shotgun, and the mother and child sprawled across the ground. There was the sight of bare earth morphing into an infantile face with a mouth opening wide to emit a loud wail.

"No," yelled Judy. "Make them stop. Make them stop."

While her eyes were closed, Judy felt an arm curl around her neck and her mother's voice say, "It's okay baby. You're safe now." Norma Parsons cried as she kept saying, "It's okay. Mother's here. You're okay now."

* * *

Homer dipped his small paintbrush in black paint and raised it to the drawing of his great grandmother's beautiful face he had drawn in the middle of the sunburst of blue paint splattered on one wall of his apartment. He was going to give the face outline and long black hair, but the face frowned at him and moved her gaze to the left of the blue sunburst.

Homer thought to himself, *What do you want me to do, G.G.?* His right hand went limp; the paintbrush fell to the floor, and his eyes closed. A soft hum sounded inside his head, and the vision of a crying baby's face appeared in his mind's eye. After that came the vision of a tiny skull, and after that came the image of a young doe and her fawn. Homer drew them all with black paint on one ray of the blue sunburst beside the beautiful face that now had a smile.

Chapter 33

Lady of Flames

Judy's nightmares finally faded under the bright sun. She stayed at Cates Memorial Hospital for observation until the following afternoon when her parents picked her up at the main entrance. Norma pushed her wheelchair out to the curb and helped her stand up. Judy grabbed her mother around the waist. "Don't leave me."

"I'm not going to leave you, honey. Mother is never going to leave you."

"I was so alone last night." Judy broke down and cried. "I was so alone. I didn't know where I was and I was so cold."

"It's okay, baby," said Norma hugging her. "We're taking you home to your own room."

"Don't leave me. Please don't leave me."

"I'm not going to honey. I'm not going to leave you."

"Is Doc home?"

"Doc is home in his own stall."

"Is he alright?"

"He's fine, honey. Everything and everybody are just fine."

When they got home, Judy stood at her bedroom window and looked out at the horse barn, the meadow and fenced field where she and Doc rode and galloped away the lazy days of summer.

She wore the nightgown her mother had brought to the hospital from home. Despite little sleep, she wasn't tired. So she got dressed in her jeans, flannel shirt and heavy socks.

She eased downstairs, put on her high-top gumboots, went out to the barn and shoveled manure out of Doc's stall.

That night Judy's sleep was free of nightmares. On the other side of Tanner's Grove, the Barnes household was not so lucky.

* * *

The man and his two daughters stepped down from the rear of the antique railroad car and stood in a cloud of steam on the station platform. The air was cold and the two girls were bundled up in heavy, fur-lined wool coats from neck to foot. Their heads were covered with plain wool scarves. The man's long skinny frame was dressed in a perfectly tailored wool suit, white shirt with high stiff collar, and black string tie. He tipped his broad brimmed hat to all the ladies he passed. The older of the two girls turned to her father. "Do we really have to do this?"

No answer.

"Please answer me."

"I have no answer for you, young lady. I raised you as best I could. I gave freely of my advice and you ignored it. What else can I say?"

"Papa, there's an old woman who lives in a cottage by the water tower."

The man grabbed his daughter's arm and whispered in her ear, "Don't you ever say one word about that old woman by the water tower. What she does is evil. What she does . . .it's . . . an abomination. You will not speak of her again. Is that clear?"

"Yes Papa."

"May God have mercy on your soul for even thinking about what she does."

"Papa, that man by the carriage is waving at you."

"There's my good man now and right on time."

A man in a plain black suit came up to greet them.

"The horse and carriage are just what I promised. The horse knows exactly where to take you."

"Very good, sir. And here's a little something for your extra trouble."

"Thank you very much, sir. Cash is always appreciated."

The man and his two daughters got into the carriage. He noticed that the horse had a long mane of blonde hair hanging down both sides of its head. The man leaned forward, his neck stretching like a stalk of taffy until his head was six feet from his shoulders. He yelled at the horse, "Pardon me, but don't I know you?"

The horse craned its neck around to look directly at the man and revealed the head of a blonde girl stuck onto the end of the horse's neck. Her own neck was ragged with severed blood vessels and mangled flesh hanging down. The girl's eyes remained closed, but the mouth opened wide in a hideous grin. Out of the mouth came five slender delicate fingers, then the hand, and finally the entire forearm with soft white skin. The hand doubled up into a fist, and the fist grew two horse's nostrils on either side of it as the girl's face and forearm turned into a horse's head.

The man drew in his neck and head and leaned back in his seat while the horse turned and trotted off down the gravel road. The man's head was between two mechanical figures operated by a pulley attached to the rear wheels of the carriage. Two little wooden men gripping hammers and hinged in the middle stood on either side of him while the pulley operated crank made them bend up and down pounding the man's bald head.

"Oh my soul! Oh my soul! Oh my soul!" he shouted.

Up ahead was a long, dark tunnel filled with tiny stars. It seemed to be carved out of the beautiful mountain scenery behind it. When the horse entered the tunnel, it started galloping faster and faster. At the end, a wooden bridge stretched across a deep gorge with a raging river at the bottom. The bridge only went halfway across the gorge, but the horse kept going until it pulled its carriage and three passengers off into midair.

They were all falling now, but below them lay a door with a flickering light coming through it. Diane suddenly realized she wasn't dreaming anymore. She was looking at the doorway of her bedroom, and in the hallway a flickering light had a crackling sound with it. *My God*, thought Diane. *The house is on fire*. She jumped out of bed and ran down the hall to Mary's room.

Diane gasped at what she saw, but terror choked the scream in her throat. Mary's bedroom was fully engulfed in flames while Mary levitated above her bed and rotated like she was being roasted on a rotisserie. Her hair stood straight out as her face turned toward Diane, her black eye sockets and mouth wide open like windows on the night sky and millions of tiny stars behind her. Diane fell back against the wall opposite the bedroom door, covered her face with her hands, collapsed to the floor and screamed. That broke the spell and Mary fell back to her bed. The flames faded leaving the room dark.

The hall light came on and Bill stood over the crumpled body of his wife. "What's going on here?"

Diane looked up at him, her hands over her mouth, and her eyes wide with fright. She pointed at Mary's room.

Bill went in and found his daughter lying still with the bedclothes thrown off her. He covered her up and went out to deal with his wife. Diane was already in the living room getting her coat on.

"What do you think you're doing?" asked Bill.

"We're getting out of here."

"What are you talking about?"

"You heard me. Enough is enough. We're not spending another night in this house."

"Where are you going?"

"Mother's house for now."

"Diane, that's not going to solve anything."

"I don't want to hear it, Bill. Get dressed. I'll get Mary
up. We're leaving."

"Diane, we aren't going anywhere. Right now I've got
a splitting headache. It feels like somebody's been pounding
on my head with . . ."

"You!" Diane straightened up from pulling on her
boots and glared at Bill. "You're having the same dream,
aren't you?"

"What dream?"

"Don't bullshit me. We're all having the same dream
and it's because of this house."

"No."

"I haven't got time to argue with you. Mary! Mary,
get up, honey. We're going to Grandma's house."

                         * * *

"You did what?"

"Mother, if we're not welcome here, we can always
rent a motel room."

"Diane, that's not the point. The point is you left Bill
back there in that house."

"He wouldn't come with us."

"Why not?"

"I don't know."

"You mean he's not afraid of that house and you are?"

"Mother, I just don't know."

"Diane, keep your voice down." Emily looked over at
Mary sleeping on the couch. "How did you get her over here
without her daddy?"

"She was asleep the whole time."

"She wasn't asleep when she came in here."

"She was groggy."

Suddenly Mary sat up on the couch. Her eyes were huge and she gasped for breath.

Emily rushed over to her. "Honey, what's the matter? Bad dream?"

Mary breathed easier when she felt her grandma's arms around her. "I had that same stupid dream again. I was falling. I was falling." She closed her eyes and rested her head on Emily's shoulder. "Oh God, I'm so tired."

Emily laid her back down on the couch and covered her with a blanket.

Diane motioned her mother over to the opposite side of the room. "We had another incident tonight."

"What happened?"

"I thought the house was on fire. When I ran into Mary's room, the walls were covered with flames." Diane began to sob and her hands trembled. "Mary was floating over her bed." She sobbed. Then regained her composure. "Her hair was standing straight out on end." She gulped down another cry. "Oh God, I thought she was . . ." Diane covered her face with her hands and cried.

Emily threw her arms around her and cooed, "Shhhhh. Now look, if you can spend a few minutes alone with Mary, I'm going over there to talk to Bill."

"What for?"

"Diane, he's your husband. You still love him, don't you?" Diane nodded. "Well then, his place is here with you. I'll be right back."

* * *

The house was dark except for the floodlight hanging from the front corner of the eaves. Emily walked up to the front door and read the note Bill had taped to the inside glass.

I spent the night at Charlie Boatright's house. I'll call you in the morning.

Chapter 34

The Black Snow Angel

The wind in the woods howled as the grandfather clock tolled the hour of ten.

A flock of starlings circled above the bluff in front of the Hanson farmhouse. The grandfather clock tolled the half hour.

The old clock ticked off the seconds and minutes and tolled the hours as it had for almost a hundred years. The portraits of Samuel and Margaret Hanson gazed out at the empty space that used to be Margaret's sewing room and where Alice had inadvertently heard an adult conversation not meant for her ears. The house was an empty shell without Aunt Alice. Cold and stern as she was, she was the focus of a tiny corner of the world around which many lives revolved. Now she was gone.

Louella Pritchett had arrived at the hospital an hour after her cousin John got there. John told her Alice's last words: *Papa was bad.* What was that all about? What did it mean?

Louella, sitting in a rocker in the front parlor, kept thinking back to grandpa Hanson's funeral when Alice had first mentioned the Hanson curse. "Something Mother and Papa and other people their age never talked about." Did the old lady know more than she revealed? Was she taking a terrible secret to the grave with her?

Louella's niece, Karen, stepped into the front parlor and said, "Aunt Louella, there's plenty of food in the house. Are you sure you don't want something to eat?"

"No Karen, I'm not hungry."

Louella had been crying for two days now. She hadn't eaten and Karen was afraid she was going to make herself really sick. She knelt on the floor beside the rocker and wiped another tear away from her aunt's cheek. "Aunt Louella, this is no good. Why don't we get you freshened up before all those people get back from the church?"

"I won't be here anyway. I'm going back to the motel before the crowd gets back."

"But they'll all want to see you."

Louella shook her head. "I don't want to see them."

"Aunt Louella, that's no way to be."

"I'm just not in the mood for it all."

"Are you still taking those sedatives?"

"Sometimes."

"Well, you're not driving with all that dope in your system."

"I don't have any dope in my system!" Louella barked. Karen's shocked and hurt expression made Louella cringe. "I'm sorry. Oh, Karen, I'm sorry. I didn't mean to hurt you."

"I know. I know." The two wept in each other's arms.

* * *

Sharon McCauley stood on the front porch, braced herself against the stiff November wind, and pulled her gloves on. John locked the front door behind them. "We should have called Louella and picked her up," said Sharon. "There's no sense in her driving to the funeral by herself."

"She called me at the office yesterday," said John. "I didn't tell you, but she's not coming to the funeral."

"Not coming? Why on earth not?"

"She was Aunt Alice's primary care giver. I think she's been so traumatized by all this, especially the way Alice died, that she can't bring herself to come to the funeral."

"But John, how is this going to look?"

"Who cares how it looks. Let's just get this over with."

They both stood on the driver's side of the car in the driveway and fumbled for their keys. "I'll drive," said John.

"I'll drive. You're upset."

"I'm not upset. Now I said I'll drive."

"John, don't push the issue." Sharon held up her set of car keys while John still fumbled through his pants and coat pockets. "You left your keys hanging on the rack in the hallway. I know you're upset. I'll drive."

"But how's this going to look?"

Sharon rolled her eyes. "Who cares how it looks? Let's just get this over with."

* * *

John sat and stared at the dirty snow, the naked trees, and the open fields of mangled cornstalks as they slipped by. "Do you think ill of me for not crying over Aunt Alice's passing?"

"You've been crying inside, John. I can tell."

"Well, she was part of our world. Her stern face was one of my earliest memories." John sighed and turned to Sharon. "Actually I cried at the hospital the night she died. I don't know why, but I did."

"She was not a loved woman, was she?"

"No. Lots of people respected her, but I don't remember anybody showing her any affection."

"She heaped a lot of affection on you. She told me all about it when we got married."

"I know. She did a lot for all of us when we were growing up. She taught me how to read. But I only remember one act of affection when I was young.

"Aunt Alice read a story to me when I was little. *The Bears of Blue River*. There's a legend in that story about a fire bear and how people are supposed to kill it. If they don't, they'll die in three days. Well, I reread that story when I got older, and I had a nightmare one night about an Indian woman coaxing me out of the house to follow her into the woods. We came upon this fire and cauldron, and when the Indian woman scooped a sample of the brew out of the cauldron and drank it she turned into the fire bear. She chased me all the way back home and would have caught me if I hadn't woke up."

John leaned back in his car seat. "I don't think I was ever so scared in my life, not even in the army. And you know, I think that's the only tender moment I remember when Alice came into my room and quieted me down and told me it was just a bad dream, and she stroked my hair and cuddled me. God, I remember that so well."

"Do you remember her showing anybody else any affection?"

"No, but she was a parent figure as much as any of our own parents." John looked away from Sharon and contemplated the passing scenery, then mused, "Strange how we knew her longer than any of our own parents. We knew she was old and was going to die someday. We just didn't expect it to end like this."

* * *

The enormous sanctuary was packed. Not another person could have found a seat after John and Sharon arrived. As he entered the main door, John couldn't shake the feeling that he was being followed. When he turned to look behind him, there was nobody close by. They looked around and breathed a sigh of relief when they were sure they weren't close to anybody they recognized. They walked over to an aisle seat along an outside wall and sat down. John still had the feeling that somebody had followed him. He forced himself to ignore the feeling and focused on how much he wished he and Sharon were somewhere else.

John had grown up in the Mount Sinai Methodist Church, listening to his Aunt Alice, his grandparents, the minister, church elders, and superintendents talk down to him with a literal interpretation of the Bible and threats of eternal damnation if he didn't kowtow to their gimcrack religion. When he became a man he joined the army, went to college, got married, had a child, and lost a child.

Lisa's funeral drew a small gathering. John thought that most people he knew from school, church, and the farm community were just too squeamish to pay their respects under the circumstances of such a tragic loss. Those who did attend seemed to say all the wrong things: *She's in a better place now. You could have other children. Why don't you adopt a child?* The world was a scary place. The Mount Sinai Methodist Church had not kept up and was no longer relevant to John or Sharon.

There were three chairs beside the elevated podium in front of the choir loft. They would be occupied by the local minister, Reverend James Sellers, who had known the Hanson family for most of his life; Alice's oldest nephew, Ronald Talland, and Reverend Chester Dale. The open coffin sat on the main floor in front of the podium. Reverend Dale was an ancient wisp of a man who could barely speak or keep his mind focused on one thing for very long. Because Reverend Sellers was too grief stricken to speak at Alice's funeral, Reverend Dale was going to deliver the eulogy. The three men gathered in the vestibule behind the choir loft and prepared to enter the sanctuary together.

"Reverend Dale, if you want to get in front, I think you should enter first," said Ronald.

"Oh, I think we should have the invocation first."

"No, I mean when we go out onto the podium."

"Oh, you mean when we enter." The old preacher's face had a perpetual surprised expression, and his head nodded constantly as he spoke. "Yes, of course." He turned to enter the choir loft door then turned back and asked, "What is your name again, sir?"

"Talland. Ronald Talland."

"Oh yes. You're giving the invocation."

"No, Reverend Sellers is giving the invocation."

"Who?"

"Reverend Sellers."

"Oh yes. Yes, of course."

Ronald Talland made a good show at not appearing frustrated, but he started to lose his cool when the preacher turned to make his entrance, then stopped and turned back.

"Who is giving the invocation?"

"Reverend Sellers," Ronald said through clenched teeth.

"No, I mean who is Reverend Sellers?"

"He is the local minister."

"I see. He was the minister to . . .What was the lady's name again?"

"Alice Hanson."

"Alice Hanson. Yes. Yes of course."

They finally made it out to the podium and sat down.

Reverend Sellers took a deep breath as he rose, then stepped up to the podium to give the invocation. "Yea though I . . .ah. He . . .He . . .that believes in me. He that believes in me . . .ah. Though he ah. Even though he dies. Yet he shall live."

He looked out over the congregation. Those who weren't looking down in their laps and wringing their hands stared at him with chagrined sympathy in their wet eyes. "Reverend Chester Dale will now deliver the eulogy." Jim Sellers walked back to his chair and sat down.

The sanctuary was stone quiet. People tried not to fidget in their seats. There was a cough here, a cough there, while Chester Dale sat like a statue.

"Reverend Dale?" Ronald Talland whispered, eyeing the congregation. "Reverend Dale, I think it's your turn."

No answer.

"Reverend Dale, everybody's waiting," Ronald said again, still watching the congregation. He did not touch the old man's hand. Otherwise, he would have felt cold flesh. He did not look in his eyes. Otherwise, he would have seen that the pupils were fixed and dilated.

The ancient head turned on its decrepit neck while the creaky voice said, "Yes, I know."

With his back perfectly straight and his head held high, Reverend Dale stood up, strode to the podium, put both hands on either side of it, and gazed out at the congregation. After a moment, he turned, descended the riser, and came up behind the coffin. The edge of that portion of the coffin lid that was raised bisected his face as he narrowed his eyebrows and cast a steely gaze at the congregation. He looked to his left; he looked to his right. He raised his head and opened his mouth of yellow teeth. A voice, not his own, bellowed from his antique throat, "Hypocrites!"

Everyone jumped and stared wide-eyed at the preacher. He turned to one side of the sanctuary and screamed again. "Hypocrites! You all came to mourn Alice Hanson. Why? She had no husband. She had no children. Why? Nobody loved her."

The old preacher walked out from behind the coffin waving his arms in mock horror. "Oh you good people, you good hypocrites do protest what I say, don't you? Well, it's the truth, and every one of you Sunday morning Christians know it! You know it!"

Chester Dale waved his arms and stabbed the air with his fingers. "You really wanted to stay away, didn't you? But you were afraid if you did, Alice would come back to haunt you. Isn't that the truth?

"Well, I'm here to haunt you now, and I say to all of you------ Hypocrites!" The old man bent forward every time he shouted, and everybody cringed.

He strode down one aisle and stopped in front of a fat, bald Doug Lassiter who was already sweating and blushing brighter with each second. "You! You were the little brat who set fire to the closet on the first floor of the old school house, weren't you? Weren't you?"

"That . . .that. . .was an accident," Lassiter stammered.

"Bullshit!" The old preacher slapped the man's face then whirled around and cast a murderous glare across the crowd on the opposite side of the sanctuary.

"You! You in the blue suit and the phony rug on your bald head." The church music director, Clarence Moore, his daughter and grandsons all squirmed at once. "You were caught with that little girl in the fourth grade in the coat room. You were caught running your hand up and down her bare leg. Weren't you? Weren't you?"

The Moore family got up to leave. Clarence kept his head down while he hustled his brood toward the outside aisle.

"Where are you going?" yelled the preacher. "Where are you taking those children? What's the matter with you? Can't you talk?" Clarence Moore was in front of the parade as the family hurried to the side door. "I said, can't you talk? Hey! Answer me! Can't you talk? You can feel, but you can't talk. Is that it?"

He heard a woman in the front pew break down in tears, and darted back to the front to stand in front of Irene Hastings. "You! You . . . perfect little angel. You horny little slut! What were you doing in the little girl's room with that coke bottle, huh? Is that why Alice had to come running in there to help you?" Irene gasped in horror and collapsed on the pew.

"Hey! Hey! Stop that." Irene's father was leaning over the back of her seat and waving his age spotted hand at Chester Dale. "Leave her alone!"

The old preacher pointed a finger at him. "You son of a bitch! You lousy son of a bitch. It's bad enough that you murdered her brother. Now you have to show your sorry carcass at her funeral."

"Who are you calling a murderer?" asked Irene Hastings' father. There were meek gasps and squeaks all around them.

"I didn't call you a murderer. I called you a son of a bitch. And you killed Alice's brother, Sergeant Victor Hanson."

"He was killed by enemy fire."

"And you were the enemy. You and that bunch of thugs who called yourselves soldiers shot him in the head and told your commander he caught a bullet when he came out of the trench, didn't you?"

No answer. The man was about to ask how the old preacher knew about this, but that would be tantamount to confession. He couldn't do that. Not here. Not now. He'd die and go straight to hell.

"Didn't you?" the preacher bellowed. "That man was going to discipline you, and make soldiers out of you, and you killed him!"

Everybody who hadn't been singled out eyed the nearest exit and shivered in fear of who might be next. But nobody left. That would call attention, and who knew what the old preacher might do then.

Chester Dale walked over to the open coffin. He mounted the casket and lay on the closed portion of the lid with his hands pressed against the cold face of Alice Hanson. His eyes got wide, and he crooned to the corpse. "Oh Alice! Alice! God still loves you. People may hate you, but God still loves you. Papa was bad, but he still loves you. Mother was mean to you, but she still loves you. Mother and Papa are waiting for you, Alice. Mother and Papa and Jesus have made a place for you, Alice. They're all waiting for you to come home now." The old preacher raised his head as he lay on the coffin and sang at the top of his lungs. "I'll be there. I'll be there. When the roll is called up yonder I'll be theeeeeere!"

The extra weight on top of the coffin made it tumble over and crash to the floor. Chester Dale, in his long black robe, rolled with the wreckage and sprawled across the floor of the sanctuary like a black snow angel.

Everybody screamed at once. As soon as the old preacher collapsed, a stiff cold wind blew across the sanctuary from the choir loft to the back of the building. It ruffled everybody's hair and blew hats off women's heads and wet handkerchiefs out of their hands. James Sellers and Ronald Talland rushed to the side of the still, cold body of Chester Dale, while the rest of the crowd stampeded out the main doors of the church.

John sat frozen to his seat. He knew the old man shouting obscenities wasn't Chester Dale. But who was he? What had possessed him?

John let everybody run out of the sanctuary ahead of him. He looked back at the front and noticed that the church office door was open and somebody was inside calling an ambulance. Chester Dale lay cold and still on the floor with the wrecked coffin and Aunt Alice's stiff body beside him.

* * *

The ill spirit sailed straight up out of the old preacher's body, out the door of the church, and high into the sky over Tanner's Grove. It flew north and spotted The Old Dog Tavern. When it penetrated the back wall of the tavern's second story, it slammed into Homer's back and sent him sprawling across the living room floor. He grunted and pushed himself up on his elbows while he struggled to catch his breath. Out of body flight never got any easier. It was getting harder now that Homer was getting older.

Anna Lee came into the living room and said, "You shouldn't do that, Homer."

"Shut up, old woman. "

"One of these times you ain't gonna make it back."

"I said shut up." Homer pushed himself up to a kneeling, then a standing position, and glared at his old mother. "The pious little prigs of this county got their tails yanked and their snooty beaks twisted. They and their daddies and granddaddies stand around and pretend they don't know nothin' about our people gettin' murdered. Ha!

"Ole John McCauley didn't spook none. He knew what was going on or close to it. I guess our daddy left him some grit before he coupled with you, Anna Lee."

Homer pranced around the room. The sunburst of blue paint with a face in the middle of it still needed some finishing touches. He picked up a small brush of black paint and finished the outline of the oblong face with a small chin and long black hair hanging down in twin pony tails. "Great Grandma's gonna make herself known, Anna Lee. Our G.G. is going to make herself known. "

* * *

Sharon McCauley wore her overcoat as she sat in the cushioned comfort of her overstuffed armchair. In a wide, sweeping motion she wrapped the yarn around her crochet needle and pulled the double loop through the back of the preceding stitch. She stuffed the needle through the second stitch and wrapped another double loop around it with a wide sweeping motion of the yarn and the needle. The repetitive exercise helped keep her warm and her attention off how frightened she was. The furnace was running; the temperature inside the house was over eighty degrees; but Sharon still shivered as she worked. She didn't look up as John walked through the door.

"What did they tell you at the hospital?" she asked.

"Chester Dale died almost instantly," John said in a dull voice. "There's going to be two funerals now."

Chapter 35

Seasons Grievings

There was a white Christmas in 1979, but the holiday frosting on the country scenery was lost on John and Louella. They spent all their spare time pouring over Alice Hanson's estate and putting her house up for sale. They got no takers.

When the trucks hauled the last of the furniture to the auction house, John stood in his aunt's front room and stared out at the dirty snow plowed out of the road and heaped on the yard. There were no snowmen with tree branch arms, no children catching snowflakes on their tongues.

Decorating a house for Christmas was really getting to be a chore. John would have let Sharon do it alone, but she needed help getting the fir tree through the front door and into the metal stand. Sharon always insisted on a live tree. She roped John into hanging the fake holly along the fire-place mantle and over the doors. And she needed help string-ing the garlands around the tree.

"You know, maybe next year we could celebrate the festival of Saturn," said John

"Whatever are you talking about?" asked Sharon.

"Well, you know Christ wasn't born on the twenty-fifth of December. That was the old Roman holiday set aside for the god Saturn. The early Christians converted it to Christmas to make it holy. The festival of Saturn surely couldn't be any more hassle than this."

"Oh John Mac, will you stop being so morose! I swear you've got to get over this horrible mood of yours!"

"Yeah, yeah. I'm sorry Sharon. Here, get down off that stool and I'll put the angel on top of the tree."

"No, you just stand down there and hold onto me like you usually do. I've got something special to put up here this year." Sharon hauled a foil-wrapped cardboard star out of a paper sack.

"Where in the name of God did you get that thing?"

"It was in some old decorations at Aunt Alice's house. Like it?"

"No."

"Why not?"

"Because I made it, that's why."

"What?"

"Sharon, I haven't seen that ratty old thing for years. I made it when I was in grammar school. Look at it. It's not even cut straight. It looks like the devil."

"I think it's lovely. Aunt Alice had this on her tree last year. Don't you remember?"

"No. You and Louella decorated her tree last year."

"I know, and when we hauled out this old star Aunt Alice took it away from me and went in the kitchen and wrapped it in new aluminum foil."

"Bless her heart." Tears welled up in John's eyes.

Sharon reached up and fingered the points of the star. "I didn't know you made it, sweetie. It looks even lovelier now."

"Thank you, Sharon."

"I guess that old lady loved you more than you thought."

"Yeah. I guess she did."

* * *

Business had been booming for Bill Barnes' welding shop. The money was coming in fast enough now that Diane was able to hire one of the office girls from Morley's Temporary Services to help out with the accounting. Since Diane no longer had two full time jobs, her spirits had improved. And the spirits in the house faded into the woodwork, replaced by a six-foot Christmas tree in the living room, bells and garlands around the doors, and lots of lights inside and outside all the windows. Everybody slept well at night.

Bill's growing enterprise needed more space. It also needed a building permit and a zoning variance. Bob Parsons provided that out of gratitude for Bill's effort to corral his prize steed, Doc.

Bill and his best friend, Charlie Boatright, took advantage of a warm spell the day after Christmas to finish enclosing the two-story addition to the south side of the house. The old garage now acted as a buffer to keep the smell and noise out of the rest of the place.

Diane walked across the garage, opened the door to the new shop, and turned her nose up at the heat and the smell. "Are you coming to bed anytime tonight?" she asked Bill.

"Not now, Diane."

"You're gonna kill yourself working like this and breathing all these fumes."

Bill took off his welder's hood and turned to Diane with tired eyes and a dirty face. "You see this? This has to be done by noon Friday."

"What is it?"

"It's money. It's worth five grand to us. I told you the money would start coming in again."

"I mean what's this thing you're welding?"

"It's a custom truck bed. Some lard head wrecked the truck, and now the boss wants to save the bed for a new truck."

"Well, what do you have to do to it?"

"I have to fix it!"

"Oh."

Later that night Diane and Bill lay in bed and stared at the ceiling. Diane said she was too tired to fall asleep.

"Bill?"

"Yeah?"

"Sharon McCauley called this morning."

"What did she want?"

"She wanted to invite us over the weekend after New Year's. She and John are having a bunch of people over."

"Aw, I ain't in the mood for that." He rolled over in bed facing away from Diane.

"Hey, what harm can it do? After all they've been through with that funeral and all. They've been nice to us and lots of other people around here. Besides, it might be good for business if you got out and met new people."

"Yeah, I suppose."

"I told Sharon we'd be there."

No answer.

"Did you hear me? I told her we'd be there."

"Yeah, yeah. That's fine."

Chapter 36

Where Lisa Lived

"This doesn't look like the house of a real estate tycoon." At John McCauley's house, Bill parked behind a long row of cars in front of an old wooden garage.

"I don't think he's a tycoon," said Diane. "The way I hear it his partner, Bob Parsons, has all the money."

They climbed the concrete steps of the front porch and knocked on the heavy glass door.

From deep inside the crowd in the front room, a tall, broad-shouldered man with curly black hair, a fairly prominent overbite, and heavy eyebrows came to answer the door. As the big guy wound his way through the crowd, Bill turned to Diane. "Good God. Kim Habowski."

"Who?"

"Kim Habowski. You remember, I told you he was one of the straw bosses at Weber Fabrication where I used to work."

"He doesn't look like a Kim."

"He's an ass."

"Bill, don't make a scene."

"I'm not going to make a scene, but he will."

Diane clutched her purse. "Oh no."

"Just let me handle this. He's going to pull his favorite trick right now just to embarrass us. Don't say a word, and I'll get him put in his place real quick."

"Bill!"

Before Diane could plead any further the door flew open, the porch light came on, and the guy with the curly hair, buckteeth, and broad shoulders called out in a high-pitched voice, "Bill Barnes! Whadya say ole buddy? Long time, no see."

Bill and Diane stepped inside the door. "Hello Kim. How ya doin'?"

"John and Sharon are in the family room. Let me take your coats. Say Bill, who's the pretty lady?"

"Kim, I'd like you to meet my wife, Diane," Bill said in a flat voice.

Diane forced a grin, gave the man a limp handshake, and tried not to notice the leering smile he gave her.

"Well now, Bill, this isn't the woman you introduced me to last time as your wife."

Diane's face turned bright red and she looked down, desperately looking for a crack in the floor to crawl into.

"Yeah, you're right, Kim. I didn't tell you before, but my first wife died." The leering grin left the big man's face like it had been slapped off. "My daughter and I were both heart broken long after the funeral. Then Diane came along. She's been a real help and comfort to me." He gave Kim a broad grin and put his arm around Diane's shoulder. He could tell by the crestfallen look on the man's face that he had just been caught without a comeback, and all three of them knew it.

A crooked grin came across Kim's face. "Touché," he said. "Score one for the skinny guy."

Bill took Diane by the arm and waded into the crowd. He said over his shoulder, "We can introduce ourselves around, Kim. Nice seein' you again."

Diane leaned against Bill and said, "You said you wouldn't make a scene."

Before Bill could answer, a large woman planted herself in front of them. "Hi, I'm Betty Habowski, Kim's wife.

You must be Bill and Diane Barnes. I know everybody else here. How are ya?"

Bill and Diane nodded and grinned as Betty shook Bill's hand, and shook and shook and shook and shook. She had the grip of a stevedore with a body to match.

She kept shaking Bill's hand as she said, "You worked for Vern Decker back at the old plant, didn't you?"

"Ah, yeah."

"I remember Vern talkin' about you all the time. He always talked like you were one of the good guys. I sure am glad to meet you."

Betty didn't stop shaking Bill's hand until she turned to Diane. "You must be Diane. I'm glad to meet you too." Diane's tiny hand disappeared in Betty's massive grip. "Now you probably wonder how I know so much about Vern and Bill here. Well, Kim brings his job and some of the guys home a lot. Shoot, he talks more than I do when you get him started. 'Course a lot of people here talk more than I do." *Man, I wish she'd stop shaking my hand,* thought Diane. Betty chuckled. "I only gush like this when I meet new people. Bill, you got a real nice wife here. Take good care o' her, ya hear?"

Suddenly Betty looked past Bill and Diane and shouted, "Do you have to go already, honey?"

Kim Habowski yelled across the room, "'Fraid so, hon. Don't worry, I'll be on vacation next week. I won't let them bother me then." He pulled on his coat and waved at the rest of the crowd.

Betty looked back at Diane and Bill, then finally released Diane's hand. "See I told ya he brings his work home. Sometimes he even leaves home to burn the midnight oil with the rest of the troops. Wait a minute, sugar. I need a goodbye kissy pooh."

When Betty was out of earshot Bill said, "Man, I had no idea Kim's wife was that fat."

"Bill, don't make another scene."

Bill looked around to make sure Kim wasn't close. "I won't, but my God, she must weigh a ton."

"Well, she's a nice lady in her own way. I like her."

"I like her too. There's just so much of her."

"Bill."

"That's okay. Some men like big women."

Before either could take a single step, a skinny man bounded up to them. "Hi there! Kyle Harris is my name. This is my wife, Phyllis."

"How do you do?" said the little round woman. She stood behind her husband and picked lint off his sweater. "Before you leave tonight I need to know your birthdays, birth years and the exact time of day you were born."

"Phyllis here has drawn up astrological charts on everybody in the group. I guess you're next." Kyle had an irritating little laugh. Bill passed it off as a nervous tick, but he still wanted to get away from him.

"We're pretty hungry," said Bill. "Where's the food?"

"Bill!" Diane sighed and looked away.

"Oh, all the men are hungry," said Phyllis. "And ill mannered. Ha ha ha ha."

"It's all in the family room," said Kyle. "Help yourself."

"Well Bill and Diane Barnes!" exclaimed Sharon McCauley, hurrying up to them. "I finally get to meet you. You'll have to excuse the informality. Just grab a plate and some food. This house is too small to get everybody at one table."

"That's alright," said Diane. "The house looks lovely, Sharon. Where did you get all the beautiful afghans?"

"Oh, I make those in my spare time, especially when I'm pulling phone duty at Parsons and McCauley Realty."

"They're gorgeous."

"Thank you."

"Does this work?" Diane pointed to an old Atwater Kent radio sitting in one corner. It fit the antique look of the rest of the room. The old console was about five feet high with elegant sculpted legs and a walnut stain finish.

"It belonged to my grandmother. John fell in love with it as soon as we got married, so Granny gave it to us just like that. We haven't had it on for ten years. I don't know if it works or not."

Sharon escorted Bill and Diane into an adjoining room where a sumptuous buffet was laid out. "Folks, I'd like you all to meet Bill and Diane Barnes. Bill, Diane, this is Jim and Carolyn Forkner." Jim and Carolyn warmed up to Bill and Diane right away. They were showing pictures of their grandson to everybody who wasn't loading up a dinner plate. Bill noticed the small liver spots on Carolyn's hands and the tiny lines around her eyes and mouth. They were her only signs of advanced age. Carolyn had a pretty smile and beautiful eyes. Bill guessed her to be in her sixties. He thought all grandmas should be that good looking.

"Folks tell me you're a welder," Jim said to Bill.

"That's right. Here, let me get you one of these." Bill fished a business card out of his wallet.

"Thanks," said Jim. "I do some consulting work for a water purification company. I may need your help later on."

"Call me anytime."

Bill and Diane grabbed two plates and stood in line at the food table. They noticed that John McCauley was holding court with his back to them in a nearby corner. His chief listeners were a young couple in their mid-twenties. The girl had devastatingly beautiful Latin features: dark eyes, heavy eyebrows, a wide mouth, and raven black hair. Her boyfriend had long red hair and black rim glasses.

The redheaded young man said, "John, I'm having a problem with the old concept of mind over matter. You know my brother, Tom, the one with Multiple Sclerosis?"

"Yes."

"Well, a few months ago he had another attack. This one really got him down. He couldn't work for almost a month. The doctors gave him more Prednisone and told him to get ready for the worst if this happens again."

"Meaning?"

"Meaning that he may wind up in a wheelchair for the rest of his life."

"And did Tom believe that?"

"Tom told the doctors that he didn't want anymore Prednisone and that he wasn't going to sit in a wheelchair forever. He's the most hard-headed man I know. But John, he's getting better. When I ask him how he does it he just goes . . ." The young man tapped his forehead.

"Do you believe that?"

"I know that a person can talk himself into being sick. But how in the world can the mind cure an incurable disease that's already there?"

"Have you and Tom talked about this yourselves?"

"Not much. I was afraid to use any hypnosis on him."

"Sounds like he's using self-hypnosis."

"I'm sure he is. But I'm afraid he may be falling into a trap you warned us about before: Using hypnosis to mask pain that's trying to tell him something is wrong."

"Is he in pain?"

"No, he was paralyzed."

"Is he paralyzed now?"

"No, but MS is a nerve disease. I mean a physical nerve disease. How can hypnosis or the power of suggestion cure that?"

"Tim, I'm sure your brother hasn't cured his disease. But he overcame his symptoms, and he's not in a wheelchair is he?"

"No, but when the spirit is willing, and the body says no . . . "

"Tim, a long time ago a wiser man than I said to me, 'You wouldn't dare imagine what the human mind is capable of doing.'"

"I think you have another visitor, John," said the black haired girl.

John's face brightened as he turned around and looked up. "Bill. Diane. God, it's good to see you. This is Tim Whitaker and Linda Toscanna. Linda works for our attorney; Tim is a local radio news announcer. Have a seat right here next to me."

"You mean like Walter Cronkite?" asked Diane as she and Bill sat.

Tim laughed. "I'm nowhere close to Walter Cronkite," said Tim. "But, maybe someday."

John took Diane's hand and said to Tim and Linda, "Diane is Pam Petersen's sister. She's Emily Petersen's other daughter."

"Pam Petersen?" Linda touched her chin. "Oh yeah. Your sister works at the deaf school, doesn't she?"

"That's right."

"I remember her," said Tim. "John regressed her to a previous life, a time when she was deaf. Now she teaches at the deaf school. Interesting how one life follows the other."

Diane caught Bill rolling his eyes at the mention of previous lives. He stuffed a cupcake in his mouth and said nothing.

"We haven't seen her for a while," said Linda.

"Pam went through a pretty nasty divorce a while back," said Diane. "She threw herself into her work to get over it."

"I've been trying to get her to teach sign language to my scuba diving club. You know, to make it easier to communicate underwater when you've got a breathing regulator in your mouth."

"You're a scuba diver?" exclaimed Bill.

"Oh yes."

Bill turned to Tim. "Wow, a jock and a beautiful woman all in the same package. Tim, you got quite a bargain."

Linda laughed and said, "I didn't feel much like a jock last weekend." She turned to Tim and said, "You want to tell them the story?"

"Oh no, you found the body."

Bill blinked. "Body?"

Linda nodded. "It was pretty awful. This guy, Ken Wallis, had been missing for about a year. We were diving in Cherry Tree Lake, and there he was on the bottom. I guess the fish had . . . well they kind of had their way with him. That's all I want to say about that. People are trying to eat."

Tim said, "They made a positive ID with dental records."

Diane decided this would be a good time to refill her coffee cup. When she came back she heard Kyle Harris, the skinny man with the irritating laugh, in a nearby corner of the room lecturing some of the women about dreams. "Dreams are very symbolic. And the symbols are very personal. What means something to one person may mean something entirely different to somebody else."

"I'm afraid to talk about my dreams," said Phyllis. "I'm always naked in them." She gave a nervous giggle.

"I know just what you mean," said Betty Habowski. "I had this dream the other night. I was swimming underwater with a crowd of people and I realized I was the only one who was nude. Everybody else was wearing some kind of black suit."

"No, no," said Kyle. "Nudity in dreams is nothing to be ashamed of. It has nothing to do with sex or exhibitionism. It means you're afraid to let people see your true feelings and personality."

"Honey, people can see all the feelings and personality I got," said Phyllis. "Just so I keep my buns covered."

"I'm not so sure about that," said Carolyn Forkner. "There's nothing about the human body we all haven't seen before. But feelings are really personal, and I think we all keep them bottled up, even when we're awake."

"Wet suits!" chirped Betty. "They were all wearing those suits like skin divers wear."

Tim Whitaker yelled across the room. "It's like Mort Sahl said one time, some women go to bed with a man to keep him from getting too personal."

Everybody laughed and Kyle said, "Phyllis, you know you're afraid of your feelings. Look at the time at your mother's funeral when your sister . . ."

"I don't want to talk about it!" Phyllis jumped up and stomped out of the room.

"I'll take care of her." Carolyn took off and left Kyle and Betty by themselves.

"No, they weren't wet suits." Betty looked around and saw that she and Kyle were alone, and Kyle wasn't paying any attention to her. So she left.

An idea, a question suddenly occurred to Diane, and the opportunity was now open. Bill was preoccupied with Linda Toscanna's good looks if not John McCauley's mysticism. Very surreptitiously Diane scooted over to Kyle's side.

"Pardon me . . . Kyle, you said something about dreams. Ah, I don't mean to be forward, but I just had a question about one of my own dreams."

"Relax. No question or subject is taboo here." *God, a beautiful woman takes an interest in what I say. What is this world coming to? And where have you been all my life?*

"Well, Bill and I have been having the same dream for some time now. Our daughter has it too. We're all in a horse drawn carriage that goes across a bridge over a big river. The bridge only goes half way across the river, but the horse keeps pulling us until we all fall off the end of the bridge."

"What happens then?"

"That's it. The dream ends and we wake up."

"You never hit bottom?"

"No."

"I'm waiting for somebody to hit bottom." *(chuckle)* "There's an old myth that if you're falling in a dream, and you hit bottom, you don't wake up."

"You die?" A worried look clouded Diane's face.

"Well, it's only a myth."

"What does it mean?"

"The myth?"

"The dream."

"Oh, your dream. Ah, well . . . a . . . life half-lived, a karmic debt half-paid. Who knows? The river? Now the river is very interesting. Rivers appear in many religions and my-thologies. The Greeks and Romans believed the dead had to cross the river Styx in order to get to the underworld."

"The underworld? You mean hell?"

"Well, it wasn't exactly hell."

"Some people believed this life on earth was the un-derworld," John said as he walked over to Kyle and Diane. "We draw much of our wisdom from the teachings of the mystery religions of Persia and Chaldea."

"Whoa! This is getting too deep," Diane chuckled.

It was getting too deep for Bill too. Once John joined the conversation, Linda and Tim's attention turned to John, and Bill scooted over to the buffet to refill his plate.

Above the din of so many wagging tongues, he heard the loud southern accent of Sharon McCauley. "Did you get all that?" Sharon put her arm around Diane's shoulder and gave her a friendly grin. Then she turned to her husband. "John Mac, you're not going to shoot your wad on this girl all in one night, are you?"

"Sharon, for God's sake!" It was John's turn to blush bright red. Sharon and Diane had a good laugh at his expense.

* * *

Diane thought the evening was going quite well. Bill was talking shop with Jim Forkner. She shared a cheese ball and rose and garden tips with Betty Habowski and Carolyn Forkner. When she was left alone, Diane searched the downstairs for evidence of children in the house and found none. There were no baby pictures, no graduation pictures, no trophies, no toys, nothing. The subject of McCauley children had simply never been broached, and Diane felt a small twinge of sadness that John and Sharon had remained childless.

Then she found a small portrait in the corner of the living room. Hanging on the wall just above the landing that preceded the main stairway was the picture of an angel faced little girl with rosy cheeks, big blue eyes, and long blonde hair. The picture frame was draped in pink satin and placed so that the first thing to be seen when coming down the stairs was the child's portrait.

"She's still here." Diane jerked around to find Sharon standing behind her. "She's still here, and she's still alive." Sharon tapped at a spot just over her heart.

"Oh Sharon, I'm sorry. I didn't mean to be nosy."

"You're not being nosy, honey. And we don't mind talking about Lisa because she's still alive in our hearts."

Diane looked at the portrait then back at Sharon. "Oh my God, she's not here anymore, is she?"

Sharon bowed her head and whispered. "No."

"Sharon, I'm so sorry."

"That's alright. We live with her pretty face and her beautiful soul every day as you can see. But she was our only child. And sometimes it hurts to know you can never hug her or kiss her goodnight." Sharon's voice began to crack. She choked back the tears and went on. "We had her late in life, and any thought of having more children was out of the question. She got sick with meningitis, suffered for about a week, then went sailing off with the angels.

"After that John and I got busy with other things. John got busier with real estate and became a full partner with Bob Parsons. I finished my master's degree and taught school for a while."

"You both seem to have handled it quite well."

"Well, I'm not so sure about that. I don't think either of us would have made it through the ordeal if it hadn't been for the love and comfort of a dear, sweet old man named Carson Sells. John met Carson when they both worked at one of the old Kirby and Bachman warehouses right after World War Two. John found out in the beginning that Carson was something of a mystic. He could read John's mind, John's mood, John's ills and pains. Carson said he was born with second sight. He was able to read auras around people's shoulders and tell what kind of health they were in."

She glanced at her daughter's portrait. "He was the first one to tell us about Lisa. I had been giving Lisa medicine for a cold. John brought Carson home for supper one night. He took one look at that little girl and told me to get her to a doctor right away. I did." Sharon's voice began to break again. "It just wasn't meant to be I guess."

"Sharon, I'm so sorry." Sharon patted Diane's hand and smiled. "Where were your families in all this?"

"Our families did the best they could for us, but it just wasn't enough. I mean what can anybody do for a couple who has lost their only child and have no hope of having more children."

"Did you ever consider adopting a child?" As soon as the words left her mouth, Diane winced. But Sharon just shook her head.

"No, we didn't. We care a lot about other people's children. Adopting Lisa's substitute was something we just couldn't handle."

"How did Carson help you when your families couldn't?"

"We had a séance."

"A séance?"

"Carson came to the house one night. He covered all the windows and doors with black cloth to block out all the light. He placed two metal pieces in the middle of the kitchen table. They looked like megaphones. Carson said they were trumpets and sometimes the dead talked through them. When we turned the lights out, it was so dark you couldn't see anything. He sat on one side of me and held my hand. John sat on my other side and caressed my shoulder. They both told me how much they loved me. They told me how much they loved Lisa." Sharon began to cry. "But we never heard Lisa's voice."

Diane took Sharon by the waist and brought her over to sit down on the couch. Sharon dried her eyes with a paper napkin. "I sat there and cried my eyes out in the dark. All of a sudden I felt Lisa's hand on my knee. I swear Diane, I wasn't imagining anything. I knew her touch. I knew the feel of that precious little hand. In my mind's eye, I saw her face looking up at me. I felt the glow of that pretty little angel face. In my mind's ear, I heard her tell me she was going away to a happy place. She told me she wasn't alone, that other souls were taking her away to a safe and happy place.

"I woke up the next morning and I still had this dull ache from not having Lisa in my arms. *(sigh)* But at least I knew she was in a safe place."

Sharon noted Diane's far off worried look. "You have an only child of your own, don't you?" Diane nodded. "I'm sorry. Some hostess I've been."

"No, it's alright. You were right to tell me all this." Diane hugged Sharon's shoulders.

"No, I shouldn't have. You folks have got problems of your own."

"You know, don't you?" said Diane.

"About the house? About the south pasture at the old Hanson farm? Of course. John and I talked with your mother the other day. She told us you've been having a pretty rough time out there."

"That's for sure."

"Maybe we can help. I just wish Carson Sells was still alive."

"Hey you two," said Betty Habowski from the door of the family room. "We're ready to start."

Chapter 37

Back in Time

Everybody sat in a circle. John McCauley sat at a card table near the kitchen door. His velvet soft baritone voice filled the room. "We have two new people with us this evening. I hope you've all met Bill and Diane Barnes. Since this is their first meeting, let me explain something about hypnosis. He turned to address Bill and Diane.

"It's trance like, but it's not sleep. It is the stage where you are highly susceptible to suggestion, but you can also be very sensitive to everything and everybody around you.

John picked up a flashlight from the table. "Sharon, please bear with me."

"Oh no, not that again," Sharon groaned.

John laughed. "When Sharon and I were undergraduates at NYU, we had a professor of communications."

"He wasn't even a professor," said Sharon.

"No, he was an ad executive. He had his own notions about the human mind. Some of them were half-baked, but some were right on target. He used a flashlight and told us to expand our minds like this." John waved the beam around making circular patterns on the walls.

Then he started making wavy patterns along the ceiling. "Moss Tyler told us that people who use their brains like this all their lives eventually emit smaller and smaller brain patterns." John traced a smaller and smaller wave pattern across the ceiling. "When the pattern becomes very small, these people lose their minds."

John laughed. "Moss Tyler taught communications like it was a course in personal dynamics. He developed somewhat of a cult following among his students. Sharon and I weren't among them.

"I tried to tell people this business with the flashlight meant nothing. I told them if they wanted to expand their minds without using drugs they should listen to what I learned from my old friend, Carson Sells, who taught me a lot about the human mind before I ever started college. He taught me the use of a relaxation patter that used highly suggestive words to put people at ease."

The relaxation patter was beginning to work on Bill Barnes. Diane knew he was bored and squeezed his thigh to keep him awake. She forgot that the tops of Bill's thighs were highly erogenous, and the fly of his pants showed it. Diane's eyes popped. She stopped squeezing Bill's leg and glanced around to see if anybody was watching. Much to her horror, everybody in the room was staring right at her. Diane knew she had missed something when she saw everybody had their hands and arms stretched out in front of them. Quickly she followed suit to get attention away from herself.

"This is just a simple exercise in suggestibility, Diane," said John. "Now I want everybody to imagine your hands in a vise. The jaws are squeezing them tighter and tighter together. The more you try to pull them apart the tighter your hands will be clenched together. Tighter and tighter and tighter together now."

He paused. "Try to pull them apart. You cannot pull them apart. They're clenched tightly together, and the harder you try to pull, the tighter they will stick together."

Some people were able to pull their hands apart instantly. Diane tried to pull her hands apart and was horrified to find that they were indeed locked together. She was helpless and was about to ask John for help when he walked over to her, then covered her hands with his.

"Diane, pull your hands apart. They're loose now, and you can pull them apart. Pull them apart now."

Diane pulled her hands apart and let her arms fall to her sides. "Whew! That was really spooky." She looked to her side to see Bill laughing at her. "What are you laughing at? You didn't even try."

Bill said with a chuckle, "I had my hands together. I just didn't get suckered in like you did. That's an old parlor trick, Diane. I'm surprised your mother and sister haven't played it on you."

John clapped his hands and laughed. "Okay, which one of you wants to go first? Bill, you might be more of a challenge."

"What are we going to do?" asked Bill.

"We're going to perform your first prenatal regression under hypnosis."

"No no," said Bill. "I'll pass."

"Go ahead, Diane," said Sharon. "You'd make a great subject."

"Oh, I don't know." Diane looked at Bill. He shrugged and motioned for her to go to the center of the room. "Okay."

* * *

Now the room was dark except for a small cone of light from a desk lamp in one corner. John sat in front of Diane and lulled her with the rich hypnotic tones that he had mastered with years of practice. "I want you to take three deep breaths. With each breath you will feel more and more relaxed. Your body will become light and airy, and you will feel no tension, no pain, and no irritation anywhere from the top of your head to the tips of your toes. You will be aware of nothing around you except the sound of my voice."

John commanded Diane to relax the muscles in her face, arms, chest, hips and legs. Diane's expression became more and more serene.

At John's command, Diane began recalling things from her past. She talked in short, halting phrases at first; finally, she became more loquacious as she began reliving a younger age.

John asked, "How old are you now, Diane?"

Diane's head tilted to one side. Her lids were closed; her eyebrows were raised. She puckered her mouth for a moment. "Six," came the squeaky reply.

"Where are you?"

Diane wrinkled her nose and said, "He stinks."

"Who stinks?"

"Ronnie."

"Who's Ronnie?

"That boy behind me."

"Where are you and Ronnie?"

"At school."

"Why does he stink?"

"I think he peed his pants again." Everybody in the room fought desperately to stifle a belly laugh. "I don't think he ever takes a bath."

"Well, Diane . . ."

"The principal sent him home one day and told him to clean himself up before he came back to school."

"Diane, I want you . . ."

"I hope they don't let any more of those kids come to this school."

John temporarily gave up trying to control the conversation and let Diane ramble on.

"Mom and Dad say those people drop 'em like kittens. Whatever that means. Nobody likes them. Everybody talks about them. I know that's not very nice, but I just wish they would take a bath once in awhile and not wet their pants like Ronnie does."

"Diane." John only raised his voice enough to get Diane's attention.

"Yes?"

"We're going to go back in time again. Now we're going back to a time before you were born. Relax, Diane. You are still in a state of total relaxation. The sound of my voice occupies all your attention."

Diane's expression went blank. Her head tilted forward on her shoulders. She appeared to be asleep for a moment. Suddenly she lurched forward as though something or somebody had hit her in the back. She lifted her face, opened her eyes, and looked directly at John. Her right eyelid began to twitch; the corners of her mouth turned down, and her lips spread open in a nasty snarl.

"Sleep!" John commanded as he pressed his thumb to the middle of Diane's forehead. "Deep, deep sleep!" He couldn't be sure what had happened, but something seemed to have taken control of Diane away from him. "You are still under the control of my voice." John kept his hand on Diane's forehead until she closed her eyes again and her body fell limp in the chair.

John reinforced Diane's hypnotic state with more relaxing patter. He ignored the super charged electric atmosphere and the shocked, worried expressions caused by Diane's sudden spasm.

Bill leaned forward as though he was about to get out of his chair. Jim Forkner put his arm on his elbow. "It's okay, Bill," Jim whispered. "John knows what he's doing." Bill sighed and leaned back.

"Diane, you're still with me, and you and I are still flying backward through time. Now we are going back to a time before you were born. You will tell me everything that you see, feel and hear. Nothing is going to disturb you."

As soon as John reassured Diane, she jerked forward and backward as if something was poking her from different directions. John recognized her body language. He had seen it before when he regressed Sharon to a prenatal state. Diane was back in her mother's womb being felt and prodded by a doctor who was trying to determine her position in the womb prior to being born.

"Back in time! Back in time!" John commanded. This was not a pleasant state to be in, and he knew it. Investigating the here and hereafter had taught John that for all the joy associated with one, and all the grief associated with the other, being born was actually more traumatic than dying.

"Tell me what you see. Tell me what you see."

Diane sat up straight in her chair with her knees together and her hands in her lap. Her expression became very stern even with her eyes closed. "I see a stone wall."

"And what else do you see?"

"What else would I see in a cloistered convent?"

"Are you a nun?"

"Of course."

"Can you tell me what else you see besides stone walls?"

"There are small windows."

"Yes . . .What are the windows for?"

"People come here to get their clothing."

"Who are these people?"

With an exasperated sigh, she said, "The poor people."

"You're handing out clothing to poor people through windows in a stone wall. Is that right?"

"That is correct."

"Is there a reason for a wall between you and the people?"

"It's just there."

"Why does it have to be there?"

She tilted her head, looking slightly puzzled. "Well . . .Why wouldn't it be?"

"What is your name?"

"Sister."

"Sister . . .That's what everybody calls you, right?"

"That is correct."

"Do you have a given name?"

"We don't use given names."

"What was your given name before you entered the convent?"

There was silence for a moment. Diane fidgeted in her chair. Finally she sighed and said, "I don't use that name anymore."

"Alright. We're going to leave this time and place now. You're going to go deep asleep again. You're going to go back in time. When I press my finger against your forehead, you will go back to the childhood of this life. You will recall your life as a young girl before you became a nun.

John waved his hand in front of her face and Diane slumped down in her chair. He told her again, "Back in time. You are going back in time again. You are a young girl now. Tell me what you see."

"It's a train station."

"A train station. Where is it?"

"Small town. I can't remember where."

"Have you just arrived here?"

"No, I'm getting ready to leave."

"Where are you going?"

"I'm going to Paris."

"Paris, France?"

"Oh heavens, no!" She smiled for the first time.

"Why are you leaving?"

"Because . . . I'm . . .My father is sending me away."

"Why is he sending you away?"

"I have . . .I . . .I'm not well."

"What's wrong?"

Diane's lower lip began to quiver. She grimaced and a tear rolled down her cheek. "I'm not well." More tears rolled down her cheeks, and she strained to get out the next words. "I am . . . not . . . worthy."

"Why aren't you worthy . . .worthy of what?"

"Father and I don't talk about this anymore."

"Do you not want to talk about it?"

"No." The answer was final. The face was set in a stone hard frown.

After a slight pause John said, "I want you to put all of this out of your mind. We're going to come forward in time. You're going to go back into a deep sleep and come forward to the present day."

John pressed his thumb on Diane's forehead and she slumped in her chair. "Coming forward in time now. Coming all the way up to the present day."

Diane's face sagged into a pout. She moved her knees back and forth and tapped her feet. Again John commanded, "Tell me what you see. Tell me what you see, Diane."

No answer.

"Diane?"

"Ain't nobody here named Diane."

"Who are you?"

"I don't talk to no strangers."

"Do you have a name?"

"Prissy."

"Prissy? Is that your whole name?"

"Thas de name Masa Harvey gimme."

John was a little confused by the dialect. "Who is Masa Harvey?"

Diane's face broke out in a broad grin. "Dat's da man who owns me." She started to laugh.

"What's so funny?"

"You da first white man I heard talk like us niggas."

"Oh, I see. You're talking about Master Harvey. Where are you now?"

"I's in da fields."

"Is this a cotton plantation?"

"Yassir."

"Where do you live on the plantation?"

"Where else? Masa Harvey's nigga quartas."

"What are they like?"

"Four walls and a tin roof, dats all."

"Does your family live here with you?"

"Ain't got no family."

"What happened to them?"

"No family! Don't tell stuff like that to no strangers no how."

"Are you married?"

"We don't get married."

"Do you have any children?"

"Don't tell stuff like dat to no strangers." The pout was now set in stone. Diane pointed her face straight ahead, with her eyes still closed, and her knees together. John decided to bring her back to the present once and for all. On the way he got a surprise.

"You are going to fall back into a deep, deep sleep again. You are going to come forward in time now. Coming back to the present. Falling deep, deep asleep, and your mind is coming back to the present day. When you wake up you will be the person we know as Diane Barnes."

Diane's face suddenly grimaced with a hard squint

that creased deep lines in her forehead and temples. She turned her head from side to side and held her hands up in front of her to ward off what John could only guess was intense heat or light. She didn't seem to be in pain so John asked her, "What is it? Tell me what's bothering you. Tell me what you see."

Diane lowered her arms and sat straight up in her chair. Her expression relaxed and a smile spread across her face. "I have just come out of the tunnel and into the light."

"Have you just passed on from the earthly life?"

"Yes."

"What happened? Do you remember how you passed on?"

"I left quietly in my sleep."

"Was it from natural causes?"

"Yes."

"Do you still remember the life you just left?"

"Of course."

"What was it like?'

"It was a test like always."

"Did the test go well?"

Diane frowned. "That depends on what you mean by well."

"Where are you now?"

"I'm in the care of others."

"Do you know these people?"

"Yes."

"Have you seen them before?"

"Of course."

"What are they telling you?"

"They aren't telling me anything. They're showing me."

"What are they showing you?"

"The sticks. There is a pattern of sticks."

"Can you tell what the pattern is?"

"I can't describe the pattern, but if I can rearrange it right I can go on to the next step."

"What is the next step?"

A wry smile spread across Diane's face. "You'll find out."

"Can you see anything here besides the pattern?"

"Not like you can."

"What do you mean by that?"

"You see reflections of things with your eyes. I see them as they really are." Diane frowned and turned her head to one side. "There is something wrong here."

"What is it?"

"There is a disturbance, an old feeling, an old familiar feeling of fear and dread."

"Whose fear? Whose dread? Is it yours?"

"No, it's yours."

A collective gasp came from the crowd around John and Diane. "I'm sorry," she said. "You were channeling her feelings to me. The fear and the dread are not yours. They belong to the one you called Alice."

John's stomach tightened. "What does she fear? What does she dread?"

Diane shook her head. "I can't tell. There's a veil." Diane caught her breath and slumped in her chair. Her lips moved slightly, but no voice could be heard.

John tried to hide the worry in his voice as he leaned forward and whispered, "What are you saying?" He watched as the corners of Diane's eyes, then her mouth, and her chin began to sag. She looked very old.

"Papa was bad," came the low, gravely voice. John McCauley felt the hair stand out on the back of his neck. He strained to keep his composure. "Papa was bad." Suddenly Diane sat up. "She's gone."

"Where has she gone?"

"I can't say. I'm not supposed to know."

"Okay . . . Let's leave this time and place. You are falling back into a deep, deep sleep. You are going to come forward in time to the present life that you know as Diane Barnes. As I count to five, you will come forward in time and reawaken in the life that you know now as Diane Barnes. One . . .starting to wake up now. Two . . . wider-awake. Three . . .coming forward in time and waking up. Four . . .becoming wide-awake now. Five . . .wide awake!"

Diane opened her eyes and wiped her cheek with the back of her hand. "Have I been crying?"

"At one point you were," said John.

Sharon turned on another table lamp at the far corner of the room. The additional light brightened everybody's mood, but their collective gaze intimidated Diane. She sat up straight and tugged at the hem of her dress. "What else have I been doing?"

"I think you may have been channeling," said John.

"What's that?"

"Somebody else was speaking through you. I don't think any harm was done." John felt Diane's neck and forehead. "You don't feel flush. Do you feel sick or dizzy?"

"No." Diane looked toward the far side of the room. "Where's Bill?"

"Bill stepped outside for a breath of fresh air," said Sharon.

John turned to look at her. The frown on Sharon's usually bright face told him there was something amiss besides stale air.

"I think I need to go powder my nose," said Diane.

"It's right through the kitchen," said John.

Everybody waited for Diane to leave, then the barrage of questions started.

"Was she channeling there at the beginning?" asked Carolyn Forkner.

"I think she was," said John.

"What was she saying at the end?" asked Kyle Harris.

"I'm not sure," said John. "I think she said 'Papa was bad'."

"John, she said you were channeling Aunt Alice at the end," said Betty Habowski. "Did you feel like you were channeling?"

"No . . .well . . .Ah, Betty . . .I think Diane's flashlight was making a circular pattern."

"A what?" asked Betty.

"You know . . ." John picked up the flashlight off the card table near the kitchen door. He snapped it on and made a circular pattern of light around the walls. "As opposed to . . ." He waved the light back and forth across the ceiling. "Hypnosis expands the mind. Diane was able to read mine."

"But you weren't channeling?" said Kyle.

"No. Diane picked up some old thoughts of Aunt Alice. Seems they've been weighing heavily on my mind lately. I suppose the funeral . . .well, the ah . . .her passing have ah . . .made things kind of bad around here."

"I'm sorry you had to go through that," said Carolyn Forkner.

"Oh, that's alright," said John. "No harm done."

John cleared his throat and broke the uneasy silence. "Well, that was an interesting study in karma. You remember Diane told us about the life of a cloistered nun. She was locked up physically and spiritually behind a stone wall that completely sheltered her from the outside world. The lack of contact with her fellow creatures had left her soul incomplete. Her next life as a black slave taught her what the other half of humanity was like. "

Jim spoke up. "You know, I'm having trouble with the

sequence of events here. Now Diane told us about riding a train to Paris. But not Paris, France. Then she told about a life as a black slave. Shouldn't those two stories be turned around? I mean trains weren't all that common before Emancipation. So doesn't some of this seem a little improbable before the mid-nineteenth century?"

Kyle Harris said, "Jim, you're getting back to our old discussion about linear time. These events don't necessarily have to be sequential.

While Jim Forkner and Kyle Harris continued to theorize, John eased his way into the kitchen. He said to Sharon, "Where's Bill and Diane?"

"They left."

"We scared Bill off, didn't we?"

"Scared? He looked like the devil was after him."

"Well, we'll get them back."

"How?"

"Patience, Sharon. Just have a little patience."

* * *

Diane grabbed her coat off the bed in the master bedroom and slipped out the front door. She stomped across the snow-covered driveway and found Bill in the front seat of the car. The engine was running, the heater was running, and Bill was smoking a cigarette with the window rolled down.

"I thought you quit that filthy habit."

"Get in the car, Diane."

"What's the matter with you?"

"I said, get in the car."

Diane got in and slammed the door. "You embarrassed the hell out of me. The least you can do is tell me what's wrong."

Bill flipped his cigarette across the driveway, rolled up the window, and drove off.

"Bill, would you please tell me what's wrong."

"I just don't like having my family on display like that."

"I wasn't on display."

"You got a better word for it?"

Silence

"You didn't have to just run off in a huff like that," said Diane.

Silence

"Is that what I get? The silent treatment?"

"Leave it be, Diane."

"I ought to make you go back there and apologize to all those people if it wouldn't embarrass me even more."

"I said leave it be!"

Chapter 38

Footsteps and Breathing

"Did you guys have a good time?" Emily Petersen asked as Bill and Diane came through the garage service entrance and shucked their coats.

"We had a nice time," said Diane. It didn't sound like it.

Bill went into the bedroom and shut the door.

"Pam said that she was going to try to make it tonight. Was she there?" asked Emily.

"No."

"Is everything okay?"

"Yes."

Emily shifted on her feet. "Well, Mary went to bed early. You guys certainly got home early. It's barely past 9:30."

Silence.

"I don't think Mary appreciated having a baby sitter. She's so grown up. I guess she's outgrowing her grandmother."

Silence.

Emily followed Diane into the kitchen, watching as her daughter reset the clock on the wall, then replace the box of baking soda in the refrigerator before taking off her shoes.

"Is something wrong, Diane?"

"No."

Emily pulled her coat off a wall hook and slipped it on. "Did you two have a fight?"

"Maybe."

"What was it about?"

"Nothing."

"Well, thank you for having me over."

Diane slipped into the bathroom and tried not to slam the door.

"Thank you, Mother." Emily muttered sarcastically under her breath. "Maybe I'll just go home and talk to the walls. I'm sure they're more civil."

* * *

Bill hovered over the bathroom sink with a hot wash-rag held up to his left ear. It hurt, but he didn't say anything to Diane. Why would she care?

"What's the matter with you?" Diane said behind him.

"Aw, probably caught cold in my ear."

"Serves you right. Sitting there like an idiot with the window rolled down."

Bill didn't answer her. He dried his ear after a few minutes and went to bed. He found Diane lying on her back with her arms folded across her chest pretending to be asleep. He considered sleeping on the couch. But he was tired, his ear hurt; and he needed his own bed.

But sleep would not come, not tonight. First, the baby started crying far off in the woods. Then somebody started walking around in the house. First in the kitchen, then in the living room where the soft white glow of new fallen snow shone through the curtains at the patio door. Now they came down the hall. The sound of the floor creaking stopped at the end of the hallway, then started coming back the other way and into Bill and Diane's bedroom.

"Mary?" Diane called lamely. "Who's there?" She knew it wasn't Mary. "Please answer me. Tell me who's there!" She trembled and sobbed. Then came the heavy breathing. Diane couldn't see the mouth or nose. She couldn't see the forehead or eyes or chin, but she felt the suffocating presence of a face hovering over her. She screamed, "NNNNOOOOOOOOOOO!!!!! Get out! Get out!"

She was still screaming when Bill turned on the light and grabbed her around the shoulders. "Diane! Diane! You're having a nightmare. It's okay. It's okay now." Bill held her close and stroked the back of her head.

Diane pushed him away and yelled, "It's not okay! It's not okay! There's something in this house. It was breathing on me. I was wide awake and it was breathing on me."

"Listen Diane. Listen . . .there's nothing. The house is quiet."

Diane knelt on the bed and tried to listen. There was only the sound of her heavy breathing.

"Now you listen to me, and you listen to me good," said Bill. "There will be no more hypnosis. There will be no more hocus pocus bullshit! You've been sick, Diane. You need a doctor. Not some old witch doctor."

"I've seen a doctor."

"When?"

"Last fall."

"You took Mary to the doctor."

"I'm fine."

"You're hearing things, seeing things."

She rounded on him. "I am not!"

"Yes you are!"

"Then we have to move out."

Bill waved a hand. "And go where?"

"To another house, an apartment."

"That's crazy."

"I'm serious. We have to move out."

"Diane, we've got a nice home, I've got a good business here."

She jabbed a finger at the doorway. "There is something in this house."

Bill shook his head. "No."

"There is and you know it!"

"Diane, it's all in your head."

"Is it? Who was breathing on me just now? "

Bill sneered at Diane in disgust. "I don't know. I told you it was probably your imagination."

Diane regarded Bill impassively. Finally she said, "We have to move out. We just have to." Diane gathered her pillow and a blanket, slid off the bed, then headed for the living room.

"I'll take the couch tonight," said Bill.

No answer. Diane flopped on the couch and cocooned in the blanket.

"Did you hear me? I said I'd take the couch."

No answer.

"Fine! Be a pig head." Bill turned on the hall light and peeked in Mary's room to see if the little tirade had awakened her.

Mary was curled up in the fetal position and she'd covered her head with her pillow. She was crying and shaking. Bill knelt beside her bed and touched her blanket covered shoulder. She rolled over on her belly and scooted away from him.

Bill took his hand away, but stayed at her bedside. "Mary, everything is going to be alright."

"It's not going to be alright," Mary cried. "It hasn't been alright since we moved in here. I hate this place. I hate that school."

Bill thought for a moment. Was there something that might brighten the gloom? Finally he said, "We're all in the winter dumps. It's less than a month till Valentine's Day. How about we decorate the house in red and white just like we did for Christmas?"

No answer.

"Well, get some sleep. Things will look better in the morning." He rose and slipped back to an empty queen-size bed. He could fix anything mechanical. He quietly chastised himself for thinking he could fix his ten-year-old daughter's foul mood.

Mary's sleep did not come to her until almost the middle of the night. Her eyes darted back and forth beneath the closed lids as she watched a man and a woman climb into a horse drawn carriage. They were arguing about how to fix something, and would anything ever be the same again. There were some angry words about moving out and going to the doctor. Then Mary got in, and the carriage took them all across the half span bridge again. Off they went into thin air, and fell toward the raging river below.

As she fell, Mary heard a woman's voice say, "I've got something to tell you when you hit bottom." But of course they didn't hit bottom. Mary woke up briefly. The house felt cold. She pulled the covers over her head, but still felt cold. So she sat up and pulled the bedspread up with the blankets, then lay down and buried her head under her pillow. Just before midnight, the footsteps started again. Mary came awake again, but the extra cover kept her from hearing the footsteps.

* * *

Bill was dreaming too. There was green grass and bright sunshine and a two-lane highway in front of his house. Cars and trucks passed each other going north and south. Suddenly there was the blast of an air horn and a soft thud, as a station wagon headed one way and an eighteen wheeler passed too close going the other way. Somebody must have thrown a ball or something out the window of the car. It was covered with some sort of yellow fur, and it rolled across Bill's front yard. He knew his daddy would spank him if he ran out the door to the front yard with nobody to look after him. But now there was somebody. She was tall and dark with twin ponytails hanging down over her chest. She grinned at Bill and invited him to come out, pick up the strange looking ball, and play with her. Bill darted out the door, across the yard and picked up the . . .Oh, God! It was bloody and had blonde hair and ragged pieces of gooey stuff coming out of it. It smelled real bad. Bill dropped the bloody thing and cried and screamed. "Mommy, Mommy!"

"Now don't think bad thoughts," said the tall dark woman. "Doesn't she smell nice? Here, throw it to me. Come on, Bill, throw it to me."

Bill screamed and ran back into the house.

"You're only dreaming," the dark woman called after him. "I can take you away from here. Would you like to go someplace more pleasant?"

Now Bill was in a strange bed, on another night, in another house. He saw a girl's silhouette pass in front of the window, and his heart started to pound hard. The exciting rush came up his chest and made him breathe harder with anticipation. She leaned over, pulled down the covers, and started fondling him. "Bill, you still like to play this?" she said.

"Yes."

She got on the bed and straddled Bill. *Oh God, that smell!* He screamed.

The girl jumped off the bed and ran into the other room. The light came on and Bill's father rushed in. "What the hell's going on up here?"

As Bill sat up in bed, he could see into the adjoining bedroom where the girl was sitting on the foot of her bed, the hem of her nightgown pulled down tight over her legs.

"Answer me," shouted Bill's father. "What's the matter with you?"

"I. . .I . . .I had another bad dream," Bill stammered. He was surrounded by four grown-ups.

"You woke up this whole household because you had a bad dream?"

The girl's mother looked into the dark adjoining bedroom. "Judy, what are you doing up? What's been going on here?"

"Nothing," said the girl.

"Yes, there has," shouted Bill's father. "What was it?"

"Frank, don't shout at the boy like that," said Bill's mother. "He's had another one of those awful dreams like he gets."

Frank stomped back toward the stairs. "Good God, I gotta drive this family back home tomorrow, and we got to get an early start. Some of us would probably like some sleep."

"Judy, what's going on?" asked the girl's mother.

As Bill writhed under the sheets in the throes of his nightmare, he failed to notice that the pounding of his heart, the quickness of his breathing, and the buzz in his libido had caused a contraction in his groin. When he woke up he felt wet shorts against his leg. "Aw shit!" Bill felt the bottom sheet. It was dry. He held up the top sheet . . . wet. "Goddamn it!"

Chapter 39

Hot Water and Flakes

It was morning, but it was still dark when Bill woke up alone in his bed. He had changed into fresh boxer shorts, but the bed sheet was still wet. It was Saturday, washday, so Diane could wash the sheets with the rest of the laundry. The first light of a gray dawn was coming through the window when he heard Diane open the drapes at the patio door. Soon she would come in the bedroom to get dressed, and Bill really didn't want to face her right now.

He heard Diane tromp to the hallway bathroom and shut the door. He got up, opened the closet door, and muttered, "God, I'm thirsty." He hauled out a pair of jeans without turning on a light. At least they felt like jeans in the dark closet. He hauled out a flannel shirt, shoes and socks. He was still thirsty, so he ducked into the bathroom between the bedroom and kitchen and downed a quick glass of water. "That's better. What's that smell?"

Once he was dressed, Bill headed for the kitchen and snatched two glazed donuts out of the refrigerator. Then he headed for the shop, newly added to the far side of the garage. The new wall clock just inside the door read 7:30. He started measuring out lengths of angle iron and cut them with the massive chop saw. It was noisy and it was Saturday. Too bad, it was time for everybody to get up anyway. "Why am I so thirsty?" He went back in the house long enough to start the coffee maker and get another glass of water.

Bill worked for half an hour. Nobody came out to complain about the noise. "Damn! I'm still thirsty." He went back in the kitchen and filled the water glass sitting beside the sink, then wrinkled his nose. "Oh my God, that smell."

"What smell?" asked Diane as she came into the kitchen still wearing her nightgown.

Bill slapped his hand over his mouth and headed for the bathroom. He barely had time to lift the toilet lid and heave everything in his stomach into the stool.

Diane hovered at the bathroom door. "I knew there was something wrong with this water." Bill didn't answer her. He heaved again. "Are you going to be alright?"

"I'll be fine. It's nothing."

"It's the water. I told you it was."

"It's not the water. It's just nerves."

"Nerves? You?"

"It's been a rough night, Diane."

"It didn't have to be."

Still clutching the sides of the bowl, he glanced up at her. "Easy for you to say."

"You feel like standing up?"

"Yeah."

"Come back in the kitchen. I've got something to show you."

Bill flushed the stool and got up. When he entered the kitchen, he glanced at the sheet of paper on the table. "What's this?"

"It's from the health department. I sent them a water sample."

"What for?"

"I told you. There's something wrong with the water."

"Don't be ridiculous. There's nothing wrong with the water. We've all been under a strain. It's just nerves."

"Oh, forget it. I'll call the health department Monday morning."

* * *

Diane killed a good portion of her lunch hour waiting on hold until a woman came on the line and said, "This is Clarice. May I help you?"

"Yes, I'm calling about a water sample I sent several days ago. I have the results back and I can't make heads or tails of them."

"Do you have the sample in front of you?"

"Yes, and all I want to know is if our water is safe to drink."

"There should be a chart showing a breakdown of the minerals and any organics. It should show actual levels and safe levels."

"Look, I'm sorry, but I don't know a thing about this stuff. I see letters like Pb, Ca, Mn, Fe, ppm. Is there anything here, or do you have any way to tell me if our water is safe to drink?"

"Let me ask you, has anybody been sick with vomiting, diarrhea, fever or stomach cramps?"

"We've all had episodes of vomiting and it's right after we got a drink out of the faucet. And it's always a drink of water that smells like perfume."

"Perfume? I've never heard of that before, but perfume quite often has some petroleum-based chemicals in it. You may have had some mineral contamination leaching into your well. Do you live close to a cultivated field?"

"Yes."

"You may have herbicide or insecticide soaking into your ground water."

"Terrific. How do we get it out of there?"

"I'm not sure it's there. Tell you what. Go to the drug store and tell the pharmacist you need a cake of camphor."

"Camphor? What's that for?" Diane got impatient and the customer service lady hastened to continue.

"Now let me explain. This little cake will be about a quarter of an inch thick and two inches square. Draw out a bowl of water from your tap and scrape some flakes of camphor into the water. Be sure you use a clean knife. These flakes should spin around on top of the water like little propellers. If they just lie there, there's some kind of petroleum based substance contaminating your water."

Diane rubbed her forehead. "What do we do then?"

"There are companies that clean up mineral contamination by injecting bacteria into the well. Or you may want to have your well digger pump the well some more. Do your camphor test first.

* * *

Diane held a white plastic bowl under the kitchen faucet and filled it. With a clean knife she scraped tiny flakes of camphor into the water. They floated, but they didn't spin. "Oh no!" She stood there staring at the reflection of her own face in the water and willing the flakes to move. She closed her eyes and opened them again, but the flakes would not spin. The plastic bowl, the surface of the water, and the camphor flakes loomed larger and larger. Her face was getting closer and closer to the surface, and tears were welling up in her eyes, making her watery reflection and the white flakes a blur. There was still no movement, but Diane felt like she was about to lose her balance.

She was now standing on the rim of the bowl, no more than a few inches above the surface of the water, and she sensed somebody standing behind her. Diane turned to see who it was and gasped at the sight of her own image magnified thousands of times. The enormous woman stared down at her with vacant eyes while Diane teetered on the edge of the bowl.

"Oh no!" She was out of her body again and falling into a lake that a moment ago had been nothing more than a two-quart bowl filled with tap water. She broke the surface, then panicked as she started to sink. She started flailing her arms and legs to get back to the surface, but an unseen force was dragging her under and she was powerless to resist it. As she sank and hit the bottom of the bowl, she looked up and saw the camphor flakes turn into human faces that shouted at her. Some of them appeared to be small children, but they had the same panic stricken expression of sheer terror.

"Help! Help! Please help us! Pleeeessseee help! Heeeelp!" The water turned blood red. The crimson ooze billowed up from the bottom of the bowl, engulfed her body, obliterated her vision, and burned her eyes. She mashed her fists into the sockets to rub away the sting. When she took her hands away and opened her eyes, she found herself standing at the kitchen sink with her feet firmly planted on the floor and the red spots in front of her eyes slowly diminishing. The camphor flakes were now spinning merrily on the surface of the water. Diane grabbed the bowl and dumped the little nightmare down the drain.

The water and camphor flowed out the main drainpipe and into the septic tank in the back yard. From there it entered the system of branched pipes, called the finger system, that sent it percolating into the ground and down into the underground river that flowed across Forest County. From there it was drawn up through an old fashioned well pump on the back porch of The Old Dog Tavern in Tanners Grove. Homer used the water upstairs in the apartment he shared with old Anna Lee. When he took a drink of the camphor water himself, he almost fainted. Fireworks and screaming faces went off in his head. He knew the water came from the old Hanson farm because he heard the screaming faces yell, "They murdered me!"

Homer leaned on the spout of the old fashioned pump and chuckled to himself. "You still gettin' their goats, ain't ya, Great Grandma? Good ole G.G., you still gettin' their goats."

Homer held no ill will against the Barnes family. But somebody in this county knew of the mass murder of his people so long ago. He and his great grandma had to start rattling cages somewhere. Why not start where it all happened? He suspected John McCauley knew about it, but he couldn't hold any ill will against him. After all, John was blood; John was family. He took another drink of water when he got back upstairs, and the fireworks and the screams exploded in his head again. This time, in the middle of all her screaming, Great Grandma showed Homer what had happened so long ago and why it happened.

Chapter 40

Max the Comet

"They keepin' ya busy, buddy boy?" Max Carter grinned as he stood in the doorway between the garage and Bill's shop.

Bill was bent over an auto frame with an acetylene torch in his hand. He raised his goggles and doused the gas flame. "Max Carter! What the hell are you doing in that uniform?"

"Reserve deputy sheriff." Max pointed at the badge on his broad brim hat while he masticated a wad of chewing gum. "Didn't you know that?"

"Hell no."

"Like I said . . .Are they keepin' ya busy, buddy boy?"

"What do you want, dirt bag?"

"Hey now, let's have a little respect for the uniform, okay?" Max pranced around the shop chewing his gum; jingling the coins and keys in his front pockets, and holding his uniform jacket wide open with his fat arms. His black shoes were spit shined to a mirror finish. His wide gun belt sported a service revolver, ammo pouch, handcuffs, and mag light. A silver lanyard was attached to the button on his left shirt pocket. It disappeared up his shoulder and under the jacket. A gold badge decorated his shirt just above his right pocket. His enormous belly led this parade of attractions by about a foot.

He stepped over pneumatic hoses, tools; he sidestepped an arc welder and racks of steel rod and angle iron. "Hell of a set up ya got here. Beats drivin' a truck for us and the old man, huh?"

"Hey! I said what do you want?"

"Now you just hold you horses there, buddy boy. I might have to shake you down for some bills of sale on all this fancy equipment ya got here."

"Yeah well, you'd need a warrant for that, wouldn't you?"

"He he he. Yeah, right."

Bill strained to hold his temper. "Alright now, what do you want?"

"You know Farley Mandon, the janitor over at the grade school?"

"Never heard of him."

"I'll bet he's heard of you."

"What?"

"The old fart had a wreck this afternoon. You know how these old people are; drive like they own the damn road. So they sent me to investigate. I checks him out, and I checks the car out. He ain't hurt. But now what do you suppose I found on his front seat?" Max pulled Bill's 357 Magnum revolver out of his jacket pocket and dangled it by its trigger housing on his fat pinkie.

"You son of a bitch!" Bill lunged at the pistol and tripped on the auto frame he was straddling. He fell prone at Max Carter's feet.

Max grabbed a steel rod and held it to the base of Bill's neck. "He he he he. Now you just stay there a minute, buddy boy. I know this hog leg belongs to you. I remember you braggin' about it to some of the boys at our shop awhile back. Now ya see the serial number ain't been filed off."

"Damn it, Max, the gun belongs to me, okay? I got a permit for it."

"Take a closer look, buddy boy." Max pointed the gun at Bill so he could see the front of the cylinder.

"Don't point that thing at me, you idiot."

"It's got hollow point bullets. Now in this county that's against the law."

"Look, the gun belongs to me; the bullets don't, and you can't prove it."

"Then how'd old Farley get a hold of 'em?"

"I don't know."

"You sold Farley this gun, didn't you?"

"Hell no!"

"Bullshit!"

"Go to hell!"

Max threw down the steel rod, and it hit the concrete floor with a bell-like clang. He grabbed Bill by his shirt and pulled him up close to his fat greasy face. "No, you go to hell. You fancy bastards move down here from the city and think you can make all of us look like a bunch of stupid hicks. Well, I got a surprise or two for you, buddy boy. You wanna play hard ball with me? I'll show you just how hard I can hit."

Max pushed Bill away and stomped out of the shop and through the garage. Bill jumped up and followed him out to the driveway. "You know I can come down and claim that gun anytime. I still got the permit with the serial number on it."

"You can't claim nothin'. It's evidence now."

"Evidence of what?"

"Illegal possession of a hand gun. Illegal possession of hollow point ammunition."

"It's still mine."

Max turned on Bill when he got to his squad car. "Back off, buddy boy! You push this, I'll have your skinny ass in a sling so fast you'll shit yourself silly."

A big black crow swooped low out of the south with a loud *Caw!* and almost clipped Max's hat off. "You son of a bitch!"

The bird was gone before Max had time to see it. He looked back at Bill Barnes standing in the garage door and laughing at him.

Max jumped into the big squad car, fired the ignition, hit the flashing lights, blipped the siren, and slammed the selector lever into drive. He charged at Bill, then stopped inches from the garage door. Bill jumped back, but he didn't offer to retaliate.

Max killed the flashing lights, backed out of the driveway and roared off into the night.

* * *

Max Carter was hot. So was his lead foot. Driving fast made him feel good. *It'd feel even better to run that little bastard down. I know the sheriff would have my balls on a spike, but it'd still feel good to ram his sorry ass into the fuckin' wall. Damn good!*

He was taking the old Coal Town Road back to Tanner's Grove. It was the long way. It would give him plenty of time to unwind, calm down. *Or maybe I'll just blow a goddamn gasket!* He was mad as hell, and he drove like it. The winding road forced him to wrestle with the steering wheel, but that was alright. He knew where he was going. He knew how fast he could go. If only he knew where he was right now.

Wait a minute, this ain't right. Max had gone around too many curves. Now he was going downhill. "Shit. I missed the turnoff. Aw, I'll just take the north road back."

He went back uphill, looking for the first road past Cherry Tree Lake. He was on familiar gravel now. Max went around another curve and back on to blacktop. *Whoaa! Where's the damn road? Oh there it is, up ahead.*

A road that looked so familiar in the daylight looked very different at night. So different that Max thought he was turning off onto a gravel lane when he was actually about to go off the edge of a cliff. He slammed on the brakes, then sat back and caught his breath, his heart pounding.

"Jesus Christ! Where the hell am I?" Max got out and walked around in front of the car. He looked out over the cliff and saw the old Hanson farmhouse and Bill Barnes' house in the valley below. "Holy shit! This ain't right. Now how the hell did I get clear up here?"

A crow called out above him.

"Goddamn it!" The big black bird swooped low again and clipped Max's hat off. "You son of a bitch!" He grabbed his hat off the ground and waved it at the escaping bird. Max noticed that he had wet his pants. "Shit. When was the last time that happened?" He jumped back in the car and charged down the road.

Now he was really mad. Or was he just beginning to be afraid? He needed something to make him feel better, and he knew what it was. Max turned on his flashing lights again. He raised his high beam headlights. Yeah, the lights made him feel real good. They made him feel good whenever he pulled somebody over and demanded their driver's license and registration. They made him feel good whenever he pulled up behind a parked car on a dark road. He'd walk up to the passenger side window just as the girl was struggling to pull her pants back up and drape her blouse over her chest. Invariably her parents would be somebody that Max knew. "He he he he he." Rousting kids, especially kids hot for each other's meat, was just the thought he needed to help him calm down. Then the damn crow screamed again.

It swooped low from the rear of the car and went sailing off in front, its black feathers gleaming in the bright headlight beams.

"Where the hell did that bastard come from?" Max shouted. "And where the hell am I?" He thought he was on the old Coal Town Road. He had started out going northwest toward Cherry Tree Lake. He had come to the cliff, stopped, then headed back to the south. But he was on the same road. Max started to sweat. It wasn't from fear. He wasn't afraid, not yet. He was just mad.

"Where in the name of all that's fucking holy is the Goddamn road!" His heart raced. He fought the steering wheel at every turn. "Aw, this is bullshit. I've driven this road a thousand times. I could drive this road in my sleep."

So that's it. This is all a nightmare. I really didn't go to Bill Barnes' house tonight. I'm not driving this fucking road. It's all a nightmare, and I'm going to wake up . . .NOW!

"Aha! There's the turnoff. To the right? No, to the left. Oh shit!" He slammed on the brakes again. The car stopped just ahead of the cliff's edge. Max got out, went to the front of the car, and saw the Hanson house and the Barnes house just like before. "Aw, Goddamn it. This can't be." He had been telling himself for twenty minutes that he wasn't afraid. So why was his heart racing? Why did his chest burn? And why were tears streaming down his face?

He shouted to the rooftops below. "Hey Bill, up here ole buddy. Up here, up high. Come on Bill. Help me out here. How about it, buddy boy? How about some help? I'll even let you have your gun back. No questions. No hassle. Come on, Goddamn it! Answer me! Shit man, I didn't hurt you that bad, now did I? I said ANSWER ME! GODDAMN IT!"

Now Max was bent over, crying like a baby. He had wet his pants like a baby. He was scared like a baby. And he was still mad. "Fuck you, Bill Barnes. You go straight to hell! AWWW Haw haw haw haw. Eat shit, motherfucker!"

"Do not curse the night," said the Indian witch. Max turned to see the lovely dark-skinned woman standing next to his squad car. She wore a short white rawhide dress with silver beads in her long braids hanging down her chest. "The night belongs to the raven, and the raven belongs to me."

Max stared in disbelief as the head of the Indian witch stretched out to form the beak and feathered head of a black bird. Feathers sprouted all over her body. The big raven spread its gleaming wings and lifted off into the night.

Max ran over and yanked open the door of his squad car and jumped in. He slammed the door and sat behind the wheel shivering. He felt safe for a short moment inside the car. It was big. It was official, and it would protect him for now until he could get home.

He told himself, "Now drive. This road's gotta end someplace. To hell with the turnoffs. If you drive far enough south, you'll wind up back at the Hanson farm. If you drive far enough north, you'll wind up at the far west end of County Line Road. Now quit your blubberin'."

Blacktop, gravel, blacktop, gravel, blacktop, gravel. Max went uphill, downhill. He turned to the left and right, fighting the steering wheel and cursing the road. "I know you end somewhere you Goddamn old road." Max felt the accelerator pedal beneath his right foot go all the way to the floor. He felt something take control of the steering wheel. And then he heard the crow or raven-whatever that spook called it - calling from above the car. He felt the crushing presence of something hot and deadly descending from above. Max could feel a dive-bombing monster coming closer and closer to him and his big, safe, official looking cocoon.

The last thing Max Carter saw before he died was a bird's flaming head coming through his shattered windshield and white hot flames going in his mouth and down his windpipe, turning his lungs to charcoal.

The big squad car was now a comet sailing off the curve in the road and over the cliff with flames streaming out behind it. When it hit the barn beside the Hanson house in the little valley below, it exploded in a white fireball that turned the moonless night to broad daylight. The explosion and fire sent flaming timbers from the barn flying across the side yard of the farmhouse and into a bay window of the downstairs dining room. The dry varnished woodwork inside the house made good kindling, and it took only a few minutes for the entire downstairs to become completely engulfed in flames. The downstairs sewing room that Samuel Hanson had added to the rest of the house in 1883, where little Alice Hanson had played with her dolls and prayed to Jesus to forgive her for hurting her mother's feelings, was filled with flames. The furniture and portraits of Samuel and Margaret had been taken away and saved, but the built-in cedar chest in front of the window and the flower print wallpaper became a charred ruins. The heavy banister post at the foot of the stairway stood indifferent witness as the flames approached, igniting the handrail and using the stairwell as a flue to send the fire racing upstairs. Fire licked out of all the windows in the house when the conflagration finally burned its way through the dry lathe boards of the ceiling and ignited the roof. Before any fire trucks arrived, the one hundred-fifty-year old Hanson house was a total loss.

The crash and white-hot fire illuminated so much of the countryside that people who lived five miles away called their local fire departments. One of them was right next door. Bill Barnes had just stepped outside to cool off a piece of hot metal in the snow when he saw the flaming wreckage soar off the edge of the nearby cliff, pierce the night air like an artillery shell, and erupt in a blaze that obliterated the barn and ignited the house. He called the Center Township Fire Department from the phone in the garage then ran inside. "Mary! Diane! Get blankets out of the closet and get outside!"

"Bill, my God, what happened?" yelled Diane.

"Something just blew up the Hanson farm. Now come on, get some blankets."

"What for?" asked Mary.

"We're going to soak 'em down and cover the windows and doors. Come on, move!"

"Bill, for God's sake, we've got to get outta here!" Diane was standing just outside the front door looking in horror at the conflagration next door. The outline of the Hanson house was now silhouetted against the billowing white-hot fire from the barn while yellow flames flickered in all the windows. Mary was already coming down the hall with her little arms loaded with blankets. One of them was dragging a loose tail that she tripped on and fell, spilling the load in front of her.

Bill glanced at Mary, then turned to Diane and commanded, "Help her. Help her right now!"

As Diane gathered the pile of blankets, Mary scrambled to her feet and ran down the hall to get more. Bill darted back into the garage, grabbed a garden hose, and ran outside to hook it up to a front spigot. He didn't notice the winter cold.

"Mary, start spraying the roof. Diane, get another hose out of the garage and hook it up in back."

They were of one mind now: Hose down the roof. Soak the blankets. Cover the windows and doors. It was no longer cold outside. Heat from the fire was turning the surrounding countryside into a sauna.

The enormous white ball of roaring flames now had to share the night with the scream of fire engines and flashing red lights. Bill and Diane and Mary had never thought the sight of fire trucks could look so good. A child-like thought about the fire raced through Bill's head: *You can't scare me now. My buddies are here to beat you up.*

The pumper and tanker trucks began lining the road in front of the Hanson house, and the radio PA horn on one of the lead trucks started squawking, "General alarm! General alarm! Engine six, engine five respond."

The big barn held nothing of value, but it had belonged to the Hanson family for over a hundred years. Now it was gone, and in its place was a tower of the hottest flames Chief Harry Mansfield had ever seen in his entire firefighting career. He climbed down from the cab of the lead fire truck and checked the direction of the wind. It was out of the north, blowing toward the farmhouse, the line of oak trees, and the house that a man and his family were struggling to save. "Could things get any worse?" he muttered.

"Get your hoses laid along that line of trees," Mansfield shouted at his lieutenant. "We have to keep them from catching fire or they'll ignite the roof of that house to the south." He shouted at his lead truck chauffeur. "Jerry, call dispatch. Tell them to call Washington Township. We need extra hose to get on the back side of this thing."

The fire silhouetted the small brigade of firemen that struggled desperately to contain the blaze. Half of them fought the fire, and the other half kept the men on the front line hosed down with other fire hoses so the heat wouldn't overcome them. They all had to be relieved every five minutes to keep from being scorched by the super heated air.

Harry Mansfield had called for assistance from nine other fire departments, but he knew none of them could fight the barn fire. It was white hot and may have been fed by magnesium or, God forbid, white phosphorus. Fighting it with water would only make it spread. He concentrated his men's efforts on hosing down the line of oak trees and fighting the house fire. He needed more help, and he was so busy coordinating the efforts of eighty men that he yelled at the chauffeur of his snorkel truck, "Call dispatch. Tell them to call Indianapolis International. We need foam and light water down here."

The chauffeur yelled back. "Foam and light water won't douse that barn fire."

"I know that," said Mansfield. But we can use it to fight the house fire."

Harry Mansfield had fought scores of fires for eighteen years, but now he felt like he was fighting the fires of hell itself. He gazed at the inferno and tried to guess how high the flames were shooting into the black sky - Twenty? Thirty? Fifty feet? And what was feeding the thing? Was it chemical? Was it gas? Mansfield kept his eyes shaded like he was looking into the sun.

Fire fighting in the wintertime had always been a cold, miserable experience. Men were quite often overcome by frostbite and hypothermia. Fire hydrants and valves on the sides of trucks would become encased in ice. Not now. It was so hot that five of Mansfield's men were overcome with heat exhaustion, and fire department ambulances taking men to the hospital joined the company of fire trucks.

Mansfield knew the house next door was in real danger so he went over to offer to evacuate the people. He found Mary and Diane Barnes on opposite sides of the house, each with a garden hose squirting water on the roof. Bill was nailing wet blankets up to the windows and doors. He marveled at the sight of the little family fighting to save their home. He yelled at Bill, "We can get you folks out of here if you want us to."

"We're staying chief," Bill shot back. "Just keep those trees wet."

"Did you see what started the fire?"

"All I saw was something that looked like a car on fire crashing into the barn."

"Have any idea what was in the barn?"

"No, I don't."

Two men ran up behind Harry Mansfield. One of them carried a large microphone on a hand held boom. The other carried a hand held television camera with the logo WTHM Ch 5 pasted across the side.

One of them yelled, "Chief, can we get some information from you about the fire?"

"Not now, boys. I got my hands full."

"The man with the mic turned to Bill Barnes. "Sir, did you see what happened?"

"Sure did," Bill said with a toothy grin.

"Phil, are you ready?"

"Go ahead." The man with the camera squinted through the viewfinder and pointed the lens at Bill.

"Just tell us in your own words what you saw."

"Well, all I saw was something on fire. It looked like a car, I think. It flew across the road and slammed into the barn on the other side of that house."

"Was anybody living in the house?"

"No."

The cameraman zoomed in on Bill Barnes profile as he turned and looked transfixed at the billowing fireball next door. "Man, whatever it was, it came straight outta hell."

"Is your own house in danger?"

"Not now, I don't think. We're keeping the roof hosed down and the windows and doors covered with wet blankets."

"Who owned the house next door?"

"Some people named Hanson. An old lady lived there until she died late last fall." With a close up view of his profile being recorded on video tape, Bill turned and looked north again at the blaze destroying a century old county landmark.

"Hey!" A uniformed fireman came up behind the camera crew and yelled. "Move that van! We gotta keep this road clear. We got tankers moving water down here!"

Bill looked out toward the road at a whole fleet of marked cars and trucks from all the radio and TV stations in Indianapolis. They were dodging the big fire department tank trucks coming and going from the fire hydrants in Tanner's Grove. He ran out and invited them all to use his frozen front yard as a parking lot. Then he ran back to the house, grabbed the garden hose from Diane, and told her that she and Mary could go inside and warm up while he hosed down the roof.

"Not on your life," said Diane. "We're not missing this for anything. Besides, it's warm out here."

Bill looked back at the yard, the road, the fire scene next door. *What a picnic!*

An army of firefighters dragging a spider web of hoses around the place to contain the blaze now surrounded what was left of the Hanson house. The red and white fire department lights flashed a surrealistic pattern of light and shadow across the trees and fields and yards. The road itself now became a racetrack for the shiny tanker trucks shuttling water to the firemen. The front yard filled with mobile news units including three vans with antennas on top that looked like laser cannons from a "Star Wars" movie.

One of the cameramen explained to Bill and Diane that they were beaming live pictures to a microwave receiving station atop the Indiana National Bank tower in down town Indianapolis.

Mary came around from in back of the house to see what was going on. She found her parents surrounded by a forest of microphones and fielding questions about what they saw when the fire started.

The big yellow fire trucks from Indianapolis International Airport finally arrived and took over the fight against the house fire. Harry Mansfield sighed in relief. For the first time in his life, he had actually considered pulling his men off the line and letting the blaze have its way. He had actually considered the possibility of something so eerie he was afraid to mention it aloud. That this particular fire was not going to die. In his experience, fires were always extinguished or eventually burned out. But the flames of this monster seemed to have a character of its own. The flames from the barn fire billowed and lashed out like angry dragons at the men on the front line. But in the end, the fire chief managed to keep it from spreading.

Chapter 41

The Devil's Fire

Nobody saw the sun come up the next morning. The overcast sky had been lit all night by the mysterious fire that overwhelmed a timid sunrise. It took nearly ten hours for ninety men to extinguish the blaze that destroyed the old Hanson farmhouse. There was nothing left of the house but the concrete front porch and a brick flue in the middle of the foundation. A few vertical timbers stood smoldering in the ruins with their charred ends pointing defiantly at heaven, while along the south yard stood a row of ice sculptures. There was an oak tree inside each one. Because of the grotesquely hot fire, it took all night for the water from the fire hoses to freeze on the trees. None of them ignited or threatened the Barnes' house next door. Everybody thanked each other for that.

The view from the helicopter overhead showed a fan shaped burn pattern on the scorched earth where Samuel Hanson's father had built a wooden barn in 1858. When the party of state fire marshal investigators inside the big state police chopper finished taking aerial photos, they flew back to the helipad in Indianapolis and drove back to the fire site. Sheriff Preston Caldwell escorted the team. Their job seemed impossible - sifting through nothing but what seemed to be blackened soil and bits of molten metal. If the blaze had claimed a human victim, he would have surely died without a corpse.

Harry Mansfield was supervising five of his men who were casually hosing down a few hot spots left in the blackened crater that used to be a barn foundation. Preston Caldwell ducked under the yellow and black tape marked "POLICE LINE DO NOT CROSS." It was stretched across the front yard and anchored to a series of iron stakes in the ground. As the sheriff crossed the icy, muddy barnyard, he glanced to the south and noticed the ice-encrusted trees where sunlight glistened off the delicate petals of ice. Caldwell stopped and looked at the frozen illusions. One looked like a face with drooping eyes, long nose, and down turned mouth. One looked faceless with long hair hanging down on both sides. Caldwell chuckled and shook his head.

He walked over to talk to Harry Mansfield whose face was ashen as he turned and said, "It was like a volcano, Preston. I swear it came out of the ground just like a volcano."

Caldwell shook his head at the sight. "It's a wonder it didn't set the trees and house next door on fire."

"It's not a wonder. It's a miracle!"

"Any idea what was burning in there?"

"No."

"Any gas mains around here?" asked Caldwell.

"We've already checked with the gas company. No gas mains." Mansfield put his hands on his hips and looked behind the sheriff at the four men in heavy fur lined jackets coming their way. "I see you brought your little friends with you."

"Who?" Caldwell looked around. "Oh them. Fire Marshal's office. Snooty bunch."

"Very smart men, Preston. Very professional. They'll look for traces of phosphorous, magnesium. They won't find it."

"What makes you say that?"

"I've seen chemical fires before. God knows I've seen some hot fires in my time. Nothing like this, not even close. This was the devil's fire."

Caldwell's eyes came up with a jerk to see the maniacal look he had never seen on the fire chief's face in over twenty years of acquaintance. "Devil's fire? Where'd you hear that?"

Mansfield motioned to the sheriff that one of his deputies wanted to see him.

"Sheriff, look at this."

"What have you got there, Maynard?"

Deputy Maynard Fallwell had walked over holding something with a pair of tweezers. "Well, it's pretty well charred, but I swear it looks like somebody's bridge."

"Bridge?" said one of the fire investigators. He came over to the little gathering with his mouth in a haughty pout and his eyebrows hanging heavy over his thick glasses.

"A dental bridge," said Caldwell. "If all the teeth are intact we might just get an ID."

"I know what a dental bridge is, Sheriff. May I have that, Deputy? Thank you very much. Now let me explain something, Sheriff Caldwell. I have a team of investigators with me who have experience totaling over a hundred years. We'll gather the evidence and find a rational cause for this fire. I suggest you and your men continue to secure the area. Do I make myself clear?"

"Yes, Mr. Caswell. I believe you do."

"Good."

Caswell turned and walked a few paces away, but the sheriff wouldn't let him have the last word. He caught up with him, turned him by his shoulder, and said, "Now Mr. Caswell, let me explain something to you. While you and I work together at this site, you will not embarrass me in front of my deputies ever again. Do I make myself very clear on that?"

"Well I . . ."

"Yes, I think I do. Thank you very much for your co-operation in this matter, Mr. Caswell."

"Sheriff, I . . ."

"Carry on."

Preston Caldwell went back to his deputies. They greeted him with broad grins, but they knew better than to say anything. One of them, Tom Wood, came up to him. "Sheriff, I just talked to the dispatcher who was on duty last night. He says Max Carter marked out of service at the house next door around eight o'clock."

"Max Carter? What was that jerk doing here?"

"We don't know. But he never marked back in service, and nobody's seen him since."

Preston Caldwell hung his head then looked back up at Tom. "You know there was talk on the television about a car on fire ramming the barn."

"You're not thinking what I'm thinking are you?"

"Max Carter?"

"Maybe."

"So one of our squad cars is in that black crater, and the ashes belong in an urn with Max Carter's name on it." Caldwell shook his head and tipped back his uniform hat. "Tom, I'm sure Max would have gone to the cheapest dentist he could find for his bridge work."

"Mr. Caswell!" Caldwell shouted across the yard.

"Yes, Sheriff."

"If you'll call Doctor Richard Cornish in Coalton, I think you'll find a match on that bridge."

"Very well. Thank you, sheriff."

"Don't mention it."

Tom said, "Sheriff, you want me to talk to the people next door?"

"Ah no, I'll do that. What's their name?"

"Barnes. Bill and Diane Barnes."

"Barnes. Yeah, okay."

* * *

Preston Caldwell and Bill Barnes began sizing each other up as soon as Bill opened the front door. "Mr. Barnes, I'm Sheriff Caldwell."

"What is it?"

"I just wondered if I could talk to you for a minute."

Awkward silence followed. "Oh, I'm sorry. Why don't you come in? We just finished breakfast but there's still some coffee left."

"That's okay. I'll just step inside." Diane came into the living room and sat on the couch. The sheriff removed his hat and nodded at her. "Mrs. Barnes."

"Good morning, Sheriff." Bill joined Diane on the couch. "Are you sure you won't have some coffee with us?"

"No thanks. I have to juggle some things next door. This won't take long." Bill and Diane stared at him. These civilians made him feel uncomfortable. Or was it something else in this house . . .something *about* this house?

Caldwell cleared his throat. "Mr. Barnes, my deputy tells me Max Carter was here last night. Is that right?"

"Yes, that's right."

"Can you tell me what he was doing here?"

"It was a personal matter."

"Personal matter?"

"Yes, I used to work for Max Carter. We didn't get along very well."

"You don't work there anymore?"

"No, I started my own welding shop."

"Did this personal matter have anything to do with your old job?"

"No."

"How about your present business?"

"No."

"Did it have something to do with a 357 Magnum?" Caldwell took note of Bill and Diane's shocked expressions and went on. "News travels fast in a small town, Mr. Barnes. Your pistol is probably buried in that black hole in the ground. I really don't think I'd worry about it."

"Did Max Carter file a report about that pistol?" Bill asked.

"If he wrote a report, it's probably out there in that same black hole. Like I said, don't worry about it. That's really not what this visit is for anyway. I just wanted to get a grip on what's been going on out here for the past year."

"Such as?" asked Diane.

Caldwell noticed Diane's pleading look and temporarily lost his train of thought. "Ah . . .well, several things really. Let's start with last night. Mr. Barnes did you see what happened? I mean did you see what started the fire next door?"

"Well, like I told the fire chief, all I saw was something on fire fly across the road. Then I saw this huge ball of fire go up behind the old Hanson house, and the place just started burning."

"Do you have any idea what was stored in the barn at that place?"

"No. Shouldn't you be asking the family about that?"

"Yes, of course. It's just that . . .Well, so many things have happened in the past year, and they all seem to come back to this house."

"For instance?"

"Somebody set fire to the frame of this house while it was being built. The drywall contractor disappeared. Fortunately, some people in a scuba diving club found him at the bottom of Cherry Tree Lake. Then there was that business last Halloween with Judy Parsons. Mr. Barnes, this is all a little too off the wall to make it an official investigation.

Maybe sometime the two of you can come down to the office."

"Sheriff, has John McCauley said anything to you about what goes on out here?"

"Diane, I think it's the sheriff's job to ask the questions."

The sheriff chuckled and said, "That's alright, Mr. Barnes. Actually he hasn't gone into any great detail. Now I wanted to ask you: You say you saw something fly across the road last night and crash behind the house?"

"Yes."

"Could you tell me exactly where it came from?"

"Well, it seemed to come off that cliff. You know, across the road."

"You mean where all the trees grow out to the edge of the cliff."

"Yeah."

"Are you sure?"

Bill got up and led the sheriff to the front door. "I'm sure. I had just stepped out in the driveway at the time. I know it came from across the road."

Preston Caldwell looked out the front storm door at the cliff. He chuckled and turned to Bill. "That's very interesting."

"In what way?" asked Bill.

"Well, the local legend has it that back in the late nineteenth century a coven of witches staged some of their rituals up there on top of that wooded bluff."

"Really? What kind of rituals?"

"No idea. I don't get into that kind of nonsense. But for years that old bluff out there was something of a rite of passage for young kids. They would dare each other to go out because there was supposed to be an old Indian witch cooking her brew in an iron caldron over an open fire. When she drank some of it she turned into a wolf, a bear, a black crow . . . God knows what all. They haven't done that since before I was born. My daddy was the one who told me about it.

"For the last thirty years that ground has been the property of the Forest County Conservation Club. They put a circular gravel road in there a few weeks back."

Bill asked, "So why would Max Carter have been running around up there last night?"

"That's a good question," said Caldwell. "Our investigation is still going on. Tell me something, Mr. Barnes. What kind of mood was Max Carter in last night when he left your house?"

"He was pretty agitated. I guess he was frustrated that he couldn't nail me on a weapons charge. Plus he just didn't like me and, believe you me, the feeling was mutual."

"I can understand that. Was there anything in particular between you two?"

"When I worked for Max Carter, I used to raise some hell about the condition of the trucks. He didn't take that too well. I really raised hell the day I quit. That was right after I lost my brakes and almost killed a bunch of people."

"None of that explains why he would have taken the long way back into Tanner's Grove."

"Or why he drove off the edge of a cliff," said Bill.

The sheriff turned to Bill and gave him an intense look. "That's true Mr. Barnes. We'll keep in touch." Caldwell left and seemed to shudder as he walked to his car.

Chapter 42

A Bizarre Offer of Help

The "Devil's Fire" became yesterday's news mostly because other events crowded it out of the headlines. There was the continuing crisis over American hostages held in Iran after the Islamic revolution, the upcoming presidential campaign, local political campaigns, and an investigation into police corruption in Indianapolis. Officially the Hanson farm fire was blamed on "an unknown fissure in the earth venting natural gas."

It was over four weeks before heavy machinery showed up to level the foundation of the old house. On a dreary Monday morning in early March, a white Town Car rolled slowly down the country road and parked across from the wrecking site. John and Sharon McCauley got out and stood watching an enormous backhoe scoop out the bricks and charred timbers of the foundation and dump them into a dump truck parked along the road.

Diane watched them as she stood at the front door. Her heart ached with their pain, the death of their only child, the tragic, bizarre passing of Aunt Alice, and now this. Diane thought that somebody upstairs really had it in for this family, or maybe it was somebody down below. She pulled on her high-top boots and her coat, then walked across the muddy front yard to meet them.

"Good morning, Diane." Sharon turned and greeted her with a faint smile. She could barely see Diane's face for the fur hood pulled up against the brutal March wind. "Why aren't you working today?"

"I called in sick this morning. Things are slow any-way. I'm so sorry about all this. I wish there was something I could say, something I could do."

"That's alright, Diane," said John. "It's all over now, and that's just as well." Diane studied John as he stared at the wreckage. "This was never a happy house. I was raised in it. I was a country boy. It was supposed to be a happy childhood. But it wasn't."

"I've got the coffee pot brewing," said Diane. "Let's go in the house. We've all got lots to talk about."

* * *

Diane chattered as they all went through the front door, took off their shoes at the little boot tray, and took off their coats. "Actually, I was just on my way over to Mother's house when I saw you guys out there. Things have finally slowed down at work. I was working so many hours there for a while. So I just called in sick today. I didn't think they'd mind and they didn't. I have to go into town today anyway and shop for seeds for the garden. It's going to be planting season pretty soon. I also wanted to set out some new rhu-barb this year. Two of my plants died last year and I need to replace them. For some reason, nobody seems to have it in stock yet."

Diane took off her coat, turned toward John and Sha-ron, and tried not to notice their shocked expressions. "Do you guys know where I can get rhubarb at a decent price?"

Diane knew what John and Sharon were looking at. She had to look at the gaunt expression, the dark circles around the eyes, and the matted hair in the mirror every morning. "Oh, I know I look a wreck. My God, where are my manners? Here, have a seat at the kitchen table."

"No, that's okay," said John. "We can't stay long. Ac-tually we came by to . . ."

"Let me at least pour you guys some coffee." Diane

rushed around the kitchen fetching coffee cups, urging John and Sharon to sit down. She brought the coffee pot to the kitchen table, poured it, and slopped coffee out of one cup. "Oh, I can't do anything right anymore. Everything I touch turns to crap." The tears rolled down her cheeks and her mouth quivered.

Sharon took the coffee pot from Diane. "Here honey, let me help you."

"I know news travels fast in a small town. You guys know what's going on here, don't you?" Diane raised her head, her wet eyes framed by lines of worry.

"Yes, we do," said John. He squeezed her hand and noticed Sharon frowning as she shook her head. "Well, we don't know everything. Diane, your mother told me you've been having visitors."

"Yes, and we had a visitor the night Bill and I left your house so abruptly. I never did apologize for that."

"Never mind that," said Sharon. "Tell us what happened."

"I woke up in the middle of the night and felt somebody breathing on me. I screamed, Bill turned on the light, and there was nobody there. I told him we had to move and I couldn't stand the place any longer." She took a deep breath and continued.

"For some reason, the next morning everything seemed to be fine. At least I seemed to be able to cope with things around me, like the water. Oh my God, the water. We all got sick from it so I sent a sample to the health department."

"What did they say?" asked John.

Diane fell silent and stared into her coffee cup. "What?"

"The water sample," said John. "There was something about the water."

"Oh…we were getting sick off the water. So we had the well tested. Well, I did."

"How did that turn out?"

"What?"

"The water test. Is the water okay?"

Diane kept looking in her coffee cup and then shoved the cup over in front of John. "Do you see something in here?"

"What are we looking for, Diane?" asked John.

"Some kind of flakes. I was supposed to scrape some flakes into the water sample. Camphor flakes, that's what they were. If they spin, the water is okay."

John and Sharon exchanged puzzled, worried looks. John looked into the cup. "I don't see any Camphor flakes. I see what appears to be a little scale. I wouldn't worry about it, Diane. We have it in our water sometimes."

Diane sighed and bowed her head. "Never mind. Sometimes I don't really know what I'm talking about. God I'm tired."

John changed the subject. "Diane, what exactly happened out here the night the farmhouse burned?"

"Bill talked to the sheriff about that. He said he saw a car or something on fire fly across the road from that cliff. The sheriff told us that the cliff was supposed to have been a gathering place for witches…way long time ago."

John frowned. "Diane, that was four weeks ago."

"What was?"

"The car crash, the farmhouse burning."

"Oh, yeah."

"What about now? Has anything happened since the fire?"

Diane stared down at her coffee cup. "No. I spend a lot of time at work. Bill spends a lot of time welding things."

"What about Mary?" asked Sharon.

Diane kept staring into her coffee cup. She started

remembering little flakes of camphor spinning around and turning into hideous faces.

"Diane, what's the matter?" asked John.

"Mary spends a lot of time with her grandmother." Suddenly Diane turned her cup upside down in the middle of the table and sent coffee splattering in all directions. When she realized what she had done, she whined in horror and rushed to the kitchen sink to grab a handful of paper towels off the rack. She came back and started wiping the tabletop, crying, "My God, I'm sorry. I don't know what comes over me sometimes. I swear this place is driving me nuts."

Sharon picked up the cups while John went over and put his arm around Diane. "Diane, we can help you and Bill and Mary. But first we need Bill on board with us. We need his approval and blessing and cooperation. That, I'm afraid, is going to depend a lot on you."

"On me?" cried Diane. "What can I do?"

Sharon told her. "Diane, Bill has got to see what life in this house is doing to you. If he doesn't, then it's up to you to move out once and for all."

"I can't do that to Mary. I always believed a child needs two parents."

John asked, "What's this doing to Mary? How is she taking it?"

"Not well. The day you met us at Doctor Blackwell's office Mary had gone to school and had no idea how she got there. Somebody had to pull her down off the schoolyard fence. She was in a horrible panic."

John sat down at the kitchen table and let out a heavy sigh. "Ladies this situation needs a woman's touch and it has to be all women."

"What do you mean, John Mac?" asked Sharon.

"I understand how Bill feels about all this and how he feels about me and what I do. But the well being of his wife and daughter are at stake here. And I think it's going to take a group of women, specifically Diane, her mother Emily, her sister Pam, and maybe even you, Sharon."

"Me?"

"Mr. McCauley, what did you have in mind?" asked Diane.

"Ladies, we're going to have another séance. Sharon, you are going to be the hypnotist. Diane, you are going to be the medium. Bill does not want me in this house and I understand that. So I'm staying out of it."

"Mr. McCauley, I couldn't do that."

"You can, Diane. You're a very good subject. You proved that the night you and Bill were at our house. You'll be surrounded by friends and loved ones. And you've got to start calling me John."

"Bill won't hold still for any of this."

"Tell him things have changed," said John. "Tell him I have nothing to do with it and that it was all Sharon's idea."

Sharon gave John an evil glare. He held up his hand for her to stay quiet, which she did, while putting a hand on one hip and the other to her head.

"I'll try," said Diane.

"Good. Sharon, we have to go now. We have an appointment with a lawyer downtown. I hope he can get Alice's estate settled before the rest of us die."

* * *

Outside Sharon was in a panic. "John Mac, you are playing with Ffire."

"No Sharon, the fire is playing with us." He pointed at the charred ruins of the Hanson farmhouse. "I'm just trying to fight back."

"Don't try to be funny. I can't do this to that girl. She's skating on the edge. I'm not going to be the one to break her delicate condition."

"She's not that delicate. What I've seen of her looks pretty solid."

"John, let me be the medium. You should be the hypnotist, the facilitator."

"No, help Diane talk to Bill. We need him on board before we ever decide who's going to do what."

"I just don't feel good about this. Can we sit on it for a few days? Maybe all our heads will clear by then, and we can see . . ."

"No, Sharon." John stopped, put his hands on her shoulders, and turned her toward him. "We have to do this *now*. We've got one chance to help this family, and we've got to take it now. Time is not on our side."

Two days later time ran out.

Chapter 43

The Reincarnation of Matthew

"Mr. Forkner?" Bill Barnes knocked on the screen door again. He knew somebody was home because the inside door was open and he heard furniture being scooted across a wood floor. "Mr. Forkner? Anybody home?" Finally he heard the shuffling of feet and Jim Forkner walked out onto the screened-in porch. Bill was shocked at his appearance. The usually neat, dapper, cheerful Jim Forkner now looked like a wreck. His stooped frame was draped in a white T-shirt, ratty old brown cardigan sweater, gray slacks and sandals. He hadn't shaved in at least a day. The long hair that he grew on the side and combed over to hide his bald pate now hung down in his face. The frown on his face brightened into a smile when he saw Bill.

"Bill! Oh my, well I almost forgot you were coming over today." He pushed the long hair out of his face. "Come on in and I'll get you the blue prints you need."

Bill followed him across the porch and through the front door. "Mr. Forkner . . .?"

"Jim. Please call me Jim. I know I'm old enough to be your father, but I like Jim a whole lot better. Mr. Forkner was my father." The old man pulled an enormous folder out of a rack of narrow shelves beside his drawing board and handed them to Bill.

At first Bill had thought that Jim was on a binge, but he was handling himself and his drawings alright. "Jim, are you alright?"

"Oh yes, my yes. Everything's just fine." Jim cleared his throat. "You think you can handle this now?"

Bill quickly scanned a couple of blueprints. "It's been a while since I read any blue prints, but this looks fairly simple."

"If you have any trouble at all, call me and I'll come over to your shop right away. I've seen your work before. Aaaand I appreciate you doing this for me."

"Thanks for your confidence, Jim. I'll do my best."

"Oh say, you're going to take my truck back to the shop with you, right?"

"That's right."

"Well, you'll need somebody to drive your vehicle back home, right?"

"Oh, I've got Diane out in the car with me."

"Oh shoot!" Jim shook his head. "I wish this wasn't happening right now. My, this would be the perfect time to invite both of you in. This is terrible."

"Jim, is anything the matter? Can I help?"

He laid his hand on Bill's shoulder. "Come over here on the couch and sit down, son."

By the time they reached the couch, Jim Forkner was trying to choke back tears. Bill had enough trouble when women cried, but the sight of a man getting soggy made him want to run the other way. They sat down and Jim patted Bill's arm. "Bill, you don't like John McCauley, do you?"

"It's not that. It's just some of the things he does, some of the things he stands for. He's a very smart man, I suppose."

"I understand. John and Sharon sometimes impress other people as being. . .well, above the rest of the crowd. They don't mean to. It's just they were educated and lived in other parts of the country. Some of their ways are . . . different. But make no mistake. John and Sharon are good people.

I've never known them to turn away from anybody that needed help. Not once."

"I'm sure that's true, but . . ."

"Now you take a situation I've got in my house right now. You see, Carolyn is in the back bedroom with our grandson, Matthew. You know we've been telling everybody that Matthew is our first grandchild. Well, that's not exactly true. You see, he's three years old, and four years ago we lost our first born grandson to crib death."

Jim wiped a tear out of his eye. He swallowed hard then said, "Matthew was born about a year later. He's been such a healthy kid, up until now.

"We took him to the doctor this afternoon. We were concerned that his cold wasn't getting any better. Now they tell us that we may have a case of Reye's Syndrome on our hands. They told us if he wasn't better by tomorrow they'll have to put him in the hospital. Bill, you know Reye's Syndrome can be fatal."

"I know," said Bill. "Where's his parents?"

"They run a traveling petting zoo. It's not much of a job, but it's all they could find right now. We called them and they're on their way back from Sandusky, Ohio. They're loving parents. They really are."

"I didn't mean to imply that they weren't."

"I understand. Listen, I was going to tell you, something came up this afternoon that may change your mind about what John McCauley stands for. Carolyn was rocking Matthew, trying to get him to go to sleep and get some of the rest he needs. Well, he was just lying there staring up at her, and all of a sudden he said something that just about knocked us both out of our chairs. He said, 'Mamaw, I don't want to die again.' Can you believe that?"

Bill frowned. "He said what?"

"He said, 'Mamaw, I don't want to die again.'"

"Why would he say a thing like that?"

"That's just it. Why would he if there wasn't something to it? Now we have never said one word in front of that kid about life after death or reincarnation."

"Are you saying that Matthew is the reincarnation of your first grandson?"

"Bill, I'll do like John does. I've told you what happened. I'll let you draw your own conclusion. But I'll tell you this: John and Sharon have stopped by already today wanting to know if there was anything they could do. There wasn't of course. But they were here for us. You see Bill they were here for us. They showed their concern and that counted for so much." Jim had to wipe more tears off his face.

"Now I don't mean this to sound like a lecture. It's just that I like you, Bill; and I like John McCauley. I just thought you two should be friends. I think it would mean a lot to both of you."

"Thanks, Jim. I'll keep that in mind."

Chapter 44

The Electric Ghost

Jim Forkner didn't change Bill's mind about John McCauley completely. Something else would do that later in the day.

Bill backed the truck into the shop, then hopped up on the flat bed and started taking measurements. He was building a tubular frame that would be anchored to the bed for long hauling to a water purification plant in Florida. It consisted of a steel floor with two upright frames in the middle and front that would hold a system of filtration tanks. Each time he completed a weld he knocked the slag off the seam with a small hammer. The bell like ring echoed off the walls, but that didn't startle him.   Something   else   would   do that . . . soon!

After the upright frame at the front of the floor was finished, Bill went to work on the middle frame. With the protective visor of his hood propped up, he checked the vertical plumb of each piece with a carpenter's level. Sunlight shining through the window made the level bubble sparkle like a Christmas tree ornament.

It would be the last glimmer of friendly light he would see that day.

Now he was ready to start welding the frame to the floor. He picked up the welding rod and its holder with his right hand and grasped the bottom edge of his protective visor with his left. When he had the rod over the spot where he would strike an arc, he pulled his visor down over his face and touched the bottom of the seam between the two pieces of steel. A brilliant arc erupted and turned the seam into mol-ten metal. Because he had done this so many times before, Bill was able to create a perfect weld that would have stood the scrutiny of an industrial X-ray.

None of this could have prepared him for what hap-pened next.

He was getting close to finishing the last seam on the tube frame. The only thing he could see behind the dark rec-tangle of protective glass on his welder's hood was the bright arc tracing the welded seam.

Then it happened.

The blue light in front of him swelled, hummed, then exploded with enough force to throw him away from the truck bed. Other than being stunned and winded by the swift thud, he was unhurt. Because his welder's hood was still over his face, he had the sensation of being in total darkness ex-cept for the huge balloon of blue light hovering in front of him. Bill heard nothing but the loud humming of the big bright blue sphere slowly bobbing up and down and scaring him half to death. He couldn't move. He could hardly breathe. Finally, the big blue ball rotated back on its horizontal axis to reveal a human forehead, then a pair of clear sparkling eyes, and finally the face of a woman with pale blue skin like the rest of the electric halo around her. The high cheekbones glis-tened and the mouth had full lips spread in a benevolent smile.

The face started to speak, but the words were drowned out by the loud hum. The mouth moved faster and wider now. The forehead wrinkled in an expression of panic. The eyes loomed bigger and bigger until they deformed the rest of the face. The entire image of blue light stretched into a hideous skull. The skull lost its shape and became a swirling mass of light and shadow that filled the entire shop. Out of the maelstrom of light and sound emerged the figure of a woman in a long flowing gown. Her long white hair blew out to her right side. It was the same woman, the same face.

What did she want? Bill wondered. *What in God's name did she want? And the smell. Dear God, that smell. There's that smell again.*

The woman floated across the garage floor and hovered over Bill. He thought he heard her say something, but again he couldn't make it out. The loud low-pitched hum seemed to assault his ears from all directions.

Please make that smell go away!

The woman was talking louder now. She looked panic stricken. Her face screwed up, her eyes getting wider; she seemed to be yelling something. Her face became larger than her body and it was getting closer to Bill's face. She was yelling louder and louder, but the loud hum drowned out her voice.

Oh God, that sickening sweet smell. Make the smell go away!

The eyes suddenly sank back into the head to leave nothing but two black holes. The mouth opened wider and wider to reveal twin rows of long sharp teeth. The lower jaw dropped wide open and the rest of the face rotated back until it disappeared. The teeth of the lower jaw started growing upward like flames. Bill felt the heat stinging his entire body and for a moment he thought that he was going to be cremated.

Just as suddenly as it had appeared, the fire and the light vanished. The garage was dark and silent as a tomb. From behind his welder's mask, Bill finally found the strength to scream like a banshee. But he couldn't move. His entire body was numb with fright.

After several minutes, Bill found his release and broke out crying and sobbing like a baby. That night Diane called John and Sharon McCauley for help.

Chapter 45

The Sweet Smell of Terror

"I ain't afraid o' nothin'! I ain't afraid o' nothin'!" Bill Barnes lay on Diane's lap shivering while she dabbed at the burn on his face. He stared up at the ceiling and chanted over and over again. "I ain't afraid o' nothin'! I ain't afraid o' nothin'!"

"Bill, hold still," Diane pleaded just as John and Sharon came rushing through the front door. They found Bill and Diane on the couch and Mary sitting on the floor looking up at them with tears streaming down her face.

"Oh, honey, this is nothing for you to be seeing." Sharon bent down and wrapped her arms around Mary.

"Diane, what happened?" asked John.

"I don't know." Diane looked up and sobbed. "He wouldn't let me call a doctor so I called you guys. Please help us! Help us!"

John knelt down beside the couch where Bill lay in Diane's lap. "What's this?"

"I put some oats in a wet towel for the burn."

John looked closely at Bill's face. "Diane, I don't think it's a burn. It looks more like hives."

"No, no! That can't be it. I found him out in the shop. He still had his welder's hood on."

"I saw it! I saw it!" Bill yelled. "My God, Diane, I saw it!' He shut his eyes to block out the vision. "It won't go away," he sobbed. "That smell. Oh God, that smell. Make it go away."

John took Bill by the shoulders. "Bill, tell me what you saw."

Bill kept his eyes shut and screamed, "No! No, make it go away!" His red face got brighter.

"Oh no, don't do that!" Diane sobbed.

"Honey, I don't think this is going to do any good." Standing behind the couch, Sharon bent down and took the towel and oats out of Diane's hand.

John said, "Alright Bill, put it out of you mind. Put it out of your mind. We're going to concentrate on something else. Keep your eyes closed and think back to last October. I want you to think back to Halloween night. Do you remember that?"

Bill nodded his head.

"Bill, tell me what happened last Halloween night."

"Noises. Something knocked over . . .something on the back porch."

"That's right. There were noises and a very frightened horse. Do you remember that?" Bill nodded. "Tell me about the horse, Bill."

"Big ole horse . . .came runnin' around the yard. Boy, he was a beauty. Ran like the devil was after him."

"What did he look like?"

"Big and gray. He was scared. God, he was scared. Eyes as big as fried eggs."

"Were you scared then, Bill?"

"No." He had calmed down a little, but his breathing was still heavy.

"You were brave then, Bill. You were calm. You could handle the situation. Tell me what you did to calm that horse down."

"I just let him run." Bill still had his eyes shut.

"You just let him run, and you let him know that you weren't afraid of him, right?"

"That's right."

"How did you manage to get him tied up?"

"I just grabbed his halter as he came by and ran him around a tree."

"Was the horse still frightened?"

"Yeah."

"But you weren't."

"No."

"Bill, whatever you saw this afternoon is tied up. It can't hurt you. It can't frighten you. Open your eyes now and we'll talk about it. You're not afraid anymore, Bill. Open your eyes. There's nothing here to harm you or frighten you."

Bill opened his eyes and looked into the ruggedly handsome face of John McCauley. The overhead light made his hair glow like a halo.

"All the phantoms are gone, Bill. Diane's here; I'm here; Mary's here; Sharon's here. But all the phantoms are gone. Now keep your eyes open and tell me what you see."

No answer, but he was starting to breathe easier.

"Tell me what you see."

"No, no. Not now, please." The angry red flush on Bill's face was gone.

"It was hives," John said matter-of-factly.

Bill got up from the couch and stood in the middle of the living room. Mary ran to him and threw her arms around his waist. "It's okay, baby. It's okay," said Bill. "Daddy's alright now."

Bill eased into his easy chair. He looked down at the floor and over at the patio door, then back down at the floor, all the while rubbing his hands together and clinching his palms until his knuckles turned white. He avoided eye contact with everybody. For one long agonizing minute he stared at the floor, then the walls, then the floor and said nothing.

Sharon broke the silence. "Bill, you're among friends.

If you want to talk about it, we'll all understand." Another long silence. "If you don't want to talk about it, we'll understand."

Bill leaned back in his chair, put his fingers over his mouth, rested his chin in his palm and eyeballed everybody in the room. John McCauley stood in front of him, his hands at his sides. Mary and Diane were on the couch clutching each other, tears streaming down their faces. Sharon sat at the opposite end of the couch.

Bill thought this was his fault; that he had put them through hell. *But by God, I had help.* Bill motioned for John to bend down close so he could whisper in his ear. "Does anybody need to know about this besides us?"

"Absolutely not," said John.

Bill put his finger to his mouth, wanting John to lower his voice. "I have something to tell you. Could you send the women out of the room for now?"

"I suppose . . ."

"Please John, man to man. I sure don't want Mary to hear this."

John nodded and shuffled over to the couch. Bill watched his tall, imposing physique bend over and whisper to the gathering of females. They left and went down the hall.

Bill stayed in his chair and kept rubbing his hands and looking around the room. John sat on the couch across from him. "If my old man saw that outburst, he would have beat me half to death."

"Why?"

"Men and boys in the Barnes family aren't supposed to carry on like that."

"What happened, Bill? What happened this afternoon?"

"I was workin'. I had the arc welder in my hand." Bill held up his right hand and wrapped his fingers around something imaginary. "I struck a spark and everything was going okay. When I got to the top of a seam, I . . .The spark . . .The spark just went VOOOOM! It slammed me against the wall. Then there was this big ball of fire and a face in the middle of it. It got so hot in there I thought the damn thing was gonna roast me." Bill jammed the heels of his hands into his eyes to dam up the tears. "I ain't afraid of nothing. I ain't supposed to be afraid."

"You're not afraid," said John. "You're not afraid now. You don't have to be afraid anymore."

Bill dropped his hands into his lap. "I thought I was over all that. Dad and Uncle Neville got me over bein' afraid of horses, and I was never afraid of anything after that except . . ."

"Except what?" John asked.

"There was something else." Bill sighed and glanced out the patio door. He leaned forward and cleared his throat. "It happened when I was five years old. We lived on a two-lane highway out in the country. One day I was looking out the front screen door wishing I could go outside. All of a sudden I heard a thud, just as a car and a big semi passed each other on the highway. Something red got splashed all over the side of the truck. This yellow ball of fur came rolling across the yard, and I ran out to see what it was. God, it was awful!"

"What was it, Bill?"

"It was a girl's head."

"What happened?"

"I don't know all the details. Folks told me later on that this girl just stuck her head out the window when the truck went by, and one of the big fender mirrors caught her across the throat and knocked her head off." Bill paused to swallow hard then went on. "You know the worst part was the smell. The girl was wearing the fruitiest perfume. Here was this head with blonde hair all matted with blood and this God-awful smell of sweet perfume.

"I had nightmares for months after that. I'd wake up screaming in the middle of the night. Dad would come down to my room and yell at me to shut up. He'd say, 'Some of us are tryin' to get some sleep. Some of us in this house have to get up and go to work in the morning.' Well, that didn't make the nightmares go away. The nightmares didn't go away until I was about eight.

"It was about that time we started visiting Uncle Neville and Aunt Betty up around South Bend. They had this daughter, Brenda. We ah . . .we got kind o' friendly."

Bill squirmed and gave a nervous chuckle. "Brenda was only ten, but she was startin' to sprout some. Every once in a while she'd let me see . . .Well, you know.

"One night she got curious about what I looked like. Well, she came in and pulled down the covers and started . . . exploring. I thought that was pretty nice until she got down on top of me. And I'll be damned if she wasn't wearing that same fruity perfume. I started screaming bloody murder; scared poor Brenda half to death. The air in that house was blue after that. My parents, her parents, all woke up and wanted to know what was going on. We never told and that made them mad as hell.

"I couldn't smell anything but that damn perfume for weeks."

Bill looked out the patio door and rubbed his chin for a moment. "Perfume. Perfume?" He got up and went to the kitchen sink. He ran water over his hand, held his fingers to his nose and sniffed.

"The water smelled like perfume," said Bill.

"Does it smell like perfume now?" John called from the living room couch.

"No. Diane had the water tested a few weeks ago. It

didn't show anything." Bill came back and sat on the couch. "But I swear the water had been smelling like perfume. How could that be?"

John sighed. "You brought a haunted past to a haunted house, Bill."

Suddenly from out of the shadows of the hallway, what looked like a disembodied arm floated into the room.

"Sharon, what are you doing?" asked John.

Sharon walked with her arm extended to the middle of the living room. "There's something here." Diane, holding Mary's hand, was right behind her. "There's a cold pocket of air right here in the middle of the room."

"Is that dust over there?" Mary pointed to a spot in front of the patio door. Everybody looked and saw a cloud of dust begin to swirl. It changed into something that looked almost human, a faint wisp with hands and feet and a vague outline of a face. The apparition folded in on itself and disappeared.

John turned to Bill, then looked at Diane. She had her face pressed against the top of her daughter's head. "Diane, do you trust me?"

"What?" Diane lifted her head.

John turned to Bill. "Bill, do you trust me?"

"What kind of question is that?"

"If you both trust me, we can channel this thing and find out what all the fuss is about. We've talked before about channeling, Diane. Remember?"

Bill and Diane looked at each other and said nothing.

"Please, trust me," said John. "We can do this. We can make this place livable. Trust me. I won't hurt you. I've never hurt anybody."

Diane looked at Bill again. He looked away and nodded. She squeezed Mary's shoulder. "Let me call Gramma. You can stay with her for awhile."

"No!" shouted Mary. "Let me stay. I'll go crazy with worry if I'm not here."

"Mary, you've seen too much already," said Diane.

"Please Mother, don't send me away."

"Let her stay," said John. "Better the devil she knows than the devil she doesn't know."

Chapter 46

The Voice of Tom Jakob

All the lights were off except the table lamp nearest the front door. The yellow umbra of light hit the ceiling and cast a soft glow over Bill, Mary and Sharon sitting close to each other on the couch. The drapes at the patio door were closed. John sat on a footstool and spoke to Diane barely three feet from her right ear. Diane sat in her favorite rocker recliner with her feet propped up and every muscle in her body relaxed by the hypnotic voice of John McCauley.

Diane stared at the ceiling. Very softly, but very firmly, John told her "Diane, you are completely relaxed, and your mind is open. You will remain aware of the sound of my voice, but you will also be aware of a presence in this room. That presence is now able to reveal itself through you." Her eyelids began to flutter and close.

John let the quiet of the moment sink in for several seconds. "Do you feel a presence in this room? Do you sense somebody here, Diane?"

"Yes," came the soft reply.

"Can you tell who it is?"

"Yes, I . . ." Diane's mouth froze open.

"Do you feel the presence of somebody no longer with us in the flesh?"

"Yes."

"Spirit, speak to me," John commanded. "Do not harm this lady. She means you no harm. We mean you no harm." There was still no reply. "Diane, tell me what you feel. Is there somebody here who wants to speak to us?"

"Yes."

"Very well, tell us who you are. Spirit in this room, tell us who you are."

Diane doubled her fists, gnashed her teeth, and furrowed her brow. Her lower lip began to quiver. Finally, the voice inside her head exploded. "TOOOOMMMM!!!!!"

The outburst made John catch his breath. He silently commanded himself to keep his cool. Bill and Mary tightened their grip around each other. Sharon patted their shoulders.

"Tom?" John repeated.

"Jakob!"

"Jakob?" John was temporarily confused by the two names.

"Tom! . . . Jakob!"

"Tom Jakob? Tom Jakob is your name?"

Diane's lower lip quivered and the grip of anguish barely allowed her to utter a faint "Yes." Between lucid outbursts, a strained keening noise of several voices came out of her mouth. The air in the room was so cold everybody could see their breath.

"Tom, you are in a quiet place now. You are among friends. We know you are troubled, and we want to help you. Tell us what happened. What happened to you?"

"They m-m-m-murdered me!"

"Murdered you?"

"They murdered me!"

"Do you know who they are?"

"I ain't never done no harm to nobody!"

"Can you tell us who murdered you, Tom?"

Diane squirmed in her chair. The corners of her mouth were turned down hard against her jaw. "Why did they do this? Why did they do this?"

"Tom, that's what we want to find out."

"I ain't never done no harm to nobody."

"Tom, whoever did this to you can't harm you anymore. Please tell me what happened."

There was a long silence as the air turned colder, then Diane spoke. "Two men . . .They came in the night."

"Yes, they came in the night."

"Set fire to the whole place."

"Then what happened?"

"They murdered me!"

John paused while the ghost calmed down. "Was this your home, Tom?"

"Yes."

"Was this a farm?"

"Yes."

"Did you have a family here?"

"I had a wife and two children."

"What happened to them?"

"We were going to have another child."

"What happened to all of them, Tom?"

"Don't know about the rest of the children."

"What happened to your wife and unborn child?"

"They butchered her!"

"Butchered her?"

"They butchered her!"

Diane's chest heaved with each breath. White puffs of vapor chugged out of her mouth along with the soft keening of many voices. John paused for a moment, then asked, "Tom, do you have any idea who did this?"

"Two men, one named Zed."

"Do you know the other's name?"

"No."

"Tom, do you have any idea why they would want to do this, any idea at all?"

"I don't know. I ain't never done no harm to nobody."

"Now Tom, I want you to know that all this is over and in the past. And I want you to tell me if there is a town close by here. Do you know the name of the closest town?"

"Place called . . .Coal town."

"Coal town?" John nodded with a knowing expression. "Tom, what year is this?"

"1889."

"Tom, that proves that all of this is in the distant past. That was almost a hundred years ago. This is the year 1980. The people who did this to you are long dead, and they have gone to meet their ultimate justice."

"They had no right to do this!"

"No Tom, they had no right to do this to you. But remember what the Bible says: 'Vengeance is mine, sayeth the Lord.'"

"Where's my wife? I want to know what they did with Elizabeth."

"She's not here anymore."

"Where did they bury her?"

"I don't know, Tom." John couldn't beg ignorance at a time like this with the ghost of a man in this condition. "But her remains . . . Elizabeth has gone on to a better life in a better world. She has probably reincarnated and is living a very happy life far from this place and time. And this is for you too, Tom. You have to go on and evolve and live a better life. You must learn to forgive those who did this horrible thing to you. Do you understand?"

"I . . . I ain't done no harm to nobody."

"I know that Tom, but you can leave this place now. You can go on and seek a better life. Do you understand?"

There was no answer, only a nod.

"Alright. Diane, you can release this spirit now. You can release him and come back to us as Diane Barnes. You can speak to me in your own voice now."

Nothing happened. John waited patiently. "Diane . . .Diane, speak to us. Speak to us, Diane."

It happened very slowly at first. Diane raised her feet off the foot rest, then her legs. She screamed long and hard. When it all stopped, she woke up and stared at John. "Is it over?"

"Yes Diane, It's over."

Chapter 47

Ten Days Later, March 14, 1980

"I don't think so.

"Are you sure?"

Clarence Blackwell looked down. "I'm sure, Diane. You are not pregnant."

Diane rose up on the examining table and let out a deep chest cough. "It still feels like there's something inside me."

"There is, Diane," said the doctor. "It's called bronchitis."

"No, no. It's something in my lower abdomen."

"Diane, we've gone all through this before. All the tests, all the exams, all the x-rays show nothing."

"I can't live through another miscarriage."

"I don't think there's much chance of that. You had a tubal five years ago."

"I know that, but sometimes they don't work."

"This one worked. You are not pregnant, okay?"

"I'm telling you, I can't live through another miscarriage."

"Could you live through another lower GI exam?"

Diane gave the doctor a dirty look, coughed again, and grabbed the top of her head. "Why haven't I had my period in over a month?"

"That's a good question. Why didn't you tell me?"

"Please . . . don't start on me." Diane was certain she wasn't going to tell the doctor about the séance and John

McCauley's conversation with the ghost. She knew Clarence Blackwell would have a hissy fit over that.

"I'm sorry, Diane." He continued in a gentler tone. "You've been under a lot of stress lately, haven't you?"

"Yes."

"Have you been taking the antibiotics I gave you?"

"Yes."

"Have you been getting lots of bed rest?"

"As much as I can. I've been going into work . . ."

The doctor sighed. "Diane, I told you to lay off work. This has been going on for over a week and it's not getting any better."

"I don't have time to lay around in bed. Things are piling up."

"Don't fight me on this. I want you home and in bed for the next three days. Then I want you back here."

Diane groaned and got off the examining table. Dizzy, she staggered and grabbed the doctor's arm.

He guided her to a chair. "I want you home, in bed, Diane. If you don't do as I say I'll put you in the hospital, and I'll use your husband, your sister, your mother, and whoever else I can round up to help me."

She leaned over in the chair against the examining table. "Oh God, I don't deserve this."

"I'll tell you what you deserve, young lady. You deserve the best care possible. You're my baby too. I delivered you. I've got a stake in your well-being.

"Now, are you going to behave yourself? If you are, I'll send you home so you can go to bed."

"I'll behave."

* * *

12:15 P.M.

Homer stepped outside the back door of the old apartment building and filled a bucket with water from the hand pump on the back porch. The Old Dog Tavern that oc-cupied the first floor had been closed by order of the county health department. Heat, electricity, and water had all been shut off, leaving Homer and Anna Lee to pump their own water, light their own candles, and heat their food and cold bodies with a propane camp stove Homer shoplifted from a local hardware store. Years of running, hiding, and fending for himself had taught him how to keep his presence a secret. But Homer knew the wrecking ball was coming soon for the decrepit building, and he would have to pack up Anna Lee and hit the road again.

He turned to go back inside when he heard the neigh-ing of a horse. When he turned around, he saw the most beautiful dapple-gray gelding he had ever seen in his life. The horse reared up on his hind legs, came back down to paw the dirt, and throw his head around. He kept neighing to keep Homer's attention, then scratched three lines in the dirt form-ing an X bisected by a vertical line. Homer walked up, looked down at the pattern, and immediately recognized the symbol of the witch.

Homer stared at the animal and the animal stared back at him. He walked up and looked closely at his eyes. "G. G., is that you in there?" The horse nodded his head and neighed softly. "Well, well. You kept your promise, didn't you?"

The horse nodded again, then trotted around to Homer's backside and stuck his head between Homer's legs. "Okay, okay. I think I know how to mount a horse."

Homer's great grandmother had entered his mind be-fore. A few months ago, when he drank Diane Barnes' water sample laced with camphor flakes, the flakes carried G.G.'s spirit into his brain and told him exactly who had murdered her and how her bones were going to be found. She told him that a horse and a girl would lead the way. Not to worry, the horse and the girl would find him.

* * *

When she got home, Diane had just enough energy to walk through the door and flop down on the couch. So it didn't lift her spirits much when the phone rang.

"Hello?"

"Diane?"

"Yes."

"This is John McCauley. Are you still sick? You sound terrible."

"I've got a little bug. *(cough)* The doctor sent me home to get some rest. I'll be alright."

"I hope so. Listen, the reason I called, you asked me last Friday about Jim and Carolyn Forkner's grandson, Matthew."

"Oh yes, how is he?"

"He's going to be fine. They had to put him in the hospital for a couple of days. His fever finally broke yesterday."

"So it was Reye's Syndrome?"

"Yes, it was touch and go there for awhile. But it looks like they'll be able to bring him home tomorrow."

"That's great news, John." As glad as she was to hear the good news, Diane's voice was still very hoarse and subdued.

"Now, I'm more concerned about you."

"Oh, I'm fine. Well, I'm getting better anyway."

"You're not there by yourself, are you?"

"I am for now. Bill should be home from Crawfordsville any minute."

"Crawfordsville?"

"Yes, he had to pick up something from a customer. He'll be home soon."

"Is there anything I can do for you?"

"No. I'm just going to take my medicine and go back to bed."

"Okay. Would you mind if I called you sometime tomorrow? I hate to be a busybody, but I'd like to make sure you're getting well."

"That'll be fine. I'll talk to you tomorrow."

"Diane?"

"Yes?"

"Is everything else okay around the house?"

"Seems to be. Why?"

"No more disturbances?"

"Oh no. None of that."

"What exactly is wrong? Is it just a flu bug?"

"Actually, it's bronchitis. *(cough)*

"Be careful. That can turn into pneumonia very easily."

Diane smiled. "I know. I'll be a good girl."

"How have Bill and Mary been getting along? Are they well?"

"Yes, they're fine."

"What kind of medicine are you taking?"

"The usual, cough medicine and antibiotics."

"Any of it making you hallucinate?"

"I don't think so."

"You haven't seen any dark-skinned men with long greasy hair have you?"

"Oh no." She coughed again.

"That's a terrible cough."

"I'll take my medicine and get over it."

"Well, if you're sure everything is alright for now . . ."

"John, there's something I just can't seem to put my finger on." Diane was desperate to shout out her concern about her condition without mentioning the ghost. The ghost was absent – so far.

"What's that?"

"It's a lot of little things. Like right now. Somehow the room seems so huge. I mean it's just a living room. But it seems so big, like I was in a cathedral or something. This morning when I got up I felt like I was walking around in a body that was about ten sizes too big for me. Does that make sense?"

"I'm sure it would if I were in Diane Barnes' body."

"Yeah, I suppose."

"Or if there were hallucinations from the medicine."

"No. Medicine has made me hallucinate before. This feels different."

"How so?"

"I don't know." She plucked at her shirt. "It's like everything inside that I know as me is getting smaller and smaller."

"I see."

"What do you see, John?"

"I'm not sure. I'd like to explore these feelings further under hypnosis when you are feeling better."

"I'm not sure I want to do that anymore."

There was a long moment of silence. Then John said, "Alright."

"Is that a problem?"

"Ah, no. These feelings will probably go away spontaneously."

"I hope so."

"The best thing for you to do is get some rest and take your medicine. Are you sure there's nothing I can do or get for you?"

"Oh no, I'll be fine. Thanks for calling, John."

John did not like the way the conversation ended. He thought for a moment. He was having a bad feeling about all this. He'd had this feeling the day before his mother died, and the day before his daughter Lisa died. Was it a premonition? The phone rang.

"Hello?"

"Hi. It's me."

"Yes, Sharon."

"I'm going to be kind o' late getting away from this office. Bob Parsons just called. Judy's missing again."

"Oh for God's sake. How did she come up missing this time?"

"Norma came home from the beauty shop. Judy's schoolbooks were on the living room couch. No sign of Judy. When she looked all over the house and yard, she found the back door standing open and the service door to the barn smashed open. Apparently Doc had busted out of his stall and run off."

"That doesn't make any sense. What did Judy do, go looking for him on foot?"

"I don't think so. The sheriff has some volunteers on ATVs combing the area around the Parsons' estate. No sign of Judy or Doc."

"Lord, this is just what we don't need."

"I asked Norma if there was anything we could do for her. She said she didn't know what it would be. She just felt the need to tell us."

"I don't know what it would be either, Sharon. We're both getting a little old for ATVs."

"Are we still on for tonight?"

"If you get home in time."

"Oh, I won't be that late. If I am, tell Linda Toscanna to stay put. I want to see what she's found."

"I will."

* * *

When Judy got home from school, she went out to the barn to check on Doc just as she had done every day since last October when she and her best friend were reunited. To her horror, she found the small service door smashed and hanging open. She ran into the barn screaming, "Doc! Doc!" The horse stall was splintered and Doc was gone.

"Oh my God! Oh my God! Doc! Doc!" Judy ran back outside, and there was Doc with a strange man straddling his bare back.

Judy was speechless, but the strange man waved and beckoned her to come nearer. "Come on, little girl. Mount up."

Judy gulped, found her voice, and shouted, "Who are you, and what are you doing with Doc?"

"Now that ain't the question. Question is: What is ole Doc here going to do with us?"

"I don't even know what you're talking about. Who are you?"

"My name ain't important. Just get over here and mount up."

"Get off my horse. You stole my horse."

"Horse came to me."

"Bullshit!" Judy headed for the house, but Doc moved over to block her way.

"How did you make him do that?" Judy froze in her tracks.

"I didn't do nothin'."

"You're a lyin' son of a bitch."

"Oooooeeee! Ain't you got a salty tongue in your pretty little mouth."

"It'll get real salty when I call the sheriff and tell him you stole my horse." Judy tried to step around Doc, but the horse moved to block her way again.

"I didn't steal your horse. I told you he came lookin' for me."

"You're a real comedian, aren't you?" Judy tried

again to maneuver around Doc and run to the house, but still Doc blocked her way.

Homer casually held the reins of Doc's rope harness between his fingers. "Comedy ain't my game. I'm here to put my people at rest."

"I still don't know what you're talking about."

"Well, mount up; and I'll show you."

Judy backed away as Doc pranced up closer to her. Homer grinned and said, "Whatchya scared of, cowgirl?" Doc leaned out and licked Judy in the face like he had done so many times before. "You're not scared of Doc, are ya? Doc ain't scared of me." Homer stretched out his hand to her. "Grab my wrist and mount up so we can get goin'."

Judy still hesitated and Doc stepped a little closer.

"Come on!" said Homer. "I know you ain't scared of Doc. Now mount up. We're goin' for a ride."

"Where?"

"Ask Doc."

"Quit messin' with me."

"I ain't messin' with you." Doc neighed and grabbed Judy by the coat with his teeth.

"Ow! Doc, you bit me."

"He didn't bite you." Homer kept his hand out. "Now get up here and quit wastin' time."

Judy grabbed Homer's wrist; he pulled her up as she slung her leg over Doc's back and sat up against Homer's back. She gagged at the stench of Homer's sweat and dirty clothes. "Pew! When was the last time you had a bath?"

"Quit yer belly achin' and hang on. We got some ground to cover."

Reluctantly, Judy put her arms around Homer's waist. "Where are we going?"

"Ask Doc."

"I said quit messing with me."

"Just sit back there and quiet your pie hole, Missy."

"My name's Judy."

"Now that we got that settled, just settle down because your old buddy Doc's in charge now."

* * *

Doc, Judy, and Homer were on the old railroad right of way trotting along the wide dirt path at a leisurely gait. "Recognize where you are?" asked Homer.

"Sort of." Judy still wasn't ready to put all her trust in Homer. So far she and Doc had gotten along fine with the strange man. "Where did you come from?"

"I was born in the big city, but I'm from just about everywhere."

"What's that supposed to mean?"

"It means I go where I can find food and shelter."

"You don't trust me anymore than I trust you, do you?"

"I don't trust nobody 'cept Doc here."

"What makes Doc trust you?"

Homer ignored Judy's question. Doc came to a stop without being reined in. "Shhh! Listen."

"For what?"

"Hear 'em?"

"I don't hear anything."

"You need to get the wax outta yer ears."

"What do . . . ?"

"Listen." There was the sound of small engines off in the distance.   "They're coming from the south. And they're looking for you and Doc."

"How do you know that?"

Homer turned around to look at Judy. "Go figure. We've been out here for a couple of hours. Somebody's at your house by now. You and Doc are missing."

Judy looked up at Homer with a smirk on her face. "You're in deep shit, aren't you?"

"I been in deep shit all my life. Right now all anybody knows is you and Doc are missing. Don't nobody know nothin' about me."

"You wish."

Homer swung one leg over the horse's head and slid to the ground. "Now you listen to me, and you listen good, smart girl. You know about all the haunting around here, don't you?"

"Who doesn't?"

"It's gonna end, and it's gonna end soon, or you and everybody you care about are gonna be mighty miserable for a long time. Your daddy and John McCauley have started building houses where my people were murdered way back long time ago. We need to find their bones and find them quick."

The sound of engines was getting closer as Homer turned his head and looked south. "We'll stay right here. It'll be dark soon. They'll call off their search. That's when we'll start lookin'."

"How are we gonna see in the dark?"

"Doc can see. So can all the other woodland critters."

"What are they gonna tell us?" Judy started crying in frustration and looking around at a landscape that was much too familiar. "Damn it. I want to go home. I hate this place. Please, just let us go home."

"You'll be home at daylight. Now get down here and hunker down. Doc and me's got a job to do."

Chapter 48

"It's Not a Game Anymore"

The day before he'd talked to Diane Barnes, John McCauley had called Linda Toscanna and asked her to help him investigate a mass murder.

"A mass murder?"

"Yes, it happened in the south pasture next to the old Hanson farm house. Bill and Diane Barnes live there now."

"So that's what all the haunting's about! How did you find out a mass murder had taken place?"

"I hypnotized Diane and she channeled one of the spirits."

"Oh, my God!"

"Linda, I have an idea that somebody in the Hanson family may have been involved. That south pasture was never used for anything. No cattle ever grazed. Nothing but weeds ever grew there. Dan Foster built a house there and there's been nothing but trouble since."

"What about now," Linda asked. "Is anything happening?"

"Apparently not. I guess I'm looking for confirmation. Let's see how much hard evidence we can gather."

Linda was so excited by the project she took two days off work to make her rounds of the libraries and newspaper morgues. By 5:00 p.m. she was home. Sadly, she had little to show for her efforts.

March 14, 7:30 P.M.

"John, Linda's here," Sharon McCauley called from the dining room.

"Hi Linda," said John. "Have a seat. I'll be right there."

"What have you got for us?" asked Sharon.

"I spent all day yesterday at the state library poring over old copies of The Indianapolis Sentinel and The Indianapolis Journal. A friend of mine in the library association helped me. She and I went back today and looked through old copies of The Forest County Gazette. I didn't find anything about a mass murder. But there's something that may or may not be important. Two copies of the Gazette from January 1889, and one from March 1889 are missing."

"That sounds suspicious," said Sharon.

"There was one thing I found interesting. During the first week in April, there were six burglaries in one night."

"Burglaries? Any details?" asked John.

"No. The article suggested people be more careful about locking their doors in the future."

John asked, "Were these in the town or out on the farms?"

"They didn't say."

"Any mention of arson?"

"No," said Linda. "Sharon, did you get hold of Connie Wilson at the county historical society?"

"Yes," said Sharon. "She came up empty handed.

Linda asked, "John did you check the abstract on the property?"

"I did that a long time ago. That south pasture has been in the Hanson family since 1850."

John pushed an old ledger book across the table to Linda and Sharon. "Here's something I found the night Aunt Alice died. I went over to lock up her house and got into a little table used as a telephone stand."

"What's this?" asked Sharon.

"Well, it's not a ledger like the cover suggests. It's Grandma Hanson's diary."

"Her diary?" exclaimed Sharon. "John Mac, why didn't you tell me about this?"

Sharon's question and tone of voice irritated John. "Sharon, a lot happened that night. A lot has happened since."

"Look at the pages," said Linda. "Some of them have been ripped out."

"There's a part of a page in there that says something about 'who will judge us all,'" John said. "There is no mention of killing or fire, but it's Grandma Hanson's diary with some of the pages ripped out. That's enough to make us wonder."

He got up and paced back and forth by the dining room table. "That brings us to another matter. I talked to Diane Barnes today."

"Diane!" exclaimed Linda. "How is she? I haven't heard from her in awhile."

"She's sick," said John. "She's got bronchitis. That's not what bothers me. She talks like she may have had some side effects from our channeling session."

"What kind of side effects?" asked Sharon.

"She tells me she feels like everything inside her is shrinking. She feels like something inside is pushing her out of her own body."

"Can't you reverse those effects under hypnosis?" asked Linda.

"She doesn't want to go through that again," said John. "And I don't blame her. It's not a game anymore."

"I didn't mean to suggest that it was," said Linda. "But what do we do now?"

John stuffed his hands in his pockets as he walked over to the far corner of the dining room and said, "I talked directly to the ghost during our channeling session, and he said that he wanted to know where his wife was. I told him she had probably gone on and evolved and reincarnated . . . " John stopped in mid-thought. After a moment he said, "But did she? Did his murdered wife go on? Or is she still here? Is she still haunting Diane?"

"What can we do about that?" asked Linda.

"I'm thinking seriously about another séance. We had one right after Lisa died, and I think it worked."

"It did," said Sharon as she gently thumped the table with her fist.

"I was hoping our research would shed some light on the subject so we could conduct a séance out of what we know, instead of what we don't know. I guess we came up a little short. And that's okay, Linda. You did the best you could. We all did."

"So when and where do we do this?" asked Linda.

"We do it at the Barnes' house as soon as Diane is feeling better."

"This time I'll be the medium," said Sharon.

"If we do it right; if we do it like we did Lisa's séance, any one of us could be the medium."

Linda looked at John then looked at Sharon. They both looked worried. "This is really urgent, isn't it?"

"Yes, it is," said Sharon.

"Linda," John said, "I've never heard Tom Jakob's name mentioned until our channeling session. I want to know what went on between him and my grandparents."

"And why would anybody want to kill him and wipe out his whole family?" asked Sharon.

"And who was he to my grandparents?" asked John. "Was he more than just a tenant farmer?"

Linda closed the diary and leaned forward with her elbows on the table. "John, I have a personal take on this."

She put her hands to her mouth and thought about what to say.

"What is it?"

Linda cleared her throat. "I've made a few friends, especially you and Sharon, since I moved here from Ohio five years ago. Now don't take this the wrong way; but you grew up around here; and maybe you haven't noticed it. But there seems to be a general . . . how can I put it? There seems to be a cold, mean, uncaring attitude in this county. Some of the people seem to be so quick to look the other way when somebody is hurt or robbed or falls on hard times. If they aren't from here and don't have family here, it's like they don't count. If they're having a streak of bad luck, it's their bad luck and nobody else's. Now not everybody is like that. You and Sharon aren't, the people in our little study group aren't."

"But my people were," said John. "You're absolutely right, Linda. Most of the Hanson's were a chilly lot, especially my grandparents.

"Now that I think about it, there's something else to consider. Diane told us those ghostly images she saw were people of color, Native Americans. In the nineteenth century, people of color were murdered in secret where nobody knew or cared, and nobody was ever brought to justice. When I think about how Tom Jakob and his family must have fared in nineteenth century Forest County." He shook his head. "My God, what were they doing on my grandparents farm in the first place?"

Chapter 49

Steamed

"Hey, what's all this noise out here?" Diane stood in the doorway between the garage and the shop and let out a hacking cough.

"What noise?" Bill poked his head up from behind the steel wall of the truck bed.

"That hissing noise." Another hacking cough. "Sounds like steam and some kind o' chugging." More coughs.

"The only noise I hear out here is you coughing your fool head off. Go back to bed, Diane."

"How much longer are you going to be out here?"

"Until I get done, okay?"

"What have you got out here that runs on steam?"

"Nothing. You're sick, Diane. You're hearin' things.

"But what is that noise? I swear I hear steam."

"It's me! I'm steamed, okay? I tell this stupid ass not to have this truck bed sectioned, but does he listen to me? Hell, no! He hauls it to some jackleg who takes the thing apart with a can opener and puts it back together with a soldering iron. Then he dumps it back on me to clean up the mess.

"Just because you're good, people expect miracles out of ya. Well I'm sick of it, and I'm about ready to take the whole damn thing over to his house and tell him to shove it."

Diane was still coughing her head off as she slammed the door to the shop, staggered across the garage floor, and went back into the house. "To hell with him. What does he care if I'm sick or dying?"

Diane noticed a light coming out from under Mary's bedroom door in the darkened hallway. The noise was still all around her. *Hisssss, Chuuuuugg!* She opened the bedroom door and found Mary in her nightgown, sitting at her little desk bent over a stack of books and papers.

"Mary, for God's sake, it's after eleven o'clock."

"I know. But this is due tomorrow."

"Mary, do you hear steam hissing?"

"No, I don't hear anything."

"I must be going nuts. What are you working on?"

"It's a research paper."

"A research paper? In the fifth grade?"

"It's for extra credit. I'm trying to make a good impression on my teacher, Mrs. Chambers."

"You won't make a very good impression by falling asleep in class, Mary."

"I'm not going to fall asleep."

"Yes you are. Now go to bed, and I'll get you up early . . ."

"I'm not going to bed! I've got to finish this!" When Mary turned around to yell at her mother, she finally saw how sick she was. Diane stood in the doorway hacking out a cough that sounded like it was going to toss a lung. Her eyes were black, her nose was red, and sweat poured off her face and arms. She wore nothing but her calf-length gown. Suddenly, Mary rushed to her mother's side. "Oh Mother, I'm sorry. I'll quit. I promise. Here, let's get you back in bed."

"I'll be okay."

Mary took her mother by the waist, walked her across the hall, into the master bedroom, and helped her lie down.

"Oh no! No covers. Please Mary, no covers. I'm burnin' up. God, I'm burnin' up."

"We need to get you to a doctor."

"I've already been to the doctor. Now go to bed. I'll be alright."

Mary rushed to the bathroom, soaked a washrag with cold water, and ran back into the bedroom. Gently, she laid the rag across Diane's forehead.

"Oh, that's nice. Thank you, sweetie. That's real nice."

"Can I get you some aspirin?"

"Already took two just a few minutes ago."

"You're burning with fever."

"I'll be alright."

"Mother please, let Daddy and I take you to the doctor."

"Doctor's office is closed, okay?"

"Then we'll take you to the hospital."

"Don't be ridiculous."

"I'm not being ridiculous. You're really sick." Mary ran the cold rag over Diane's face, neck and shoulders.

"That's nice, baby. Now go to bed, or go work on your paper if you like."

"I'm going to ask Daddy . . ."

"No! No! Don't do that." Diane's outburst strained her whole body. She sighed heavily to catch her breath. "Don't bother your father. He's having a hard time of his own. Now I'll be all right. I'll go back to the doctor in the morning, okay?"

Mary was not consoled, but she said, "Okay."

Diane kept the cold rag on her forehead. It did not make the fire go away, and it would not make the steam go away. *Hiisssssssss. Chuuuugg!*

She might have drifted off, she wasn't sure. But the clock now read 12:15. Bill's side of the bed was still empty. Diane got up, yanked off her nightgown, and went into the bathroom to stand under a nice cold shower. She hung onto the shower nozzle while the water hit her head and cascaded down her back. "Oh, I could die under here. What a nice way to go."

She turned off the water, stepped out of the tub, walked down the hall, then eased Mary's bedroom door open. Her daughter was bent over her desk sound asleep. Diane didn't have the strength to pick her up and put her in bed. "Well, at least she's asleep."

Diane looked down and noticed that it was raining on the carpet. "Oh no, that's me. I'm dripping wet. Better dry off. Then again, maybe not." The fire still burned inside her, and all around her was that unceasing *Hiiiisssss Chuuuug!*

She staggered through the house looking for Bill. He wasn't in the bedroom, the kitchen, or the living room. How about the garage? The light was still on. No sign of Bill. The door leading into the adjoining shop was open. She stepped out into the garage and called out in a faint hoarse voice, "Bill!" No answer. Diane walked naked and wet across the cold concrete floor. She put her hands against the door jam in the shop, leaned in and called, "Bill." No answer. Nothing except: *Hiiissssss Chuuuuggg!*

She walked across the shop floor and called again, "Bill?" Her wet, naked body contrasted sharply with the battered work benches heaped with tools, gas and pneumatic hoses snaking across the floor, and the battered truck bed in the middle of it all. All around, there were pieces of mangled metal that threatened to slash her feet if she didn't watch where she walked. When Diane came to the open back of the bed, she bent over with her hands on her knees and looked underneath. Bill lay on a mechanic's creeper under the floor of the truck bed snoring peacefully. "Good. That takes care of him."

She picked her way across the cold concrete floor and went back in the house. It was the middle of March; she was wet and naked; and still she was on fire.

Hiiiissssss Chuuuug!

She walked into the dark living room and gasped. Mary's favorite peppershaker had come to life. A life-sized Pepper Jane bent over the coffee table, brushing it with a feather duster. She looked exactly like the little ceramic figurine, down to her yellow headscarf, yellow housedress, white apron, and broad black face with thick ruby lips. But tonight there was no ivory smile. When Diane came through the door Pepper straightened up, turned and looked up and down the naked body. Her eyes gleamed in the darkness. She had the look of a tent preacher ready to condemn the naked woman to hell fire and damnation. Instead, she said to Diane, "Better get some clothes on, honey, afore yous gets your death of it."

Diane still had her hand over her mouth as Pepper turned, left the living room, and walked down the hall to the master bedroom, entered and slammed the door. Diane caught her breath, but she remained stuck to her spot in the living room. When she finally was able to move, her feet felt like lead as she walked down the hall and stood in front of the closed bedroom door. She put her hand on the doorknob and turned it very slowly until the latch retracted, and the door swung open. She stepped into the dark room, and the oncoming steam locomotive engulfed her in its fiery boiler. *Chug , Chug, Chug, Chug, Chug, Toooot!*

Through the firebox, through the cab, through the coal hopper, into the passenger car, down the aisle she sailed. She wasn't naked anymore, but she had a hard time staying dressed. One set of clothes after another wrapped around her only to be blown off as she flew down the aisle of each railroad passenger car. Robes, blouses, shawls, hoop skirts, bonnets, scarves all clung to her only to be blown away by the wind she made as she sailed along. Her skin kept changing color from white to red to black to white to red to black. Finally she came to a sudden stop in back of the trailing car, leaning over the railing of the rear platform and looking at the tracks and ties speed by. A bonnet and a long plain brown dress covered her from head to foot. A man and a girl grabbed her by the shoulders and pulled her back.

"Good heavens, child, you almost fell off the train," the man exclaimed.

"Sister, are you alright?" asked the little girl.

"What in the world were you doing back here?" asked the man.

Diane was too stunned to answer. The man and the little girl looked exactly like Bill and Mary.

"What were you doing back here?" the man repeated.

"Let's get her back to her seat," said the conductor standing in the doorway.

"Come on, child," said the man. "My Lord, you could have been killed."

Diane staggered down the aisle and sat down between the young girl and the man.

They were her daughter, her husband, her sister, her father from a previous lifetime. She remembered her father was sending her away because she carried an illegitimate child. She was aware of a lot of things.

She could feel every thread of her ancient clothing against her body. The dream was so real she was aware of everything on, inside and under the train. She saw without eyes, felt without touching, heard without ears. She knew how fast the push rods were working around the drive wheels of the locomotive. She felt the tug of every draw bar between every car. She could even count every fiber of wood in every panel of every passenger car.

"Tickets, please. Tickets, please," the conductor said. When he came to the man and the two girls he asked, "Are you folks going to the end of the line?"

"Is the river at the end of the line?" asked Diane.

"There is a river at the end of every line," came the reply.

"Is there anything beyond the river?"

"You'll have to find out for yourself," said the conductor.

"Where are we?"

"You are in a nightmare, and it's going to get worse."

Chapter 50

Hitting Bottom

On they rode through the green Indiana hills and lush meadows. On they rode past the farms and hamlets and forests. Diane rocked gently in her seat as the steel rails and steel wheels whined beneath her. The long ride, monotony, and constant rocking did not lull her to sleep. Too many new sensations were coming at her like the morning sun rising high in the sky, bringing with it an awareness of the circle of time that Diane had never known before. The earth orbited the sun. The sun orbited the galaxy. Events past and future orbited each other in Diane's new concept of the present. And the flowers and the trees, and the woodland creatures, and the fish in the streams, and the animals in the fields, were all living and giving birth and dying. Diane was aware of them all.

The train slowed and Diane saw that they were pulling into an ancient depot. The conductor walked up and down the aisle and called, "Paris. This is Paris, Illinois."

There was a crowd of waiting passengers standing on the wooden platform in front of the depot. The sign dangling from two chains that identified the town had been ripped apart. Half of it was gone; the other half had twisted around on its chain to conceal the lettering. When the train stopped, the man and the two girls got off and got into a carriage behind a lone horse hitched up and ready to haul them away. In this dream, there were no words between them because there was no time for talk.

As the horse pulled its load down the dirt road, Diane relished every piece of scenery around her. She admired the texture of every leaf and tree bark, the smell of every blossom, and the sound of every barking, chirping, howling animal. All along she had been aware of the presence of new life inside her body. But she was also aware of the thoughts inside her father's head, and they were not pleasant. The songs of the robins and the sparrows were pleasant though. But she heard more than their songs. She heard the straining and laying of eggs in the birds' nests. She saw the trees and flowers like she had never seen them before. They were real, so unlike the illusions that passed for flowers and trees back on earth.

The horse trotted faster. Up ahead lay the dark tunnel filled with stars. Now they were in the tunnel, and a magnificent array of heavenly bodies stretched out all around them. As they came out of the tunnel, the bright sun blazed down, and a wooden bridge stretched out in front of them. There was only half a bridge across the gorge, but that was alright because after all they were going to the river. Diane knew that once they got there everything would be fine.

They could see the end of the bridge now and the horse ran at full speed. He ran so fast that when he got to the gorge the horse and carriage and all its passengers became airborne for a brief moment, then everything and everybody started falling.

This time Diane Barnes hit bottom.

Chapter 51

"Live Diane, Live!"

At the moment the horse-drawn carriage sailed off into midair, Mary awoke with a start. She sat up in her chair and stared at the diagram of the solar system taped to the wall behind her desk. At first she wondered what it was. Then she looked down at the sheets of paper that had stuck to her arms while she snoozed. She raised her arms, peeled off the papers, then looked at the heading of the first page: **The Solar System**. Below it was a wet spot where she had drooled as she slept. Then she remembered promising her teacher that she would have a special report ready by tomorrow. Or was it today? What day was it? Mary looked at the diagram of planets and moons and sun and stars. Its oval lines indicating the orbits of the planets made her feel queasy and afraid. Orbiting planets, orbiting the sun, falling people, falling horses, falling and spinning around and around. All around her the house seemed deathly still and silent. Was she alone in the house? Better find out.

She got up and went looking for her mother. "I suppose she's in bed, but why is the bedroom door closed?" Mary turned on the hall light, crept across the hall, then slowly opened the master bedroom door. The narrow column of light streaming in from the hallway illuminated nothing in the darkened bedroom except the nude body of Diane Barnes lying face down and diagonally across the bed with her feet hanging over the edge. Mary stepped back in shock for just a moment. She hadn't seen either of her parents naked for a long time. She had to force herself to go in and see if her mother was alright.

One touch of her cold skin made Mary think the worst. One hand on her bare back told Mary her mother wasn't breathing.

"Mother? Oh God, no! Mother!" She shook her shoulder and Diane's body bounced lifelessly on the bed. "Mother! Mother! Oh God, please, help her! Help her!" At that moment Mary wasn't sure that God was around. The more she panicked, the more the whole world blurred. She finally mustered the presence of mind to go look for her daddy.

She found her way back out into the hallway and took a couple of moments to decide which way to run. Was he in the bathroom? No not there. She ran down the hall screaming. "Daddy! Daddy!" He wasn't in the kitchen. He wasn't in the living room. A parade of horrible thoughts flashed through her mind as she ran through the house: living the rest of her life without her mother, cooking her own meals, washing her own clothes, keeping her own head on straight instead of her mother doing it for her. The thought that Diane would grow old and die someday within Mary's lifetime had never entered her head.

"Daddy! Daddy!"

Mary threw open the garage door and was momentarily heartened to see the light on, but there was no sign of her father. She raced across the garage floor and into the welding shop. Where was he in all this junk? She kept calling for him between screams and sobs and ran barefoot through the maze of tools, hoses, and jagged metal. Was he behind that metal thing? Was he under it? Mary sliced the instep of her right foot on a piece of angle iron and left bloody foot prints on the floor as she ran around to the back end of the truck bed and found two feet sticking out from under it.

"Oh my God! Is he dead too?" Mary grabbed Bill by the shoelaces and dragged him on the mechanic's creeper out from under the bed while she screamed at him. "Daddy! Daddy!"

* * *

Bill Barnes sailed through space under a bright sunny sky, then he suddenly felt himself being sucked into a dark tunnel. Now somebody was screaming at him, and the ribs of the steel tunnel were flashing before his eyes. For an instant, he thought he was going over the edge. He sat up before coming out from under the truck bed and hit his forehead on the rear bumper. It opened a gash above his right eyebrow and sent blood streaming down his face.

"There's something wrong with Mother! I think she's . . . Oh God, help us!" Mary ran back in the house with Bill in hot pursuit. He still hadn't come wide-awake, but he heard the words come out of Mary's mouth: *Mother . . . Help us!*

He was barely awake until they entered the bedroom and Mary hit the light switch on the wall. Bill was horrified at the sight of his wife's lifeless nude body on the bed, but he turned her over and felt for a pulse in her neck. Nothing. Blood from his face dribbled onto the bedclothes and Diane's chest. He scooped her up and laid her on the floor and dribbled more blood on her chest and the yellow carpet.

"Oh no! No! No! Don't let them find her like this!" Mary screamed. "Cover her up! Cover her up!" She ripped a blanket off the bed and started draping it over Diane.

Bill grabbed her by the shoulders and yelled, "Listen to me! Listen!" His one eye was closed to the stream of blood running down his face. But his other eye glared with desperation. "Go to the phone! Dial 911. Tell them we need an ambulance out here now! Go! Do it now! Your mother's life depends on it!" Bill pushed Mary over toward the bedside phone then went to work on Diane.

He was bleeding all over her so he pulled off his flannel shirt and wrapped it around his head like a turban, covering his bleeding eye. Then he tilted Diane's head back, opened her mouth, pinched her nose, and blew three short bursts of air into her windpipe. Now he had to concentrate. "Fifteen chest compressions and five breaths of air. No, Five . . .No! That's right fifteen chest, five mouth. Damn it! Do it right." He placed two fingers at the base of her sternum, then put the heel of his other hand directly on top of the breastbone and stiffened his arms so they were directly under his shoulders. "Push damn it!" he told himself through clenched teeth as blood oozed out from the flannel shirt bandage he had wrapped around his head. "Live Diane! Live! You think you're gonna leave me alone in this world? You're crazy!"

The emergency medical technician in the back of the big ambulance continued the CPR. No luck. He was still pumping Diane's chest as she was being wheeled into the emergency room. The doctors and nurses tried in vain to shock her back to life. They pumped her chest, pumped her lungs full of oxygen, and shot her heart full of adrenaline. No luck. Diane Barnes was pronounced dead at 3:57 A.M.

Chapter 52

One Step Beyond

Diane was vaguely aware of air being pumped into her windpipe, something hard pressing on her chest, electricity shooting through her, and that old shrinking feeling making her feel disconnected from her body. She thought all the fuss was rather silly. People all over the world were dying at this exact moment. She was amazed and downright giddy to realize that she knew all of them and that she was going to join them in peace and paradise. But first she had a trial to endure.

Diane sank deeper and deeper into a muddy river bottom until the ooze squeezed her in a warm cozy shroud. She shut her eyes and realized she could see without eyes. She held her breath to keep out the water and discovered she no longer had the urge to breathe. Up ahead there was a face that had been badly burned and covered with blisters and charred skin. The face was framed by long black hair tied in pigtails. It was the conductor she had seen on the train, but she had seen him before; she was sure of that. Diane felt herself falling into the face, closer and closer to one eye, closer and closer to the pupil in the beautiful brown iris, now deeper and deeper into the black void beyond the eye. Strange feeling, she was falling up, not down.

She fell through the man's face and the river's muddy bottom and hit hard rock. She felt her clothes being ripped off as she passed through a hole that opened in the stone floor. Beneath the floor was a narrow room with stone walls and another floor covered with straw that cushioned her fall. Her body was swollen and pain shot through her belly.

Suddenly, two women jerked her to her feet. The two nuns on either side of her supported her as the pain raced through her groin and abdomen, and water cascaded down between her thighs. Slowly, she sank to her knees and screamed with pain.

A tiny pointed head popped out between her legs. A shoulder came next, then another shoulder and two arms. The nuns were still holding her arms as the lifeless infant squeezed out of her body and dropped in a still heap. One of the nuns pressed on her belly and the bloody placenta dropped from between her legs.

"It's best this way, my dear," said the other nun as she poured water over Diane's head and shoulders. "His little soul is in heaven now." The burning, stabbing pain was slowly flowing out of her.

The nuns stood her on her feet and dressed her in a long habit just like their own. One of them cut her hair with a pair of scissors very close to her scalp. It was then that Diane noticed there were windows on either side of the stone room. There were people behind each window yelling for help. Diane started walking, but she looked at each face as she passed each window. She was finally seeing them as she should have seen them before. She felt their pain and knew their suffering. Their faces were no longer a blur as they had been before, but their burdens weighed heavily on her shoulders, and once again she turned away from them.

She heard their voices. "How can she be the bride of Jesus and be so cold to us?"

"Come here, Sister. Come here," cried an old man from behind one of the windows. Diane walked over to him and recognized him immediately. The last time she had seen him he was begging money to buy booze. She remembered him now. He represented life on the other side, her life as Diane Barnes, Diane Barnes dressed up in a skirt and blouse and high heels, standing in an office building on the other side of the circle of time.

"You're going to need this, sister. You were as kind to us as you knew how to be. But from here on out, you're going to need this." He handed her a straw hat. "The hot sun is going to bear down on you soon, so take this as a token of our kindness to you."

Diane took the hat and pulled back the scarf of her habit to reveal her closely cropped hair. She bowed her head, put on the straw hat, and when she looked up she knew her whole being had changed. There was no mirror to look at now, but the feel of her mouth told her that her lips were thicker, and one look at her bare hands told her that her skin was now black. She felt a thud and a shooting pain across her back and shoulders. She fell down, turned over, and looked up into the face of a skinny, wretched white man standing over her with a hoe. He was silhouetted against the bright sunny sky.

"What the hell's 'a' matter with you, nigger?" he yelled. "You wanna start bustin' up them clods and pullin' them weeds with yer bare hands? Now grab a hoe and get yer black ass back to work!" The white man kicked her in the rump and sent her on her way.

This time her way was between endless rows of cotton being cultivated and weeded by hundreds of her fellow slaves. They all swung their hoe handles and sang the same song. Diane couldn't understand all the words or pick out any rhythm. It all sounded like a cacophony of squeaks and grunts muttered lazily to ease the monotony of the back breaking labor in the hot midday sun.

Diane heard a young girl scream and she looked around to see where it was coming from. Nobody around her looked up except the big round woman with charcoal skin, a yellow dress, white apron, and yellow scarf. She turned her broad face to Diane and her big eyes glared with fright, anger, urgency. "Go to her, Prissy," said the big woman. "It's one of your children. I do declare it's the baby."

Why it's Pepper Jane, Diane thought. In this life and the next, Pepper Jane was there all the time. And she wasn't Diane, and she wasn't Sister. She was Prissy. She looked for the overseer. He was busy with another slave. So she ran to the edge of the nearby meadow. The girl's muffled screams were coming from behind a tree. A sense of outrage over-powered her. It was her little one. It was the baby. Prissy hid behind the tree and peeked around the corner, then gasped at the horrible sight. Three white boys had the little girl held fast by her arms. One of them held his hand over her mouth to silence her. The other held a knife to her throat.

A third boy stood in front of her and pulled up her dress. Then he glanced over at Prissy and yelled, "Look! Nigger spy! Let's get her."

Prissy knew she was had. She turned and started to run. But it took no time for the boys to catch up with her and drag her to the ground. The pain in her back was horrendous. She knew she was being stabbed, but when they rolled her over she found herself looking up into the face of a white woman in a white coat, a long hypodermic needle in her hand, and a worried expression on her face. The woman was look-ing off to the side and listening to a high-pitched tone. She looked down at Diane, shook her head, and pulled a white sheet over her face.

Diane felt a snap in the middle of her body. The sense of boundary that had defined the shape of her body all her earthly life disappeared. She floated up and hovered over the gurney where her white shrouded body lay and noticed that a silver umbilical cord was unwinding out of her navel and ex-tending down to an opening in the white sheet. She soared up through the ceiling of the hospital emergency room and passed through one layer of concrete after another. There were brief flashes of light between each layer. Then Diane flew above a tall building and soared higher and higher into the night sky.

The black sky split open as if it had been cut with a razor. White light spilled out and engulfed Diane in its warmth. Now everything around her was white and everything was moving. She fell up through a spectacular tunnel of light that was so bright it illuminated the sky and the cosmos above her, the earth and sea below her. Waves of energy, harmony and music surrounded her. The music was not the crude striking of sound against a fleshy eardrum. It was the movement of fragments into creation, dissonance into harmony, chaos into order, imbalance into symmetry. It was music that transcended the weakness of voice and the imperfection of instruments.

She looked around her and saw every soul that had ever lived. She knew when they were going to be born and when they were going to die.

In the hereafter Diane saw, and felt, and heard new concepts of the soul. Love and hate, fear and envy, pity and shame, lost all meaning. In their place stood knowledge of things unknowable in the earthly plane, things unknowable to a mortal being. But then the being that had been called Diane Barnes was not a mortal anymore, not in this place, not in this time.

In the river were reflections of things past, reflections of Diane as a little girl, reflections of the realization that Diane no longer belonged to any parent or child or husband. She belonged to all souls alive and departed.

It all seemed so natural that she could know everything that was going on in the earthly circle of time and the circles of time and space beyond. She was aware of every atom and every molecule in every plant, mineral and animal.

The light filled her with ecstasy and with music and voices that stretched across an infinite span of the cosmos. How sweetly the angels sang to her!

Suddenly the angels stopped singing, and another chorus of voices spoke to her.

"You have seen the river.

You have seen the light.

The light and the river are life everlasting.

But your life on the other side of the circle of time

Is not yet fulfilled.

Your life on the other side of the circle of time

Must go on."

The loudest voice in the chorus belonged to a man who had left his earthly plane and his body of blistered and charred skin, dark hair, and flashing eyes. Diane recognized him as Tom Jakob. He was part of a chorus of guides who had flown and paddled and run through the river of time for thousands of earthly years.

Tom came out of the crowd and wrapped his arms around Diane. He carried her through a dark tunnel to the edge of what she recognized as blue sky, sunlight, and the gateway to the earthly plane. Tom said nothing to her. He pushed her gently through the gate and Diane started falling.

She fell backward through the tunnel of light. All around her she heard the wailing of the mourners and the dead, the killers and the lovers, the creators and the destroyers.

Chapter 53

Emergency Traffic

Louella Pritchett had nodded off in the motel office, then woke with a start when the loud voice came over the police scanner.

"Medic One. Medic One, standby, I've got a hysterical child on the line." The dispatcher's voice was faint in the background, but Louella could make out: "Calm down. Calm down. County road . . . " The voice became louder. "Medic One, start a run to County Road 600W. I'm getting an exact house number now."

There was silence for a moment then, "Medic One, that's 4771 North County Road 600W. Medical emergency, 4771 North County Road 600W. Medic One respond. Zero three hundred hours. KMX965, Center Township."

Louella sat for several seconds wondering if she had heard the dispatcher right. "County Road 600W? That's Bill and Diane Barnes' house. My God, what's happening now?" She reached for the phone to call her cousin John.

He had been pacing the floor all night. As soon as the phone rang, John knew his world was about to cave in around him. When Louella gave him the news, his heart sank to the bottom of his stomach. Before hanging up he said, "I'm on my way to the hospital now."

Sharon looked up at him. "It's about Diane, isn't it?"

"I'm afraid so," said John as he rushed out the door.

"Wait. I'll go with you."

"You're not dressed. I am," John called over his shoulder.

* * *

As soon as John entered the hospital emergency room, he checked with the front desk. "Excuse me," he said to the harried nurse. "I'm looking for information about the Barnes family. Can you help me?"

"I'm sorry, sir. What was the name again?"

"Barnes."

"Barnes? That sounds familiar. Oh, here we are . . .ah. . .I guess we have a whole family of Barnes. One was a DOA."

DOA! Hearing it was like inhaling gasoline fumes. The sensation of fire erupted in John's chest, and his heart raced. "No, that's impossible," he said. "I'm looking for a Bill or Diane Barnes. They're a young couple in their thirties."

"Yes, sir. We have a Diane Barnes, white female, 32." The nurse spoke matter-of-factly, then looked up at John. "I'm sorry, sir. Are you a relative?"

John stared at the nurse and, with no consideration about how sick he knew Diane to be, he said, "I'm a friend. Now you don't understand. I'm referring to a perfectly healthy woman. There's no way she could be DOA."

The nurse regarded John with pity, looked down at her records, then back at John. "I'm so sorry. Diane Barnes came in a little before 4:00 . . .DOA."

John sighed and asked, "Is the family here yet?"

"If you didn't see them in the north hallway when you came in, you might go through that door and check the south hallway."

"Thank you. I'm sorry I spouted off like that."

"Sir, I'm sorry for your loss," said the nurse.

John turned away from the desk and headed for the south hallway. He knew Diane hadn't been well. Why, he wondered, had he said she was? And now she was dead. He couldn't accept that. He walked into the crowded hallway abuzz with doctors and nurses and paramedics scrambling in all directions. He almost collided with Clarence Blackwell.

"John, what are you doing here on a night like this?" Doctor Blackwell asked.

"I'm looking for the Barnes family. Have you seen them?"

"Yes. Did they tell you about Diane at the front desk?"

"Yes."

Doctor Blackwell sighed, shook his head, and almost broke down in tears. "John, we did everything we could to save that girl. I saw her this morning, and I knew she was sick; and I ordered some tests on her."

"What was wrong with her?"

"We still don't know. She was complaining about a stubborn cough. I examined her, ordered a chest X-ray. My diagnosis was bronchitis. For some reason, she thought she was pregnant again. I ran a test and told her she wasn't. It just doesn't make any sense at all."

John's heart pounded harder now, and he was afraid Clarence Blackwell was going to ask about matters of the occult John was not prepared to deal with right now. "Where is the rest of the family?"

"I think they're at the end of the hall. The husband and the little girl are still being treated."

"For what?"

"There was some sort of accident at the home. In addition to Diane, Bill cut his eye on something; and the little girl stepped on some jagged metal. They could sure use a friend like you right now, John. They're all in pretty bad shape."

John leaned against the wall and pushed a lock of hair off his forehead. "This is all insane. I just...I was just talking to her this morning."

"I hear that all the time. Spend a week or two down here. It'll show you just how fragile life can be."

"Thanks, Doctor Blackwell. Thanks for being here."

Pam and Emily, wide-eyed with shock, were settled on a long bench against a white wall. At the sight of John McCauley, Pam jumped to her feet and fell into his arms.

John looked down at his old friend, Emily Petersen. "Emily, what in the world happened?"

"John, we just don't know," she said between sobs. "Mary woke up in the middle of the night. She found her lying there. She was so still."

"John, we can't go back in that house just yet," said Pam. "None of us can bear the sight of that place right now."

"Listen," said John. "You don't have to. I'll go over there and make sure all the doors are locked. The place is empty I suppose."

Emily nodded her head. "I suppose."

Pam said, "Oh, we need to call Charlie Boatright. He's Bill's best friend. Charlie will want to know."

"Do you have his number?" asked John.

"I don't have it," said Pam. "It's probably on the desk directory in the living room. Oh, you might need a key."

"I've got a key in my purse," said Emily.

In her struggle to find the key, Emily spilled the contents of her purse all over the terrazzo floor in front of her. "Oh God, I can't do anything right," she sobbed. Pam tried to pick up the mess.

"Pam, take care of your mother," said John. "I'll find the key."

* * *

Clarence Blackwell watched John McCauley leave after he picked up the contents of Emily's purse. Pam and Emily were still crying. It broke the doctor's heart, and he knew he couldn't leave them like this with nothing to hold onto. He hurried back to the emergency room and entered just in time to see a woman doctor pull back the privacy curtain and reveal a shrouded body on a gurney. Doctor Blackwell walked up to her. "Let's leave the curtain pulled for now. I want to let the family have a final goodbye. Where are the husband and daughter?"

"They're on the opposite side over there." The woman doctor pointed to a far corner of the big treatment area.

"Okay. I'm going to bring the mother and sister in here. We can at least do that much for them. It'll only take a few minutes."

Clarence Blackwell peeked in one of the curtained treatment areas and found Mary Barnes strapped to a gurney, shivering and crying, while one of the interns stitched together a bloody gash in her foot. Her eyes were squinted shut as tears streamed down her face and her mouth quivered. Blackwell found Bill Barnes in the next curtained area sitting in a chair while another intern stitched a bloody gash in his forehead. Bill had his eyes shut as he breathed heavily with the back of his head pressed firmly against the wall. The old doctor walked back to the hallway and found Emily and Pam sitting patiently on the same hard bench staring into space. He walked up and touched Emily's shoulder. "If you ladies want to do this, I have arranged to have Diane left in the ER for awhile. It's not the best place to say goodbye, and you don't have to . . ."

"Thank you, Clarence," said Emily. "Would you lead the way?"

As they entered the big treatment area, Blackwell took her by the arm while Pam took her other arm, and walked Emily up to the side of Diane's corpse.

Clarence Blackwell very delicately raised the end of the cover and folded it down revealing the comatose face of Diane Barnes. Emily gasped and burst into tears. Pam grabbed her around her shoulders, closed her eyes, and rested her chin on Emily's shoulder while she cried and cried.

Emily broke away from Pam, grabbed Diane by the shoulders, hugged her, and sobbed hysterically while Pam reached under the sheet and took Diane's hand. Clarence Blackwell knew he wasn't needed here for a few moments, so he slipped around the curtain and stood in the middle of the treatment area. He had never felt so helpless and angry, not knowing what killed Diane or what could have been done for her.

The hapless doctor stood and stared up at the overhead lights while tears welled up in his eyes. He knew he couldn't perform miracles or save all his patients. He had lost patients before; most of them very old. But Diane was so young and full of life and so very special. He loved her like a daughter, having delivered her and her daughter Mary. With the privacy curtains between him and Diane's family, Clarence Blackwell broke down and cried his heart out.

As he cried, Clarence heard a woman singing, not knowing if it were Pam or Emily. She was singing the Lord's Prayer with a strained, pitiful falsetto ring to the melody. The song came to an end with both women crying, and suddenly there were screams from behind the curtain. Emily and Pam shouted together, "She's alive!"

Chapter 54

Blood and Cotton

At first it was so beautiful. A woman's voice was close by and singing, not reciting, but singing so very softly, "Our father which art in heaven . . ."

The music was old and familiar and the voice was near and dear to her. She could see, but she couldn't see all around her like before. She could hear that lovely voice, but it wasn't as clear as the music she had heard before. She was flesh and she hurt all over. There was a hand holding her hand and warm breath caressing her face. Reflexively, she opened her eyes and squeezed the hand and winced as screams pierced the air and rattled her eardrums.

Then there was movement and voices all around her, and hands all over her, and a blur sailing by as she was pushed along under bright lights. They hurt her eyes so she kept them closed and stared at the glowing blood vessels behind her lids. There were people around her pushing her down a tunnel. Their footsteps clattered along as they ran alongside her. They shouted about giving her something. There was talk about blood pressure, IVs, some kind of scopes. There was the smell of cotton sheets. This was not good. There was something bad about cotton, something about cotton and hoe handles, and a white overseer and the overseer's son forcing her daughter to . . . Her daughter! She had a daughter. Her name was Mary. "Run Mary! Run!" Diane shouted.

"Mary's okay," she heard a woman say close to her ear. "Mary's fine. Everything's fine."

Everything was not fine. The smell of cotton made her sick with fright. It made her taste something she didn't want to taste, the bile sliding out of her stomach and flowing up her esophagus. She started to heave.

"Roll her over!" a male voice shouted. "Roll her over! She's going to vomit."

Another voice: "Aw, God, it's going to go all over."

"I don't care. Get her on her side before she chokes."

The smell of cotton was replaced by the smell of a rich, pungent fluid coming out of her mouth and splattering on the floor below.

"Get an orderly up here. Get this mess cleaned up."

"Never mind that. Keep moving. Get her to ICU."

Suddenly it felt like her insides had been torn apart. "It hurts," Diane whined. "Oh God, it hurts so bad."

"What hurts?" asked the male voice. "What hurts, Diane?"

"I just had a baby." Diane sobbed hysterically. "It's dead. Oh God, it's dead. It's all my fault."

While Diane wailed, a soft hand stroked the side of her head. "There's no baby, Diane. The hurt isn't from a baby. We'll make the hurt go away in just a little while."

* * *

There were bloody footprints across the living room carpet when John McCauley entered the front of the house. All the lights were on as he walked down the hall and into the bedroom. The covers had been ripped from the bed and thrown all over the floor. There was blood everywhere, all over the bedclothes and the carpet. Clarence Blackwell had said that there had been an accident. What kind of accident? This looked almost like a murder scene.

John thought, *I came here for something, something on the desk in the living room. What was it? A phone directory. What was the name? I think it started with a B.*

The phone in the living room rang and John ran to pick it up. "Hello?"

"John, Diane's alive! My God, she's alive!"

John didn't recognize the frantic voice at first. "Who is this?"

"It's Pam. John, she's alive. She's alive."

"Pam, I . . .are you . . ?" He sighed. "I'm sorry Pam. I've had a bit of an overload tonight."

"John, did you hear me? Did you hear what I said?"

"Yes, it's a miracle."

"Listen! John for God's sake, we all thought she was dead. Mother . . . Oh God . . .Mother."

In the background he heard Emily say, "Give me that phone." When she came on the line Emily shouted, "John, Diane is alive. I swear to God she's alive. And you know what?" Emily gasped and choked and coughed, and John couldn't tell if she was laughing or crying or both. "You know what John McCauley? I brought her back to life. I did. I swear. I could not let my daughter go. I sang right into her ear and pleaded for her to come back to me. Guess what? She did! She did it John. She came back to me."

John heard what he thought was Emily sobbing and the phone receiver falling on the floor. Pam came back on the line and said, "Are you still there, John?"

"I'm still here. What about Diane? Where is she now?"

"She's in intensive care. The doctors are dumbfounded. They can't believe it either. John, did you hear what I just told you?"

"Yes, she's in intensive care."

"She's alive. John, Diane's alive! I held her hand . . . and . . . she . . . she squeezed my hand . . . and she's alive. Oh my God, she's alive."

"I heard that. What about the rest of you? What about Bill and Mary?"

"We're fine. Bill and Mary are fine."

"Bill and Mary were hurt."

"They're fine now."

"You sent me over here for something. What was it?"

"I don't remember, John. Just get back here."

Chapter 55

Their Delicate Conditions

The Intensive Care Unit at Cates Memorial Hospital was on the second floor. Only one member of the immediate family was allowed inside the room, but John found Pam sitting in the small waiting area in the hall outside. Sharon was with her.

"Sharon, what are you doing here?" asked John.

"Why shouldn't I be here?"

"I'm sorry," said John. "I'm just . . . I guess it's my night to say all the wrong things." He took a chair next to Pam. "What happened here?"

As Sharon sat on the other side of her and patted her shoulder, Pam said, "She died. The doctors pronounced her dead and were ready to take her into the operating room to do a post mortem. Doctor Blackwell was good enough to let us say goodbye to her in the emergency room. While we were there, Mother took her face in her hands and sang the Lord's Prayer right into her ear. I was holding her hand and all of a sudden Diane squeezed my hand." Pam's voice cracked and she started to cry.

Sharon got up and walked over to the entrance to Diane's room and looked in. She came back and sat down by Pam. "Emily and Diane are both resting peacefully right now."

"What kind of shape is Emily in?" asked John.

Sharon said, "She's sitting in a chair next to the bed with her head resting on the side guard."

"Have the doctors given any explanation for what happened?"

"None," said Pam.

"Where are Mary and Bill?"

"They're still in the emergency room," said Pam. "Mary . . . Poor little Mary . . . She's the one who found her mother. They tell her she's dead, then they tell her she's alive. It's just too much for a little girl. They gave her a sedative to calm her down and kept her on a stretcher . . . or a . . . whatever you call those things."

John took a deep breath. "So they don't know what she died of, and they don't know how she managed to come back to life."

"I don't even care about that anymore," said Pam. "She's alive. She's my little sister, and she's alive." Pam leaned on Sharon's shoulder and cried.

Sharon said, "Honey, we'll stay at the hospital with you and your mother if you want us to."

Pam shook her head. "That won't be necessary. We have each other."

"What are they doing for Diane?" asked John.

"I don't even know," said Pam. "They come in and draw blood and leave."

"It's probably too soon to tell what to do," said Sharon.

Pam looked at Sharon then at John. "You guys are welcome to stay, but you don't have to."

There was little John and Sharon could find out at the hospital and little they could do for Diane or her family. They drove home as the sky was showing a faint glow of pink shining through the early morning haze. John flopped on the living room couch and fell asleep almost instantly.

* * *

A beam of sunlight coming through the front window, and a ringing phone, shook John out of his sound sleep. He rolled off the couch and grabbed the phone sitting on top of the old Atwater Kent radio. "Hello?"

"John, it's Norma. I wonder if you and Sharon could come over right away. We found Judy. Or . . . I guess . . . ah . . . I should say she found her way home. She and Doc both. Bob said you might be able to help out with . . .with our little situation here."

"What's wrong? Is Judy alright?"

"I think so. Please . . . could you come right away. Please."

"We'll be right there."

* * *

John drove into the circular drive in front of the Parsons' mansion and stopped along the side of the garage. The house was a classic antebellum structure of all brick with a colonnaded portico in front. The garage door was on the side of the house facing away at a right angle to avoid detraction from the rest of the neo classic architecture. John and Sharon walked around to the open service door and gasped at what they saw.

The overhead door was closed. Inside, there was a thick bed of straw on the floor, and Judy Parsons' beautiful gray gelding lying in the middle of it. He had his head resting in Judy's lap as she stroked his neck. She looked up, her blond hair hanging down in wet tangled strands, her face dirty and pale, and her eyes empty of all expression. The little bucolic scene contrasted sharply with the workbench, tools, and shelves of paint and cleaning supplies around the walls. When John and Sharon entered, Doc raised his head, looked at them, and neighed softly.

"My God, are they alright?" asked Sharon.

"Doc is just tired," said Norma. "We're worried about Judy." Bob stood behind Norma, both of them in jeans and T-shirts with their hair disheveled and their eyes reflecting how tired they all were.

"They were out all night," said Bob. "Doc came trotting in here about 7:00 this morning. Judy was so tired she fell off Doc's back. I had to catch her to keep her from hitting the ground." Bob stepped lightly over to Judy, squatted down, and put his hand on her head. She jerked away from his touch and stared down at Doc as she kept stroking his neck. Bob looked up at John with a worried look. "She won't talk to us. When she does . . . it's like . . . crazy talk."

"What does she say?" asked Sharon.

"She says . . ."

"I know where the bones are buried." Judy did not look at John or Sharon or her parents.

"What bones?" asked John.

"Murdered bones. Murdered me. They murdered me." Judy kept staring at Doc and stroking his neck.

An electric buzz ran through John's chest and arms. He could feel goose bumps all over them. *Murdered me? She's seen the ghost. She's been with the other ghost, the ghost of Tom Jakob's wife.* "Judy, did you see somebody last night?"

"Yes."

"Who?"

"I don't know. I think I was dreaming. Maybe not. But I saw her. I saw her in the flash of a blast . . . a . . . shot, gun . . . gun shot."

"Where did you go last night?" asked John.

"To the woods. That man said the bones were buried in the woods."

"What man?"

"A man. Strange man. I don't know. Me and him . . . we rode Doc out into the woods."

"Where in the woods? Do you remember where?"

"I don't know." Judy started to cry and laid her head on Doc's neck. "I'm so tired. Poor Doc's so tired. We looked for the bones all night."

"Did you find them?"

"I just want to sleep."

John looked up at Bob and Norma. "We need to get her in the house. I don't know about Doc here."

"Doc needs to stay where he is until I get the barn fixed." Bob bent down and stroked the horse's withers. "God help me, I thought we lost them for sure this time." He reached out to touch Judy's head, then jerked his hand away when she woke up with a start and pushed herself to a sitting position with her eyes bugged out.

"They're here!" Judy gasped. "That woman said they were right here."

"Right where?" asked John. "What woman are you talking about?"

"The woman with the baby. Oh God! Somebody shot her."

Doc stirred, raised his head, and waved his front and hind legs around. The small effort wore him out and Judy stroked his neck to calm him down. "Shhhh. It's okay, baby. We're in a safe place now."

"What woman?" John asked again. "Where were you?"

"I . . . I can't remember exactly." She stared into space for a moment. "The deer . . . that's it, the deer and her baby. They showed me the way to the house."

"What house?" asked John.

Norma spoke up. "We need to get her to a doctor."

"No!" said Judy. She took a deep breath. "I remember now. The deer and her baby showed Doc and me how to get back. They showed us where the bones were buried and showed us . . . way off in the distance. There was a light. It was the light from a house. Your house. It was your house, John.

"No! It wasn't your house. But you were there. You were there last night."

"Last night? I was there last night? At what house?"

"I don't know."

John silently chastised himself. He knew what house, the Barnes home. "Was this house on the other side of an open field?"

"Yes." Judy looked at John with an expression of recognition.

"You came to the edge of the woods and saw a light on at the house."

"And your car parked in the driveway. That's it. Now I know."

"Judy, could you find your way back there?"

"Back where?"

"To the field, the woods, to where the bones are buried?"

"I don't know."

"Do you think Doc could find his way back there?"

"I don't know."

Bob said, "John, don't lean on her. We need to get her to a doctor."

"No! I can find my way. I think I can find my way."

John stood and pulled Norma and Bob together. "Last night we almost lost Diane Barnes. She and Bill and Mary were at Cates Memorial . . .and . . . we don't know what was wrong with her, but she almost died."

Norma said, "She almost died? Oh my God. Is that the house with all the ghosts?"

"Yes."

"You're not getting my daughter near that place," said Bob.

John looked at Norma, then at Bob. "Listen to me, both of you. This ground has been cursed and haunted for three generations. I think we may have a chance to stop it once and for all. Whether you like it or not, Judy is as involved as anybody."

"What do we do now?" asked Norma.

"We let her show us where the bones are buried . . .if she can. Lord help us all, I pray so hard that she can."

"For God's sake she's just a kid," said Bob.

"Bob," said Norma. "That kid has done a lot of growing up since last fall. Let's follow John's lead."

"Thanks, Norma," said John. "Judy's going to need a while to get rested. Until then . . . I just wish I knew who she was out with last night."

Chapter 56

Four Days Later

The moving van that had brought the Barnes family to their new home was the same one now parked in front of the house waiting to move them out. The truck driver had a different helper with him this time, and the helper didn't like being here at all. He got down from the cab and looked around with wide, anxious eyes, lips pursed tightly together, hair slicked back against his head, and his hands stuffed deep in his pockets. He was stone cold sober, but the gin blossoms on his cheeks belied an old habit. He looked at the house for a long time, then turned back toward the truck and shivered.

"Hey, what's the matter, Fred?" the driver asked.

"I don't like this place. I've been here before."

"Really? When?"

"Over a year ago. I pushed out the crawl space. This place has been giving me the creeps ever since."

"Why?"

"That's the worst part. I don't know why."

In front of the moving van sat Charlie Boatwright's Ford Ranger and Bill Barnes' black Dodge Ram pickup. The big white Pontiac screeched to a halt behind the moving van, and John McCauley jumped out and stood at the foot of the driveway while Bill Barnes exited the garage carrying a large miter saw. Charlie was right behind him with a load of kitchen utensils. "Bill, what's going on here?" asked John.

"What does it look like? We're leaving. We've had enough. It's over, John. The only way to get rid of the ghosts is to leave." Bill laid the big miter saw in the back of the truck bed and slammed the tailgate shut.

"Bill, you don't have to do this. I've got Bob and Judy Parsons in the car with me," said John. "We can . . ."

"John, it's over. We tried. We all did. I'm sorry it didn't work out. I'm sorry I ever bought this house. I thought we were getting a good deal."

"You were."

"No. I wasn't."

"Where are you going?" asked John.

"We're putting our stuff in storage for now. Then we're going to live elsewhere."

John stood back and shook his head while he watched Charlie and Bill walk back into the house and come back out, each with a load of clothes they stuffed into the back seat of Bill's truck.

John walked over to Bill and said, "Bill, it's not over. You can still have a life here; you can still have a business here, a good life, a good business."

Bill slammed the door of the truck and turned to John. "I told you it's over. Don't try to change my mind now."

"Bill, we can end this misery right now, today." John followed Bill and Charlie back to the front door. "Please, if you'll just give me a chance to explain."

Charlie stopped and turned to Bill. "Why don't you guys stay out here and talk? I can haul some more kitchen stuff and some tools out."

"I ain't got time for that," said Bill.

"Yes, you do," said Charlie. "Now quit being such a pig head and give the man a chance."

Bill stayed at the front stoop and took a deep breath. "What do you want?"

"First of all, where's Mary?"

"She's at the hospital with Pam," said Bill.

"How is Diane doing?"

"She's sedated most of the time," said Bill. "Her bronchitis is still bad, and the doctors are afraid it's going to turn into pneumonia."

"Where's Emily?" asked John.

"She's at home resting. This thing almost killed her too. She looks like hell."

"Listen to me," said John. "Diane is going to survive, right?"

"I'm sure she will." He grimaced. "I hope she will."

"And when she comes home from the hospital, she's going to need to come home to a familiar house."

"Not this house," said Bill.

"Then where?"

"We're moving in with Emily. I don't want to, but we don't have a lot of choice."

John sighed. "Bill, with all due respect to your mother-in-law, you're going to an unfamiliar, crowded, and unsettled home for Diane. Emily didn't move into that house until I sold it to her twelve years ago. If it was the house that Diane grew up in it would be different, but it's not. This is her house, right here. This is her home."

"Not anymore."

John sighed and took a step back. "I've got Judy and Bob Parsons out in the car. Judy can help us."

"How?"

The two-man moving crew was close by and hauling load binder straps out of the utility boxes on the under side of the truck. John glanced at them and lowered his voice. "Bill, Judy has had a vision. She told me all about it on the way over here. She had a vision like yours. Remember? Out in the shop, you were welding that truck together; and one of the ghosts appeared to you too."

"I don't want to talk about that anymore," said Bill

"You don't have to. The ghosts who've been dogging

you all this time, Judy knows where their bones are buried."

"I don't want to talk about that either. I just want out of here."

Charlie Boatright was coming out the door with another box of tools as John said, "Please, Bill. This moving business is never pleasant even under better circumstances. Now you've got a sick wife and a terrified daughter, and you're right in the middle of doing something that may make them worse."

Bill got in John's face. "Don't tell me what to do, old man. We're all scared to death of this place now. And we're moving out, and we're moving out now. You got that?"

John didn't back down. He saw Charlie come up and slap his hand on Bill's shoulder. "I don't get it. Bill, too many people have put out too much sweat and tears to let it all end this way. That includes you, and you can help us put this thing to rest once and for all."

Charlie turned Bill around and forced him to walk away from John. From the short distance between them John heard Charlie whisper, "Give the man a chance." His voice faded to a whisper John couldn't make out. When Charlie finished, he walked up to the moving crew. "We need to put this move on hold. We'll call you when we need you."

The moving van driver looked flummoxed, and he started to say something to Charlie. But Charlie turned and walked away before he had a chance to say a word. The driver and his helper finally shrugged and got back in the truck.

Bill turned back to John. He still looked angry and upset. "You and your friends there have until the sun goes down. After that the house is vacant."

* * *

The three men and a teenage girl walked across the backyard, across the open field toward the woods. Bob Parsons held Judy's hand until they got to the edge of the field where Judy shook loose from his grip and started taking long strides across the rows of mangled corn stalks.

As she walked, she kept turning and looking back at Bill and Diane's house. Suddenly she froze in her tracks and looked up as a huge crow screamed and flew up above the treetops. John came up alongside her and saw the look of fear on her lovely upturned face. "It's alright, Judy," he said. "Nothing's going to hurt you out here now."

"I know. I'm just trying to keep my bearings."

She watched the crow fly out of sight, then she turned around and looked at the three men behind her. Her father's worried face was wrapped in the upturned collar of his fur-lined coat. Bill fidgeted and shuffled his feet. He kept his black cowboy hat pulled low over his eyes. John McCauley was the only one who looked confident. The wind ruffled the fur of his sable hat as he smiled at her. She returned the smile, her blue eyes flashing, and her pretty mouth creasing her porcelain face.

Her father glanced over at John. "Are you sure you know what you're doing?"

"No. But Judy does."

Bob shook his head. "You always do this to me. You talk me into something that I know is no good, and about half the time we both wind up in trouble."

"I've never gotten us into any trouble we couldn't get out of."

"Well, sometimes it's wound up costing both of us a lot of money. Besides, this is my daughter we're talking about, John. Now she needs a doctor. You understand what I'm saying to you? She needs a doctor."

John stepped closer. "Not now Bob, we're on a roll. Judy's on a roll."

"On a roll?" He waved his arm. "John, look at us, three bozos out in the boonies leading her on a wild goose chase."

"She's not chasing, Bob. She's leading. Come on, let's go. We're all doing fine."

They were almost to the tree line on the east side of the field when a sudden movement from out of the corner of her eye caught Judy's attention. She turned with a jerk just in time to see a doe and her young fawn bound across the furrows and disappear into the thicket. "This way!" she shouted and started running toward the spot where the deer had entered the tree line. She scrambled part way through the woods then stopped to look around. "There they are!" She pointed at a small clearing beyond the twisted brambles then looked back at the men. "There they are!"

Her excited look clouded over when she saw the looks on everybody's face. They all shrugged and shook their heads. "What are they?" asked John.

"Look at her!" Judy shouted impatiently. "A doe and her fawn. She's standing right there, pawing the spot where . . ." Judy turned to look back at the clearing. "Oh, they're gone now."

Judy ran toward the clearing, batting tree branches and twisted vines away from her path, and never looking down. The three men were close behind. When they came to the small clearing, Judy stopped and looked down at what appeared to be a perfect circle of snow in the middle of a bare patch of ground. She knelt down and began brushing the snow away. Bob wanted to get closer, but John stopped him.

The bare ground was moving. First, it caved in a little. Then small protrusions began to erupt in the bare earth to form a brow, nose, chin and lips of a human face. The mouth opened wider, and a baby's loud wail came out of the ground. It was so loud it sent shock waves through the forest and made everybody hold their ears. Judy stood, held her ears, and backed up across the little clearing. She stumbled and landed at her father's feet looking straight up at him. Bob grabbed her and buried her in his embrace. As soon as he did, the wail of the baby came out of Judy's mouth. Bob looked at her and blanched at the sight of her wide eyes and wide-open mouth with the infant's screech coming out of it. He pressed her body closer and said to John, "This is your fault. You need to make all of this stop." He looked up. "Make it stop, John! Make it stop!"

Judy quit crying and went limp in her father's arms. Her eyes fluttered, and she looked around wondering what had knocked her down.

John eased over to the bare spot in the snow and looked into a shallow grave. A tiny human skull was in the middle of it with some bone pieces scattered around it. "She knew where the bones were buried." John reached out to touch the tiny human skull then drew his hand back. There was something unholy and unknowable here that made even John McCauley squeamish. What was it, the skull of an infant and the scream in broad daylight where he used to hear a baby's mournful cry late at night when he was a small boy and still afraid of the dark?

"I'll go get the sheriff," said Bill.

"I wouldn't bother," said John. "There's nothing left now but bones and ghosts."

"To hell with your ghosts," yelled Bob Parsons. "To hell with your haunted houses. I'm taking my little girl home."

* * *

They came through the back door and found Emily Peterson sitting at the kitchen table with one of the men from the moving company. Emily ran to Bill. "My God, what happened out there? I heard screaming."

"Emily, what are you doing here?" asked Bill. "You need your rest as much as Diane does."

"No. I need to be a part of this. I thought you were moving."

"Who's your friend?" asked John.

"My name is Fred Grider," said the stranger. "I've got some old business to attend to out here. So I had my boss run me back here."

"What's your business, friend?" asked Bill.

"About a year and a half ago I was working for an excavating outfit, and I was pushing out the foundation for this house. Well, the whole time I was doing this I felt like somebody was looking over my shoulder." Fred took time to shiver for a moment. "I'd look around and there'd be nobody there. Then I heard this voice in my head. It kept saying, 'Murdered me. Murdered me.' I suppose that means I'm nuts; and I been known to drink a lot in the past; but that's over. I swear it's over."

Fred stood up, shoved his hands in his pockets, and looked at the floor. "I know this don't make no sense. All the time I was digging that foundation I felt like I was digging into something dead. God, I felt so awful. I drove as fast as I could into town to get me a nip so's I could feel normal. That's the way it was. I tried to quit on my own and wound up shakin' like a scared pup. Trouble was I got me a drink and still heard that awful voice."

John put his hand on Fred's shoulder. "We all have some unfinished business at this house to attend to. But the first thing we need to do is get our wits about us.

"Emily, take Judy down to one of the bedrooms and let her lie down. Stay with her. Keep her company. The rest of us need to have a talk."

The four men sat around the kitchen table leaning on their elbows. They had all refused offers of fresh coffee from

Bill who now sat and resisted the urge to grab an ashtray and light one up. John looked out the window for a minute then turned to Fred Grider. "Fred, I guess you used a regular bull-dozer to dig this foundation hole, right?"

"Yeah, we were gonna use the backhoe and dig the footings at the same time, but I told Rick Mundy I had to leave early that afternoon to take my wife to the doctor."

"When did you feel like you had done something wrong?"

"As soon as I got started."

"How long did it take you to dig the crawl space?"

"Couple o' hours, maybe . . . I really can't remember for sure."

"Did you just do the excavating, or did you backfill the foundation too?"

"Oh no! I ain't been by here since a year ago last summer."

"Bill, when did you guys move in?"

"Last June."

"Was the yard finished then?"

"Pretty much."

"Did you see anything that looked outta place?"

"Like what?"

"Old tools, scraps of metal or stone, or . . . "

"Bones?"

John smiled. "My guess is that Fred unearthed some human remains when he dug the foundation hole. They got buried in the pile of earth at the edge of the crawl space then got pushed back around the foundation."

"I sure hope they're not buried under the house," said Bill.

"I don't think they are," said John.

"Wait a minute! We had trouble with the well one night. Some guy came out and got under the house, fixed the problem, then came runnin' outta there screamin' and yellin'."

"What did he see?" asked John.

"I never found out."

"Did you hear anything besides his screaming?"

"No."

"Bob, Judy found some bones for us," said John. There's probably more buried around the house. We can't just leave them lying there. Gentlemen . . . .We need . . . .to have a funeral."

"A funeral?" said Bill.

"These people were murdered in life," said John. "In death they have been treated no better. It's worth a shot, Bill. We've tried everything else. How about it?"

"Well, we haven't tried everything," said Bill. "We haven't moved out." He chuckled and thought to himself, *Worth a shot? The wise old man with all the answers, reduced to shooting craps. How sad.*

"We'll do it right. We don't know exactly what kind of people we're dealing with here. So we'll cover all our bases. We think Tom was part Indian. He may have also been Christian because of his first name. For now I'm going to need some things. Bill, I need a couple of wooden boxes built like old-fashioned coffins. You know, wide at the shoulders, narrow at the foot."

Bill nodded. "I can handle that."

"We're going to need a metal detector."

"I can get us one," said Fred.

Chapter 57

The Boxes

"Is this going to work?" Emily asked Bill as she came into the living room.

"We can only hope. If it doesn't, I guess we've got no choice but to move."

Emily took one long look at the living room and shuddered. It contained the same familiar blue carpeting, the same white couch and matching chair, the same blue drapes with antique credenza at the window, the same leather recliner, the same walnut end table, desk, and lamps. The coffee table had been removed and in its place sat an unfinished plywood riser. On top of the riser sat an unfinished old style coffin.

Sharon McCauley came through the front door. "Hi everybody. Can I help?"

Emily exclaimed, "Sharon! Oh God, it's good to see you."

"Emily, why don't you join Pam at the hospital. I can help the men dig. My daddy raised me on the business end of a shovel when I was little."

"Oh Sharon, that's so sweet of you."

"How's she doing?"

"They are cutting back on her medication. She's getting a lot better."

"Good. Now skedaddle."

* * *

Two days before, John McCauley and Bob Parsons had dug up the shallow grave in the woods. They found the skull of a child and one of an adult, a few rib bones, a couple of broken leg bones; and they all went into the first wooden coffin. Both adult and child skeletons were very incomplete. The ghost of Tom Jakob had said that his wife was butchered. John reasoned that as long as they had the heads and a few other body parts that would be sufficient for a decent burial. They still hadn't found the bones of Tom Jakob.

Outside the yard had been marked off with wooden stakes and rope to form a grid. Each square was about four feet on a side. Fred Grider was carefully walking through each square and waving a metal detector over the ground. Bob Parsons walked along behind him with two sets of wooden stakes. When Fred found something, Bob drove a stake in the ground with a red flag on top of it. They had started at the foundation wall of the house and worked their way out. John McCauley was guessing that a funeral would appease the spirits better if they humored the primitive notion of taking one's personal effects into the after life. First they had to find them.

When Fred finished with his metal detector, he and Sharon McCauley painstakingly dug up the yard where the red stakes marked something metallic. They found roofing nails, somebody's pocketknife, and a few things that had obviously belonged to somebody a long time ago. There was a gnarled pick ax head, some old kitchen utensils, a dagger with nothing left but the blade and handle stub, and what Emily guessed to be an old picture frame. The picture was long gone - just like the Jakobs.

Now it was time to look for the rest of the bones. Bob Parsons, Fred Grider, Bill Barnes, and John McCauley were all digging around the foundation wall of the house. Sharon had to move all of Diane's rose bushes into pots. She hoped a few of them survived, but right now that didn't matter. John reminded everybody that they were digging for human remains. "Take very small bites out of the ground," he said. "We don't know what kind of shape his bones are in, and we don't want to miss anything."

While all the digging was going on Emily, Pam, Bill, and Sharon took turns keeping a bedside vigil with Diane, She was out of the hospital and staying with Emily. There was not one mention of a near death experience.

On the first day of spring, Bill hauled the second coffin out of the garage and laid it on the ground outside Mary's bedroom window. Everybody was down on hands and knees carefully picking through the dirt with their fingers. As each bone was unearthed, it was carefully, reverently placed in the coffin. They only found half of what John guessed to be Tom Jakob's skull. Along the same front wall they found a rib bone, part of a leg bone, and part of what looked like a shoulder blade. They put the bones, the utensils, the dagger, and the picture frame into the coffin.

To the casual observer the scene may have appeared gruesome and macabre. Bill felt a sense of relief. The manifestations of things unseen could now be measured by something real. Tom Jakob was no longer a phantom, and Bill held the bones in his hand as proof of his existence.

Fred had been digging in the dirt most of his life. Never before had he gotten his hands so dirty and felt so good about it as when he gently scraped the mud out of the eye sockets of a man shot to death years before Fred was born.

I ain't never done no harm to nobody. The words of Tom Jakob kept echoing in John McCauley's head. *No you didn't*, John thought. *And we mean you no harm.*

Chapter 58

The Graves

Emily Peterson, Bob and Judy Parsons, John and Sharon McCauley, and Fred Grider arrived at nine o'clock on Sunday morning. The four men went out into the woods with shovels and an ax and dug two graves. The women opened the dining room table and put in extra leaves for a large pitch-in dinner later in the day.

Bill used an ax to carve the outline of a cross in the trunk of an old maple tree at the head of the graves.

"Nice piece of art work," said John.

Bill turned. "Thanks. Let me relieve you on that shovel, John."

"You finish what you're doing there. I'm alright."

Bill watched the man, thirty years or so his senior, mash the spade into the earth. John's lean old body performed well even though he was sprouting lines in the back of his neck and lines along his temples. A lock of salt and pepper hair hung over his forehead. "You're a piece of work yourself, John."

John grinned and kept digging.

When he finished his carving and dug for a while, Bill Barnes stood only knee deep in the grave. For every shovel full of earth he threw out, a dozen roots had to be chopped off.

"We should have figured this," said Bill. "Diggin' out here in the woods. There was bound to be lots of roots."

John looked around the landscape like he was searching for something. "What's the matter, John?" asked Bob.

"Does anybody see anything out in the woods?"

Everybody looked then shook their heads.

"Funny. I've had this feeling we're being watched since we've been out here."

Everybody looked around again. "Still don't see anything," said Bob.

"Probably nothing," said John.

"Let's hope so." Bill handed his shovel to Fred.

Fred got down in the hole and started digging. "You know it's funny. I had a light breakfast and I still ain't hungry."

John looked at his watch. "After 11:00. Is anybody hungry?"

"I am," said Bill. "But let's just finish this."

* * *

When the men got back from the woods, everybody took turns showering in the same bathroom and getting dressed up in the two bedrooms. In just a few days they had become a close-knit family, and now the somber mood had changed to something more resembling a festive gathering for Thanksgiving or Christmas.

They all wore their Sunday best when they walked out to gather up the coffins, the rope, and the shovels. Fred wore a topcoat he had borrowed from Bill to cover his sweater and black jeans. The coat cuffs came well above his wrists, and there was no way he could button it around his husky frame. The rest of the men wore suits and ties, and the women all wore plain white blouses and black dress slacks under their dress coats. They all wore gumboots to wade through the mud of the dense forest.

Bill Barnes raised the overhead door and bent down to hoist one end of one coffin on his shoulder. There, standing in the driveway to greet the little party, was the tall, lanky figure of Sheriff Preston Caldwell.

"Afternoon folks," said the sheriff. His squad car was parked in the driveway behind him. The engine was off and there were no lights flashing.

Everybody stood straight and faced the lawman. John McCauley said, "Good afternoon, Sheriff."

Caldwell looked at the coffins. "What's in the boxes?"

John and Sharon McCauley looked at each other then, with deadpan expressions, they replied, "Bones."

"Bones?" said the sheriff. "Whose bones?"

John cleared his throat and said, "Sheriff, there was a mass murder on this property almost a hundred years ago. The victims are getting a decent burial."

The sheriff just nodded.

"Sheriff Caldwell, that's the truth," said John.

"Sounds strange enough to be the truth," said Caldwell as he pursed his lips. "Listen, the reason I'm here . . . Dan Foster called our office this morning about a stolen pickup. He said he saw it going north on the Old Coal Town Road headed in this direction."

"He could be headed for Cherry Tree Lake," said John.

"And why would he do that?" The sheriff looked puzzled.

"Why would he come here?" asked John.

"That's a good question, Mr. McCauley." The sheriff grinned. "So is mine."

"Did Dan get a good look at the driver?"

"No."

"Did he steal anything else?"

"No. But he was headed in this general direction."

"Excuse me," said Bill. "Who's Dan Foster?"

"Dan built your house," said John.

Bill shook his head. "So that's it. And everything seems to come back to this house."

"It seems to," said Caldwell. "Well, if you see an old four-wheel drive Ford F-250 with a wood platform in place of its bed, please call our office."

"I can assure you we will," said John.

"Where are you burying the bones?"

"Back in the woods. On private property."

"That's okay. You folks sure look like you're dressed for a funeral." The sheriff glanced back at his squad car. "Need an escort?" he chuckled.

"I don't think that'll be necessary," said John. "We're not going that far."

Preston Caldwell looked around, looked down at his shoes, stuffed his hands in his uniform jacket then looked back at John. "Who killed the people in the boxes?" asked Caldwell. "Any ideas?"

"None at all," said John. "One thing's for sure, they're dead too."

The sheriff nodded his head. "Everybody gets to meet the same judge eventually.

"Oh by the way, Mr. Barnes, how's your wife doing?"

"She's at her mother's house, and she's getting better."

"So she's going to be alright?"

"Yes. Thanks for asking."

"I'm glad to hear that."

Preston Caldwell opened his squad car door, and just before he got in he turned to Bill and said, "Mr. Barnes, I know you and your family have had a rough time here. But you're good people; you run a good honest business here. I hope you stay."

"That means a lot to us," said Bill. "Thanks for the kind words."

"That's okay," said the sheriff, then he got in his squad car and drove away.

Chapter 59

An Unholy Place

They walked across the muddy cornfield, with Judy and Sharon leading the way, each carrying a coil of rope. Behind them John and Fred shouldered the coffin containing the bones of Tom Jakob. Bill and Bob carried the other coffin filled with the remains of Elizabeth Jakob and a small child whose name had remained unknown to anybody in this lifetime. Mary and Emily walked close behind them, each carrying a shovel on her shoulder.

Mary walked with her head held high, staring at the coffins on the shoulders of the men. Emily looked over at her and saw a tear stream down Mary's cheek.

"You okay, baby?" asked Emily.

"I'm okay."

"Why are you crying?"

"I'm not. The wind makes my eyes water."

"Oh." Emily went back to watching her feet step over the bent cornstalks in the muddy furrows. She looked over at Mary after a few minutes and asked, "Honey, are you sure you're alright?"

"I'm fine."

"I'm sorry. I don't mean to bug you."

"You're not."

"You've had to do a lot of growing up this year, haven't you?"

Mary looked puzzled. "Growing up? Well, I hadn't thought much about growing up." She glanced at the coffins.

"Gramma, I just thought of something. The night Mother almost . . . "

After a few seconds, Emily broke the heavy silence. "Yes, Mary?"

"That night I was working on my paper about the solar system. I remember something Carl Sagan said in that TV series, *Cosmos*. He said that everything and everybody came from the big bang. So we're all made of the same star stuff. I guess in a way we're all the same age, aren't we?"

"Well, I suppose . . . "

"I mean if what you and the McCauleys believe is true, we've all lived before. Do we all go back to the beginning? And does that make us all the same age?"

"I guess in a way it does. You're a very wise ten-year-old, Mary."

The more they walked, the more Emily noticed Mary's slight limp. "Mary, you're limping. Do you want to go back to the house?"

"No, I'm alright."

"Are you sure? We don't want to bust those stitches open."

"I'm alright."

Emily heard Bill talking to Fred as they walked ahead of them. "Hey Fred, slow down. The side of the coffin's banging you in the head."

"I know it is."

"Well, take it easy, man. You're getting your ear all bloody."

"Too bad. I deserve it."

"What do you mean by that?"

"'Cause I been a drunk and a no-good husband. The day I dug your crawl space I went off and got tanked. I was supposed to take my wife to the doctor and see about her ulcer. Well, that was the day she bled to death inside because I wasn't there." His voice cracked, and he struggled through his tears to say, "I wish so many times it'd been me instead of her."

Fred quit talking and there was more silence. John finally broke it. "Keep talking, somebody. This is good. This is good for all of us." They were nearing the edge of the woods. Judy and Sharon led the procession to the entrance of the path that had been beaten down in the brambles. John said,   "Bob, what's going through your mind right now?"

"Nothing."

John chuckled, "Don't say nothing. Might be bad for business.

"Let's just get this over with. That's all I've got to say."

Sharon turned to Judy. "Your turn, girl. What are you thinking just now?"

Judy turned and looked back at the rest of the funeral procession. "There's a baby in one of those coffins. If that baby had been allowed to grow up, he might have a great grandchild right now. That child might be older than me by now. Who knows, the world might be very different because of that."

"How about you, John?" asked Sharon. "What are you thinking?"

"Watch out Sharon. You're about to get slapped by a branch." Sharon turned and ducked just in time.

"Thanks, sweetheart. Now you were saying?"

"I was thinking about that fire bear. When I was a boy I wanted to play in these woods, and Aunt Alice wouldn't hear of it. Then one night I had a nightmare about being chased through the woods by a bear with fire all over its fur. God I was scared."

"Are you scared now?" asked Sharon.

John took a while to answer. "I'm not scared. Just . . .

uneasy? I'm not sure that's the right word. Let's just do this."

Finally they came to the little clearing with two graves where a man in a hooded parka was shoveling dirt back into the holes.

John McCauley yelled, "Hey! What are you doing?"

The man pushed back the hood of his parka and turned to face the crowd. Fred and Judy recognized him immediately. Same devilish eyes, same hair lip, same bent nose. Judy gasped and dropped the rope she had been carrying. "Get him away from here. He's the one who stole Doc."

"Now I told you a thousand times, I didn't steal him. He came to me." Homer took a step toward Judy. "We found the bones. Remember? Doc showed us how to find our way out here. And in the dark too. Ha ha ha ha ha!"

"Why are you filling in those graves?" asked John.

"You got the wrong ones," said Homer. "This place is not holy."

The men put the coffins on the ground as John confronted the grizzly man. "What do you mean it's not holy? It's going to be…"

"Two holes in the ground," said Homer. "Now don't you worry brother, I got a couple of fresh graves dug elsewhere for them coffins."

Fred glared at Homer and said, "You're trespassing on private property. We need to call the sheriff back out here."

Homer stuck his shovel in the dirt. "Why sure thing. You got a phone handy? Check and see if there ain't one over there on that tree trunk."

"Who are you?" asked John.

"That there's Homer," said Fred. "He swilled moonshine at The Old Dog Tavern in town."

John was getting irritated. "Where did you come from?"

"Well, brother, I come…"

"I'm not your brother."

"Ha ha ha. Oh, yes, you are. You're Ken McCauley's boy." Homer stared at John and walked closer to him. "And so am I."

An icy chill shot through John's chest. "I don't believe you."

"He's drunk!" shouted Emily.

"Now I ain't drunk; but I had a hellacious week." He looked around the clearing and barely kept himself vertical. "And I got a powerful lot of talkin' to do about this place. Let me start with you and me, John.

"You know you had a mighty fine looking mama. And you got a good brain in that old noggin of yours. But our daddy was nothin' but a broken down old relic from the war. When he left you, he hitched up with my mama; and my mama was nothin' but an old gypsy from an old gypsy family. And the daddy of them all was none other than Tom Jakob."

John said, "But they were all wiped out in the massacre."

"Not quite," said Homer. "Now let me explain. Tom was part of a wagon train that went around tellin' fortunes, sellin' old Indian medicine, and healin' folk with ways of the Indians. They come up from down around Natchez, Mississippi; and they got away with what they was doin' until they got to Indiana. Bunch of 'em landed in jail for fortune tellin' and peddlin' evil spells. So old Tom broke away and tried his hand at farmin'. That's when he met up with your grandpa. But his oldest daughter left the farm and went to work sellin' potions and tellin' fortunes in the big city. She knew trouble was comin' so she hit the road and saved herself." Homer nodded his head, let out a big sigh, and said, "That lady was my grandma, Anna Lee's mama."

John shook his head. "How do you know all this?"

"How else would I know? Family all told their history to the youngins."

"I don't believe any of it."

"Well, now, why wouldn't you? I'm just a poor old sinner from the big city. How would I know to come down here and get inside all your lives if it weren't true?

"Tell 'em, Judy. Tell 'em how Doc showed us where the bones were buried.

Bob walked over and put his arms around Judy. "She's not talking to you." Judy hugged her daddy but looked at Homer with a mixture of curiosity and fear.

"How did you find the bones?" asked John.

Judy said, "A deer and her young fawn lead us out here."

"In the dark?" asked Bob.

"There was a full moon and Doc could see . . ."

"Doc was possessed by the spirit of my murdered great grandmother. Old G.G. knew it all." Homer looked at Judy's shocked expression. "It's true, girl. How do you think a stranger like me managed to ride him?"

A man he had just met had handed John half his pedigree. After recovering from the revelation and hearing Homer's story, he asked, "Where did our father meet your mother?"

"He was workin' for an orphanage in the big city washin' windows and sweepin' floors. One of the children was Anna Lee. When she turned eighteen, they threw her out 'cause she was too old. 'Make your own way,' they told her. So our daddy took her in and kept her until he finally drank hisself to death. By then she had me, and I was fightin' and stealin' and whatever else I had to do to keep both of us alive."

Homer's attention was suddenly diverted toward Mary and Emily.

"Who killed Tom Jakob and his family?" asked John.

Homer was still looking at Mary and Emily. "What's that you say?"

"I said, who killed Tom Jakob?"

"Who do you think?" Homer glanced at John with an evil stare.

"I can't believe my grandfather acted alone."

Homer looked back at Mary who was hanging onto her grandmother. "He didn't. He hired two drifters to do it for him."

"Why?"

Homer glanced back at John. "'Cause they was witches, that's why. And they was half-breeds." Homer turned away from John and pointed at Emily and Mary. "I want you to set that little girl down on that there coffin lid right now."

"What for?" asked Bill.

"'Cause I says so," said Homer.

Bill looked over at Mary who was still hugging Emily and grimacing with pain. "You're scaring her. You're trying to scare all of us."

Emily said, "Bill, help me. She's about to pull both of us down."

Bill and Emily grabbed Mary by the shoulders and sat her down on the nearest coffin. Bill asked, "Mary, what's wrong?"

"It's my foot. I think it's bleeding again, and it hurts."

"I knew we shouldn't have brought you out here," said Emily.

Homer squatted down in front of Mary, grabbed her heel and lifted her leg. "It's alright, honey. Just keep that right foot up here in front of my face." Homer pulled her boot off to reveal a bloody white sock around a bloody foot. He cradled her ankle in one hand.

"Oh God," said Emily. "Mary, we have to get you back to the house."

"Stop! Don't anybody move!" Homer removed his dirty gloves then looked into Mary's wide eyes. "This leg is stiff as a board right now. It gonna stay that way 'till I says otherwise." Very deftly he pulled the sock off Mary's foot and unwound the crimson gauze as blood continued to dribble on the ground. Then he squeezed the sole of her foot with the heels of his hands until the blood stopped flowing. Homer's eyes were closed, his head shivered, and his hands quaked. He started mouthing some words, but his voice was silent.

After several agonizing seconds, Homer took his hands off Mary's foot to reveal a completely healed wound. Nothing showed but some bloody smudges along a thin line with ragged sutures around it. Homer cradled Mary's foot gently in one hand as he swiped blood off the sole of her foot with the other and snatched the stitches out of her old wound with his teeth. Mary flinched and batted her eyes as each stitch came out in Homer's mouth, but she didn't cry out.

Homer was still cradling Mary's foot as he looked up and crooned. "Bless her soul! Bless her sweet little soul! G.G. left me a fine gift to heal with." He looked over at John. "Just like she healed your grandpa."

"How was that?" asked John. His expression was grim, his eyes darted back and forth between Homer and Mary.

Homer wrung the blood out of Mary's sock and put it and the boot back on her foot. "John, your grandpa Hanson was sick with a tumor, and my great gramma cured him. Shameful! Shameful! Goin' to a half-breed heathen witch doctor. What would the good Christian souls of this county think?

"But most of all, Tom Jakob wanted the south pasture for his own. Get it? Make the old man well. Barter for the land. But Samuel Hanson wouldn't hear of it. No sir! They couldn't have the land. It was Hanson land. They could have money, but no land.

"So they threatened squatter's rights to make it their own. That's when the old man got rid of 'em."

"Squatter's rights?" said Bill.

Bob Parsons spoke up. "It's also called adverse possession. Samuel Hanson was too sick to work all that land, but Tom Jakob was well enough. That's probably how he threatened to take over, by invoking adverse possession."

"But he'd need a lawyer to do that, wouldn't he?" said Bill.

"Be that as it may," said John. "All my grandfather needed was a threat from anybody to make him hit back and hit back with a vengeance. My God, what a family we came from."

Homer grinned and said, "My G.G. could hit back too. Then come 'the Hanson curse'."

"How do you know all this?" asked John.

"Aw John, my dear old Great Grandma Jakob left me a piece of her soul. All I have to do is close my eyes; and I see faces; and I go places." His expression turned devilish again. "And I make up rhymes. And just in time. Haaaaaaa! Ha ha ha ha ha ha!"

Homer staggered, regained his balance, leaned back, and clasped his hands above his head as if he was holding something. "I see all your dreams, and I'm **in** all your dreams and the dreams of souls long departed. I know what you hate and what you fear. Most of all I see the witch. I see the witch holding her dagger over her bowl of magic potions and weaving her wondrous spells to heal the sick and make the lame strong again."

He dropped his hands to his sides. "I go to sleep and I dream about a man walking across the meadow, and he's coming this way. He knocks on the door of the witch's house. She lets him in, sits him down, and gets ready to make him well again. This man has a hurt in his belly. This man is in pain. He's in hooooorrrrible pain!" Homer reached up and pulled off the black bandanna binding his hair to reveal a medallion and chain tied around his head. The medallion was made of three silver bars arranged to look like an X bisected by a vertical line.

"But the witch, she calls up her powers from the mother earth; and she reaches down his throat and yanks that nasty ole tumor right outta his belly and makes him feel soooooo much better!"

Homer staggered again, and the medallion and chain shook loose from the crown of his head and dropped down around his neck. He sighed, "Now I see two men coming in the night. The witch makes the man feel so much better, and how does he repay her? How does he repay her?"

Homer's head drooped, the corners of his mouth turned down, and his eyes sagged like those of an old bloodhound. "He butchered her! He butchered her!"

The hair bristled on John and Bill's necks, and Mary gasped as she covered her face with her hands. The expression on Homer's face turned to a grimace of extreme pain. The keening and wailing that they first heard with the voice of Tom Jakob returned, and this time there was a new voice, or was it an old voice?

"Papa was bad."

It's Alice! John thought as his heart pounded in his chest. "Homer, let her go! You've got Alice in there with you. Now let her go!"

"Papa was bad." The voice began to squeak.

"Let her go, Homer!"

"Papa was bad."

"Did you hear me? I said let her go!"

"Papa was baaaaa. . ." The voice trailed off, and only the keening and wailing came out of Homer's mouth.

There was a loud screech from above, and a black crow swooped down and sailed over the heads of the little funeral procession. Homer was the only one who didn't flinch. He chuckled and kept his eyes closed. His jaw went slack as a low rumble came out of his mouth, followed by several moments of silence as his head tilted skyward, and his eyes slowly opened to twinkle in the late morning sun. There was a slight breeze as he said, "She's gone. They are all gone. They are all at peace."

Homer bowed his head then looked up to stare dead-pan at the gathering. "Now if you gentlemen will heft them coffins up on your shoulders again, I got a little conveyance to take you where you need to go."

Chapter 60

The Final Resting Place

It sat in the woods next to the little clearing that had been excavated just hours earlier. Homer's little conveyance was the old four-wheel drive pickup truck with the enclosed bed replaced with a long, flat wooden platform. Bob, Bill, Fred and John loaded the coffins onto the truck while everybody climbed up and sat down next to the wooden boxes.

Fred shouted at Homer, "If you promise not to take us on some wild goose chase, I promise I won't tell Dan Foster who stole his converted pick up truck here."

"I ain't taken you on no wild goose chase," said Homer. "This here little lorry is going back to its own garage when I get done."

"I'll bet," said Fred.

Homer drove them out of the forest and onto the country road. He only had to drive a short distance to the stone bluff overlooking what was left of the Hanson farm. There he turned left and wound his way down Cherry Tree Road and into another dense forest.

The road was narrow and had lots of hills and curves and hairpin turns. The farther they went into the deep woods the darker the afternoon light got. They passed a sign that read: *No Trespassing Property of Forest County Conservation Club.*

Fred Grider shouted above the noise of the straining truck engine and manual transmission. "You're trespassing again, Homer."

Homer shouted back, "You'd be surprised at how many times I've trespassed up here."

"You're going to get us all shot," shouted John.

"No I'm not," said Homer. "Shooting range is five miles that way." He pointed to his left.

He came to a wide place in a curve and stopped. "Have a look along the edge of that wide place in the road," said Homer.

Everybody got off the truck and walked to the edge of a cliff. Below them were Bill and Diane's house and a black crater where the old Hanson barn used to stand. "That's where ole Max Carter took his ride to glory."

"I remember that," said Bill. "How did you know about it?"

"It was on the news."

"But they didn't say a word about Max," said Bill.

"They didn't say a lot of things about that night. Just like folks didn't say a lot of things about how they murdered my people. I come up here all the time late at night and have all kinds of dreams including the sight of a man getting hit by a raging black bird and sailing off that there cliff in a ball of fire. Now get back on here, and I'll take you where you're supposed to be."

Homer wound his way around another curve and up a hill. He parked along the road and killed the engine. "Graves are about sixty yards that away." He pointed across the left headlight. "I'd take you there, but the ground is too soft. All you have to do is fill them in. Don't bother markin' them. Don't nobody care no more anyway."

Homer seemed devoid of any emotion. He stared straight ahead as he said, "Get your coffins over there. Say your piece, then get back here. I'll take you home."

They got to the little gravesite deep inside the forest and put the coffins in the ground. John McCauley opened his

Bible to the fourteenth chapter of the Gospel according to John.

"Let not your heart be troubled: ye believe in God, believe also in me. In my father's house are many mansions: if it were not so, I would have told you. I go to prepare a place for you. And if I go and prepare a place for you, I will come again and receive you unto myself: that where I am, there ye may be also. And whither I go ye know, and the way ye know."

He closed his Bible and looked at everybody around the grave. "The earth forgives. Let not the earth forget." John cleared his throat and hung his head. There were several moments of agonizing silence before he said, "Well now, wasn't that poetic." He pulled a folded piece of paper out of the pages of his bible, unfolded it and said, "Grandma Hanson said it more appropriately. In her old diary she wrote, 'The earth does not care. The good mother was born of fiery upheaval herself, and over the ages she adapted to the violence of human kind by covering the graves of the wicked and the good with the same soft soil that grows new crops of tall grasses and golden rod to dapple the green pasture.'"

John looked around at the faces of Mary, Emily, Sharon, Bob, and Judy Parsons. He looked at the comical figure of Fred Grider with his enormous hands hanging limply at his sides, the too small coat strained by his massive shoulders. John studied Bill's grim face, then said, "Thanks for building the coffins, Bill."

Bill looked at John with tears in his eyes and said, "You're welcome, John."

"It still seems like we should mark the graves some way," said Sharon.

"Homer said not to. These were his people. I'm sure he had his reasons."

"Thanks John, said Bill. "Thanks for all you've done for us."

"Seems like Homer should be thanking us too," said Bob.

Judy turned to her father. "After what was done to his people, I don't think he owes any of us any thanks."

John handed his Bible to Sharon. "Let's cover the graves."

Bill and Fred began shoveling dirt back into the open graves. Judy stood and cried softly as she buried her face in her father's chest. Bob stroked her head and shamelessly let the tears stream down his cheeks. Mary, Emily, John, and Sharon gathered up the shovels and the ropes.

* * *

As they walked back to the truck, Bill came alongside John and asked, "Did we do the right thing? I mean did we really know what we were doing back there?"

John gave a soft chuckle. "Bill, we did the best we could." He shook his head and looked down at the rough ground as he walked. "Did we know what we were doing? I don't know. God help me, I've spent a lot of time saying I don't know lately. But . . . what am I supposed to do? It was just a simple act of kindness, Bill; and that's all any of us can ever hope to do in this life. Was it the *right* thing to do? Only time will tell."

And so it did.

Epilogue

Forest County, Indiana, present day

The little funeral worked . . . sort of. The old troubled spirits remained rested in their unmarked graves, and the ground around them remained pristine and undisturbed.

The living did not fare so well. Out of the seven mortals standing at the graves of Tom Jakob and his family, only two are known to have survived. Fifteen years after burying the bones, John McCauley was struck dead by a cerebral hemorrhage. His widow, Sharon, was shocked and devastated and couldn't bear to spend one more day in Forest County after John's memorial. She had him cremated, hauled his ashes back to her native Georgia, and directed Bob Parsons to sell the house and donate the proceeds to charity. None of John's and Sharon's friends or family in Indiana has heard from her since.

Bob Parsons was diagnosed with Alzheimer's seventeen years after the funeral. He died at home at the age of eighty-two under the constant care of his wife, Norma. Their daughter Judy had received a real estate license, a degree in accounting and marketing, and had taken over the business. After her wild teenage years and her near brush with all the poltergeists around the old Hanson farm, Judy became aloof, straight-laced, and all business. She never married.

Bill Barnes' welding shop became a huge success and Bill became a victim of that success. He worked long hours inhaling fumes from his welding torch and never, never took a vacation. He died of emphysema twenty years after the funeral.

Poor Fred Grider had no family or friends to help him stay on the wagon. Despite his good intentions, he could never keep away from booze for more than a month or two. One night a convenience store clerk on the edge of Tanner's Grove noticed a foul odor coming from a car in a neighboring parking lot. He saw a man slumped over the steering wheel and called the sheriff. The deputies found Fred stiff, cold, bloated, and covered with flies laying their eggs on his rotten face. The car had over a hundred empty whiskey bottles in the front and back seats.

Mary got her college education in North Carolina and that's where she stayed. She and her husband, Brad Shockley, have five children. The only time they came back to Indiana was to mourn and bury Mary's father.

Emily Peterson died of congestive heart failure seven years after the murdered family was laid to rest. She was seventy-two, and her family thought that was rather young for somebody who had never been sick and only went to a hospital to have both of her daughters. Her other daughter, Pam, shocked the gathering at the funeral with a little impromptu eulogy: "Mother was not all that old when she died, but she lived as long as she could. She didn't suffer a lot, but she didn't die instantly. Just before she passed, Mother told me she has concluded that the secret to a long life is a four-letter word ending in u-c-k, first letter - L. Any other explanation for a long life is dishonest and a load of bull scat."

My name is Tim Whitaker and I got all this information from Diane Barnes who survived the two-year long nightmare with more tenacity and strength than anybody else. I had met Diane and Bill only once at one of John McCauley's gatherings. I knew about all the trouble with their house because my stepfather, Dan Foster, built it; and I helped him while I was between jobs as a radio news announcer. It was only recently that Diane and I got well acquainted, and that was because we both needed to reinvent ourselves. The radio business really didn't work out so I came back home, lived and worked with my stepdad while I served a four-year apprenticeship with the electrical workers' union.

After her husband Bill died, and her daughter Mary was rearing her own family in North Carolina, Diane was left alone in that little house in the country. She turned Bill's welding shop into a garden store, added a greenhouse in back, replaced the roof, and hired Dad and I to do the work.

My parents are long gone and I'm semiretired; but Diane still calls me to do odd jobs around her place even though I'm getting a little long in the tooth for some of them. Diane is almost seventy and occasionally she will talk about selling the house and shop and moving to Indianapolis. I hate to think when that's going to be. You see, I never married; and Diane is widowed and so pretty, so easy to talk to, so easy to be around and really not that much older than I. She has finally opened up to me about something she never told to anybody else; not her mother, not her husband and not her daughter.

Diane decided one day she wanted to finish a project that Bill had started just before he died. She hired a carpenter to finish the porch on the front of the house and hired me to put lights in the overhang.

While I worked, Diane transplanted new rose bushes around the front of the house. The more she worked the slower she worked. Finally she stood, arched her spine, and massaged her lower back. She looked up at me as I stood on the stepladder and said, "Tim, I'm going to take a break and go inside. You're welcome to join me if you like."

"As soon as I button up this junction box, I'll do that."

We sat in the kitchen for several minutes as Diane brewed two cups of coffee from her Keurig coffee machine for us. She said, "If I had any sense I'd sell this place, but I don't know where I would go."

"Diane, as long as I'm around to help, you can stay right where you are." I blushed as soon as I said it. I guess I was getting brave in my old age. I knew Diane when she was married, and much younger, and I was sure that, even if she was single, she was way out of my league.

"Oh, you don't say." She raised her eyebrows and smiled. "Well, I'll remember that Tim."

The brewing machine coughed out its last batch of hot coffee for the last cup. Diane got up and fetched the two mugs. "You're a sweetheart, Tim. You know that? Let's move this into the living room and get comfortable."

She sat in her favorite rocker recliner with her shoes off and her feet curled up under her while she smiled and looked at me with those devastating blue eyes. "I have something to tell you that I've never shared with anybody. It's something I haven't thought about for over thirty years." She paused to take a sip of coffee. "John McCauley told you all about the trouble we were having at this house many years ago, didn't he?"

"Yes."

"Did he tell you I died at one point?"

"My God, no."

"My family and I never talked about that very much. Everybody knew I was sick. Not many knew I came back from the dead.

"There are times when I'm out there digging in the dirt in the garden when I start remembering that thing of dying and sinking into a muddy river bottom and falling into a horrible place." Her voice began to crack. "And then I come out of it and go sailing off to heaven."

I couldn't believe it. This woman who I knew so little about, who had occupied such a small corner of my world, was sharing such a personal secret about her encounter with the final frontier. "Diane, are you telling me you had a near death experience?"

"I guess that's what they call them."

"Have you told anybody else about it?"

"Not a soul."

"Why me?"

"Why not you. Mother, Bill, John, they're all gone."

"How about your sister Pam, and Mary?"

"Pam was so traumatized by what happened, I really don't think she wants to hear any more. Mary . . . I think Mary has grown a lot closer to her husband's family. You and I aren't getting any younger."

Diane took a sip of her coffee and looked out the front window. "Oh Tim, that was such a scary thing. I didn't talk about it; I tried not to think about it; but I couldn't put it out of my mind. Mother always said I was good at clamming up when something was bothering me. That bothered me a lot. God, I was scared."

"Really? Most accounts I've heard tell of people going to heaven and not wanting to come back."

"I didn't want to come back once I got to heaven, but I had to go through hell first. I had to relive two previous life times before I came back. She looked close at me. "I realize now that what I went through . . . I should have shared it with people closest to me. They had a right to know, and I should have told them. But I was so scared, and I wanted so bad to put all this trouble behind me." She sighed. "Over the years, Bill and Mary would look at me like they didn't know me sometimes. My sister Pam told me I wasn't myself anymore, and I wasn't. I was changed."

"How so?"

Diane took another sip of her coffee and made a face. "Well, for one thing, my taste buds got more sensitive." She walked into the kitchen, took a small bottle off her spice rack, and shook something into her cup. "They never put enough chicory into these blends."

When she came back, Diane stood with her hands wrapped around the mug and her shoulders hunched forward. "I don't sweat the small stuff anymore. It's not worth it. I've learned we're all in this together; we're all a part of all creation; and I'm more inclined to treat people better without being so high strung."

"Diane, what did you see that changed you that much?"

She smiled, took a sip of coffee, and looked at me. "Tim, why don't you stay for supper; and I'll tell you the whole story."

Author's Post Script

This story was based on a real life event that I witnessed many years ago. I was a member of a study group that investigated the paranormal. We studied books about Edgar Cayce, one of the world's most gifted and famous psychics. A man identified in my book as John McCauley headed up the group. He taught us hypnosis, self-hypnosis, prenatal regression and the idea that we have all lived before.

One of the married couples in that group lived in a house that they claimed was haunted. It got so bad that, one night, the wife awoke to the sensation of somebody unseen breathing on her. She screamed, and that's when they called John for help. He hypnotized the wife, and she channeled the spirit of a man murdered on the site of her house almost a hundred years before. John recorded the channeling session and played it back at one of our meetings. When I heard the voice of the ghost of a murdered man scream out loud, "They murdered me," the hair on the back of my neck stood out straight. The woman who channeled the ghost was in the room as the recording played back, and she was visibly shaken.

I was going to write an article about the haunting and how John urged the ghost to go on and leave the house. But the lady of the household was rather cool to the idea; I was getting ready to take a job in another city, so the little project fell apart.

Many years later I got the idea that this was still a great story and that it would probably make a darn good novel. I hope you have enjoyed it.

R. S. Craig